PUFFIN BOOKS
Editor: Kaye Webb

THE PICTS AND THE MARTYRS

'Look here,' Nancy told Dick and Dorothea. 'There'll be no adventures this time, not until Mother and Uncle Jim get back. But they'll be back in eleven days and after that the Swallows are coming and, with three boats and all our tents, we'll work out something really splendid. But till then we've jolly well got to see that nothing happens at all.'

'Just being here's lovely,' said Dorothea.

But next morning the blow fell: the pirates' awful Great Aunt (the one in *Swallowdale*) had heard that Mrs Blackett had gone away, leaving Nancy and Peggy alone, and she was coming to take charge of them – and she would be even more disapproving of Mrs Blackett if she knew that Dick and Dorothea were staying there as well.

There was only one thing to do: Nancy and Peggy had to sacrifice themselves, wearing best white frocks, practising the piano and winding the Aunt's wool, while Dick and Dorothea disappeared to live in the woods.

It was not as easy as it seemed. Nancy herself had a dreadful time being so good, and more and more people, the postman, the milk boy, and the doctor, had to be let into the secret, until half the countryside was wishing she had never thought of her plan. And then, to crown it all, the Great Aunt disappeared!

THE PICTS AT HOME

The Picts and The Martyrs:

OR, NOT WELCOME AT ALL

ARTHUR RANSOME

ILLUSTRATED BY THE AUTHOR

PUFFIN BOOKS

Puffin Books, Penguin Books Ltd, Harmondsworth, Middlesex, England
Penguin Books, 625 Madison Avenue, New York, New York 10022, U.S.A.
Penguin Books Australia Ltd, Ringwood, Victoria, Australia
Penguin Books Canada Ltd, 2801 John Street, Markham, Ontario, Canada L3R 1B4
Penguin Books (N.Z.) Ltd, 182–190 Wairau Road, Auckland 10, New Zealand

—

First Published by Jonathan Cape 1942
Published in Puffin Books 1971
Reprinted 1972, 1974, 1976, 1977, 1979

—

—

Made and printed in Great Britain
by Richard Clay (The Chaucer Press), Ltd,
Bungay, Suffolk
Set in Monotype Caslon

To
AUNT HELEN
C.F.C.A.

PLUS 100. A1

(These letters mean Certificated First Class Aunt. There are Aunts of all kinds, and all the good ones should be given certificates by their nephews and nieces to distinguish them from Uncertificated Aunts, like Nancy's and Peggy's G.A.)

CONTENTS

ILLUSTRATIONS

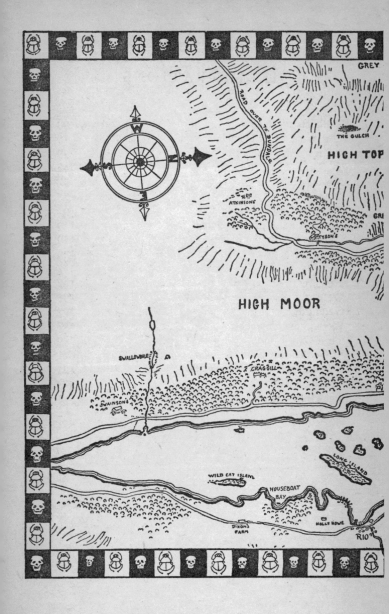

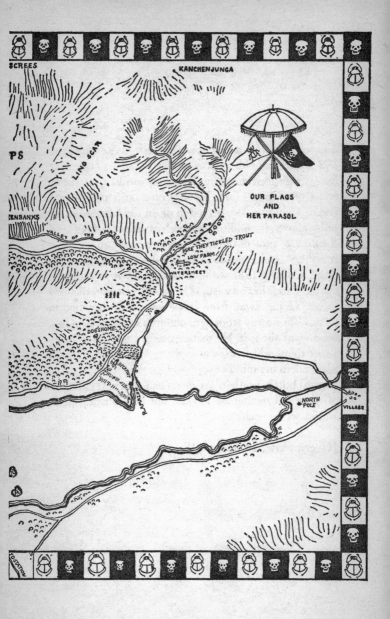

I have been often asked how I came to write *Swallows and Amazons*. The answer is that it had its beginning long, long ago when, as children, my brother, my sisters and I spent most of our holidays on a farm at the south end of Coniston. We played in or on the lake or on the hills above it finding friends in the farmers and shepherds and charcoal-burners whose smoke rose from the coppice woods along the shore. We adored the place. Coming to it we used to run down to the lake, dip our hands in and wish, as if we had just seen the new moon. Going away from it we were half drowned in tears. While away from it, as children and as grown ups, we dreamt about it. No matter where I was, wandering about the world, I used at night to look for the North Star and, in my mind's eye, could see the beloved skyline of great hills beneath it. *Swallows and Amazons* grew out of those old memories. I could not help writing it. It almost wrote itself.

A.R.

Haverthwaite, 19 May 1958

CHAPTER I

VISITORS EXPECTED

'It's not what I call homely,' said the old Cook, standing in the doorway of the spare bedroom at Beckfoot and looking at an enormous skull and crossbones done in black and white paint on two huge sheets of paper and fixed with drawing pins on the wall above the head of the bed.

'Dot'll think it's just right,' said Nancy, who was kneeling on the pillows putting a last touch to one of the bones.

'A death's head like that to watch her go to sleep. And she won't like that yellow and black thing either,' said Cook, looking at the two flags on little flagstaffs fixed at the foot of the bed. 'Isn't that what you had out of the window when your face was swollen up with the mumps?'

'It's the L flag,' said Nancy, leaning back to get a good look at her work. 'It does mean leprosy and plague and things like that, but it's the only one we've got handy that's the right size. She won't mind.'

'And that inseck. It's enough to make her think the bed's alive. I don't know where you've seen such things. Not in this house anyway . . .'

'It's a scarab,' said Nancy.

'More like a bug,' said Cook.

'Well, it *is* a bug really, a sort of bug . . . It's a beetle thousands of years old. A sacred beetle. Egyptian. It's the flag for their new boat.'

'I don't know what your mother'll say when she comes back and sees it. And your uncle's room with a death's head, too. Nice way to welcome visitors, it seems to me.'

'It all depends on the visitors,' said Nancy, scrambling off the bed and joining Cook in the doorway to get a better view.

'Yes. I think we'll have another skull and crossbones at the foot of the bed. It looks a bit tame without. Hi! Peggy! More paper. I'm going to do another skull for Dorothea and another for Dick as well.'

'So long as you don't drop paint on the carpet,' said Cook.

'I won't. That was only one spot on the pillow. Accident. We'll do the rest of the painting in the garden. All right, Cookie, darling, we've promised Mother we're going to be almost sickeningly good. You'll see. Haven't we been good so far?'

'Well, I must say, Miss Ruth, you haven't had much time . . .'

'Jibbooms, bobstays and battleaxes,' exclaimed Nancy. 'If you call me Ruth again . . .'

'All right, Miss Nancy . . . though Ruth's a nice name, I must say.'

'Not for a pirate,' said Nancy. 'And you know the only person who calls me Ruth now is the Great Aunt, and she doesn't count. She even calls Peggy, Margaret.'

'I don't what you might say see eye to eye with your Aunt Maria,' said Cook.

'We none of us do,' said Nancy. 'Not even Mother or Uncle Jim.'

'Well, Miss Nancy,' said Cook. 'With you doing the housekeeping, if you can take your mind off them death's heads, you'd best be coming into the kitchen like your mother to talk to me about the day's meals. There's that bit of roast mutton, cold. There's the brawn, and I was thinking of a treacle pudding . . .'

'Oh, bother,' said Nancy. 'I won't start housekeeping till tomorrow. Ask Peggy. Or, you do just as you like. Only no tapioca. Or sago. Never. We can't stand them and I expect Dick and Dot hate them just as much as we do.'

Peggy came across the landing with paper for more skulls and crossbones.

'Here you are,' she said. 'Come and look at Dick's room. The skull and crossbones looks fine over Uncle Jim's bed. I wonder he never thought of it himself. And I've put the big telescope on the table by the window. Dick'll feel at home right away.'

'You will do the painting in the garden, won't you?' said Cook. 'I'll have to put on a new pillowslip as it is.'

'No need,' said Nancy. 'Dot won't mind. I'll tell her it's a drop of blood gone black.'

'She won't thank you,' said Cook and went off downstairs to her kitchen.

*

Influenza was the reason that Nancy and Peggy were alone with Cook at Beckfoot. Examination papers was the reason that they were expecting Dick and Dorothea Callum to join them. Mrs Blackett had had influenza very badly and had been ordered to go away for a complete rest. Her brother Jim, generally known as Captain Flint, had taken her off for a sea voyage and a cruise round the coasts of Scandinavia. It meant being away for the first ten days of the summer holidays and Mrs Blackett at first had refused even to think of it. But Captain Flint had pointed out that that was much better than spoiling the whole holidays by having a break-down and in the end she had agreed that it would not do Nancy and Peggy any harm to manage by themselves at Beckfoot. 'Jolly good for them to have a chance,' Captain Flint had said. 'And old Cook'll see they're properly fed, and Timothy Stedding'll be hanging on in the houseboat and going to and fro to the mine. He's got a job to do in my den. He'll be looking in on them every other day. They'll be right as rain.' Then had come the news that Dick and Dorothea Callum could not be taken in at Dixon's Farm, because it was full up with other visitors, and Professor Callum had to be busy for a fortnight in London correcting examination papers. So Mrs Blackett had invited

Dick and Dorothea to join Nancy and Peggy. 'Dick's a sensible chap,' said Captain Flint, 'and Dorothea's got some sort of head on her shoulders. They'll be ballast for the party even if they are a bit younger, and that young Dick can give Timothy a hand.' Before leaving, Mrs Blackett had visited Nancy and Peggy at their school. 'No wildnesses,' she had said doubtingly. 'If I thought there was any risk of your getting into trouble, I'd much rather stay at home. I don't know what Aunt Maria would say if she knew I was leaving you alone.' 'As tame as tame can be,' Nancy had promised. 'You go off and get well. We'll be so jolly good nobody'll know us. And then, when you come back, we'll have a lot of wildness stored up, and we'll fairly take it out of Uncle Jim.' And now they were back from school and looking forward to being model hostesses. Not one single thing was to be allowed to happen that would make their mother wish she had not trusted them to run the house themselves.

*

They came in to their midday dinner, leaving the two new specimens of skull and crossbones spread on the lawn, with stones to keep them from blowing away, while they dried in the hot August sunshine. They were talking of the boat which Professor Callum had asked their uncle to order for Dick and Dorothea, and were hoping it was ready so that its crew could get the hang of it before the Swallows turned up, who were coming in a fortnight's time to stay at Holly Howe on the other side of the lake.

'Timothy said yesterday he didn't think it would be done by today,' said Peggy.

'We'll go and look at it on the way from the station,' said Nancy.

'They'll be bursting to see it,' said Peggy. 'I say, Nancy, is a boat she or it before it's launched?'

Nancy never answered. The telephone bell was ringing in the hall.

'Who's that?'

'Somebody for Cook, probably. Butcher, perhaps.'

They heard a clatter as Cook put down the pudding dish on the table in the hall. Then they heard her at the telephone. 'Hullo ... Hullo ... Telegram, did you say? ... Eh? ... Mrs Blackett is away ... Miss Ruth Blackett ... Wait a minute ... Hold on, please. I'll call her ...'

Nancy had already jumped up from her chair.

'It's a telegram for you, Miss Ruth ...'

Even in that moment, Nancy shook her fist at Cook.

'Miss Ruth Blackett,' said Cook firmly. 'That's what they said.'

Nancy was already at the telephone in the hall.

'Yes ... Peggy, don't make such a row with your hoofs! ... I can't hear ... Wait a minute while I get a pencil ... Hi! ... Pencil! Peggy! ... All right now ... Ready ... Go on ... Reply paid ... I heard that ... Never mind about the address ... "Are ... you ... alone ... at ... Beckfoot ... when ... does ... your ... mother ... return ... Maria ... Turner ..." Gosh! Sorry. Nothing. I was talking to somebody else. Yes ... That's all right. I'll send the answer in a minute or two. Thank you.' She hung up the receiver. 'Gosh!' she said again. 'Giminy! It's the Great Aunt. She's found out about Mother being away.'

'What business is it of hers?' said Cook. 'You come along and eat your pudding. No call for you to get worried. Miss Turner's far enough from here. And she can't stop your mother now.'

'We've got to send an answer,' said Nancy. 'It was reply paid.'

'Time enough for that,' said Cook.

Nancy, while eating her pudding, scribbled between mouthfuls. She covered a sheet of notepaper with possible telegrams, not one of which seemed fit to send. 'The main thing is to quiet her down,' she said. 'How can we squash her in twelve words?'

'We can't,' said Peggy.

'We couldn't in twelve thousand,' said Nancy. 'But we've got to do something. Don't you see? It's Mother she's getting at, not us. "Are you alone at Beckfoot?" She's prickly with disapproval.'

'We aren't alone,' said Peggy. 'Tell her Cook's here.'

'Twelve words,' said Nancy. 'And the address takes four. That's eight for what we've got to say.' She crossed out a few words on her last draft, added three more, and read the result. 'No. Cook is here. Mother comes back thirteenth. Nancy.'

'You could say "returns" instead of "comes back",' said Peggy. 'And, I say, won't you have to sign it "Ruth" for the G.A.?'

Nancy made a face, crossed out 'Nancy,' wrote 'Ruth' with an angry pencil, and saved a word by using 'returns'.

Peggy read it. 'She'll think it means we are alone. She'll read "No cook is here," because of their never bothering to put in stops. She'll think it means "Not even Cook".'

'Shiver my timbers!' said Nancy, and altered the telegram again. '"Not alone. Cook here. Mother returns thirteenth. Ruth." Ugh! Ruth! That makes twelve words with the address.'

She showed the telegram to Cook.

Cook read it aloud, word by word. 'You ought to tell her there's nowt amiss,' she said.

'Extra words,' said Nancy. 'But perhaps I'd better. After "Cook here," I'll put in "Everything scrumptious".'

'Slang,' said Peggy, doubtfully. 'She won't like that.'

'Everything splendid,' said Nancy. 'She won't really like that either. I'll just put "All very well." Three words. Only threepence anyhow. Worth it. And it'll be in the telephone account. Mother won't mind.'

'NOT WHAT I CALL HOMELY'

She went to the telephone with Peggy and Cook, neither of whom could think of any improvements. She rang up the exchange, asked for 'Telegrams', gave the Beckfoot number, explained that this was the answer to the reply-paid telegram, gave Miss Turner's address in Harrogate and read out the final version:

'Not alone. Cook here. All very well. Mother returns thirteenth. Ruth.'

She waited while the telegraph clerk repeated the message, said that it was all right and put down the receiver. She looked at Cook. 'I hope it *is* all right,' she said. 'Anyway, it's the best we could do.'

'You can't do better,' said Cook. 'Eh, but I'd like a word with the meddlesome busybody that let Miss Turner know your mother was away.'

'She can't do anything about it now,' said Nancy, 'but I bet she'll go and be beastly to Mother as soon as she comes back.'

'Mother'll have had her holiday by then, so it won't matter,' said Peggy. 'At least not as much as if she'd got at her before she started.'

'Bother Aunt Maria,' said Nancy. 'Keel haul her. Fry, frizzle and boil her.'

'You've sent your telegram now,' said Cook. 'Best forget it. Time's running on and we've enough to do with them two coming.'

'Giminy!' said Nancy. 'It's a good thing whoever told her Mother was away didn't tell her we were going to have visitors.'

'They'll be here before you're ready for them,' said Cook. 'One of you ought to run round to Mrs Lewthwaite's to tell Billy he'll be wanted to drive the car.'

'We're not going to meet them in Rattletrap,' said Nancy. 'They wouldn't care twopence about driving round the head of the lake. They'll want to sail across. And they'll want to look at the new boat.'

'And what about their luggage?'

'They won't bring much. We'll get it down to the steamer pier in the bus.'

'And if there's more than what you can carry?'

'Billy Lewthwaite can fetch it in Rattletrap tomorrow. Come on, Peggy. We haven't finished the decorations yet. And we've got the boathouse to get ready for *Scarab*. And we didn't finish *Amazon*'s rigging.'

'It won't do for you to be late at the station,' said Cook.

'We aren't going to be. Come on, Peggy. That black paint'll be dry by now.'

CHAPTER 2

THE VISITORS ARRIVE

WHILE Nancy and Peggy at Beckfoot were making ready for their visitors, the train for the north, flashing through all but the biggest stations, was bringing Dick and Dorothea. Dorothea had been seen off by her mother at Euston. Dick, coming straight from school, had joined the train at Crewe, after a frantic run along the platform before he had found the through carriage and seen Dorothea waving from a window. After the first few minutes of exchanging news, and rejoicing that they had been allowed to go north at once instead of having to waste the first fortnight of the holidays sweltering in London, Dick had opened his suitcase and taken out a thin blue book, *Sailing*, by E. F. Knight, on which he meant to put in some hard work during the journey.

'What are the other books?' asked Dorothea.

'*Pocket Book of Birds*,' said Dick, 'and *Common Objects of the Countryside . . .*'

'Oh,' said Dorothea. 'Nothing to read at all?'

'You really ought to read the sailing book, too,' said Dick. 'Perhaps we'll be launching *Scarab* tonight, and it'll be awful to make mistakes with Nancy and Peggy watching.'

'I'm half-way through *The Sea Hawk*,' said Dorothea.

'Telescope, compass, microscope, collecting box,' said Dick, making sure he had forgotten nothing that mattered.

'Are those all the clothes you've brought?' said Dorothea.

'I shan't want any more,' said Dick, closing the suitcase and pushing it away under the seat. 'And there wasn't room anyhow. All the rest have gone home.'

'Have you had anything to eat? Mother told me to have lunch in the train.'

'I had mine at Crewe. I had thirty-seven minutes to wait before your train came in.'

'Good,' said Dorothea, and, while the train rushed northward, the two of them settled to their books.

Dick was a slow reader, Dorothea a fast one. Dick read the chapter on the theory of sailing, three careful times, then the chapter on small boats. He had gone back to the chapter on knots and was trying each one of them with a bit of string and being polite but firm to an old man sitting next to him, who knew no more about knots than Dick but kept on wanting to show him how to tie them, when, as the train slowed down for the last time, Dorothea closed *The Sea Hawk* with a sigh.

'It all came right in the end,' she said. 'The horrid brother had to own up and everybody knew Sir Oliver wasn't a murderer. Dick! There's the lake! We're nearly there.'

Books were hurriedly stowed. Dorothea wrote 'Arrived safely Dick and Dorothea' on the addressed postcard her mother had given her to be sent off from the station. The train jerked to a standstill. The old man said 'Good afternoon' and stepped down to the platform, and they saw the red caps of Nancy and Peggy dodging quickly through the crowd.

'Scarabs, ahoy!' cried Nancy.

'Hullo!' called Dorothea.

And then, it was as if Nancy had suddenly remembered something she had forgotten. She became a different Nancy.

'We are delighted to see you. I do hope you had a pleasant journey.'

Dorothea stared. 'Yes, thank you,' she said. 'It was very kind of you to invite us. I am so glad we were able to come.' She had understood that Nancy, who was very good at being a pirate, was now being a hostess instead.

Nancy laughed. Nobody could keep up that sort of thing for more than a sentence or two.

'Heave it out,' she said. 'And the next.'

Between them she and Peggy swung the two suitcases down to the platform. 'Is this all you've got?' she asked.

'Yes,' said Dorothea.

'Well done. We can manage these easily. Cook thought you'd have a ton of luggage. She wanted to send Billy Lewthwaite with Rattletrap. Come on. Two to a suitcase. We've got to lug them to the bus.'

'We're going down to the boat landing,' said Peggy.

'Is *Scarab* ready?' asked Dick.

'She must be, pretty nearly,' said Nancy. 'We'll know in a minute. We hadn't time to stop on the way up. Touch and go getting here to meet the train. Hullo! Here's Timothy. I thought he'd missed it.'

'Squashy Hat,' exclaimed Dorothea, who had seen him at the same moment, a tall, thin man, with an old tweed hat, working towards them through the crowd.

'We don't call him that now,' said Peggy.

'We've spent the last two holidays breaking him in,' said Nancy.

'He's still shy of everybody except us,' said Peggy. 'Look at him waiting while those farmers stand jabbering. Captain Flint would have barged through in two jiffs.'

But the tall man had seen them, waved his hand and was presently beside them. 'Hullo, partners,' he said. 'I had a few stores to get, and I thought I might as well see if you'd really arrived. Better let me have those suitcases.'

'How are you getting on with the mine?' asked Dick.

'Not so bad. We've cut into the vein at eleven places now, and got a lot of samples. Jim tells me you're going to give me a hand with the assays.'

'I'd simply love to,' said Dick.

'Look here,' said Nancy. 'You aren't going to make him do stinks when they've got a new boat.'

'Not unless he wants to. But I've promised Jim to get those assays done before he comes back.'

'We can't be sailing all the time,' said Dorothea.

'Nancy would if she could,' laughed Timothy.

'Qualitative or quantitative analysis?' asked Dick. 'I've only got as far as qualitative at school.'

'Quantitative,' said Timothy. 'Assays. We know what's there, but we want to know how much to the ounce.'

'We're going to miss that bus,' said Nancy.

'We're not,' said Timothy, and, after Dorothea had dropped her postcard into the letter-box by the booking office, the five of them squeezed into the last four seats of the station bus, and the conductor found room for the suitcases. The bus swung out of the station yard, and down through the village on its way to the steamer pier.

'When are we going to start the assays?' asked Dick.

'Working in the houseboat tomorrow,' said Timothy. 'The day after tomorrow I'm going up to the mine. We might get at the assays the day after that.'

'Not unless there's a dead calm,' said Nancy.

'If you want to have a look at your mine, you could come up to High Topps with me the day after tomorrow. I'll call for you on the way.'

'Look here,' protested Nancy. 'They've got a boat.'

'They've never seen the mine since last summer,' said Peggy.

'There isn't much to see,' said Timothy. 'The interesting stuff is what Dick and I are going to do in your uncle's study.'

'Just stinks,' said Nancy, but Dick and Timothy looked at each other with a private grin.

*

At the steamer pier they left the bus, and Timothy carried the suitcases out along one of the small landing stages. Two boats were tied up there. One was the *Amazon*, with her Jolly Roger fluttering from her masthead. The other was the old grey rowing boat that usually lay against fenders alongside Captain Flint's houseboat. Her stern was full of parcels, for Timothy Stedding had been buying stores. He now unfastened his painter, stepped in and put out his oars.

'See you the day after tomorrow,' he said. 'No need to come up to the mine unless you want to, but I'll look in just in case.'

'Aren't you coming to see their boat?' said Nancy.

'Not now,' said Timothy. 'I'm a working man. Busy. I'll see her soon enough when you come sailing along and fetch up with a bump against Jim's new paint.'

'We never do,' said Nancy. 'Remember when we came and made you and Uncle Jim walk the plank last summer? We were aboard and rushing the cabin before you knew we were anywhere near.'

'I'll look in early the day after tomorrow,' said Timothy. 'So long, partners!'

They said 'Good-bye,' and watched him as he laid to his oars and went rowing away between Long Island and the point with the boatbuilders' sheds, on his way to Houseboat Bay.

'Boats mean nothing to him at all,' said Nancy. 'He always says he'd rather walk. Uncle Jim says he's first-rate on mountains . . . Uncle Jim's too fat . . . And he says it wouldn't do for everybody to be web-footed. Come on, Dick. You've seen enough of Timothy. Hop in. You sit on the suitcases, Peggy, and Dot in the stern. I'll row across the bay.'

Five minutes later *Amazon* was slipping alongside one of the little landing stages that ran out from the boatbuilders' sheds. Wherever the new boat was, she was certainly not in the water. The old boatbuilder saw them rowing in, and came out on the stage to meet them.

'Isn't she ready?' asked Nancy.

The old boatbuilder did not even think he needed to say he was sorry. 'You'll be wanting to see her,' he said, making fast *Amazon*'s painter. 'But you must let the varnish dry. And the sail's been dressed. I've got it drying now in the loft.' He led the way into the shed and Dick and Dorothea saw for the first time the first boat they had ever owned. She lay upside down on trestles, her bottom shiny with smooth black varnish, her sides gleaming gold in the sunshine that slanted through the open door.

'Is she only thirteen feet?' asked Dick. 'She looks much bigger.'

'She's as near the same as your boat as we could make her,' the old boatbuilder said to Nancy. 'That's what Mr Turner said was wanted. You'll be racing, I dare say.'

'Yes, yes,' said Nancy. 'But the holidays have begun and they want her now. Uncle Jim's quite right. You know what he said?'

'Nay, I don't.'

'He said you were bound to be late with her because the only boatbuilder who ever finished a boat on time was Noah, and he only did it because he knew he'd be drowned if he didn't.'

'He's one for joking, is Mr Turner,' said the old man.

'But when will she be ready?' asked Nancy.

'Last coat of varnish . . . trifle of rigging . . . another coat to the oars . . . anchor should be here in the morning . . . You can have her the day after tomorrow. Better say the day after that.'

Dick knelt on the ground to look up into her from below. Dorothea, hardly believing that she was really looking at their own boat, twisted her head to read the name, SCARAB, upside down on her transom. Dick got to his feet again, saw her rudder leaning against the wall of the shed and, privately, felt the tiller in his hand.

'That's quite all right,' he said. 'We don't want to put her in the water till she's ready.' He turned to Nancy. 'We'll be able to go to High Topps the day after tomorrow without wasting any time.'

'We'll leave her tomorrow and the next day,' said Nancy. 'But the day after that we'll come for her.' She looked hard at the boatbuilder. 'She really will be ready for them by then?'

'She will that.'

'If she isn't,' said Nancy, 'we can't raise a flood, but we'll jolly well burn down the shed.'

'And welcome,' said the old boatbuilder. 'But you won't need to. She'll be afloat and waiting for you.'

*

With white sail set and a southerly wind, the *Amazon* ran swiftly back across Rio Bay and away on a straight course for the Beckfoot promontory, where a Jolly Roger had been hoisted on the flagstaff in honour of the visitors. Dorothea and Dick took their turns at steering, just to remember what it was like. They had often sailed before, both on the lake and on the Broads, but it felt different to be sailing now when in only two days' time they were going to have a boat of their own. And for nearly a year they had not been in the north. There were the hills, with patches of purple heather, glowing in the evening sun. There were other boats. A steamer came out of Rio Bay, and shook them with its wash, as it churned past on the way to the head of the lake. There was the distant peak of Kanchenjunga. Somewhere behind the nearer hills to the south of the great peak lay High Topps where they had been prospectors, found copper and ended by fighting a fell fire. Looking astern over Rio Bay, they could see High Greenland on the skyline. No matter where they looked, there was always something to remind them of the adventures of the past.

Nancy seemed to know what they were thinking. 'Look here,' she said. 'There'll be no adventures this time, not until Mother and Uncle Jim get back. We've promised. But they'll be back in eleven days and after that the Swallows are coming and, with three boats and all our tents, we'll work out something really splendid. But till then we've jolly well got to see that nothing happens at all.'

'Just being here's lovely,' said Dorothea.

'There'll be sailing, of course,' said Nancy.

'We won't have time for adventures,' said Dick. 'There'll be *Scarab*. And the work I've got to do with Timothy. And the heather's out. I promised another man I'd try to get him a fox moth caterpillar. There's always a chance of finding them on the heather. And I've got a list of birds to make. Hullo. There's the first of them anyway. I've been hoping we'd see one.' He pulled out his pocket-book, wrote 'Cormorant' and, until he lost sight of it in the shadow of the western hills, watched the big black bird flying close above the water.

'There's lots and lots to do without adventures,' said Dorothea.

'That's all right,' said Nancy.

'We knew you wouldn't mind,' said Peggy. 'So long as you know what to expect.'

They rounded the point and turned in between the reed-beds at the mouth of the Amazon River. The ridge of the promontory cut off the wind. They lowered the sail, pulled up the centreboard, and rowed slowly upstream to the old Beck-foot boathouse, with its skull and crossbones, fading now but still to be seen, painted over the entry.

'It could do with a lick of paint,' said Nancy when she saw what the visitors were looking at.

'Where's the launch?' asked Dick as soon as he could see into the boathouse.

'Having a new plank put in,' said Peggy.

'Good thing, too,' said Nancy. '*Scarab*'s going to have her place. We've got it all ready. Look out for heads while I lower the mast . . .'

'She's going to lie against those fenders,' said Peggy, and

29

Dick and Dorothea, looking at the rope fenders, saw in their minds' eyes their ship already in her private dock.

Amazon was tied up and the four of them carried the two suitcases across the lawn to the house.

'Here they are!' shouted Nancy, and old Cook came out from her kitchen to meet them and ask if they had had a good journey, tell them they'd grown since last year and remind Dick of all the plates she had broken when, a year ago, he had startled her by making the homing pigeons ring a bell.

Dick had a queer feeling that they had never gone away. Over the telephone in the hall, just where it had been last year, was Colonel Jolys's card, giving his telephone number in case of fires on the fells. He pointed it out to Dorothea:

DROUGHT   FELL FIRES

IN CASE OF FIRE RING FELLSIDE 75

T. E. JOLYS (LT-COL.)

Nancy laughed. 'Nothing for him to do this year,' she said. 'Too much rain. I bet he's simply praying for somebody to light a fire on purpose . . . No more telegrams?' she asked, turning to Cook.

'No,' said Cook. 'One's enough.'

'Good,' said Nancy, and explained to Dorothea. 'It's only our Great Aunt. She found out somehow that Mother was away and sent a telegram. I squashed her all right. Come along upstairs and look at your rooms.'

'What do you think of it?' said Nancy, as she flung open the door.

There was a moment of startled silence.

'We'll have them death's heads down in two shakes, if you like,' said Cook. 'I wouldn't care to sleep with them myself.'

'But they're simply splendid,' said Dorothea.

'Just to remind us that piracy and all that's only put off for a bit,' said Nancy.

And then Dorothea saw the beetle flag.

'Dick! Dick!' she cried. 'They've made the flag for *Scarab*. I'd been thinking about it at school but I wasn't sure how it ought to be made.'

'Peggy made it,' said Nancy. 'I only made the flagstaff.'

'Thanks most awfully,' said Dick and Dorothea together.

'Is it the right kind of beetle?' asked Peggy.

'I'm not sure about the legs,' said Dick. 'Scarabs are mostly made of clay or stone, and I think their legs are tucked up against their bodies.'

'But our scarab's alive,' said Dorothea.

'Of course it is . . . she is . . .,' said Dick. 'The legs are just right.'

Then there was Dick's room to see, but, though he admired the skulls, he admired still more the big telescope that made his own look small. 'I say,' he said. 'You can see a lot of sky from here. I'll look at stars tonight.'

'You'll be asleep before it's all that dark,' said Cook from the doorway. 'And now, Miss Nancy, I've supper ready, and they'll be wanting it.'

'All right,' said Nancy, remembering that she was in charge. 'I dare say you'll want to wash your hands after the journey. Come down as soon as you can.'

At supper, in the Beckfoot dining-room, Nancy sat at the head of the table, Peggy at the foot, their guests on either side. As Dorothea said to Dick afterwards, 'No one ever would have thought that Nancy could be so polite.' It was clear that, in spite of skulls and crossbones, plans, for the present, were for a quiet house-party, with reformed pirates entertaining the most civilized of visitors.

After supper, however, memories of the past kept crowding in. Dick, thinking of the work he was going to do with

Timothy, wanted to have a look into Captain Flint's study. Their hosts took them in and, remembering the tall, lean man who had met them at the station, they laughed at seeing the hutch that had been made for him when they had thought that he was probably an armadillo. The hutch was now used as a boot-cupboard, but it still had Timothy's name painted on its door. That, of course, reminded them of their pigeon post, and they went out into the yard to see the pigeons. Dick climbed the steps to the loft to find out if his bell was still working. He set the gate with the swinging wires but found that nothing happened when he pushed his hand through.

'It's not broken,' said Nancy. 'We undid the wire from the battery. We'll use it again this summer when Uncle Jim and Mother come back and we start stirring things up.'

As it was growing dusk, they went out over the ridge to the end of the promontory, and hauled down the skull and crossbones. Just for a moment, on their way back into the house, they had a glimpse of the old Nancy.

'There's something different about the house,' said Dorothea. 'It wasn't quite like that. Was that trelliswork there last year?'

'No,' said Peggy. 'It's for climbing roses. Uncle Jim had it done for a present for Mother.'

'Jolly useful,' said Nancy. 'Of course, when the roses grow up . . .'

'It'll be lovely,' said Dorothea.

'It won't be so much use,' said Nancy. 'Too beastly prickly. But now . . .'

She put the folded flag between her teeth, ran up the trellis like a monkey, and disappeared into her bedroom window.

'Uncle Jim says he's sorry he had it made so strong,' said Peggy.

From inside the house came the noise of someone coming downstairs in flying leaps, and, a moment later, Nancy was at the garden door. 'Pretty good, isn't it?' she said, and then,

A GREAT IMPROVEMENT TO THE HOUSE

remembering again her good resolves, she became the hostess once more. 'You must be very tired after your journey,' she said. 'I should think, for the first night, you ought to go to bed early.'

And the reformed pirates took their visitors upstairs to their bedrooms, lit their candles for them, asked them if they had everything they wanted, and left them for the night. In spite of the big telescope lying handy, Dick decided not to wait for the stars. Dorothea blew out her candle and settled herself in the middle of the big spare-room bed. An owl called in the woods. 'Not a barn owl, but a tawny,' thought Dick, listening to the sharp 'Gewick! Gewick!' as he fell asleep. A smell of new-mown hay drifted from the meadows on the farther side of the river. 'There isn't a lovelier place in all the world,' thought Dorothea. London last night, and now Beckfoot. The summer holidays had begun.

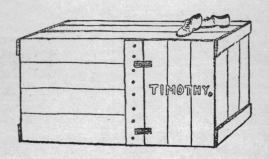

CHAPTER 3

OUT OF THE BLUE

No one could have guessed from the way the day began how differently it was going to end. There was a dip in the river before breakfast, when Dick added three more birds, waterhen, wagtail and swan, to the list he had begun the night before. Breakfast, like supper, was a formal meal, with hosts being polite to guests and guests refusing to be outdone in courtesy by their hosts. They talked of plans, but these were all of the tamer kind.

'You do understand, don't you?' said Nancy. 'It's no good thinking of anything tremendous. It's got to be plain ordinary life, to show Mother it was perfectly safe to leave us by ourselves.'

'Of course,' said Dorothea. 'We don't mind. I've got a new story to write.'

'And there's the boat,' said Dick. 'And birds, and that chemistry I'm going to do with Timothy. There wouldn't really be time for anything else.'

'Good,' said Nancy. 'It feels a bit rum planning for nothing to happen instead of stirring things up, but that's what we've got to do. There's one thing about it. It's easy.'

'It's going to be perfect,' said Dorothea.

And then, soon after they had finished breakfast, the blow fell.

A bell rang somewhere in the house, followed by a double knock on the front door.

'Postman,' said Peggy.

She and Nancy ran out into the hall.

'There won't be a letter for us yet,' said Dick.

35

'There might be,' said Dorothea, and they went out after the others.

The postman was just handing the letters over. 'Nay,' he was saying, 'they're not all for your mother, nor for your uncle either. There's a postcard for each of you ... Bergen postmark ... Fine-looking place ... And a letter for Miss Ruth Blackett ... Eh? I'm glad to see you back and hope you're well ...' He smiled cheerfully at Dick and Dorothea, whom he remembered from the year before.

'Thank you very much. I hope you are, too,' said Dorothea.

'Nowt to go back?' said the postman.

'Not today,' said Peggy, and the postman went trudging off to his bicycle, which he had left by the gate.

'Is something the matter?' asked Dorothea.

Nancy had hardly glanced at the picture-postcards. She had dropped the letters for her mother and Captain Flint on the table in the hall. She was staring at the letter addressed to herself.

'Something *is* the matter,' said Dorothea, and Dick, who had been looking at the postcards with Peggy, glanced up at Nancy's face and saw that Dorothea was right. Nancy was holding the envelope in her hand almost as if she were afraid to open it.

'Harrogate postmark,' she said, 'and calling me Ruth ... It's a letter from the Great Aunt.'

'Open it. Open it,' said Peggy. 'Let's get it over. It's bound to be beastly. Like her nosy telegram,' she explained to Dorothea. 'The Great Aunt never writes to us except for birthdays to hope we're turning over new leaves.'

Nancy opened the letter. Her face went crimson. She stamped her foot. 'But I told her we weren't alone,' she said. 'Whatever are we to do? Cook!' she called. 'Cooky! The most awful thing has happened ...'

Dorothea stared at her. How could a letter from an aunt

be so upsetting to an Amazon Pirate? She thought of other aunts they knew, most friendly, kindly creatures. Were Great Aunts somehow different? Dorothea could not believe it. She thought a Great Aunt must be something like Mrs Barrable, with whom they had been sailing on the Broads. And a letter from Mrs Barrable was always good fun for everybody with the little pictures her pen kept making when she let it run away. But there was Nancy, at first afraid to open the Great Aunt's letter, and then looking as if it had brought dreadful news.

'Is someone dead?' said Dorothea.

'Ten times worse than that,' said Nancy.

'What is it?' said Cook, who had come to the kitchen door.

'Read it,' said Nancy.

'Nay, I can't read it,' said Cook, 'not without my spectacles.'

'Well listen,' said Nancy. 'It's Aunt Maria. She's coming here.'

'She can't do that, with your mother away,' said Cook.

'That's why she's coming,' said Nancy.

Nancy read the letter aloud:

My dear Ruth,

I have just learnt with surprise that your mother has chosen this time to go abroad with your Uncle James. Neither of them has thought fit to let me know of their intentions. I am horrified at the idea that you and Margaret are alone in the house. I cannot consider Cook sufficient guardian in your mother's absence. It may have been from a wish to spare me anxiety that your mother did not tell me she was to be away from home when you returned from school for your vacation. A little more thought would have shown her that I should have preferred to hear from her than to receive such disturbing news at second hand. However that may be, my duty is plain. Inconvenient as it is for me to disarrange my plans, I cannot permit you two children to be thus abandoned to your own devices. You tell me your mother returns on the thirteenth. On that

day I am expecting a friend whose visit I cannot defer. I have, however, cancelled all my engagements until that date, and am coming
to Beckfoot tomorrow to take charge of the house till the eve of your
mother's return, when I shall have to leave you to prepare for my
visitor at Harrogate. I shall be glad if you will ask Cook to air the
spare-room bed for me. I have made, by telephone, my own
arrangements for a conveyance to meet me at the station, and expect
to be at Beckfoot between six thirty and seven o'clock.

Believe me, my dear niece,

Your affectionate Aunt,

Maria Turner.

'Beast! Beast! Beast!' said Nancy. 'And we can't stop
her. We can't do anything. And she's going to be here
tonight.'

'If Miss Turner thinks I'm not fit to look after you, I'd
best be packing,' said Cook. 'I'll not stop in the house with
her.'

'Is she very awful?' asked Dorothea.

'She jolly well is,' said Nancy. 'You ask the Swallows.
They know what it's like when she's here. She spoilt everything for all of us. We had to be in for meals and learn poetry
and wear best frocks and be seen and not heard and all that
sort of rot. Ask Cook. She knows her, too. She fairly danced
when she went away. Yes, you did.'

'I wasn't sorry to see the back of her,' said Cook. 'Sitting
down to meals before I had 'em ready. Looking at her tumbler
and wiping it with her napkin. She's one of them that can't
keep their eyes off the clock when other folk are a bit behind.
If she hadn't gone when she did she'd have had your mother
in bed with all her worriting.'

'Last time she was here,' said Nancy, 'Uncle Jim told
Mother she must never have the G.A. here again except in
term time. And Mother said she never would.'

'Let's take to the hills,' said Peggy. 'Let's clear out to
the island. Cook can come, too. We'll leave the key for the
G.A., and she can stew in Beckfoot all by herself.'

Dorothea looked at Nancy. This was the sort of plan that Nancy herself might have made in ordinary times. But Nancy, in charge of Beckfoot, was a different Nancy.

'We can't,' she said. 'No camping till Mother comes back.'

'She'll ruin everything,' said Peggy.

'I know,' said Nancy. 'But it's not that that matters. Can't you see? It's Mother she's hitting at, not us. She means to make Mother wish she'd never gone away. She means to make her wish she'd never been born.'

'Well, I wish she hadn't.'

'Don't be a butter-brained galoot,' said Nancy. 'Mother, not the G.A. She's going to make Mother wish she herself had never been born. We've got to stick it. So has Cook. We've got to soothe the savage breast. We've got to be so jolly good that she simply can't not realize that it was all right for Mother to go away.'

'I'd like to ramscramble the one that put it into her head to come,' said Cook. 'Where are we going to put her, I'd like to know. Air the spare-room bed for her! I'll have to put her in your mother's room.'

'Oh, look here, we can't do that. She jolly well shan't sleep in Mother's bed.'

'Where else?' said Cook. 'She don't know you've got visitors . . .'

'She'll be more furious than ever when she finds out.'

'She will that . . .' And then, Dorothea saw that Cook had something to say that she did not want those visitors to hear. Cook was going back into her kitchen, and Dorothea saw her give Nancy a beckoning nod.

'It's all right, Cooky,' said Nancy. 'Spit it out. We've got no secrets from them.'

'You come in here for a minute,' said Cook.

'Go on,' said Dorothea. 'Dick and I don't mind. We'll be in the garden . . . Come on, Dick.'

Dick followed Dorothea out through the hall door at once, but even so they could not help getting a hint of what was in Cook's mind. 'Visitors while she's away . . .,' Cook was saying. 'Your poor mother'll never hear the last of it.'

*

'We may have to clear out,' said Dorothea. 'Did you hear what Cook said?'

'Go home?' said Dick. 'But we can't. There's *Scarab* nearly ready. And I've got to do those assays with Timothy. And we've only just got here.'

'It can't be helped,' said Dorothea. 'I'm in the spare room and the Aunt wants to sleep in it.'

'They'll fix up a bed for you somewhere else.'

'That isn't all,' said Dorothea. 'You heard that letter. She thinks Mrs Blackett oughtn't to have left Nancy and Peggy. And Cook says it'll be worse when she finds they've got visitors.'

'But Mrs Blackett asked us.'

'That's just it,' said Dorothea. 'Look here. I've got to tell Nancy we'll go. I'd better tell her at once . . .' She went back into the hall. A tremendous argument seemed to be going on in the kitchen. She heard Cook, Peggy and Nancy all talking at once. 'Hi! Nancy!' she called. The talking stopped suddenly.

'Come on in,' called Nancy. 'Cook says . . .'

'Don't you think we'd better go home?' said Dorothea. 'We could come back after she's gone.'

'What about Dixon's farm?' said Nancy, and Dorothea knew that her instinct had been right.

'I thought of that,' said she. 'And Holly Howe. But they're both full up. That's why Mother wrote to Mrs Blackett. We'd better go home. We can come back after she's gone.'

'We don't want you to go,' said Nancy. 'And Mother

wouldn't want you to go. She'd be as sick as anything. It's only that the G.A.'s going to undo all the good of Mother's holiday. Cook's right about that. She'll go for Mother for having you here at all ... But why should you go? Why shouldn't Mother ask you here if she wants to? Why should the G.A. be allowed to barge in and spoil everything? Hullo, Dick's got something to say.'

Dick had come in, and was standing in the doorway, wiping his spectacles with his handkerchief. Nancy, like Dorothea, knew the signs.

'Spit it out, Professor,' she said.

'Couldn't we be badgers?' he said.

'What?'

'Couldn't we go on being here and never let her see us? Like badgers. In lots of places people think they're extinct. But they aren't. Only they never let themselves be seen.'

'She'd hear you moving in the house,' said Nancy. 'And it wouldn't be any good talking about ghosts to the Great Aunt. She'd go on the prowl till she found you.'

'Things'd be a sight worse then,' said Cook.

'Need we be in the house?' said Dorothea. 'Our tents are here from last year.'

'No camping,' said Nancy. 'We promised that.'

'If only the igloo wasn't on the other side of the lake,' said Dick.

'We could have lived in that all right,' said Dorothea. 'We'd be Picts.'

'Picts?' said Nancy.

'Ancient Britons,' said Dorothea. 'Prehistorics. Original inhabitants. They had to hide from the invaders and went on living secretly in caves and in the end people thought they were fairies and used to leave milk outside the door for them. Something like that. I heard Father talking about it . . .'

'What about the Dogs' Home?' said Peggy.

Nancy jumped off the ground with both feet at once. 'Well

done, Peggy,' she cried. 'Well done, Dick! I was a galoot never to have thought of it. They could be Picts there for a hundred years and all the Great Aunts in the world would never know. Come on. Let's go and have a look at it at once.'

'That old place,' said Cook. 'There's no glass in the window and the roof's likely enough down by now.'

'Bet it isn't,' said Nancy. 'Glass doesn't matter. Fresh air's all right. And there's a grand fireplace. And plenty of wood everywhere. Look here, Cooky, they could live in the Dogs' Home as comfortably as anything till Mother and Uncle Jim come back.'

'What about their meals?' said Cook.

'Easy. Dorothea's a splendid cook.'

'I never *have* cooked,' said Dorothea. 'But I've often watched Susan.'

'There's nothing in cooking,' said Nancy. 'Not the sort you'll have to do. And we can smuggle food out to you.'

'Can't you come too?'

'She knows we're here. We can't escape. We've got to bear it. But it'll be a lot easier if she isn't made worse by finding we've got visitors.'

'I don't know what your mother'd say about it,' said Cook.

'Look here,' said Nancy. 'Mother wouldn't want them to go home. She'd planned everything. Only she never thought the G.A. would be here. They're jolly well going to stay. They'll be all right in the Dogs' Home. The G.A. won't know anything about them so there'll be one thing less for her to complain to Mother about. And if we can only manage to be angels for ten whole days she won't have anything to complain about at all. Come on.'

'She'll be here at half past six,' said Cook suddenly. 'And you've got the spare room looking like a nightmare.'

'You get at it right away,' said Nancy. 'We'll tear down the skulls and crossbones when we come back. We must just see if the Dogs' Home's fallen down.'

'But . . .'

'Settled,' said Nancy. 'It's the only possible way. Come on, the Picts.'

And leaving Cook worriedly fingering Miss Turner's letter, Nancy and Peggy, followed by Dorothea and Dick, went out of the kitchen, through the yard and turned right outside the Beckfoot gate along the road that led up the valley under the steep woods.

'But what is the Dogs' Home?' Dorothea asked Peggy.

'You'll see,' said Peggy.

EGYPTIAN SCARAB

CHAPTER 4

THE DOGS' HOME

NANCY was racing ahead. 'Hammocks,' she said over her shoulder. 'You'll do better in them than sleeping on the ground.'

'There might be a rat or two,' said Peggy.

'How far is it?' asked Dorothea.

'No way,' said Peggy. 'That's the beauty of it. It's up in the wood just round the first bend.'

Dick and Dorothea knew the road that passed Beckfoot, turned inland to the bridge over the little river, and divided into two, one road going to the head of the lake, and the other going on up the valley and past High Topps over to Dundale. But they had never been up into the woods that sloped steeply down to it behind Beckfoot.

'If only it hasn't tumbled down,' said Nancy.

'We haven't been up there for ages,' said Peggy. 'It's where we used to go when we were young, before we had *Amazon* and before we discovered Wild Cat Island. It's a jolly good place.'

'It's a jolly good place to be hidden in,' said Nancy. 'No one can see it from anywhere and we can slip up there ourselves if ever we can escape.'

'Just the place for badgers,' she said a moment later. 'Or Britons, or whatever it was you said.'

'Picts,' said Dorothea.

'This way, the Picts!' said Nancy, and turned off the road through a gap in the low stone wall at the bottom of the wood.

*

Dick and Dorothea followed breathless, not so much because they were hurrying as because of the speed with which things were happening. Plans for a quiet life had been blown away in a moment. That letter from the Blacketts' Great Aunt had changed everything. Why, even Cook, who had seemed so pleased to see them, had been as much upset by it as Peggy and Nancy. At breakfast they had been welcome visitors, but after the coming of that letter even Cook had not been able to pretend that it was not a pity they were there. What could the Great Aunt be like? And then a word from Dick about being badgers, a word from Dorothea about being Picts, and already they were looking for a hiding place. Better than going home, of course, but . . . a dogs' home, kennels . . .

'Buck up, you Picts!' said Peggy.

*

There was a belt of tall pines and larches along the side of the road. A path from the gap in the wall led suddenly from sunshine into shadow. For twenty yards or so there was a clear track covered with brown needles. But beyond the pines and firs was coppice, oaks and hazels and silver birches, and the Picts could seldom see more than a yard or two ahead. For a little way the path was good enough under foot, and then, suddenly, it turned into something like the bed of a dried-up mountain stream, sharp-edged stones and rocks with here and there a tiny pool. Dick and Dorothea found it pretty hard going, stepping from one stone to another, and at the same time fending off the hazel branches.

'A bit of a beck crosses it higher up,' said Peggy, waiting for them. 'That's why it's like this. When there's a lot of rain the beck overflows and comes sluicing down here, and you have to wriggle up through the trees instead.'

'It's all right,' said Dorothea. 'Only it takes time. How much farther?'

'Nearly there.'

'Where does the beck go?' asked Dick, remembering that he had seen no bridge.

'It's only a little one,' said Peggy. 'It goes through a pipe under the road and then through our coppice to the river.'

They climbed on. Nancy, charging up the rough path with her arms before her face because of the branches, was already out of sight.

Suddenly they heard a joyful shout above them in the wood. 'It hasn't tumbled down yet.'

They came to the place where the beck crossed the path.

'Hullo,' said Peggy. 'Somebody's put down stepping stones. There never used to be any.'

On the other side of the beck some of the trees had been cleared long ago and in the open space was an ancient old hut, built of rough stones. A window gaped empty. The roof was covered with huge slates, green with moss. Here and there grass was growing on it, and there were ferns sprouting from between the stones of the chimney. Somebody, once upon a time, had painted the words 'THE DOGS' HOME' in big clumsy letters on the door. The paint had faded, but the words could still be read.

'It's come down a bit on this side,' said Nancy, from behind the hut.

They went round and found her looking at a heap of stones that had fallen from the wall at the back.

'Lucky they built the walls so thick,' she said. 'There's plenty of it left. It'll last another week anyway. And jolly lucky it isn't the wall with the fireplace. If the inside's all right it'll do. Let's see what it's like.'

'Hullo,' said Peggy at the door. 'Somebody's been using it for something. The door's tied up.'

'Rot,' said Nancy. 'There's nobody to use it.'

'Come and look,' said Peggy.

'IT HASN'T TUMBLED DOWN YET'

'It's been tied up a long time,' said Dick. 'You can see by the string.'

Once upon a time there had been a chain and perhaps a padlock to fasten the door from the outside. Nothing of that

was left but a staple in the door and another in the doorpost.
A bit of string had been put through the two staples and tied.

Nancy looked at it. 'Tied in a bow,' she said. 'No sailor
anyhow. Nobody we know would tie the thing like that. But
you're quite right. Somebody has been using it. Look at those
hinges. Oiled. They used to be a mass of rust.'

'There's a lot of stuff inside,' said Dorothea, who had been
trying to look into the gloom through the glassless window.
'Why is it called "The Dogs' Home"?'

'Joke, I expect,' said Nancy, plucking at the string.
'Uncle Jim says the woodcutters used it long before we were
born. And he used it when he was a little boy. Rotten luck for
us if anybody's using it now.' She opened the door.

No one can see much when they look through a small
window into a dark room, and what little Dorothea had been
able to make out in the gloom had not been cheering. When
the door was opened and the light poured in, the hut at first
looked even less like a place in which it was possible that
anybody, unless perhaps real Picts, savages or badgers, could
settle down to live. It was like peering into a wood pile.
A huge mass of firewood seemed to fill the hut. Dead branches
of trees had been hauled into the hut and thrown one above
another on the earthen floor.

'If somebody's using it, we're done,' said Peggy.

But Nancy was forcing her way in between wall and firewood. Dorothea and Peggy followed her. Dick, after one
glance, went back and came in through the window instead.

And suddenly the thought of living in the hut began to
seem more hopeful. Once past that great barricade of tree
branches there was room for them to move about, and they
could see that whatever the hut lacked it had something that
in houses matters more than anything else.

'What a gorgeous fireplace,' said Dorothea.

'I told you it was a good one,' said Nancy.

It was an enormous fireplace, taking up nearly half of one

wall, a huge cavern of a fireplace, of the old kind, built for burning wood, with no grate, but an iron bar, very rusty, stretching from one side to the other with a great hook hanging on it.

'That's for a kettle,' said Peggy.

'Yes,' said Dorothea.

'This is something new,' said Nancy, looking at a wooden chair that had lost its back. 'There wasn't any furniture when we were here.'

'What are those pegs for?' asked Dick.

He was looking up at two great beams, black with age and smoke, that stretched from one side of the hut to the other under the ridge of the roof. Huge wooden pegs, a yard or so apart, stuck out of the beams.

'Hanging things on,' said Peggy. 'Guns, perhaps. Uncle Jim says a gamekeeper lived here before the woodcutters.'

'Jolly useful,' said Dick. 'And that shelf over the fireplace is just the thing for keeping books on, and my microscope . . .'

Dorothea looked at him. Well, if Dick thought it was all right . . .

'Nobody's using it,' said Nancy suddenly. 'If anybody was there'd be some bedding about, and there isn't. Let's make a fire and see what it's really like.'

'It doesn't smell really damp,' said Peggy.

'All hands to breaking up wood,' said Nancy. 'Whoever was here has left a good lot of logs as well as all that small stuff. But we want sticks to get it started. Small twigs first. Who's got any matches?'

'I have,' said Dick, who had put a box in his pocket before leaving school to be ready for such moments as this.

'Good,' said Nancy. 'Look here. The twigs aren't too dry. Handful of dry leaves . . . We'll get a fire started and then we'll clear all these sticks out and have room to turn round . . .'

Dick, climbing out through the window, was back in a

moment with some dry leaves. Nancy made a little heap of them in the old fireplace on the soft grey ash of old fires. She put a match to them and as they flared up built them in with twigs. The twigs caught fire, little jets of flame spouting from their ends. She built the twigs in with sticks, and as these too crackled and flamed, she added bigger sticks and small logs that someone had left piled neatly in a corner. The fire roared cheerfully up the chimney.

'It must have taken somebody an age to collect all these sticks,' said Dorothea.

'It won't take ten minutes to get them out,' said Peggy, and, with all four of them working as hard as they could, the pile of dead branches that had half filled the hut soon began to grow smaller.

'Make a proper wood pile outside,' said Nancy. 'It'll all come in handy. They'll want a saw to cut it up.'

'There's a saw here,' said Dick. As the pile of branches grew lower in the hut he had seen something hanging on the wall behind it. He had worked his way in between the wood and the wall till he could reach it, and was looking at it now, feeling its blade with a finger. He brought it out into the sunlight. 'Jolly well hidden,' he said. 'And properly looked after. Whoever it belongs to put grease on it to stop it rusting. Fingerprints on it,' he added. 'A bit smaller than mine . . .'

'Won't do it any harm to use it,' said Nancy.

'But perhaps there's a sort of Pict living here already,' said Dorothea.

'Couldn't be,' said Nancy. 'Where could he sleep with the whole place bung full of sticks like it was?'

'Just somebody collecting wood and leaving a saw behind,' said Dick. 'Jolly useful for us.'

Even when all the branches were cleared out, the floor was left covered with broken twigs, but, somehow, the hut, that had seemed very small at first, had seemed to be growing as branch after branch was lugged out into the open. Now, with nothing but small stuff left on the floor, it seemed quite roomy. It was unfurnished, except for the chair that had lost its back, and the shelf that ran along the wall above the fireplace, but Dick and Dorothea, picking up broken sticks and throwing them on the fire, were already beginning to think of it as a home.

'Where will we have the hammocks?' said Dorothea.

'We could hang them under the two big beams,' said Dick. Nancy and Peggy were watching them hopefully.

'Will it do?' said Nancy at last. 'Do you think you could manage?'

'There's a three-legged stool in our bedroom,' said Peggy. 'You could have that.'

'We'll have to do something about a table for you,' said Nancy.

'Picts never had tables,' said Dorothea.

'We'll fix up something,' said Nancy. 'If you're writing a story you'll want one. But the point is, will it do?'

'It's going to be splendid,' said Dorothea. 'It's a perfect place to write in.'

'Jolly good for watching birds,' said Dick. 'Butterflies, too. I saw a red admiral and two fritillaries just outside. And I'm pretty sure I heard a woodpecker.'

'The main thing is it's so near the house,' said Nancy. 'And utterly out of sight. Once we've nipped out without being spotted we can be up here in two shakes. Ten times better than if you had to clear out altogether or be on the other side of the lake. And you can go past Beckfoot and out on the promontory . . .'

'To get *Scarab* out of the boathouse?' said Dick.

'Giminy,' said Nancy. 'I forgot that. We'll have to make a harbour for your boat somewhere up the river. It wouldn't do for the Great Aunt to find her in our boathouse. What's the time?'

'Half past twelve,' said Dick. 'Twenty-seven and half minutes to one.'

'Less than six hours and she'll be here,' said Nancy. 'Come on. We've got to fix up your hammocks. We've got to bring bedding. You'll want stores and cooking things. We've got to turn Dorothea's lair back into a beastly spare room. And then we've got to be all proper in party dresses ready to soothe the savage breast when the Great Aunt comes gorgoning in. We'll manage her all right so long as we can keep your secret. What her codfish eyes don't see her conger heart can't grieve over. I think it's splendid of you and Dick.'

'We'll have to pack our things,' said Dorothea.

'We'd better hurry up,' said Peggy. 'Cook'll have grub ready soon, and you'd better tuck in while you can if you haven't done much cooking.'

'I can manage eggs anyhow,' said Dorothea. 'And I'll soon learn.'

'Of course they'll manage,' said Nancy. 'And old Cook'll smuggle things out to them. It isn't as if they were going to be a hundred miles away. Come on. No, don't put any more on the fire. We can light it again if we want it. And look out for broken ankles hurtling down the path.'

CHAPTER 5

TRANSFORMATION SCENES

'I've the sheets off,' said Cook. 'But I won't make the bed till you shift them death heads. And I'm thinking if Miss Turner's to be in the spare room, I'd best make up your mother's bed for . . .'

'Dorothea won't want it,' said Nancy. 'The Dogs' Home is just right. We're taking hammocks for them. And you'll give them the camping kettle and our big saucepan and a couple of mugs, and stores. . . . All right. All right. We'll clear the spare room in two jumps of a weasel. Give us time to pack . . .'

Cook looked at Dorothea.

'We're going to be very comfortable,' said Dorothea.

'I don't know what to do,' said Cook. 'There's this room a nightmare, and I must run a duster over the drawing-room. A body could write their name in the dust on the piano.'

'Piano,' exclaimed Nancy. 'Jibbooms and bobstays! She'll be making us play the beastly thing. Come on, Peggy. You go and get the drawing pins out on the other side . . . carefully, or we'll tear it. We'll want a Jolly Roger or two to cheer up the Pict's Home.'

'You be getting them things down,' said Cook, 'and I'll have your dinner on the table. Days like this a body wants two pairs of legs and a dozen arms . . .'

'It isn't really that you want,' said Nancy, pulling out drawing pins from the skull and crossbones over the head of the bed in which the Great Aunt was to sleep. 'It's time. It always goes too fast or too slow. Here's the G.A. coming and minutes fly like seconds and yet when we're at school waiting for the end of term the days drag out like years. Look out, Peggy. Hold your side up till I get out this last pin . . .'

Dick had gone off to his room that was really Captain Flint's, and was collecting everything that was his and putting it on the bed. Dorothea was putting back into her suitcase the things she had taken out the night before.

'We won't lug the suitcases up the wood,' said Nancy. 'Take just the things you can't do without. We can stow the suitcases here.'

'The suitcases'll be pretty useful,' said Dorothea. 'Like a chest of drawers.'

'All right,' said Nancy. 'Of course it would be pretty awful if she started prowling round the box-room and found them here. We'll get them up somehow.'

'Torn,' said Peggy. 'Can't be helped. Anyway the big one's all right.' She folded the remains of the Jolly Roger that had been on the foot of the bed. 'What about the flags?'

'They'll want the scarab flag for their boat. They won't want the other.'

'Come and eat your dinner,' called Cook from downstairs and at the same time banged loudly on the dinner gong.

*

Lunch in the Beckfoot dining-room was like the last meal in a house before people are moving to a new one. The dining-room looked the same as usual, but it was as if the carpets were up, and the furniture half packed, and a van waiting outside for the rest of it. They could hear Cook pushing the spare-room bed about (at least that was what it sounded like) while she was hurriedly making it up anew for the unwelcome visitor. Nancy and Peggy were snapping out single words, 'Hammocks' . . . 'Hammer' . . . 'Nails' . . . 'Bedding' . . . 'Grog' . . . 'Pemmican' . . . 'Tin opener' . . . their minds darting this way and that through the memories of camping expeditions, trying to be sure that nothing should be forgotten that the Picts would need. Dorothea was looking

54

ahead into the housekeeping that she would be doing for the first time. Dick was thinking of the hut as a forest base for a naturalist. He was almost sure that was a woodpecker he had heard . . . But neither Dick nor Dorothea got very far with their thoughts. Those single, practical words, snapped out by the experienced Amazons, kept breaking in with new ideas. Five minutes after they had finished not one of them could have said off hand what they had eaten or whether they had eaten anything.

*

'We've got to get Cook working on their stores,' said Nancy. 'She must have done that room by now.' For a few minutes the noises from upstairs, of brushes banging against walls and catching against chairs and bed-legs, had come to an end. Suddenly there was a new noise of drawers being pulled open and banged shut.

'She's done,' said Peggy. 'She's just looking in the chest of drawers to see there's nothing of Dot's left behind.'

They went up and found Dorothea's suitcase on the landing outside the spare-room door. Cook was looking anxiously round.

'If there's owt amiss, Miss Turner's the one to see it,' she said.

'There's nothing amiss,' said Nancy. 'It's the same dull room it always was. And after all the work we put into it, cheering it up for Dot.'

'She likes a box of biscuits by her bed. And a glass and a jug of water,' said Peggy.

'Flowers,' said Nancy. 'We'll do that. At least . . . You go and pick some flowers for her, Dot; Peggy and I have got to raid the kitchen . . .'

'That you haven't,' said Cook. 'I'll get that kettle for them in a minute. Happen it *will* be better if they're out of sight.'

'We'll come with you,' said Nancy. 'They'll want all our

camping things. Give them just what you give us when we camp on Wild Cat Island. Fill up the puncheon for them. Lucky you made a lot of lemonade before they came . . .'

'What flowers shall I pick?' said Dorothea.

'Deadly nightshade would be best,' said Nancy. 'Only there isn't any. Or garlic . . . that's got a lively smell. No. The whole thing is to keep her happy. Better give the beast roses.'

Dorothea came back with the roses and met Nancy staggering across the hall with a bundle of brown netting.

'Hammocks!' said Nancy, and dumped them on the floor. 'I'll get you some vases. Hi! Peggy! Take down the Jolly Rogers from Dick's bed. She's bound to poke her nose in and want to know what Uncle Jim was doing with them. I say, Dot, when you've plunked the roses in her room . . . Some on the dressing-table . . . Some on the mantelpiece and some with the biscuit tin by her bed . . . just make sure Dick's got all his things . . . Coming . . . COMING! Jibbooms and bobstays! We've only got four hours left . . .' She was gone and back again in a moment with three glass vases for the flowers. 'Water in the bathroom,' she said. 'I've got to keep an eye on Cook and the stores.'

Ten minutes later not a trace of Dick and Dorothea was left in the rooms that had been theirs. The spare room, gay with roses, was ready for a guest of a very different kind. Even the two suitcases were down in the hall, with the hammocks, kettle, hammer, a tin of nails and a huge pile of rugs.

In the kitchen Cook was filling tins with tea and sugar and Peggy and Nancy were packing things into knapsacks. 'And a cake,' said Cook. 'And a beef roll to start on, and a dozen eggs. Dearie me, I wish I knew if I'm doing right or wrong.'

'Right. Right. Right,' said Nancy. 'There's nothing else to be done and you know it. Look here, if you and Peggy and I all fairly bust ourselves being angels she'll simply have to let Mother alone. But if Dick and Dot are here she'll be down on

MOVING HOUSE

Mother and down on us and down on them and we'll never be able to hold in and everything'll be ten millions times worse.'

'Well, I'm doing it for the best,' said Cook. 'And if it turns out bad . . .'

'It won't. Their house is splendid. They'll be better off there than here. And you'll be able to smuggle grub to them. Where are our mugs and the camping spoons and knives and forks?'

'Out of my kitchen all the lot of you,' said Cook. 'We'll be having her here before they're out of the house. Miss Peggy, come out of my larder . . .'

'All right, we'll leave the rest of the stores to you. We'll be getting on with all the other things. Giminy, there'll be a lot to carry. And we can't use dromedaries either. Nobody could push a bicycle up that path . . . Come on the Picts. Everybody cart what they can.'

*

For the next few hours even the Great Aunt herself was forgotten in the rush of house moving. They had not far to go, but every single thing had to be carried by hand. There were the two packed suitcases, that the four of them, two to a suitcase, found quite enough to manage, going up the steep place through the hazels where the overflow from the beck had washed the path away. There were the hammocks, a three-legged stool, a Tate & Lyle sugar case for a table, a hurricane lantern, the scarab flag, the folded paper skull and crossbones, the big camp kettle, a huge saucepan, a teapot, mugs, spoons, knives, forks, plates and more stores than would go into all four knapsacks. There was the little barrel, filled with lemonade, that had to be slung from a pole and carried up by Nancy and Peggy, who explained that in the ordinary way they carried their grog slung beneath an oar.

Down at Beckfoot, as they came dashing in for fresh loads, they found Cook getting hotter and hotter, shaking out rugs, dusting and generally trying to do twenty-two things at once.

'And what about your tea?' she said late in the afternoon, as Nancy went off for the last time with a knapsack in each hand.

'No time,' said Nancy. 'We'll hang on till supper. There's an awful lot to do.'

'And them two?'

'They're all right. Rigging hammocks with Peggy.'

'You'll be back before Miss Turner comes?'

'Back and beautiful,' said Nancy. 'Be an angel, Cooky, and save time by digging out our best frocks.'

*

Up at the hut in the wood, the pile of things dumped outside it was dwindling. The two hammocks had been slung under the big cross-beams. Stores and crockery had been allowed to share the shelf high above the fireplace with Dick's microscope and books. The huge skull and crossbones had been fixed up on the wall. A soap box, in a corner well away from the fire, was being used as a larder. The sugar case made a table and store cupboard in one.

'We've forgotten something,' said Dorothea. 'What about our sleeping bags? They're put away somewhere with our tents.'

'Have you ever tried to get into a sleeping bag in a hammock?' asked Nancy. 'It can't be done . . . not unless you're a sort of eel. That's why we brought the rugs.'

Dick was looking at the hammocks. He was wiping his spectacles. Dorothea knew that he was trying to work out the scientific way of getting into a hammock slung far above the floor. But he did not say anything, and neither did she. That sort of thing they would have to find out for themselves.

'Barbecued billygoats,' said Nancy. 'Who slung those hammocks?'

'I did,' said Peggy. 'Is anything wrong?'

'Let go this end of this one,' said Nancy, 'while I do the other, and then make it fast again with a bowline. Then they can undo them and roll them up during the day. We'll roll them up now.'

'No, no,' said Dick. 'Please leave them so that I can have a good look and be able to do it tomorrow.'

Tomorrow. By that time they would have slept in those hammocks . . . if they could ever get into them. Dorothea looked hurriedly away.

'It's a lot better than the igloo,' said Nancy. 'And it'll be better still when you've lived in it a bit.'

'Let's start the fire again and make tea,' said Dorothea.

'What's the time?' said Nancy.

Dick pulled out his watch. 'Twenty-two minutes to six.'

'Good-bye, Picts,' said Nancy. 'She'll be here before we're ready if we don't go.'

'Do you think she's really going to make it very awful?' said Dorothea.

'Pretty awful, I expect,' said Peggy. 'She usually does.'

'It would have been a jolly lot worse for everybody,' said Nancy, 'if she found visitors in the house with Mother away. We've saved that anyhow, thanks to you people not minding being kicked out.'

'We're going to be all right,' said Dorothea. 'But what about you?'

'We'll keep her purring somehow. Come on, Peggy. You've got a smear right across your face. Hurry up. Soap and water. White frocks. Oh gosh, and party shoes. Come on. Look here, we'll never be able to give her the slip tonight, but one of us ought to be able to dodge out in the morning. One of us'll have to, or you won't have milk for breakfast. Good-bye. Picts for ever!'

'Picts and martyrs!' said Dorothea.

'Now to meet the lioness,' said Nancy, and, with Peggy close behind her, was gone.

CHAPTER 6

'SHE'S HERE!'

THE noise of footsteps died away below them in the wood. Dorothea stood listening till she could hear them no more. Everything had happened with such a rush, there had been no time to think. Now, suddenly she began to wonder if after all they were doing the right thing, and, even worse, if they were going to be able to do it. She was sure they were right in clearing out from Beckfoot. What else could they have done? Nancy and Peggy were older than they were and had wanted them to go. Even old Cook had been thinking they would be better gone. But wouldn't it have been better to go away altogether? Down at Beckfoot it had seemed quite simple, just to go and live in a hut in the wood. It had seemed easy till Nancy and Peggy had gone. Now, just for a moment, she found herself wanting to run after them.

She turned to look at the Dogs' Home that was now to be a house for Picts. Were they really going to live in that old hut, alone, high in the wood, with no one else within sight or call? Were they going this very night to sleep in it, and wake in it tomorrow alone and secret, like escaping prisoners hiding in a hostile country? They had never even camped except with other tents close by and with John and the capable Susan taking charge and doing the housekeeping for everybody. Was she going to be able to manage by herself? Wasn't the whole idea a mistake?

She looked at Dick and saw that he had no doubts at all. For him there had been a problem to solve and a solution found for it. If they could not live at Beckfoot, they must live some-where else. Why not here? And she saw that Dick was already looking warily into the trees and trying to get a better view of some bird of which he had caught a glimpse. Dorothea pulled herself together. Nancy and Peggy down there at Beckfoot with the Great Aunt were going to have the really difficult time. And, whatever happened, she and Dick must not be the ones to let them down.

'Come on, Dick,' she said. 'Let's see what wants doing to our house.'

They walked round it and decided that the wall was so thick that there was no need to worry about the few stones that had fallen from it. A little moss well pushed in would stop any holes in the roof. 'It's a good solid house,' said Dick, 'and quite big enough, and it couldn't be in a better place.' Dorothea, after walking round it, and remembering that at least there was no danger of its blowing away like a tent, half thought they would make a bit of a garden for it, but decided that the few foxgloves growing close to the hut were really better than anything planted on purpose. 'We'll not bother about a window box,' she said, 'but we'll have some flowers in a jam-pot. I found an empty one when we were clearing the sticks out. I wish I'd thought of taking some roses when I was picking them to go in the spare room.'

'I wonder who left the jam-pot,' said Dick.

'Some Pict or other before us,' said Dorothea. 'It doesn't matter so long as he doesn't come back while we're here.' She looked in at the door of the hut. 'I'm sure Susan would say we ought to have brushed it out first, before putting the furniture in. But we haven't a brush.'

'I can make one,' said Dick. 'Where's that saw the other Pict left?'

In a very few minutes he had cut some young birch shoots and tied them into a firm bundle round one end of a straight ash sapling. Meanwhile Dorothea had pulled all the furniture out once more, the packing-case table, the soap-box larder, the three-legged stool, the chair with a broken back, the two suitcases. Then she set to work with her new broom and the hut filled with choking clouds of dust.

'Better not sweep all the floor away,' said Dick.

'I'll just get the top layer off. It's mostly twigs. I'll sweep it into the fireplace ready for when I start the fire again for supper. Look here. You'd better be cutting logs.'

Dick, while the dust came rolling from the door and window of the hut, set to work outside on the huge pile of dead branches. There was an old tree stump in the clearing, just the right height for him to use in sawing the thicker ends of the branches into short lengths. The thinner branches he broke across his knee, or by putting a foot on them and lifting. He had made two piles, one of small stuff for firelighting, and one of thicker bits, and was resting for a moment, to open and shut his fingers, cramped with holding the saw, when Dorothea came out to him with something in her hand.

'Dick,' she said. 'Somebody really has been using our house. Look at this.' She held out an open clasp knife with a bone handle.

'Not very rusty,' said Dick. 'Where did you find it?'

'I nearly brushed it into the fireplace,' said Dorothea and stiffened . . . 'Listen!'

'Only a motor car,' said Dick.

'It's her,' said Dorothea.

Dick stood listening, the knife forgotten in his hand. Above the noise of the little beck, above the noise of rustling leaves, above the harsh shouting of some jays below them in the wood, they could hear a motor car coming along the road. They heard it hoot at a bend. They heard it passing.

'Perhaps it isn't going to stop,' said Dick.

They heard it hoot again.

'It's turned into Beckfoot,' said Dorothea. 'She's getting out now. This very minute. Nancy and Peggy are saying "How do you do?" They're carrying her things in and asking if she's had a pleasant journey . . . just like they asked us . . .'

Presently they heard the motor car hoot again. They heard it pass once more along the road below the wood. They heard the noise grow fainter in the distance.

'They're in for it now,' said Dorothea. 'We all are.'

Things felt suddenly different, even for Dick. Before, somehow, the Great Aunt had hardly seemed a real person. All these preparations, the turmoil at Beckfoot, the sudden change from being visitors into being Picts hiding in a hut in the forest, might have been just part of one of Nancy's games. The noise of that motor car coming along the road to Beckfoot and going away again had altered everything. It was like the moment in a game of hide and seek when a whistle blows far away and the hider knows that the search has begun and that it is not safe for him to stir.

For some minutes they stood silent.

'It's no good wondering what's happening,' said Dorothea at last. 'We can't do anything to help them.'

Dick found suddenly that he was holding a knife in his hand.

'It isn't one of their knives,' he said, looking at it carefully. 'At least, I don't think so. Nancy's has a lot of tweaks in it, tin-openers and corkscrews and things. And Peggy's is a scout knife with a marline spike.'

'If there's another Pict ...' Dorothea shook herself. 'Anyway, that string on the door had been there a long time. The only thing to do is to hope he won't turn up. I've done the floor. You've got a grand lot of wood ready. Give me a hand in getting the things in again, and then I'll get the fire going and you take the kettle and find a good place to fill it from the beck.'

They were given yet another hint that someone else had been using the hut when, after the furniture had been taken in and arranged on the floor now swept clear of rubbish, Dick went off to fill the kettle.

He crossed the clearing to the beck and only a few steps

from the path found what he wanted, a tiny pool with a foot-high waterfall dropping into it over the edge of a rock. He filled the kettle by holding it under the waterfall and saw that, though there are always plenty of little pools in a beck finding its way down a steep hillside, this pool had been improved by someone who had built a dam across it at its lower end. 'Wash basin,' said Dick to himself. 'And we'll be able to wash up by putting plates and things where the waterfall drips on them.' He went back to the hut and found Dorothea on her knees before the fire, blowing at the rubbish, which had not flamed up as easily as she had expected.

'But this is awful,' she said, when Dick told her about the pool. 'It's that other Pict again.'

'Well, it's going to be very useful,' said Dick.

Then, as the flames began to leap, and Dorothea hung the kettle on the iron hook and begun to look among the stores, he turned to the hammocks. How, exactly, had Nancy fastened the ends that were to be let go in the day-time?

'I'm not going to do anything difficult the first night,' said Dorothea. 'We'll start on the beef roll. It'll go bad if we try to keep it. I won't open a tin. Beef roll. Bread and butter. And there's any amount of cake for pudding.'

'All right,' said Dick. 'I've found out about the hammocks, how she fastened them, I mean. The only thing I haven't found out is how to get into them.'

'They're a long way off the floor,' said Dorothea.

'We'll have to use the stool for a step.'

'I say. Do take care,' said Dorothea two minutes later, reaching for the loaf of bread which had been kicked out of her hands almost into the fireplace.

'Sorry,' panted Dick, who was lying on his stomach across a hammock that had somehow twisted itself into a rope. Flying legs felt desperately for the stool, but it had fallen over. The only thing to do was to go on. He held tight to the hammock and went over it in a somersault, landing safely on his feet. 'Sorry,' he said again. 'It's no use trying to get into it head first. Of course it won't be so bad when the rugs are in it. But I think the proper way must be stern first.'

'We've got to learn everything,' said Dorothea, who had began by cutting the first slice of bread before putting the butter on, and only then remembered watching Susan who always spread the butter on the loaf and then cut off the buttered slice.

'Stern first *is* the way,' said Dick, 'and it's much easier if you get on the packing case first.'

Dorothea turned round to see Dick lying in his hammock and looking very pleased.

'It's quite easy,' he said, 'once you know. You pull one side of the hammock down and go at it stern first till you're sitting in it, and then you swing your legs up.'

'How about getting out?'

'Legs first. Then slide. Like this . . .' And Dick stood breathless on the floor beside her.

'Kettle's boiling,' said Dorothea.

They were a long time over that first meal in their own house. Somehow, though there was no cooking to be done, the different courses fell apart. In that big fireplace wood burned very fast, and by the time they had eaten their slices of beef roll, they had to bring in more of the logs Dick had sawn, and once they had begun doing that, they went on till they had a good pile waiting ready in a corner of the hut. Then they ate their cake. After that they still felt hungry, wondered what supper had been like at Beckfoot, and went on to eat bread and marmalade. By the time they took their dirty plates, mugs, spoons and the one sticky knife that had been used for everything, and went out to the washing basin in the beck, the sun had gone far round and the clearing in the wood was in shadow.

Washing up was not a success.

'It's doing it with cold water,' said Dorothea. 'I ought to have remembered that Susan always uses hot.'

'Leave everything under the waterfall,' said Dick, 'and it'll be clean by morning.'

'We'll have hot water another time,' said Dorothea.

It was growing dusk when they heard steps coming up the path from the road.

'It's that Pict,' said Dorothea. 'What are we going to do if we have to clear out now?'

'It's somebody pretty large,' said Dick.

'She's found out already,' whispered Dorothea. 'It's the Great Aunt herself coming up to bring us back.'

'Mercy me, it's a pull up that brow,' panted old Cook as she came up out of the trees into the clearing. 'And the path grown over with trees and underfoot them stones enough to break your legs. There's one thing. We shan't have Miss Turner walking up here. I thought I'd drop that dish a dozen times. Eh me, I hope we're doing right.'

'Come in and look at our house,' said Dorothea, able to breathe once more.

'I've brought you the apple pie they had to their suppers. They didn't eat much. Happen it'll put you on a bit . . .'

'Thank you very much. Has she really come? We thought we heard the motor car but we couldn't be sure.'

'Aye, she's come,' said Cook grimly. 'She's come, and trouble with her. Girt auld hen 'at wants to be cock o' t' midden. She's begun by clearing Miss Nancy off from the head of the table and taking the mistress's place herself. And I'd put Miss Nancy's napkin ring there, so there could be no mistake. And it isn't as if Miss Nancy's the little lass she was.'

'What did she say?' asked Dorothea.

'Miss Nancy? I couldn't have believed it. "Cook," she says, "Aunt Maria likes that end of the table better. And she's the visitor so she must choose. Peggy and I'll sit one each side of her." Miss Turner looked at her a bit flummoxed, but she didn't oppen her gob ... I mean, she didn't say nowt about it, and after that Miss Nancy was saying how she hoped the weather would keep fine for her visit, and Miss Peggy chipped in asking if she liked sitting facing the engine in the train or the other way and did she have a corner seat?'

Cook was looking this way and that round the inside of the hut. 'Not but what it's better'n I thought,' she said. 'But there's Mrs Blackett trusted me to look after you, and here's two of you gone already. Miss Nancy does fair rush a body off their feet. Not but what Miss Turner wouldn't be letting her tongue off if she knew you were staying at Beckfoot with the mistress away. But it'll be worse if she finds out now, and how we'll keep it from her, I don't know. There's one thing. You've a roof over your heads ... not but what it could do with patching ...'

'Will you have a cup of tea?' said Dorothea. 'I can make one in a minute.'

'Not I,' said Cook hurriedly. 'Thank you kindly, but I must away down. I had to run up to see where Miss Nancy'd put you before I could be easy in my mind. Not that I'm that easy now. But it's better'n I thought. Nay, nay, I mustn't stop. Miss Turner'll be ringing that bell, and no one to answer it ... Not but what no one can say I haven't as much right as other folk to put my nose out of doors.'

'What are they doing now?' asked Dorothea.

'When I slipped out they were sitting in the drawing-room,' said Cook. 'Good thing I dusted that piano. Miss Turner run her finger over it first thing.'

They went down with her as far as the road. Somehow, old Cook, stumbling down that rocky path and grumbling at the branches that met across it, made Dorothea feel that they were not yet altogether out of touch with Beckfoot.

By the gap into the road they stopped, and waited there while Cook hurried away in the dusk.

'Listen,' said Dick suddenly.

In the quiet evening they could hear the faint tinkling of the Beckfoot piano.

'Let's go a bit nearer,' said Dorothea. 'If they're all in there it's quite safe.'

They tiptoed along the road and waited opposite the house. The noise of the piano came clearly through the trees.

'That's the third time she's got stuck,' whispered Dorothea. 'It must be awful for the one who isn't playing, just sitting there and watching the Great Aunt's face.'

'There she goes again,' said Dick.

'It isn't Nancy's sort of tune,' said Dorothea. 'She's quite all right with one finger doing that pirate song of Captain Flint's.'

'Let's go home,' said Dick suddenly. 'I want to have another go at the sailing book. *Scarab*'s going to be ready the day after tomorrow.'

They tiptoed away round the bend in the road and began to climb once more up into the wood. Dorothea felt suddenly very much alone. Dick was there, of course, but, with his mind on the new boat, or on birds, or on cutting up wood in a scientific way, he did not seem to realize that they were going to sleep in a hut in the wood with nobody in it but themselves, a hut with holes in its roof and no glass in its window. Dorothea did not know which was worse, to think of it as a hut in which for perhaps twenty years no one had lived, or to think of it as a house from which in the middle of the night they might be turned out by the rightful owner coming home. It was not at all like sleeping in a tent in camp with other friendly tents close by.

The first call of an owl sounded in the valley.

'There's that tawny owl again,' said Dick. 'I heard him last night, but I'm not putting him down on my list till I've seen him.'

Of course it was all right, thought Dorothea. The ghostly

wood all round them was only full of natural history. And Dick knew all about that. All the same . . . 'Alone in the Forest' by Dorothea Callum. She started violently as a couple of woodpigeons clattered out of the branches of a tree close to the path.

'Roosting already,' said Dick.

Back in the hut, Dick lit the hurricane lantern and took his sailing book from the shelf over the fireplace. Dorothea divided the rugs and laid them in the hammocks. There were three for each of them.

'There aren't any pillows,' she said.

'Knapsacks,' said Dick. 'With clothes in them.'

Dorothea shut the door and put more wood on the fire. 'We'd better be too hot than too cold the first night. And with no glass the window's open anyway.' The sticks flamed up and shadows flickered over the walls except for the square gap where there should have been glass. Through it she could see the dim shapes of trees and a patch of sky on which were the first stars. Dick was already sitting on the three-legged stool, reading as much by firelight as by the light of the lantern.

'Let's put the light out and go to bed,' said Dorothea.

'Just one chapter,' said Dick.

He read steadily on about the theory of sailing till he heard Dorothea again. 'Much better go to bed. There's all to-morrow.'

He looked round and saw Dorothea looking down over the edge of her hammock.

'I say. You got in jolly quietly.'

'It was easier than I thought. Dick, I do believe it's going to be all right.'

'Why shouldn't it be?' said Dick.

Five minutes later he too had worked himself into his hammock, had put his torch and his spectacles in a safe place on the top of the beam above his head, had folded his rugs over himself and was trying to find a soft place in his knapsack.

'It's rather like being a caterpillar,' Dorothea heard him say.

'What?'

'Lying in a hammock. Really it would be better to be a caterpillar, because they've got joints all the way along.'

Dorothea, lying in her hammock, very tired and already half asleep, was feeling much better about things. They had had their first meal. They had gone to bed. The Great Aunt had not found out about them and come raging up to bring them back to Beckfoot. No other Pict had come to turn them from his home. They had only to go on like that and all would be well. It was Dick and not Dorothea who thought of a new danger ahead.

He had been lying there, thinking of *Scarab* and of all they had planned to do. Suddenly he started up.

'Dot. We've forgotten something. Timothy's coming tomorrow to take us to the mine. As soon as he comes to Beckfoot he'll ask where we are.'

'Nancy's sure to have thought of that,' said Dorothea.

'Listen. Listen,' said Dick a moment later. 'There's that tawny owl again.'

'I heard it.' Dorothea's voice was muffled by the rug she had pulled over her head. The owl, heard from the hut in the wood, was nothing like so friendly and holiday a sound as it had been when heard from the spare room at Beckfoot. And the thought of Timothy, though she had told Dick that Nancy would have remembered about him, kept her lying awake long after Dick had gone rather uncomfortably to sleep. If Timothy was going to walk into Beckfoot and blurt out the whole secret first thing in the morning, it would have been better, far better, if they had never turned into Picts.

CHAPTER 7

SECONDHAND NEWS

DOROTHEA was waked by the squawk of a cock pheasant in the wood. There was a feeling of stiffness in her back. Her bed seemed to have sagged in the middle. She opened her eyes and saw that the high ceiling of the spare room had dropped and turned into a dark oak beam. And the skull and crossbones from the head of her bed had gone. And what had happened to the wallpaper? No. There was the skull and crossbones, fastened against a stone wall. She remembered where she was and looked out past her feet through a great hole in the wall to green leaves and the trunks of trees. That tinkling noise was water dripping down into one of the little pools of the beck.

She remembered everything now. The Great Aunt of whom everybody was so much afraid was sleeping in that spare-room bed where she herself had slept the night before. Life at Beckfoot was going on without herself or Dick. It was as if they had slipped through a hole in the floor. They had fallen out of that life into another, in which, for the first time, she, Dorothea, had a house of her own. Nobody was going to say, 'Buck up, Dot. Breakfast's nearly ready.' If there was going to be any breakfast, she ought to be getting it now. She looked across at the other hammock. Dick was still asleep. Getting down was not going to be too easy. She pulled loose the edges of the rugs that she had tucked in under herself, swung her legs over the side, felt for the chair and kicked it over, held firmly to the hammock, kicked again, let herself slide and found herself standing on the earthen floor.

She put on her sandshoes, took soap, toothbrush, towel and

kettle, opened the door and went out into the morning sunshine. There was that pheasant again. And now a new noise, the tap, tap of a hammer on a tree-trunk. For a moment Dorothea stood still, listening, half thinking that there might be someone working in the wood. Then she remembered that she had heard that noise before, last summer, in the woods below High Topps, and Dick had told her what it was. A woodpecker. No. There was nobody about. She and Dick were the only people in the world. And Dick was asleep. She had the world to herself.

She filled the kettle at the pool in the beck, washed her face and hands and cleaned her teeth. She thought of a new name for a story. 'Ten Thousand Years Ago . . . a Romance of the Past,' by Dorothea Callum. No. No. With breakfast to get, this was no time to think of stories. She gave her face a last towelling, took the plates and mugs and spoons from under the waterfall and set off back to the hut to light the fire. As she came out into the clearing she saw a wisp of blue smoke above the huge old chimney. The smoke thickened and climbed straight up in the still air. And there was Dick, in his pyjamas, coming out to look for her.

'Hullo, Dot. Why didn't you wake me?'

'I've only been to wash and fill the kettle. I say, you'd better wash, too, and get dressed. What have you been doing to your face?'

'I started the fire with some of the sticks that hadn't burnt away last night. Some of them were almost charcoal. And then I went and rubbed my eyes by mistake.'

'Here's the soap and towel. Get your toothbrush. Take your clothes with you.'

'All right. I only used one match for the fire. Dry bark makes splendid stuff to start it.'

'Good. Hurry up and get dressed and I'll have breakfast ready by the time you come back.'

Dorothea put the kettle on, dressed in two minutes and

was laying plates and mugs on the sugar case that was the Picts' table before she remembered that they had used the last of the milk the night before. That meant no cornflakes and milk as usual. And no tea. 'Oh bother,' thought Dorothea. 'I ought to have kept some from yesterday and kept it in a cool place.' Housekeeping was not as simple as people thought who had other people to do it.

Dick came back dressed, looking a different colour with the charcoal washed from his face and hands.

'No milk,' said Dorothea. 'Not till one of them comes. I expect they'll bring it.'

'Let's be all ready before they come,' said Dick. 'They may want us to do something about stopping Timothy. If they go out in the boat and we go along the road . . .'

'Oh, I say,' said Dorothea. 'I'd forgotten Timothy. We won't wait for milk. We'll be all right with cocoa. It says on the tin it's cocoa, sugar and milk all in one. It only needs hot water. And we can have eggs and bread and butter and there's a pot of marmalade.'

'There's all that apple pie,' said Dick. 'We can eat it out of the dish and it won't be so sticky to wash up.'

The woodpecker spoilt the eggs for them. Dorothea had put them in the saucepan of boiling water and pushed it in at the side of the fire. She was hard at work stirring the cocoa first in one mug and then in the other and Dick was timing the egg-boiling with his watch, when he heard that tap, tap, close outside the hut. 'A minute and a half gone,' he said. 'I'm sure that's a woodpecker . . . Two minutes . . .' He moved quietly, watch in hand, to the doorway. The tapping seemed to come from a tree behind the hut . . . Dorothea added more water and went on stirring, wondering if breakfast was over at Beckfoot and how soon one or other or perhaps both the martyrs would escape and come racing up through the wood. 'It must be four minutes now,' she thought, and was not at all sure whether Susan boiled eggs for four minutes or for three.

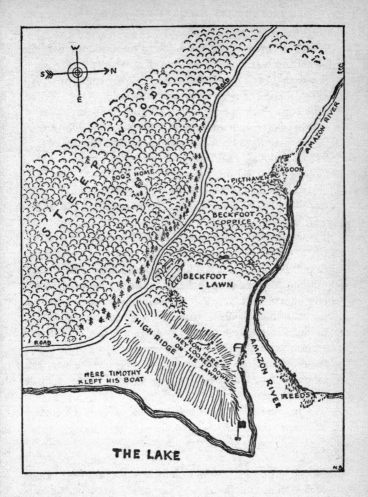

'Dick,' she called. There was no answer. She went out and could not see him. 'Dick!'

'He's gone. But I saw him all right. Great Spotted. Black and white with a red patch.' Dick slipped his watch back into the breast pocket of his shirt and pulled out his notebook.

'But the eggs,' said Dorothea.

He looked at his watch again. 'I can't remember where the minute hand was when we started. I'm awfully sorry.'

She darted back into the hut and took the eggs out with a spoon. 'I expect they're ready now,' she said.

The eggs when opened were as hard as bullets.

'Perhaps even four minutes is too much,' said Dorothea.

'They may have been in much more than that.'

'They make an awful mess when they're runny.'

'These aren't runny, anyway,' said Dick.

'Hard-boiled,' said Dorothea.

'Steel-boiled,' said Dick. 'My fault, watching the woodpecker.'

They washed the eggs and bread and butter down with the cocoa, but were glad to get to the last course – the Beckfoot apple pie. It had been baked in a deep oval dish, with an egg-cup upside down in the middle of it to keep the pastry from sagging down. Yesterday, in the Beckfoot dining-room, the Great Aunt had opened it carefully with a knife, and served small slices from it for Nancy, Peggy and herself. Dick and Dorothea, with the pie-dish between them, set to work at opposite sides of the neat three-cornered hole she had left. They could have finished it, but kept a little for dinner in the middle of the day.

'It's just the thing after eggs and cocoa,' said Dorothea. 'Cool and wet and not sticky at all.'

*

They washed up by the beck, with a kettleful of hot water that made things much easier. They rolled up their rugs, un-slung the hammocks and hung them against the wall. They decided to put no more wood on the fire and to light it again in the evening. Every now and then they listened for footsteps coming up through the wood.

'I wonder why they don't come,' said Dick.

'Perhaps they have breakfast later with the Great Aunt here.'

'It'll be too late to do anything about Timothy now.'

Dick sawed and broke up a lot more of the firewood they had cleared out of the hut. Dorothea made a neat pile of them at the side of the fireplace. There was no sign of either of the martyrs from Beckfoot.

'It's a good thing we didn't wait for the milk,' said Dick.

'Let's go down and wait for them at the bottom of the wood,' said Dorothea.

They had left the coppice and were going cautiously down through the larches when they heard a rattle. A man got heavily off his bicycle by the gap into the road. He had come so suddenly that he was already looking up the path at them before they had time to dodge back out of sight. He swung a bag round from his shoulder, put his hand into it and brought out a letter.

'It's the postman,' said Dorothea. 'If he's been to Beckfoot with a letter for us we're done.'

'I've a letter for you,' said the postman. 'Addressed to Beckfoot. Miss Turner at Beckfoot wouldn't take it. She wrote on it too.' He gave Dorothea the letter, and on it, pencilled in a clear sloping hand were the words 'Not known here.'

'It's from Mother,' said Dick.

'You didn't say you'd seen us yesterday?' asked Dorothea.

'It was on the tip of my tongue,' said the postman. 'But I saw Miss Nancy. She was there making faces at me, and I could see she meant me to say nowt. So I said nowt, and took the letter. Least said soonest mended I thought to myself. "Not known?" All right. Take it back to the Post Office.'

'But . . .'

'I'd nobbut got back to my bike when a stone come by my ear as near as nothing, and there was that young limb beckoning at me over the garden wall. She's a terror, Miss Nancy.

"About that letter," she says. "And whatever you do don't bring any more letters for them to the front door." "But Miss Turner says they're not here," says I. "They are here," she says, "but Aunt Maria mustn't know. Mother knows they're here. She invited them. But Aunt Maria doesn't." And then she says where you was at, and she says I'd better bring you the letter to make sure. "What if Miss Turner asks me what I've done with it? There'll likely be trouble for me," I says, "if I do as you say." "There'll be much worse trouble for us if you don't," says Miss Nancy. "And don't you talk so loud. And there'll be much worse trouble for Mother. That's why they've gone. You ask Cook," she says. "Well, I've had trouble with Miss Turner," I says. "I'll take them the letter. But you'll have to clear me if there's questions asked." "There won't be," says she. Here's your letter. But what am I to do if there are any more?'

'You mustn't take them to Beckfoot,' said Dorothea.

'Couldn't you put them in a hole in the wall?' said Dick. 'And we'll come down and collect them.'

'If they're addressed to Beckfoot it's to Beckfoot I should take them,' said the postman.

'It's just till Mrs Blackett comes back,' said Dorothea.

Dick had gone down to the wall. 'There's a good place for letters here,' he said.

'It matters most awfully,' pleaded Dorothea.

'So she says, that young limb,' said the postman. 'Well I'll do it, but it'll go hard with me if it all comes out. Nobbut what the letter's for you. Nowt wrong but the address.'

'We can't give another address,' said Dorothea. 'It's got to be secret till Mrs Blackett comes back.'

'I'll do it,' said the postman. 'But I don't like it. And that's what I says to Miss Nancy. "And lucky it was," I says, "you didn't hit me with that stone." "It wasn't lucky at all," says she. "I could hit you every time if I tried, but I didn't."

She's a limb, is Miss Nancy, but if it's to save trouble for Mrs Blackett I'll take the risk and say nowt about it.'

'Thank you very much,' said Dorothea.

'The hole between these two stones will be the letter-box,' said Dick. 'And this smaller stone will do to shut it up with when there's a letter inside.'

The postman nodded, mounted his bicycle, and rode away.

'That letter might have spoilt everything,' said Dick.

'It's not going to be half as easy as Nancy thought,' said Dorothea opening the letter. 'We never thought of the postman.'

'And now there's Timothy,' said Dick. 'He may be charging in any minute to take us up to the mine. And he's sure to ask for me straight off because of the work we've got to do in Captain Flint's study.'

'One of them'll be coming along soon,' said Dorothea.

'If she was coming, why didn't Nancy keep the letter?'

'She had to let the postman see for himself that we were really here,' said Dorothea. 'Let's get a bit back from the road, so that we can dodge out of sight if there's anyone else.'

They sat down to wait under the larches close to the place where the path climbed into the coppice. Two steps up that path and no one would be able to see them from the road.

Dorothea read her letter aloud, a pleasant cheerful letter from their mother, hoping that they would both have a happy time at Beckfoot, hoping that the new boat was ready, and that they would presently be teaching her and their father how to sail, urging them not to take risks at first, and saying that she was really rather glad that while that sensible Susan was not there to look after things they would be sleeping in a house and not miles from anywhere in tents on an island or up in the hills.

'Well, we *are* in a house,' said Dick.

'There's a postscript,' said Dorothea. '*Whatever you do, I'm sure you'll try to do nothing to make Mrs Blackett wish she had not let you come while she was away*. It's all right. Mother would have done just the same. We've just *got* to be Picts to save Mrs Blackett from the Great Aunt. Anyway, we couldn't say No when even Cook thought it would be better if we did.'

'I wish there was some way of reminding them about Timothy,' said Dick. 'Shall I scout along towards the house?'

'No good,' said Dorothea. 'One of them's sure to be here in a minute, because of bringing the milk.'

'I'm going to look for a goldcrest,' said Dick. 'Larches are always likely trees for them.'

Five minutes later he came hurrying back.

'Quick. Quick,' he whispered. 'There's someone in the wood. Coming this way.'

There was hardly time for them to get into the cover of the coppice. 'Don't move,' whispered Dick. 'You can't help making a noise on the stones ... Look. I can see his legs.' Dick was crouching low, looking out below the leafy branches.

'It's Squashy Hat himself,' said Dorothea. 'It's Timothy. Hi!'

The tall thin man hurrying through the larches stopped short as they ran out.

'Hullo!' he said.

'You mustn't go to Beckfoot,' said Dorothea. 'Or have you been?'

'You mustn't say anything about us,' said Dick.

Dorothea was not sure whether Timothy was blushing or whether it was that he was hot. His lean face was much redder than usual.

'What's going on at Beckfoot?' he said. 'I was just turning the boat to row into the boathouse when I saw Nancy and Peggy with an ancient dame. And the clothes! I hardly knew them. The old lady didn't see me. No more did Peggy.

But Nancy did and looked scared out of her life. She waved me away down the river. So I went out round the point and landed there close under the road. I really did not know what to do. But I've got to get up to the mine. So I came along the road, and bless me, as I was turning the corner by Beckfoot there they were again. Nancy, Peggy and the old lady, all three together.'

'What did she say to you?' asked Dorothea. 'You didn't ask about us?'

Timothy turned a little redder. 'I . . . Well, you know how it is. I never can stand meeting strange people. I just nipped over into the wood and dodged past them through the trees. Only thing I could do . . .'

'Thank goodness,' said Dorothea.

'They may turn round and come this way,' said Dick.

'I'd better get on,' said Timothy. 'If she comes along here . . .'

'We'll keep out of sight. Come and look at our house and we'll explain.'

'What house?'

'We aren't at Beckfoot any more,' said Dorothea.

'What?'

'We don't exist. That's why it's so important that when you go there you mustn't ask about us. That was Nancy's and Peggy's Great Aunt you saw. She's turned up to look after them and Nancy thought we'd better clear out.'

'But bless my soul,' said Timothy. 'You're staying there.'

'Not now,' said Dorothea. 'You see the Great Aunt found out that Nancy and Peggy were by themselves at Beckfoot and she's furious with Mrs Blackett. Nancy says she always is about something or other, and it would be much worse if she found out that Mrs Blackett had let them have visitors while she was away. So we've just moved into our own house. You'd better come and see it, and then we can talk without so much danger of people hearing. If she's

81

out walking, she might turn back and come this way any minute.'

'It's up here,' said Dick, and led the way up the path.

'So that's Miss Turner is it?' said Timothy. 'Jim's told me about her. And that's why I hardly knew them when I saw them looking at the flower beds. Dressed up like that. Not much of the gold prospector about Nancy when she's . . . Yes, I know. Of course it isn't her fault. But look here, if that old lady's staying at Beckfoot, how can I ever go in there to work in Jim's den?'

'It's all right for you,' said Dorothea. 'You can just walk in and be introduced.'

'Not after she's seen me shinning a wall to get away from her,' said Timothy. 'No, thank you.'

'All that matters is that you mustn't let out anything about us.'

'Well, let's have a look at your house,' said Timothy.

They walked up the rough path, where Timothy had to stoop and push his way through the branches. He seemed only half to hear what was said to him. He kept on muttering to himself.

'This is the house,' said Dorothea as they came out into the clearing before the old hut. She looked anxiously at Timothy, half expecting that he would disapprove.

'I've slept in much worse places,' he said. He went in with them and looked round. 'You want a bit of moss in those holes,' he said, looking at the roof.

'I thought of that,' said Dick.

'But you've a good fireplace and hammocks and not too far to go for your water . . . No, you might be much worse off. It's not that. But hang it all, I promised Jim I'd keep an eye on you. And we've work to do in Jim's den before he comes back.'

'Dick can't go there now,' said Dorothea.

'We're badgers,' said Dick.

'Picts,' said Dorothea. 'Chased out, you know, but keeping alive underground. At least not exactly underground, but in secret.'

Timothy shook his head. 'How long do you think you can keep a secret like that? You can't. The old lady'll hear of it, and things'll be worse than if she'd found you the moment she arrived.'

'She'd have had a fit if she'd seen the spare room as it was,' said Dorothea. 'There was this over the top of the bed.' She pointed to Nancy's skull grinning on the wall above its crossed bones.

'How many people know already?' asked Timothy.

'Nancy and Peggy,' said Dick.

'And old Cook,' said Dorothea. 'And the postman . . . Nancy had to tell him this morning . . .'

'The whole countryside will know if the postman knows,' said Timothy.

'It's only for ten days,' said Dorothea.

'She'll find out in two,' said Timothy. 'And then there'll be the dickens to pay. I wish Jim were here to deal with this.'

'Nancy'll manage,' said Dorothea. 'Of course the other way would have been to do some of the things Nancy said she'd like to do . . . You know . . . Putting gravel between the sheets and the mattress, putting a drop of paraffin in her morning tea, cutting the butter with an oniony knife, and so on, till she boiled over and went home. Only that way, she would have worked out her rage on Mrs Blackett. This way, Nancy's going to keep the Great Aunt happy, so that she won't have any excuse for being down on anyone. All we've got to do is to keep out of sight. Nancy and Peggy and Cook are going to deal with the Great Aunt and do every single thing she likes. It's the velvet glove instead of the iron hand.'

'The trouble with Nancy's velvet glove is that it's usually got a knuckleduster inside it. And you never know who's going to get hit. When Miss Turner finds out about this, it won't be only Nancy who gets into trouble. It'll be you and me and Cook at Beckfoot and the postman and everybody else who happens to get dragged in and Mrs Blackett most of all.'

'What about those assays for Captain Flint?' asked Dick.

'Can't do them at Beckfoot, that's one thing. I'll have to do them in the houseboat. I'm not ready for them yet.' He saw the disappointment in Dick's face. 'You'll have your own boat, won't you? You'll be able to come.'

'We're going to keep her up the river,' said Dick.

'Good. Well, are you coming to the mine with me today?'

'Not without the others,' said Dorothea. 'They'll be coming here to look for us the moment they can get away.'

'No good waiting for them,' said Timothy. 'I must get on. And if you see Nancy, tell her you know somebody who'd like to wring her neck.'

'Who?' said Dick.

'Me,' said Timothy.

'It's a very lucky thing he is shy,' said Dorothea when the sound of his footsteps had died away. 'If he'd said "How do you do?" to them and been introduced, he'd have been sure to ask where we were and everything would have gone wrong the very first day. I bet Nancy and Peggy were glad when they saw him bolt.'

If the Great Aunt was walking with her nieces it was hardly safe for the Picts to be near the road. Nor was it safe to go the other way and explore the upper part of the wood, because at any minute, Nancy or Peggy or both of them might escape from her and come to the hut, with perhaps only a minute or two to spare before racing down again. Dick settled down to sawing wood so as to have a lot ready cut for the fire. Dorothea went carefully through the provisions, making a list of them in an exercise book in which she had meant to write a story. She crossed out 'Scarab Ahoy! A tale of Adventure', and wrote instead 'STORES'. Then she put down everything they had, the tinned foods, soups, steak and kidney pie, corned beef, stews, peaches and sardines; the fresh food, half a beef roll, one third of an apple pie, six bananas, twelve oranges, ten eggs, half a loaf of bread, then other things, such as marmalade, potted meat, corn flakes and chocolate. They were certainly not going to starve. Old Cook, who had provided for many expeditions of the pirates, had seen to that. Then, remembering the careful Susan, Dorothea began to plan her housekeeping, and set out, on another page, to make lists of food for separate meals, breakfasts, dinners and suppers. Finally, she took a writing block and a stamped envelope from her suitcase, and wrote a letter to her mother. She told of the journey and seeing the new boat and crossing the lake to Beckfoot. She went on:

Nancy's and Peggy's Great Aunt has come here unexpectedly. This is a great misfortune but it can't be helped. We are living in a house of our own. It is in the wood close to Beckfoot and Dick and I have it all to ourselves. Please ask father about Picts. He said something about people thinking that fairies and things were invented because of the Picts who were living secretly in caves and only coming out at night long after other people had conquered the land. I know it was something like that. Please ask him. I am doing the housekeeping so I shan't have much time for writing. Dick is cutting wood and making a list of birds. He says a woodpecker and a goldcrest are the two best so far. He says there are two kinds of owls, but we haven't seen them yet, only heard them. No time for more because I have to think of dinner.

Much love from both of us,

Dot.

P.S. Please don't forget to ask Father about the Picts. We'd both like to be sure.

She folded her letter, put it in the envelope, addressed it and put it in her pocket. She would have to ask the others about getting it posted or lie in wait for the postman in the morning.

Dick came in with an armful of small logs.

'What's the time?' she asked.

'Twenty-nine minutes past one.'

'Dinner,' said Dorothea.

For dinner, they finished the beef roll and ate the last of the apple pie, washing it down with lemonade from the pirates' grog-puncheon which Nancy and Peggy had set up on stones, so that it was high enough off the ground for anyone to fill a mug at the tap.

'I believe something's gone wrong,' said Dick. 'If it hadn't, Nancy or Peggy would have been here by now.'

'It's all right,' said Dorothea. 'If the Great Aunt had found out, she'd have sent up here right away to haul us down. I'm sure it's all right. The postman was an awful danger and so was Timothy but they're not any longer, and there can't be anybody else . . .'

'Listen!' said Dick.

The next moment Peggy, in a white frock that startled them both, was in the doorway. She was almost too much out of breath to speak.

'Quick. Quick!' she panted. 'Here's the milk. Sorry I couldn't bring it before. You ought to have rinsed the other bottle. Never mind. Come on. We've got to stop the doctor. She's sent for him. She always does. We ought to have warned him but we forgot. Come on. He knew you were coming and if we don't catch him he'll go and blurt out something the moment he opens his mouth.'

CHAPTER 8

DEALING WITH THE DOCTOR

'THE doctor?' said Dorothea. 'Is she ill?'

'Not a bit,' said Peggy. 'She's full of beans. Only she always likes to have a doctor hanging about like she has at Harrogate. She telephoned to him and he'll be here any time now. Never mind about putting things away. Giminy, it's been the most awful morning. Much more difficult than Nancy thought it would be. Look here. Where's that apple pie?'

'We've eaten it,' said Dick.

'Cook said you would have done. That's all right. She's going to make another quick and cut it up and slosh it over with custard.'

'But it was very good as it was,' said Dorothea.

'It's not that,' said Peggy. 'After breakfast Cook asked Nancy to order meals, and the G.A. said that she would do that herself, and Cook was pretty mad, but bore it and went back to the kitchen, and then, just now, the G.A. remembered there was a lot of pie left and rang the bell and told Cook she'd like it brought in for supper ... But that's only one of the awful moments. ... Hurry up. Never mind about putting things away ... First of all we never had a chance of getting away to bring you the milk. Good thing we didn't. We'd gone out in the garden with her after her kick up with Cook, and there was Timothy just rowing into the boathouse. The G.A. was looking the other way but Nancy saw him and he saw Nancy shooing him off ...'

They were hurrying down the path with Peggy in front throwing bits of news over her shoulder.

'We'd forgotten about Timothy ...' she explained.

'We remembered about him last night and didn't know what to do,' said Dorothea.

'He rowed away, and we were saved for the moment. And then just when we were all in the hall ready to go with her for a walk the postman came with a letter for you. When the G.A. said you weren't known and gave the letter back, he jolly nearly let out he'd seen you yesterday. Nancy managed that somehow.'

'We got the letter,' said Dorothea.

'And now we've got our own letter-box in the wall by the road,' said Dick.

'Good,' said Peggy. 'But that's not all. We started for a walk, one each side of her, awful, and we hadn't gone a hundred yards before we met Timothy coming along the road. Our hearts nearly knocked our teeth out from inside. But Timothy was just like he was last year before he knew us. He took one look and bolted over the wall into the wood and we were saved again. The G.A. said he was a dangerous tramp, so whatever happens he mustn't come to Beckfoot now.'

'He isn't coming,' said Dick. 'We've seen him.'

'Well that's all right,' said Peggy. 'We went on walking and spotted where he'd left his boat. Just below the road beyond the point. You can't miss it. Nancy says he's got to have the pigeons in case of anything urgent. But there wasn't time for everything. We've put the pigeons in their cage and hidden it behind the wall at the bottom of the wood. There's a bag of pigeon food, and Nancy's written him a letter explaining. You'll find it all right. And you're to take the cage and the food for the pigeons and put them in his boat . . .'

'Now?' asked Dick.

'Not now,' said Peggy. 'When we've gone back to tea.'

'Where's Nancy?' asked Dorothea.

'She's bringing *Amazon* up the river, with a scythe.'

'For cutting hay?' asked Dick.

'Waterlilies,' said Peggy. 'Reeds . . . She's going to make the harbour for *Scarab*.'

'Here's our letter-box,' said Dick, and showed her the hole in the wall.

'Good,' said Peggy. 'Do for us too. Half a minute while I see if the road's clear.'

She went through the gap and into the road, looked right and left, beckoned silently, turned left and ran. Dick and Dorothea hurried after her. She was waiting for them round the next corner where the Beckfoot coppice ended and a field began. 'Bit near the house,' she said. 'She's probably in the drawing-room waiting for the doctor to take her temperature, but we mustn't risk being seen together . . . Nancy's orders. Nancy'll be here in a minute . . .'

'She's here now,' said a cheerful voice. 'You've been an age. But I don't think we've missed him.' Nancy, complete savage, in bathing things, was climbing over the gate out of the field. She had a letter in her hand.

'Another letter for us?' said Dorothea.

'No. It's the G.A.'s letter. I've got to show it to the doctor. Did you get yours all right? It was pretty awful when the postman gave it to the G.A.'

'Yes,' said Dorothea.

'Where's *Amazon*?' asked Dick, looking through the gate across the cut hayfield to the tall reeds that hid Octopus Lagoon.

'Close here,' said Nancy. 'Peggy, you'd better go and get into your bathers. Have the others brought theirs?'

'We haven't,' said Dick. 'Shall I go back for them?'

'Waste of time,' said Nancy. 'Peggy and I'll be doing the really wet work. Buck up, Peggy. And look out for the scythe. It's a brute in the boat. I've tied up at the usual place. All right to land at, but no good for a harbour. We're going to make you a beauty in the lagoon. Get it done today if only that doctor doesn't keep us too long.'

Peggy was already over the gate and hurrying along the edge of the coppice. She disappeared into the trees.

'What will the doctor want us for?' asked Dick.

'He doesn't want us,' said Nancy. 'We want him. He's like the postman and Timothy. He knows you're here, and we've got to stop him from letting it out to the Great Aunt.'

'We've seen Timothy,' said Dick.

'So've we,' said Nancy . . . 'Listen! There's a motor car coming now . . . Spread out. Don't give him a chance of charging past. Ahoy! Hey! Stop!'

The motor car came to a standstill close to them. The doctor put his head out.

'Nancy, you young donkey, you'll be getting yourself run over if you play the fool like that. If I hadn't good brakes and wasn't one of the world's most careful drivers, you'd be a patient this minute instead of the usual pest. What are you stopping me for? Why! Hullo! Dick Callum, isn't it, and Dorothy?'

'Dorothea,' said Dick.

'Dorothea,' said the doctor. 'So it is. Well, you never got mumps that time. You'll get them sooner or later. Out of the way, Nancy. Can't stop now. I've got an appointment to keep with Miss Turner.'

'That's just it,' said Nancy. 'When you see her you must be jolly careful not to say one single word about Dick and Dorothea.'

'What?' said the doctor. 'In disgrace already?'

'SHE DOESN'T KNOW THEY'RE HERE.'

'Where does she think they are? Doing holiday tasks on a fine day like this?'

'SHE DOES NOT KNOW THEY ARE HERE.'

'Well, I don't see that it matters.'

'Shiver my timbers,' said Nancy. 'You don't understand. She doesn't even know they exist. She's never heard of them. And she jolly well mustn't.'

'But aren't they staying at Beckfoot? Your mother told me . . .'

'They aren't. They're in the hut in the wood. Cook knows, but the Great Aunt doesn't and mustn't. Listen. Mother and Uncle Jim didn't tell her they were going away. Some horrid old cat must have told her. Mother never asked her to come and stay with us. She jolly well wouldn't. Mother meant us to be in charge. She said so. The Great Aunt came on her own. She simply said she was coming and came. She'll make it beastly for Mother anyhow. She always does. But she'll make it much worse if she finds out that Mother let us have Dick and Dorothea to stay with us while she was away. You know the G.A. You know what it was like when she was here last time.'

'I do,' said the doctor. 'But what's all this about your Mother not inviting her?'

'Read this,' said Nancy. 'Then you'll understand. Cook didn't know she was coming. We didn't know. Mother didn't know. It's all her own idea. She sent a telegram and I tried to squash her but failed. She sent this letter. Read it. Read it.' Nancy passed the Great Aunt's letter through the window of the motor car. The doctor looked at the address on the envelope.

'She wrote to you,' he said.

'Of course she did. But she didn't give us time to stop her. You just read it and you'll see what Mother's in for.'

The doctor pulled off his gloves and took the letter out of its envelope. They saw his lips curl into a smile and then grow serious again.

'Why didn't you put the Callums off?'

'They were here when the letter came. The only thing we could do was to get them out of the house. Even Cook agreed.'

'I don't suppose you gave her much of a choice.'

'Do you think we ought to have gone home?' asked Dorothea.

'Of course not,' said Nancy. 'Mother had invited you herself.'

The doctor read the letter through again and then a third time.

'I expect Miss Turner knows perfectly well they are here,' he said.

'She doesn't,' said Nancy. 'The postman brought a letter for Dorothea this morning, and the G.A. wrote "Not known here" on it, and gave it back to him. It was the narrowest shave. If he hadn't seen the faces I was making at him he'd have gone and told her. I explained to him afterwards and he was quite decent about it.'

'He's going to leave our letters for us in a hole in the wall,' said Dick.

'Nancy,' said the doctor. 'You are the most dangerous animal ever let loose in this world. Poor old postman'll be in trouble if this gets found out.'

'And so will Cook, and so will we, and Mother most of all,' said Nancy. 'It's just not got to be found out. That's why you've got to be careful. The G.A.'s going the day before Mother and Uncle Jim get back. We've only got to hold out till then, and everything'll be all right. Peggy and I are being angels all the time, keeping her happy and wearing best frocks.'

'Best frocks?' said the doctor with a grin, looking at the half-naked Nancy.

'All the time,' said Nancy, 'except when we can get out of her sight. Then we jolly well wear comfortables or bathing things just as if Mother was at home.'

'What about that friend of your uncle's . . . Stedding. Isn't he keeping an eye on you?'

'Oh, Timothy!' said Nancy. 'I nearly forgot. You mustn't say a word about him either. She's never heard of him. We met him this morning when we were being taken for a walk . . . white frocks and all the rest of it. He bolted at the sight of us. The G.A. said he was a dangerous-looking tramp.'

'And hasn't she friends here? Somebody's sure to give you away.'

'Nobody will unless you do,' said Nancy. 'Everybody she used to know here has gone except Miss Thornton at Crag Gill and she had a row with her ages ago. They haven't been on speaking terms for years.'

'Well, it's no good trying to drag me into it,' said the doctor, giving her back the Great Aunt's letter. 'You can keep your hornets' nests for other people.'

Nancy stamped her foot. 'Coward,' she said. 'And traitor. Wait till Uncle Jim comes home and hears you've been the one to get Mother into trouble . . .'

'Shut up, Nancy,' said the doctor. 'Let me think . . . What, exactly, are you asking me to do?'

'We're not asking you to do anything,' said Nancy. 'We're only asking you not to do something. Don't say anything about Dick and Dot. Don't say anything about Timothy. Just do the usual thing. You know. Holding her claw and taking her temperature and telling her she's got to be careful. That's all she wants you to do. And . . . oh yes . . . if you want to help a bit you could tell her she must always lie down for a rest in the afternoons. That'll give us an hour or two every day and if we can never get away at all we'll simply bust. Dick and Dot have got a new boat. And we've got to help them to get her going.'

'But if she asks about them?'

'She won't.'

'Well,' said the doctor. 'I'll do that much for you. If she doesn't mention them first, I'll say nothing about Dick and Dorothea. And I'll say nothing about the wretched Stedding. He must look after his own skin. But if she asks any questions I'll have to answer them.'

'That's all right,' said Nancy. 'And you needn't think you're doing it for us. You're doing it for Mother. And it's better for the G.A. too. We're going to keep her happy all the time. We're practising on the beastly piano. We're wearing party frocks. We're even doing our holiday tasks. Learning poetry and spouting it at her with our hands behind our backs. We're going to keep her happy if it kills us. You're simply helping the good work.'

'Nancy,' said the doctor.

'Yes,' said Nancy.

'I wish you were at the bottom of the deep blue sea.'

He slipped in his clutch and the car moved on.

'Don't forget she's got to lie down in the afternoons,' called Nancy.

'Timothy said something like that,' said Dick as the car disappeared. 'A message. He said we were to tell you that he knew somebody who'd like to wring your neck. He meant he would, but he didn't say why.'

'Natives are all alike,' said Nancy. 'But it doesn't matter.'

'Is the doctor going to be all right?' asked Dorothea.

'He's never as bad as he pretends. But we'd better make sure. Somebody'll have to wait in the road till he comes back. We can't all wait because if we don't start making that harbour at once we'll never get it done. And *Scarab*'ll be ready to-morrow.'

'Shall I wait for him?' said Dorothea.

'Right,' said Nancy. 'I can manage with Dick and Peggy. Come on, Dick. We'd better get started anyhow. But if he hasn't told her to lie down we'll have to give up and go back.'

'Do you think he'd post a letter for me?' asked Dorothea.

'Of course he will.' Nancy was already over the gate. Dick was climbing after her. 'Good excuse. Give him your letter. Ask him if he's been a traitor or not? And find out if she's in her lair or on the prowl. And then come and squeak gently in the coppice as near the lagoon as you can get. Come on, Dick. We're going to have a job cutting those reeds. And the waterlilies are worse!'

*

Dorothea watched them race along the edge of the wood and dive into the trees near where the river must be. She tried to get some of the creases out of her letter, which did not look as fresh as it had before she squashed it into her pocket. Peggy's scraps of news had set her thinking of what was happening at Beckfoot, of Nancy left in charge of the house, deposed from her place at the head of the table, not allowed to order meals, made to wear the clothes she hated, forbidden this, forbidden that, and in spite of all, determined to keep the Great Aunt happy. And Peggy was the same. There they were, the two of them, their own holiday spoilt but determined to see that she and Dick had just the holiday Mrs Blackett had planned for them. And yet there was Timothy wanting to wring Nancy's neck. And kind old Cook bothered out of her life. And the postman in a stew. And now the doctor. If only it had been a story, things would have been simpler. In a story, villains were villains and the heroes and heroines had nothing to worry about except coming out on top in the end. In a story black was black and white was white and blacks and whites stuck to their own colours. In real life things were much more muddled. Real life was like one of those tangles of string where if you found an end and pulled you only made things worse. Nancy had turned them into Picts simply because it was the best she could do to save her mother. And now, look at all the other people who were getting mixed up in things. Anybody could see that Nancy was doing her best. But look at the doctor. Instead of being eager to help her he was wishing she was drowned. Dorothea liked the doctor and if she had been writing a story she would have counted on the doctor to be on Nancy's side, and to pull his hardest in the white team . . . Why, in a story he would have ladled out pills and other medicines and kept the Great Aunt not exactly ill but anyhow not well enough to be a nuisance. Instead it was almost as if the doctor and Timothy and the postman were wishing the Great Aunt had been allowed to find Nancy and Peggy with visitors in the house and no natives about except Cook.

Dorothea was looking far away up the valley to the high slopes of Kanchenjunga. The sun was pouring down on purple patches of heather. Dorothea did not see them. It was as if she were looking at the hills with blind eyes. A horrible thought had struck her. What if the doctor and Timothy were right? What if the whole plan was a mistake? The Great Aunt was cross with Mrs Blackett anyhow. Her letter showed that. Would she have been very much crosser if she had come to Beckfoot to find Dick and Dorothea as well as her nieces? Now, of course, if she were to find out that they were being Picts, living in a hut in the wood just round the corner, she would be very cross indeed, much crosser than if Nancy had just let things slide. She would be cross with Nancy and Peggy as well as with Mrs Blackett. She would never think for a moment of how Nancy and Peggy were doing every single thing they could to keep her happy and contented.

And with that Dorothea shook herself and saw things clear once more. There could be no going back now. At all costs the Great Aunt must not be allowed to find out. Nothing must happen that would mean that Nancy and Peggy had been martyrs all for nothing.

She heard a heavy splash from behind the reeds on the other side of the field. For a moment she thought Dick had fallen in. Then the clear ring of Nancy's laughter. It couldn't be anything serious. But splashing and laughter so near the house was serious enough. That was a risk that need not be taken. Wouldn't it be better to let *Scarab* stay at the boatbuilder's till the Great Aunt was gone? Dick would be disappointed. She saw him sitting in a corner of the railway carriage reading the book on sailing. But, after all, theirs was the easier part, just being Picts in a house of their own. And Dick had his birds. She was sure he would agree. If Nancy and Peggy could be martyrs in a good cause, she and Dick could do without *Scarab*. And even if the harbour was already made it would be a pretty big risk, keeping the boat in the river that flowed past the Beckfoot lawn. Bother the doctor. She wanted to get down to the river at once to tell them that *Scarab* could stay in Rio till the Great Aunt had gone.

But the doctor was coming, coming now. She heard the hoot of his motor car as he turned out of the Beckfoot gate. There it was and in another moment the doctor had pulled up beside her, where she stood waving her letter.

'Have you told her she must lie down?' she asked.

'Not because of any game of Nancy's,' said the doctor hurriedly. 'Nothing to do with Nancy. I'd have given her the same advice in any case. Yes. I've told her it would be as well if she made a practice of resting after luncheon.'

'And you haven't told her anything about us?'

'No, I haven't,' said the doctor almost angrily. 'She didn't ask any questions. But I'll be in trouble if she finds out, just the same.'

'Thank you very much indeed,' said Dorothea.

'Don't you dare to thank me,' said the doctor. 'I haven't done anything for you. I won't do anything for you. I won't have anything to do with it. Good-bye.'

'Can I tell Nancy it's all right?'

'You can tell her I haven't said anything to make it worse than it is.'

'That's all right,' said Dorothea.

'No, it isn't.'

He was just starting off again when Dorothea asked him if he would post her letter for her. 'It's to Mother,' she said.

'Of course I'll post it for you. Have you told your mother about this mess?'

'But there isn't any mess,' said Dorothea. 'I've told her Dick and I are being Picts.'

'Picts?' said the doctor. 'What are Picts? Is that another of Nancy's?'

'Oh no,' said Dorothea. 'That's us. Picts were the people who went on living secretly when everybody thought they were extinct. At least I think so. I've asked Mother to find out from Father. He'll know.'

'Beyond me,' said the doctor. 'Well, I'll post the letter. Good-bye and, if you don't mind, I'd very much rather not see you again.'

Something in Dorothea's face stopped him. 'Nothing against you,' he added. 'Only, if you're supposed to be extinct, I oughtn't to be able to see you except in a museum. Good-bye.'

The motor car shot away, and Dorothea climbed the gate and hurried along the edge of the wood. The doctor's news was good as far as it went, but the sooner they stopped worrying about *Scarab* the better. At least that would be one risk the less.

CHAPTER 9

HARBOUR FOR *SCARAB*

WET work was being done in Octopus Lagoon. Dick and Nancy had found Peggy already changed into bathing things, waiting in *Amazon* ready to push off. Dick had been put at the oars, because Peggy, being larger, was better fit to balance Nancy and to keep the boat upright, more or less, while Nancy was busy with her under-water scything. A few strokes had taken them up river and into the lagoon, and Nancy, working away with the scythe, had begun cutting a fairway through the waterlilies. 'The harbour's got to be right in the corner down there, not where there's nothing but field behind the reeds . . . there, by the willows. Get her in there and nobody'll be able to see her even from the road.'

Cutting the stems of waterlilies deep below the surface is no easy business from a small boat. Dick did his best to keep *Amazon* steady, pretending to himself that already he was handling *Scarab*. Nancy, astride the bow thwart, leaned over, sunk the scythe as far as she could reach and swept it round, while Peggy hung her weight as far over as she could on the opposite side, as if they had been sailing with a stiff breeze on the port tack. That splash that Dorothea had heard from the road was Peggy falling backwards overboard when Nancy after nearly overbalancing to starboard had jerked herself suddenly upright.

Peggy came up again with a mouthful of water, and grabbed the gunwale of the boat. Dick let go of an oar, but caught it again, very nearly dipping the gunwale as he did so. Nancy laughed.

'All right, Peggy,' she said. 'My fault really. Good thing

we left our party frocks ashore. Work round to the stern and come in over the transom ... Sit still, Dick. She'll manage.'

In another moment Peggy was aboard again, shaking her wet hair and dripping water as she went back to her place. 'I ought to have had a foot under the thwart,' she said. 'All right, Dick, you needn't grin. Who went overboard on the Broads?'

'I wasn't grinning because of that,' said Dick.

He had not known that he was smiling at all. The smile that the dripping Peggy had seen was one not of amusement but of admiration. Nobody in all the world could have fallen overboard and climbed in again with less fuss. And already Nancy was working her scythe under water as if nothing had happened. They really were sailors these two, and more than sailors. While cutting the channel, already wide astern of them, they had been talking. He had heard more of the Great Aunt's arrival. Peggy had copied Cook's voice in greeting the unwelcome guest, and the Great Aunt's in announcing to Cook that she and not Nancy was going to do the house-keeping. He had heard Nancy's story of her dealings with the postman. He had heard of Timothy rowing hurriedly away at the sight of the Great Aunt outside the drawing-room window, and of his panic-stricken dodging into the wood on meeting her taking her nieces for a walk. 'Good thing really,' said Nancy. 'I'd made up my mind to give him a glassy look and pretend we didn't know him, but he might not have taken the hint. And there wouldn't have been a chance of warning him. "Where's Dick?" he'd have said, thinking of his stinks. And the G.A. would have said nosily "Who's Dick?" And then we'd have been all in the soup together ... Pull right a bit. That's it. Hold her there ... As it is, it's going to work out beautifully. He'd have been one of the worst dangers. Now, it's quite safe. He'll never come near the house. I've told him about it in my letter. He'll do his stinks in the house-

WET WORK IN THE LAGOON

boat, and when he wants you all he'll have to do is to send off a
pigeon, and we'll get a message up to you.'

'They've got a good letter-box in the wall,' said Peggy.

'We'll be able to shove a dispatch in that,' said Nancy.

'Even if we can't get up the wood. Shove her forward again, Dick ... You'll have *Scarab* tomorrow, so you'll be able to get to the houseboat. Everything that was planned is going to get done just as if the G.A. wasn't here.'

It was little wonder that Dick was smiling. Everything was going to be all right after all, and the doubts even he had had were gone. With people like Nancy and Peggy who fell in and got out again as if it was part of the day's work and set themselves without a murmur the dreadful task of keeping the Great Aunt happy, how could anything go wrong?

They had cut a way through the waterlilies almost to the edge of the reeds, when they heard a quiet 'Ahoy!'

'Dot,' said Peggy, and quacked like a duck.

'She doesn't know that signal,' said Nancy, and called out 'Coming.'

Dick rowed stern first through the waterlilies, catching an oar now and then in the tough stems on either side of the cut channel.

'No good making it wider,' said Nancy, watching. 'You don't want it so that everyone can see it. You'll have to work her in and out by sculling over the stern.'

'Yes,' said Dick. That was yet another thing to learn. He could row very well with two oars, but sculling over the stern with one ... Well, he had seen Tom do it in *Titmouse*, and noticed that sideways waggle and twist of the oar's blade, making it work something like the blade of a screw. There was nothing about it in Knight on Sailing, but he would find out by experiment.

Once clear of the waterlilies he turned *Amazon* round, and rowed down stream. Dot was waiting under the trees at the edge of the river by the two white blobs that were the clothes shed by Nancy and Peggy. He worked the boat's nose in towards the bank.

'This side of that tree root,' said Nancy. 'Good. You don't manage her half badly. Hop in, Dot. I'll keep the scythe out of the way. Get to the stern. Pole off, Dick. Well? Is it all right?'

Dorothea had meant to tell them her new idea before getting into the boat, but, somehow, she found herself sitting in the stern, with the boat afloat and Dick pulling upstream before she had had time. She answered Nancy's question.

'He hasn't told her about us,' she said.

'I knew he wouldn't,' said Nancy. 'He's never as bad as he makes out. But what about her lying down?'

'He's told her to take a rest every day after lunch.'

'Good. That means two and a half hours clear for us,' said Nancy. 'We'll manage with that.'

'I've been thinking,' said Dorothea.

'Pull left, Dick . . . Left again . . .'

'Stop,' said Dorothea. 'Wait a minute . . .'

'What is it? Go on, Dick. You're heading for it now.'

'I've been thinking,' said Dorothea. 'Don't let's do it . . . The harbour, I mean. You see the only thing that really matters is that she shouldn't find out we're here. And we oughtn't to take any risks at all. And having the harbour so close to the house . . . Much better not. Dick and I can easily wait for *Scarab* till she's gone.'

Dorothea saw the disappointment on Dick's face. She went on hurriedly. 'It's only for a few days. And it won't be much good having *Scarab* if you can't sail too. And she's much less likely to find out, if we simply stay in the wood.'

Dick stopped rowing. The boat slid silently on towards the waterlilies.

'It would be a bit safer,' said Peggy.

Nancy turned her head sharply. 'And let her win?' she said. 'Of course not. Look here, Dot. Mother asked you two to come here. Uncle Jim did all the arranging about *Scarab*. They planned for her to be ready when you came. If the boat-builders weren't boatbuilders and always late you'd have had her already. Mother thinks you're having a lovely time sailing every day. She'll be awfully sick if she finds you've been cooped up doing nothing.'

'What about you?' said Dorothea.

'That's got nothing to do with it. It can't be helped about us. Go on rowing, Dick.'

'There's lots for us to do in the wood,' said Dorothea. 'We can easily wait for the sailing. I've got housekeeping to learn and Dick's cutting wood. And there's birds and caterpillars . . . We won't mind a bit just waiting for a few days.'

Dick was watching Dorothea's face. 'Dot's quite right,' he said.

'No she isn't,' said Nancy. 'Shiver my timbers. Just you listen to me. Nobody invited the G.A. Mother invited you. Everything was planned beforehand. There's *Scarab* ready tomorrow and you're jolly well going to have her. And it isn't just for fun either. There's a reason.'

Dick's hopes rose again.

'You've forgotten the main thing you're here for. What about the mine? What about the stinks that have got to be done? Timothy and Dick were to get them done before Uncle Jim came back. Well, they can't do them in Uncle Jim's den. But they can do them in the houseboat. And how's Dick going to get there if you haven't got *Scarab*? So no more gummocking about doing without. It isn't safe for you to use *Amazon* or to keep *Scarab* in our boathouse . . .'

'I'd forgotten about the assays,' said Dick.

Dorothea looking from Dick to Nancy and to Dick again made up her mind once more. 'I suppose it's the only way,' she said.

'Of course it is. And we've nearly got to the reeds already. Steady, Dick . . .'

They were back in the cut channel. Already the oars were lifting loose waterlily leaves.

'Don't you ever try bathing here,' said Nancy.

'Peggy's been in,' said Dick.

'Pretty beastly with waterlilies,' said Peggy. 'I don't wonder Roger called them octopuses when they caught the oars. They're worse when they catch your legs.'

'I heard a splash,' said Dorothea, and Dick knew that she was no longer thinking of making Nancy change her plans. *Scarab* tomorrow. Sailing. And then assays in the houseboat with Timothy. If it had not been that he could not let go of the oars he would have taken off his spectacles and wiped them with relief.

'Good thing we got into bathers,' said Nancy. 'Pretty awful if Peggy'd had to turn up at tea with her frock all over green slime.'

'The harbour's going to be by that bush,' said Dick. 'The willow. You can see it above the reeds.'

'Get your weight on the same side as Peggy,' said Nancy, who was again working her scythe. 'Don't lean over too far or you'll be in, too.'

Foot by foot, yard by yard, they were coming nearer to the deep bank of tall reeds at the edge of the lagoon. There was a little open water between the last of the waterlilies and the reeds. The boat slipped forward and then stopped.

'Hold her so,' said Nancy.

Bit by bit she cut her way in, reaching down with the scythe to cut the reeds as far below the surface as she could. It was hard work even for Nancy, and the others said nothing, but did their best to help. Dick found he could touch the bottom with an oar. Peggy took one and he kept the other, prodding at the bottom while Dorothea took hold of the reeds and pulled to keep the boat from slipping back as they forced their way slowly in.

'We're not going straight for the willow,' said Dick.

'That's all right,' panted Nancy. 'We want a bit of a bend in the channel so that it'll look like solid reeds from the other side of the lagoon. Then nobody'll be able to see her from anywhere. Shove her stern round a bit now. Gosh, my arms are nearly busting.'

Dorothea looked back. It was as if they were in a narrow alley between tall reeds with feathery tops just stirring in the wind. The water astern of them was covered with cut and floating reeds. Through the mouth of the alley she could see waterlilies out in the lagoon, and, beyond them, the reeds that fringed the other side. Presently, as the boat moved forward on a new line the opening narrowed and disappeared. There was nothing but reeds to be seen. There was more hard work by Nancy. Dick and Peggy, poling the boat with their oars prodding into the soft bottom, watched her. They did not wait for orders, but moved the boat forward as Nancy cut a way for her. The reeds suddenly seemed thinner before them. The top of the willow tree showed above their heads.

'Shove her in now,' said Nancy. 'Both together. Let go of those reeds, Dot, or you'll get your hands cut. Now. One two, push . . .'

The boat shot forward and grounded, close beside the willow.

'Soft bottom for her and roots to land on,' said Nancy. 'I had a look first. And jolly well hidden. She won't be seen here even if anybody was looking for her. And the harbour's going to be useful even when the G.A. goes back to her horrid Harrogate. We can use it as a lurking place when the Swallows come and we start a new war. Roger'll remember the octopuses and they'll never think of our being able to hide a brig here. What's the time, Dick?'

'Three minutes past four.'

'Giminy. Hop out, you two. We've got to get home. I've got to get cool somehow. How's your hair, Peg?'

'Pretty dry.'

'It's got to be perfect with a ribbon round it before we go in to tea. And we've got to get out of bathers into beastlies. We haven't a minute. All right, I'm holding the scythe well out of the way.'

'The ribbon's dry but you can see where it's been wet,' said Peggy.

'Well, don't try to explain if she spots it,' said Nancy.

'What shall I say?'

'Say "Oh Aunt Maria, how careless of me", and go and dig out another. Grab the willow, Dot, and jump on that root. Now look here. You know what you've got to do next? I've told Dick. The pigeon cage is hidden behind the wall nearly opposite our gate. Wait till we're in having tea. Then go and lift it and cart it down to Timothy's boat. You'll see it from the road beyond the promontory. And then you'd better dodge back. You never know. She might want to walk that way again after tea.'

'What about tomorrow?' asked Dick.

'We ought to be able to tuck her up by about two. Go along the road past Beckfoot. Climb up the promontory from the other side. All rocks and heather on the top. From there you can look down on our garden, and you'll see when we're ready. We'll get *Amazon* out and pick you up below the boat-house. We'll take you across to Rio, and get *Scarab* and then you'll sail back by yourselves. You'll have her in your own harbour tomorrow night. Time, Dick?'

'Seven and three quarter minutes past four.'

'Giminy,' said Nancy. 'I've simply got to get cool.'

She stepped over into the water beside the *Amazon*, paddled her feet, and scooped handfuls of water over her shoulders.

'But how will you get dry?' said Dorothea.

'That doesn't matter so much,' said Nancy, climbing into the boat again. 'My hair's better than Peg's anyhow. We ought to have brought a comb. Shove her off.'

'Are you going to be there in time?' said Dick.

'We jolly well are. You'd better sneak through the trees

till you can see the lawn. Then you'll know when it's safe to go for the pigeons.'

Already the two half-naked savages were poling their boat out stern first through the new-made passage in the reeds. They disappeared round the bend in the channel and a moment later, Dick and Dorothea, still waiting by the new harbour, heard the grunt of rowlocks and the steady noise of rowing.

CHAPTER 10

PIGEONS FOR TIMOTHY

'I'm jolly glad we're going to have *Scarab* after all,' said Dick.

'I'd forgotten about what you've got to do with Timothy,' said Dorothea. 'And anyway, the harbour's made now. All the same, we'll have to go right past the house every time we take her in or out.'

'Anybody can use the river,' said Dick. 'Even if she saw us, she wouldn't know who we were.'

'With more and more people knowing, it's getting riskier every minute,' said Dorothea.

'We'll be able to tie her up to the willow tree,' said Dick, thinking not of the Great Aunt but of *Scarab*. 'And the reeds on each side will work like fenders. She's going to be quite safe here.'

'Do you think they're going to be in time?'

'We've got to go and see,' said Dick.

'We might run right into her.'

'Too jungly for that,' said Dick.

They left the secret harbour and set off through the coppice towards the Beckfoot garden, moving like hunters and wishing the twigs underfoot were not so dry and crackling.

'Don't go so fast,' whispered Dorothea. 'They can't be there yet. They've got to land and change out of their bathing things first. Listen!'

Somewhere to the left of them Nancy and Peggy must be turning themselves from savages into suitable nieces for the Great Aunt. But there was not a sound to be heard.

'They're being awfully quiet.'

The Picts went carefully on, Dick leading the way. They came to an overgrown path, and crossed it. Paths, in enemy country, were things to be avoided. They stepped across a narrow trickle of a stream that they guessed must be the same that filled their washing basin up in the wood.

'We must be close to the house now,' whispered Dorothea.

And then, only a little way ahead of them, they heard someone call. 'Ruth! Margaret!'

They froze.

'Her!' whispered Dorothea. 'Cook wouldn't have called them that. Dick! Dick. We've heard her voice. Do you think we'll be able to see her?'

'They're going to be late,' whispered Dick. He crept slowly on, putting each foot down as if he were walking on eggshells and afraid of breaking them. He had often stalked a bird in the same way, hearing its call and trying to come near enough to see it. Dorothea crept after him. He stopped, and crouched lower and lower, signalling with a hand to Dorothea.

She crouched beside him. Looking out, from among the bushes, with their heads close to the ground, they could see the long daisy-covered grass of the Beckfoot lawn stretching down to the boathouse and the river. They could see nothing of the house, but dared not move again.

'Ruth! Margaret!'

The Great Aunt herself could not be more than thirty yards away.

'She's in the garden,' whispered Dick.

'We oughtn't to be here,' whispered Dorothea.

'Listen!'

They heard the splash of oars.

'Just coming, Aunt Maria.' That was Nancy's voice, but oddly gentle, not like her usual cheerful shout.

Then they both gasped at once. The boat had come into sight below the lawn, gliding down the river. They had last seen it with a crew of wet dishevelled savages. Now it was being rowed by a girl in a white frock with a pink ribbon round her hair. Another girl, just like her, was sitting in the stern, idly trailing a hand in the water. The boat turned into the boathouse. A minute later, they saw the two girls walking hand in hand towards the house.

Dick looked at his watch. 'Half a minute to half past four,' he whispered. 'They've done it.'

'I say,' whispered Dorothea. 'How many more days? They'll never, never be able to keep it up like that.'

They could not see the meeting of the Great Aunt and her nieces, but there was talking and then silence and then the noise of a door closing.

'They're in at tea,' said Dick. 'Now's the time. Quick, Dot. This way. We've got to get the pigeons to Timothy's boat before they've finished and come out again.'

*

It would have been safe to go straight to the road while the Great Aunt was indoors having afternoon tea, but instinct made the Picts swerve to the right, away from the house, and they climbed over the wall into the road only a few yards from the field gate where they had met the doctor.

'Hurry. Hurry,' said Dorothea, and they raced along as far as the gap where the path led up to their house.

'She said they'd hidden them behind this wall,' said Dick. 'I'd better go along inside the wood so as not to miss them. It'll take longer if we have to stop and look over the wall every other minute.'

'I'm coming, too.'

'You'd better keep along the road,' said Dick. 'We've got to get the pigeons over the wall.'

'I'll keep watch at the same time.'

'Good.'

It was a low tumbledown wall, only a few feet high, and here and there broken down altogether. Dick raced through the pines and larches, looking along the wall for the old pigeon cage he remembered from the mining expedition of last year.

'Don't you think we may have passed it?' said Dorothea from the road, when they were already almost opposite the gate into Beckfoot.

'Not yet,' said Dick. 'I say. Better go quick when you pass the gate.'

'Or slow,' said Dorothea. 'So long as I don't look as if I belonged.' All the same she walked a little faster while passing the big open gateway.

'Got it,' said Dick a moment later. 'They said they'd put it somewhere close opposite. I say, it's bigger than I remembered.'

Dorothea came to the wall and looked over.

'There's a gap just a little farther on,' she said. 'We'll get it through there.'

She came round, to find Dick testing the weight of the cage, and looking at an envelope, sealed with black sealing wax, and tied to the cage with a bit of string that had been threaded through a small hole in one corner.

"Pict Post," read Dorothea. 'She oughtn't . . . Oh well, I suppose it doesn't matter. "Private. Personal. Urgent." ' The envelope was one of Nancy's best, addressed to 'Timothy Stedding, Esq., S. A. and D. Mining Company', with a skull and crossbones instead of a stamp.

'This bag must be the food for them,' said Dick. 'I'll put it on the top of the cage. Look here, if you'll take that end, I'll walk in front and take the other with my hands behind my back. Then we'll both be able to walk straight ahead. Quicker than if one of us has to walk backwards.'

'Pheeu . . . Pheeu, Pheeu. Pheeu.' Dorothea made a noise to reassure the pigeons, as like as she could make it to the noise she had heard Titty making for them last year.

'It's Sappho and Homer,' said Dick. 'Or Sappho and Sophocles . . . That's Sappho anyhow. I don't remember which of the others they said they lost.'

'Sophocles,' said Dorothea. 'I'm awfully glad they've

still got Sappho. It was Sappho who took the message to Beckfoot that brought the firelighters just in time.'

'She's the one who sometimes didn't hurry about getting home,' said Dick.

'I expect they'll have told Timothy in the letter which one he can count on.'

They took the big cage through the gap in the wall and then set out along the road, up the steep slope over the shoulder of the promontory and down again on the other side towards the lake shore. Dick was keeping a look out for the grey rowing boat, and presently saw it, with its nose well pulled up on the shingle beach. They left the road, struggled through some high bracken and came down to the water.

'It'll just about fit across the stern,' said Dick. 'Look out. Just hold steady with the end on the gunwale while I get in.'

The long narrow boat listed sideways with a loud creak as Dick climbed in.

'It's all wrong pulling her so far up on the stones,' he said. 'But I suppose he was thinking of the wash from the steamers. He hasn't got her in a very good place . . .' He worked his way along the boat with one end of the cage while Dorothea held up the other walking on the shore till she could go no farther without stepping into the water.

'Shall I get in, too?'

'I can manage now,' said Dick. 'Hang on to the pigeon food till I get the cage fixed.'

'Just right,' he said a minute later. 'It almost might have been made to fit.'

'Twist the envelope this way so that he can't help seeing it,' said Dorothea, handing Dick the bag of pigeon food. 'He's sure to be surprised when he sees the cage, and if he doesn't see the envelope with his name on it he might think someone had put it in his boat by mistake.'

'And I'll put the pigeon food just in front of it on the

bottom boards, so that he can't help noticing it when he sits down to row,' said Dick.

'Well, we've done it,' said Dorothea. 'Let's be quick. She's probably pouring out second cups by now. It's drawing-room tea, you know, balancing bits of bread and butter on the edge of a saucer.' In her mind's eye she was seeing the Beck-foot drawing-room, and Nancy, Amazon Pirate, holding her cup and saucer in one hand while, without spilling her tea, she offered her aunt a plate of cakes with the other.

'Can't we wait and see him?'

'They said we'd better get back while it was safe,' said Dorothea. 'And he may not come for ages. And there's all our housekeeping to do. Tea and supper all in one,' she went on. 'Come along. Let's get up home and be Picts and perfectly invisible. Much better not take risks when we needn't.'

Dick had had a look at the anchor that Timothy had laid out up the beach. He was now bending over the knot with which, to make sure, Timothy had fastened his boat's painter to the stem of a hawthorn tree.

'John, or Nancy, or Tom Dudgeon would never have tied it like that,' he said.

'He's a miner, not a sailor,' said Dorothea.

'I know,' said Dick.

His mind leapt forward to the work he and Timothy were to do, making analyses of different samples of copper from the mine. Real analysis, not just copying experiments out of a book, and dipping bits of litmus paper and seeing them turn blue or pink when you knew they were going to anyhow. And they were going to work in the houseboat. And that meant sailing in *Scarab*. And *Scarab*'s harbour was ready. And *Scarab* was ready. And tomorrow, at last, they would be sailing her.

'Dot,' he said gravely. 'It was awful when I thought we'd have to do without *Scarab*.'

'It would be a lot safer if we could,' said Dorothea. 'But I'd forgotten that you've got to be able to get to the houseboat.'

'We've got to get the assays done before Captain Flint comes home,' said Dick. 'I wish we could start tomorrow.'

'He'll send a pigeon when he's ready to begin,' said Dorothea. 'Come along. Better get a lot of wood ready now so as not to have to bother with it when you're working all day.'

Dick hesitated no longer. They left the grey boat and the pigeons waiting for Timothy, hurried safely past Beckfoot and up to their hut. Everything was just as they had left it, and the Picts settled down to home life. Dorothea looked through her stores list and decided on a steak and kidney pudding, because the directions on the tin were very simple. Dick burnt his fingers getting the tin open after its long stay in boiling water, but the pudding was well worth it. They made ready much more wood than they used in cooking their supper. They heard a nightjar. Dick had a good view of the tawny owl flitting through the trees. Dorothea found her empty jam-jar, filled it with water, put some wild honeysuckle in it, and set it on the window sill. They washed up beside the beck. Tonight, they did not go down in the dusk to hear if Nancy was playing her pieces on the piano. What with the postman and Timothy and the doctor and the harbour and the pigeons, Dorothea felt there had been more than enough risks taken for one day. They set up their hammocks early, found them more comfortable than they had the night before, and were asleep soon after dark.

CHAPTER II

'A BETTER PICT THAN EITHER
OF US'

'LISTEN!'

Dorothea stopped with an egg balanced in a spoon just as she was going to lower it into the water already boiling in the saucepan. The Picts had slept well their second night in their own house, and there was no real hurry about getting up. But it was not light enough in the hut to read while lying in a hammock, and, with *Scarab* to be launched that day, Dick wanted to put in every minute he could at the sailing book. He felt as if he was going to sit for an examination and he wanted to make no mistakes with those two old shellbacks, Nancy and Peggy, as examiners. So he had slipped out, dipped his head in the pool in the beck, cleaned his teeth, dressed, set the three-legged stool in the doorway and settled down to work. Dorothea had not felt like lying in a hammock with Dick already up and about, so she too had got up, washed, dressed, brought mugs and plates from under the waterfall where they had been rinsing all night, lit the fire with two matches (she would have done it with one if only the first had not broken as she was striking it) and now had breakfast all but ready.

'Listen!'

Dick lifted his head from his book.

'It's somebody coming,' he said, 'but it isn't Timothy, or Nancy, or Peggy . . .'

'Not unless they're walking on skates,' said Dorothea.

Footsteps were coming quickly nearer up the path through the wood where the overflow from the beck had washed the stones bare, and with every step there was the sharp click of metal.

'Friend or enemy?' Dorothea whispered.

Dick picked up his stool and came into the hut.

'They may go straight past.'

'Not with smoke coming out of the chimney,' whispered Dorothea. 'And the door open ... No ... No ... Keep still. It's too late now.'

'We couldn't put the fire out anyhow,' said Dick.

The steps were almost silent now. Whoever it was had crossed the beck and was on the grass of the clearing. A stick cracked close by. A smallish boy, yellow-haired, blue-eyed, and red-faced, stood in the doorway, holding out a quart bottle.

'Here's your milk,' he said, looking curiously round the hut.

'Thank you,' said Dorothea. 'Did they send it from Beck-foot?'

'Aye. And I've to bring you a quart in the morning and you'll give me the bottle to go back.'

'The bottle from the day before?'

'Aye. Not this yin.'

The boy was digging in the pocket of his short corduroy breeches. He pulled out a crumpled envelope. 'For you,' he said.

'Is there an answer?'

'Nay, they didn't say. They heard somebody a'coming downstairs and they pushed me out quick and shut t'door on me.'

There was nothing written on the envelope. Inside it was a small bit of writing paper with a hurriedly scrawled skull and crossbones in one corner, not one of Nancy's best. Under-neath it was written, 'Bit of a row last night. She told Cook she was being extravagant with milk. Cook held her peace though nearly busting. Yours is to come separately. Give him yesterday's bottle. Now listen. Orders for the day. Be where I said at two o'clock sharp.'

Dick and Dorothea read it together, while the milk-boy's eyes roamed this way and that, over the hammocks, the skull and crossbones on the wall, and the packing-case table on which Dorothea had been making ready for breakfast.

'No, there isn't an answer,' said Dorothea.

'Where's t'other bottle?'

'Sorry,' said Dorothea. 'I'll give it you in a minute. I saved some milk in it from yesterday. I'll just pour it over our cornflakes.'

She took the half empty bottle from the floor by the wall farthest from the fire. The small boy watched her. She was just going to pour it over the cornflakes which were already heaped in two saucers, when the small boy said, 'Smell ut.'

'It's gone sour,' said Dorothea a moment later. 'How did you know?'

'That's no place to keep ut this weather.'

'It's so hot everywhere,' said Dorothea. 'Well, it doesn't matter if you're bringing another bottle tomorrow.'

The boy put out his hand. Dick took the bottle from Dorothea and gave it to him. He sniffed at it, held it up, looked at the milk through the glass, emptied it on the ground just outside, came back and leaned against the doorpost as if he meant to stay.

Dorothea, who had put the spoon with the egg in it on the packing-case table while she was reading Nancy's message, picked it up and lowered the egg carefully into the saucepan. She put a second egg in the spoon and lowered that in, too.

'Look at your watch, Dick,' she said. 'We'll try to get these just right.'

'Three minute and a half,' said the small boy. 'That's what my mother gives 'em.'

Dick looked at his watch and waited, holding it in his hand. This time, at least, there should be no mistake.

NOT LOOKING AT ALL LIKE GOING

Dorothea began cutting bread and butter.

The small boy stood there, his eyes alert, not looking at all like going.

'What's your name?' asked Dorothea, uncomfortable at being watched in silence.

'Jacky. Jacky Warriner. What's yours?'

'Dorothea Callum and Dick Callum.' Dorothea suddenly reddened. Ought she, or ought she not, to have told their names to a stranger? But it must be all right, she thought, or he would not have been sent to them.

'You'll be visitors?'

'Yes, in a way,' said Dorothea.

The small boy pointed at the hammocks.

'Sleep here?'

'Yes,' said Dorothea, uncertainly, wondering how far Jacky had been let into the secret.

'She don't know, I reckon?'

'Who?'

'That Miss Turner.'

'No.'

'I thought there was summat . . . when they threw me out so quick.'

'Two minutes,' said Dick, looking at his watch.

'Doing for yourselves?' asked Jacky, shifting his weight from one doorpost to the other.

'Yes,' said Dorothea.

'Plenty of food?'

'Yes,' said Dorothea.

'My mother don't think much of tinned stuff.'

An idea came to Dorothea. 'Have you had your breakfast?' she asked.

'Six o'clock,' said Jacky scornfully. 'We've had cows in and milked since then. What are you doing for your food? Catch trout in t'beck?'

Dick looked up. He had been thinking of that himself. 'We haven't got a fishing rod,' he said.

'Rod!' said Jacky. 'You don't want a rod to catch trout.'

'How do you catch them?'

'Guddle 'em,' said Jacky. 'What about rabbits?'

'We haven't got a gun.'

'Gun? What for? You don't want a gun for rabbits. Have you got a fry pan?'

'Only a saucepan,' said Dorothea.

'You want a fry pan for trout.' Jacky shifted again, but showed no signs of leaving them.

'Oh, I say, Dot. I'm awfully sorry. Five minutes. I've done it again.'

Dorothea hurriedly scooped first one and then the other egg out of the saucepan. 'Never mind,' he said. 'We'll get it right tomorrow.'

'You want a fry pan for eggs, too,' said Jacky suddenly, and came a step into the hut. 'Break 'em into boiling water and you can see 'em turn white. Or stir 'em up with butter over t'fire. I'll lend you a fry pan.'

And, while they watched open-mouthed, Jacky walked across the hut, took hold of a loose stone in the wall close to the fireplace, shook it a little and pulled it out. Then he took a second stone out, reached in and brought out an old blackened frying pan.

'You take this,' he said. 'Put it back when you're done wi' ut. Like nuts?' he asked, and, reaching again into the hole in the wall, brought out an old flour bag and emptied some brown nuts on the ground beside Dorothea.

'Oh!' exclaimed Dorothea. 'Have we taken your house? We didn't know. I'm awfully sorry. We knew somebody had been here because of the wood and the ashes in the fireplace, but we thought it was a long time ago.'

'I'm not wanting it,' said Jacky.

'They didn't know at Beckfoot.'

'Nobody knows nowt about ut,' said Jacky. 'Nobbut me. You're welcome. And I don't mind your using my saw.'

'That's awfully good of you,' said Dick. 'We've nowhere else to go. And I'm sorry I took the saw without asking.'

'You weren't to know,' said Jacky.

'This must be your knife,' said Dick, taking it from the shelf over the fireplace.

'I'm right glad to have it,' said Jacky. 'Where was it? I thought I'd lost it in the wood.'

'We found it on the floor,' said Dick.

'You've been putting things to rights,' said Jacky, opening his knife and trying the blade with a finger.

'Were you sleeping here?' asked Dorothea.

'Nay,' said Jacky. 'Not I. I've cows to milk morning and evening.'

'It's a lovely house,' said Dorothea.

'Aye, it's a good spot,' said Jacky. 'See here. If you come up as far as t'bridge and I see you, I'll show you how to guddle trout for your suppers. Our farm's just above the bridge.'

'We can't come today,' said Dick, thinking of *Scarab*.

'Tomorrow likely,' said Jacky. He took another look all round the hut. 'I'll be seeing you in t'morning. It's a snug spot and you're welcome to it for me. You'll put they stones back in t'wall after. We don't want all folks wi' their nebs in my cupboard.'

'Well, it's jolly decent of you not to mind,' said Dick.

'Nay, you're welcome,' said Jacky, and he went off with the empty milk bottle.

A moment later he came back. 'You don't know nowt about milk,' he said. 'You don't want to keep it where you did. You come along wi' me.'

They followed him out of the hut. He went straight to the beck, to the pool they had already discovered. On the far side of the pool was a patch of pale green moss. A large flat stone was lying on the moss. Jacky lifted it, and showed them a deep hole scooped in the moss beneath it. 'Yon's where I put my bottle o' tea in hot weather like this,' he said. 'You put your milk in there and it won't turn. Butter too. You'll be right enough now. So long . . .' And this time, satisfied that his house was going to be properly used, he went off down the path and did not turn back.

'I ought to have seen that that stone couldn't have been lying on the moss unless someone had put it there,' said Dick to Dorothea.

'We've got to have breakfast anyway,' said Dorothea as if she were thinking of something else.

They ate their cornflakes with the fresh milk that Jacky had been taking from the cow while they were still in their hammocks. The eggs, boiled for five minutes, thanks to Jacky's visit, were not as bullet-like as those that had been boiled for more than ten, thanks to the woodpecker. They drank their tea. They ate bread and marmalade. The tried Jacky's nuts. Some were very good, though others had dried up inside their shells. Somehow, the hut did not seem as much theirs as it had been. Jacky had been there first, and had done the thing better than they could hope to do it, living on trout and rabbits and having his own store of nuts like any squirrel.

'All the nicest houses have been lived in for hundreds of years,' said Dorothea suddenly.

'That boy was a sort of Pict, too,' said Dick. 'It sounded as if nobody knew he'd been here.'

'They didn't at Beckfoot anyhow,' said Dorothea. 'Or Nancy would have said when she brought us up here. She thought there'd been nobody since the woodcutters. He's a better Pict than we are. But I say, that's another person now who knows where we are, besides Cook and the postman and Timothy and the doctor.'

'I wonder how he does catch trout.'

'Dick,' said Dorothea. 'We haven't really begun to know how to be Picts.'

'We're going to learn,' said Dick.

CHAPTER I2

A SIGNAL FROM THE LAWN

Two o'clock sharp.

Dick and Dorothea, after a Pictish morning exploring the wood, had had an early dinner, had skirted round above Beckfoot while they knew the Great Aunt must be safely lunching, and, complete with telescope and the book on how to sail, were lurking in the rock and heather at the top of the ridge of the Beckfoot promontory.

There was no one in the garden. They looked cautiously down on the big Beckfoot lawn, half of it level where once upon a time people had played lawn tennis or croquet, and half of it sloping gently to the river. They could see part of the house, with the rose trellis up which they had seen Nancy climb to her bedroom window. Much of the house was hidden by trees. Beyond the lawn was the coppice, behind which lay Octopus Lagoon and the secret harbour for their boat. Beyond the coppice they could follow the winding line of the river. They could see where the bridge must be and in the woods below Kanchenjunga the white speck of the farm where their morning visitor milked the cows. They could see the great peak of Kanchenjunga where they had visited Slater Bob in the underground workings of long ago miners, and far away the fells where last summer they prospected for gold and found the copper for which Timothy had been looking. To the right, and close beneath them, they looked down on the river and the roof of the Beckfoot boathouse.

'Not one single human being,' said Dorothea.

'They may have gone to the boathouse before we got here,' said Dick. He looked back over the lake. 'They haven't taken her out already or we could see her.'

'It's only just two o'clock,' said Dorothea. 'We were here before she said. Look here, Dick. I'd better have another look at the sailing book. You must know it by heart.'

'I very nearly do,' said Dick. 'But I'll probably forget it when we're really in *Scarab*. The thing you'd better read is the bit about sailing against the wind. There isn't going to be much of it. Nearly a calm. Just look.'

Half a mile away on the other side of the lake a yacht with a big white sail was ghosting along in glassy water, hardly stirring the reflection that she made.

'Good,' said Dorothea. 'We don't want a lot for the first time.'

'We want some,' said Dick. 'It's awful steering when there isn't any wind.'

'We can row,' said Dorothea. 'All that matters is to have her safe here.'

'Timothy may want me tomorrow,' said Dick. 'There may be no time for practice before we have to use her in a hurry.'

He handed over the book and Dorothea did her best to put her mind to it, though it was not her sort of book and, no matter how she tried, her mind kept slipping off from the diagrams that showed just how the wind blowing on a sail made the boat move forward. She was all the time seeing pictures instead of the diagrams, pictures of Nancy hammering at the piano, pictures of the Great Aunt sitting listening, very upright in a chair, with her lips primmed together. Down there, the house was silent, but in Dorothea's head bits of dialogue kept breaking through the sailing book's explanations ... The Great Aunt telling Nancy how many hours a day she used to practise when she was a girl, and Nancy bottling up her shivering timbers and barbecued billygoats and saying 'Yes, Aunt Maria' and 'No, Aunt Maria' in the right places.

Dick took off and cleaned his spectacles. It was no good

getting in a dither, but he could not help it. Two o'clock sharp, Nancy had said in her note. If they were starting now they would only just have time to get across to Rio, take *Scarab* from her builders, hoist sail and have the shortest of short trials before Nancy and Peggy would have to leave them and be bolting home to drawing-room tea. And they were not starting now. Minute after minute was passing. Minute after minute was being simply wasted. Dorothea had the sailing book which would perhaps have helped him not to worry, but it was a good thing that she was trying to read it. Nancy and Peggy would be watching while they tried the new boat and he knew very well that Dot was not as clear about the theory of sailing as she might be. Dick took a last desperate glance at the deserted lawn, and then, wriggling backwards down the ridge, so that he could stand up and still be out of sight from the house, plunged into natural history. One of the things he had set himself to find these holidays was a Fox Moth caterpillar. Heather, he knew, was where to find it. Heather was all about him, and he worked slowly to and fro, searching clump after clump, trying hard to think of caterpillars and to forget how the minutes were slipping by. He could not forget and he had no luck in his search. He decided that Fox Moth caterpillars were probably only to be found on higher ground. He was sitting, looking out over the lake, watching yachts that were hardly moving, and a steamer that left a trail of smoke hanging above the water like a whitish slug, when he heard a very slight noise somewhere above him. He looked round and saw Dorothea beckoning to him.

Dorothea put a finger to her lips. She was still lying where he had left her, on the top of the ridge. Dick climbed quickly.

'It's the Great Aunt herself,' whispered Dorothea, and Dick wormed himself back to his old place and looked cautiously down into the Beckfoot garden between two clumps of heather.

Nancy was there, and Peggy, both in their white frocks.

They were listening to an old lady who seemed to be showing them something on the lawn, pointing this way and that with a blue parasol.

'Oh, Gosh!' groaned Dick. 'They'll never even try to start while she's there.'

'I wonder if they know we've come,' whispered Dorothea. 'Shall I signal while she's got her back to us?'

'No. No. If they saw, she'd know in a second and turn round to see what they were looking at ... I say. She's sent Nancy on a message.'

Nancy went off at a run round the corner of the house. The Great Aunt stayed on the lawn talking to Peggy.

'She ought to be lying down already,' said Dick.

They heard a door slam somewhere behind the house. Then they heard a whirring noise. Then they saw Nancy coming back to the lawn, dragging something behind her.

'Mowing machine,' said Dick. 'Oh I say, she can't be going to make them mow the lawn *now*.'

'They're all going back to the house,' whispered Dorothea.

The mowing machine stood alone in the middle of the lawn. Nancy, Peggy and the Great Aunt were on the path under the windows of the house. Then Nancy and Peggy went in.

'If she doesn't go in herself, they'll never risk going to the boathouse,' said Dick.

But the Great Aunt stood there waiting. Nancy and Peggy came out carrying a long garden chair between them. They set this up, and the watchers could see that the Great Aunt was showing them just where she wished it to be. They went in again. Nancy brought out a little table; Peggy, a book and a basket.

'What's that green stuff in the basket?' whispered Dorothea.

'Green wool, I think,' said Dick after a careful look through the telescope.

'It's her knitting.'

'They'll be free now,' said Dick.

'If only they could get her properly settled,' whispered Dorothea not very hopefully.

'It'll be all right if even one of them gets away,' whispered Dick.

But, after the Great Aunt was comfortably in her chair, with the table where she wanted it, at her elbow, and her knitting on her knees, she still seemed to have something to say to her nieces. Peggy ran off and came back with a small chair. They saw her sit down. They saw her open the book.

'Peggy's being made to read aloud,' gasped Dorothea. 'And Nancy . . .'

Nancy was walking across the lawn to the mowing machine. Just for half a moment. Dick thought that perhaps she was going to the boathouse. But she took hold of the handles of the mowing machine and gave it a sharp push, so that the blades spun.

'She's going to cut the grass,' whispered Dorothea. 'And there's miles of it.'

'Pretty shaggy,' said Dick.

'She's going to mow the whole lawn,' said Dorothea. 'Look she's going to start at the river and work up.'

Nancy, dragging the mower behind her, had left the level part of the lawn and was crossing the long slope to the edge of the river. Just for one moment they saw her glance up at the ridge where the watchers were lurking. She never looked up again. Suddenly she turned and began to push the lawn mower instead of pulling it. They could hear the whirring blades.

'She hasn't begun cutting,' said Dick. 'She's got the blades off the ground . . . Now's she's beginning.' Cut grass suddenly began to fountain from the spinning blades into the big green box on the front of the machine.

'Why isn't she doing it in straight lines?' Dick whispered.

LOOKOUT POST ON THE RIDGE

'She must be furious at being made to do it at all,' whispered Dorothea.

Nancy, instead of mowing in straight lines seemed to be running the lawn mower aimlessly about. She ran it round in a big curve, then straight for a few yards, then back the way she had come, then round again in a complete circle. . . .

Suddenly they understood.

'She's writing,' gasped Dorothea.

Under the very eyes of the Great Aunt, Nancy was writing them a message. The Great Aunt, from where she sat by the house, could not have read it even if she had been looking. But the Picts, lurking behind rock and heather on the top of the ridge, were looking straight down on the lawn instead of across it. They could read it easily, a message written in the broad trail of the lawn mower that left a different green behind it from that of the long, uncut grass. Four letters Nancy wrote. Two short words. A melancholy message. But there it was, plainly written on the lawn.

NO GO

And Nancy, a virtuous martyr as before, was driving the machine in a straight line from one side of the lawn to the other as if she had never thought of doing anything else.

'It means they can't come at all,' said Dorothea.

'And we can't go and get *Scarab* without them.'

They lay watching Nancy steadily at work, pushing the mower to and fro until she had covered the ground where her

message had been written. In front of the house Peggy was reading aloud and the Great Aunt's fingers were flickering about her knitting.

'It's no good stopping,' said Dick. 'We'd better go away. That's what she meant to tell us. We'd better go and have a look at the harbour.'

'All right,' said Dorothea.

'Wasted day,' said Dick grimly, as they climbed back into the road after coming silently down from their look-out post above the garden.

'It's much worse for them,' said Dorothea.

'It's a wasted day for all of us. A whole wasted day. It means we can't get *Scarab* till tomorrow, and there's all that work to do for Captain Flint and Timothy may be sending a pigeon any minute to say he's ready for me to come to the houseboat and help.'

'It's much worse than that,' said Dorothea. 'Why didn't the doctor tell her to go properly to bed. If he just told her to take a rest, she may go and lie in a chair every afternoon and keep them busy all the time.'

EASY FOR CATERPILLARS

CHAPTER 13

TICKLING TROUT

THERE was nothing they could do to the harbour until they had a boat to berth in it. They stood for a few moments looking at the narrow lane of clear water through the reeds. By now, if only things had not gone wrong, they would have had their ship.

'Listen,' said Dorothea.

Faintly, from the other side of the coppice, they could hear the whirr of the mowing machine on the Beckfoot lawn. Whirrr ... rrrrr. On and on, and then a change of note, almost a scream, as Nancy came to the edge of the lawn, gave an extra hard push, and sent the blades spinning with no grass to cut.

'It wants oil,' said Dick.

'It's like listening to the prisoners working a treadmill,' said Dorothea.

'They don't have treadmills nowadays,' said Dick.

'Well, listen to it,' said Dorothea.

And then, while Dick was looking for caterpillars on the under sides of the willow leaves, she began her favourite game, trying to think herself into the minds and skins of other people.

'Of course you can't really blame her,' she said suddenly.

'Who?'

'The Great Aunt. She didn't know they were meaning to take us across to fetch *Scarab*. If she had ...'

'Everything would be even worse,' said Dick.

'I know. I know. But I'm just trying to be her for a minute. You see, not knowing, she can't be doing it on purpose. She's thinking they've got nothing to do, and she's thinking of Mrs Blackett coming back and finding the lawn all nicely cut in spite of Captain Flint not being here to do it.'

'It *was* a bit shaggy,' Dick admitted.

'She's thinking of how they ought to be brought up, and killing two birds with one stone . . . I'm sure that book she's making Peggy read must be one of their holiday tasks. She's wanting them to get it done. Like eating bread and butter first instead of starting on cake. She's thinking . . . You know the funny thing about people is they always think they're doing right.'

Dick became interested from another point of view. 'Like natural history,' he said. 'There's no good in hating wasps because they sting. What matters is to understand how they do it. It works both ways. When you understand you don't mind it so much even if it's you who get stung. Like that mosquito. I forgot how beastly he was when I was watching him and saw him uncurl his proboscis and shove it in and start sucking blood up out of the back of my hand . . . Of course, it was scratchy afterwards just the same.'

'I know,' said Dorothea. 'She thinks she's doing good. It's no good blaming her, but it doesn't stop things being beastly for them. Did you hear? The mowing stopped for a minute, and now it's started again. She must have sent Peggy to tell Nancy to come and read, and now it's Peggy's turn at the treadmill. And we can't do anything to help. Let's go farther away where we can't hear it.'

They left the harbour and the trees, skirted round the reedy shore of the lagoon, and walked along the river bank. They startled a water rat and watched it swim across, push upstream close under the farther bank and disappear into a hole. Dick had a kingfisher to add to the list in his pocket-book. They saw or thought they saw several trout. Here, where it flowed between the meadows, the river was smooth and deep enough for a boat. It was silent, but, as they followed it towards the bridge where the road crossed it, they began to hear it, tumbling and rushing over the shallows and rocks above the bridge, just as they had heard it last summer when camped beside it in Mrs Tyson's orchard.

'You can't hear the mowing machine now,' said Dick.

'No,' said Dorothea, 'but I can't help thinking about it.'

'They'll finish the lawn today,' said Dick.

'Tomorrow she may go and think of something else,' said Dorothea.

They climbed over a stile into the road and stood on the bridge looking at the river. There could be no doubt about the trout now. Dick counted seven, three in the smooth water close under the bridge, one behind a stone in midstream, another in front of the stone, another in a smooth patch a few yards higher up, and another in some rippled water. This one he could see only when it splashed up after a floating fly. Every now and then the splash came in the same place, and, by keeping his eyes on that place, he saw the trout itself, a head, a flash of silver, and then nothing but rippling water as before.

And then something happened that for the moment put martyrs and *Scarab* and chemistry and treadmills clean out of their minds.

'Hey!'

They looked up and saw the small boy, Jacky, hurrying towards them with an old rusty tin in his hand.

'Thought you said you couldn't come today,' he said as he joined them on the bridge.

'We were going to do something else,' said Dorothea, 'but it's been put off.'

'Lucky I happen to see you coming up t'beck.' Jacky crossed to the other side of the bridge and hove himself up so that he lay with his stomach on the parapet.

'There's a big yin down yonder.'

The other two, who could look over the parapet without having to lie on the top of it, stood on each side of Jacky, watching the water flowing away from under the arch. They saw a sudden ring of ripples that drifted with the stream and was gone.

'That's him,' said Jacky. He was scratching at the moss between the stones, and they saw him reach out a hand and let something slip from between his fingers.

'You'll see him now . . . now . . . Nay, it's passed him . . . See him get ut . . .' There was a swirl in the water and they had all seen the flash as the big trout turned.

'What did you drop?' asked Dick.

'Wingy ant . . . Here's another.'

Again the big trout rose. Dick, too, began hunting.

'Will any insect do?'

'Ay. But ants is best or flies. Bracken clock's best of all when you can get 'em.'

'What's a bracken clock?'

'June beetle,' said Jacky. 'Here's an ant. You take ut. You mun drop ut in t'reet spot.'

The ant floated away a bit to the side of the place where the big trout was lying. It was taken by a much smaller one farther down the river.

'I don't see how you can catch them without a fishing rod,' said Dick.

'We'll not catch yon,' said Jacky. 'You come wi' me. I'll show you.'

He wriggled down from the parapet and led the way from the bridge along a cart track above the river. They passed a gate where the cart track turned through trees towards the white farm house. They kept on by a footpath close to the water and came to a place where a smaller stream came hurrying down from Kanchenjunga to join the bigger one.

Jacky stopped. He dropped on his stomach and wriggled to the edge of the stream. He pulled up his sleeve and, as it slipped down again, took his coat off and rolled up the sleeves of his shirt.

'You aren't going to catch them in your hands!' said Dick.

'Whisht!' said Jacky, and Dick and Dorothea, Picts with everything to learn, watched in silence.

With his head close to the ground, Jacky was dipping his arm under water. He wriggled a little nearer. His arm went in to the elbow. They saw one of his feet that had been moving stop as if it had been suddenly frozen. Half a minute went by like half an hour. Suddenly Jacky rolled sideways. His arm shot up out of the water and something flew through the air over the heads of the watchers. The next moment Jacky was on his feet searching the brambles where it had fallen. They saw his white arm plunge. They saw him bang something on a stone. He came back to them grinning with a small trout in his hand, and blood trickling from a scratch on his forearm.

'Get 'em away from t'water quick's you can,' he said. 'Or you'll lose 'em sure.'

'But how did you catch it?' said Dick, looking at the trout.

'You've scratched your arm,' said Dorothea.

'That's nowt,' said Jacky, licked the scratch and began to explain how the thing was done.

'Easy,' he said. 'You've nobbut to guddle 'em.'

'But how?' said Dick.

'Why don't they just swim away?' said Dorothea.

Jacky held the dead trout in his left hand as if it was swimming. He brought his right hand towards it, with all his fingers gently moving.

'You mun do it artful,' he murmured. He looked away, as if to show that he could not see the trout that he was holding. The fingers of his right hand were never still for a moment, like weeds stirring in a stream. He shut his eyes. Dick and Dorothea saw the moving fingers coming nearer and nearer to the trout. They touched, but still kept moving till the tips of them had worked up from underneath and round the body of the trout. Suddenly the fingers closed. Jacky's left hand was empty. His right hand held the trout. He opened his eyes, looked at it as if surprised to see what he had caught, and grinned happily at his pupils.

'Got him!' he said.

'But why doesn't the trout just bolt?' said Dick.

'It's the guddling,' said Jacky. 'If you go for to take him he's gone. You mun keep guddling and guddling till you've your fingers round the middle of him. He'll lie quiet. But you mun keep guddling. And you mun keep clear of his tail or he's off. Let's see you get yin. There's aye a good yin under yon stone.'

He put the dead trout in his tin, and warily moved back towards the beck, pointing out the stone he meant.

Dick rolled up his shirt sleeves and crawled to the edge of the stream.

'Nay,' squeaked Jacky. 'Put your hand in below him. You don't want to give him your fist to smell. Aye. Yon's t'place . . . Is owt there? . . . Can you feel him?'

One of Dick's feet waved in the air.

'He's found one,' said Dorothea.

'Keep guddling,' urged Jacky. 'Get your fingers round the thick of him . . . Eh, but you lost a good yin there.'

Dick's arm had plunged to the shoulder. A sharp V of ripples shot across the pool.

'I'm awfully sorry' said Dick.

'I'll catch another,' said Jacky. 'There's plenty more fish in t'beck.' He pushed his tin at Dorothea, and went quickly up the stream, stooping as he went.

'You've got your shirt wet,' said Dorothea.

'Never mind,' said Dick. 'I felt him. I felt his fins waving and then I wasn't sure. I must have let my fingers stop. Come on. Let's see him catch another.'

Jacky was already down on his stomach, clinging to a tree with his right hand, while his left reached down into the water that ran under it. He had lain there hardly more than a few seconds before he was scrambling to his feet with a small trout.

'Easy, that yin,' he said.

He banged its head on a stone, dropped it into the tin that Dorothea was holding, and darted off to another favourite place. He changed his mind. 'Nay, you get this yin,' he said. 'Right under t'bank.'

'How do you know?' asked Dorothea.

'I've had many a trout from yon spot,' said Jacky. 'Catch yin today and there'll be another in t'same spot in t'morning.'

This time he did not wait to watch, but hurried on up the side of the stream.

'I'm going to get this one,' said Dick, and he did.

'Oh, well done,' cried Dorothea, and Jacky came running back, to bang the trout on the head and put it with the others.

'I felt his fins tickling my hand. At least it wasn't his fins. It was the stir they made in the water. It's quite easy if only you can keep your fingers moving all the time.'

'Plenty more likely spots along here,' said Jacky. 'I'm going higher up. See who can catch most.'

Dick chose what he thought was a good place, but there was no trout in it. He tried again and after long careful tickling caught a small stick that he had made sure was a fish. Then he had two failures with trout that darted away before he had made up his mind that he had worked his fingers into position. 'Go on, Dot. You try. We've simply got to learn.'

Dorothea, after several tries in places where there were no trout, caught one to her own surprise. 'Jacky,' she shouted, and got an answer from much farther up the beck. Dick had failed again and yet again, and they hurried along to find Jacky, who was sitting by the stream with a row of seven small trout on the mossy bank beside him.

'Bang ut on t'neb,' said Jacky jumping up when he saw that Dorothea had something leaping in her cupped hands. 'You'll lose ut in t'beck if you don't look sharp. I telled you,'

FEELING FOR A TROUT

he added as the little fish fell on the bank, flapped its tail, and, before she could pick it up, had dropped with a splash into the water and was gone.

'Never mind,' said Dorothea. 'I say, you have got a lot.'

'Nay, we want more nor that,' said Jacky.

Tickling trout takes longer than telling about it and it was late in the day when they came back to the place where the small beck ran into the Amazon river, and laid out the catch. There were thirteen. 'Lisle yins,' said Jacky, 'but them's the sweetest.' Jacky himself had caught all but five, Dick had caught three, and Dorothea two.

'It isn't only the tickling,' said Dick. 'It's knowing the right places.'

'Nay, you've done none so bad for a first asking,' said Jacky. 'It's a gey good supper, but they won't look so big when you've fried 'em.'

Dorothea did not think they looked very big even before frying, but she did not say so.

Jacky began separating them into two lots, but he changed his mind and put them all together.

'I can get plenty more,' he said. 'You put 'em in my fry pan wi' a dollop of butter. Have you got any butter?'

'Yes.'

'Swizzle it round the fry pan,' said Jacky. 'Real hot. Lay 'em in and turn 'em after. Turn 'em over when they start curling. Eat 'em as hot as you can lay your tongue to.'

'Put them in just as they are?' asked Dorothea.

'Gut 'em,' said Jacky. 'I'll show you.' He pulled out the huge pocket knife they had found when cleaning out the hut. One by one, he ripped up the little fish and scraped their insides out over the beck. 'My mother rolls 'em in flour,' he said. 'But there's no need. Or you can made do wi' bread-crumbs.'

'Jacky! JACKEE!'

'That'll be my supper,' said Jacky. 'And hens to feed and cows to milk and what all.' He jumped up after putting the last of the little fish into the tin where they were packed like sardines, and gave the tin to Dorothea.

'Thanks most awfully,' said Dorothea.

'Thank you very much,' said Dick.

'Nay, I can do better for you nor that,' said Jacky. 'And happen I will before morning.' And he bolted off towards the farm-house.

'They'll have done the lawn by now,' said Dorothea, and with that they remembered that while they had been learning to tickle trout, Nancy and Peggy had been having a dreadful time.

They crossed the bridge and hurried along the road.

At the gap in the wall they waited and listened. There was no sound of the treadmill.

Dick had a look at the hole in the wall that was to be their letter-box. He knew the postman did not come in the afternoons, so he was not expecting a letter. He was wondering if the postman would find the right hole if there was a letter in the morning. But there was a letter in the hole already. He pulled it out.

'From Nancy,' exclaimed Dorothea, as she saw the skull and crossbones. There was no other address on the envelope. Dick tore it open, and read the note inside.

'Sorry about today. Couldn't be helped. Better luck tomorrow. Same place. Same time. She got a headache. Serve her right. No hope of getting out this evening. Hope you got your milk.' There was no signature, but there was no need of one.

'Good,' said Dick. 'There's been no message from Timothy.'

'If we'd come back a bit sooner we might have seen them just for a second,' said Dorothea.

'They probably only just had time to jam it in and bolt back,' said Dick.

'It's simply a miracle,' said Dorothea.

'What is?'

'Three whole days already,' said Dorothea. 'And Nancy keeping it up all the time. I thought Peggy might manage, but I never thought Nancy could hold in for half as long.

I suppose it's because she's made up her mind. I expect the real martyrs were just the same. The more the lions roared the less they let Nero or anybody see they cared.'

'It's all right so far,' said Dick. 'So long as we get the boat before Timothy's ready to start work.'

*

Things were certainly easier for the Picts. They went up through the wood, to their own house, where there was no Great Aunt to tell them what to do or not to do. They lit their fire and set up their hammocks for the night. Dorothea crumbled some dry bread, got some butter melted and bubbling in Jacky's frying pan, rolled each little fish in the crumbs and laid it in the pan. Then, shielding her face from the hot fire and the spitting butter, she watched till the trout began to curl. She turned them over to brown them on the other side. There was one bad moment when she remembered that she had forgotten the salt, but it was not too late to put that right, and presently the smell of fried trout was mingling with the smell of the wood fire, and soon after that, the Picts were licking their fingers and dropping fins and backbones to sizzle in the flames.

Dorothea put four of the trout aside. 'We'll have those cold for breakfast,' she said. 'I say, Dick, that's our first real meal.'

'Why our first?'

'Food that we got for ourselves,' said Dorothea. 'In my next story I'm going to let the people have no food at all except what they can get in the forest where they live.'

'There's blackberries,' said Dick. 'And nuts.'

'If Jacky was living here instead of us,' said Dorothea, 'I'm perfectly sure he'd manage without any bought stuff at all. There were no shops for the Picts. And no things in tins.'

Dick thought for a moment. 'They would have used them if they could have got them,' he said.

CHAPTER 14

'THEY CAN'T BE GOING TO SAIL...'

'WE'LL be sailing today,' said Dick almost before he opened his eyes, and saw that Dorothea was already up and dressed and busy about breakfast.

'Hurry up then,' said Dorothea.

The kettle was boiling when Jacky came stumbling up the path with the milk. He held out the bottle, but kept one hand behind him.

'Told you I could do better for you nor trout,' he said with a wide grin.

'They were awfully good,' said Dorothea. 'We had them for supper last night and we're just going to eat the last four for breakfast.'

'What about yon?' said Jacky, who brought his hand suddenly from behind his back and showed them a rabbit.

'Did you catch it?' said Dick.

'I thought there might be summat doing,' said Jacky. 'Fine night and all. I catched three.'

He held out the rabbit to Dorothea, who took it gingerly by its hind legs.

'But don't you want it yourself?' she said.

'Nay. Mother says she don't want but two. You're welcome. And here's an onion to go with it. My mother says a rabbit's not worth cooking without.'

'Thank you very much,' said both Dick and Dorothea at once.

'I'll show you where to hang ut,' said Jacky, and took them round to the north side of the hut and showed them a big wooden peg driven between the stones of the wall just about as high as he could reach. 'Fox won't get ut there,' he said as he hung up the rabbit by the loop of string he had used to fasten it to the handle-bars of his bicycle. He stood for a moment admiring it. 'Have you got a bottle to take back. I mun be getting along. Summer and back end's our busy time.'

'Whose busy time?' asked Dick.

'Farmers,' said Jacky as if he owned a thousand acres. 'Aye busiest when other folk are having holidays. I'se going wi' dad to market today. We've young pigs to sell.' And with that, taking the empty bottle that Dorothea had rinsed in the beck, he hurried away down the wood.

*

The little beck trout were almost better cold than hot, and while they were washing up after breakfast, the Picts planned to go guddling again.

'We'll get a whole lot,' said Dick. 'We know how. It only needs practice. And then we can make a feast for the others.'

'The sort of meal real Picts would give them,' said Dorothea. 'Trout, and perhaps Jacky'll get another rabbit . . . I'm going to cook this one for dinner . . . But I don't suppose the others'll be able to get away.'

'We needn't stop being Picts even when she's gone,' said Dick. 'Though there won't be any need.'

'We could be a whole tribe,' said Dorothea. 'If only something doesn't go wrong while she's here.'

'We'd better go down to the road,' said Dick. 'Something may have happened already. There may be a message in the letter-box to say it's no good again today. . . .'

They went down to the gap in the wall, but found nothing in the letter-box.

'Let's hang about a bit. One of them may escape for a moment.'

'Not too near the road,' said Dick.

They were lurking just where the path left the larches and climbed into the thick undergrowth of the coppice, when they heard the rattle of a bicycle.

'Postman,' whispered Dick. 'Lie low. Let's see if he puts a letter in our box.'

'We'd better stop him and make sure,' said Dorothea. 'It would be too awful if he went and took another to the Great Aunt.'

But, before they had time to move, they heard his feet on the road as he got off his bicycle. Looking down through the trunks of the trees they saw him come into the gap, swing his bag round, dip into it and take out a bundle of letters. They saw him take one letter from the bundle. He stooped and poked it into the wall.

'He's done it all right,' said Dick.

'Wait just a minute,' said Dorothea. 'If he's like the doctor he'd much rather not see us. And there's no need now.'

They waited till the postman had had time to go on to Beckfoot, and then ran down to the wall.

'It's for you,' said Dick, pulling the letter from its hole.

'From Mother,' said Dorothea.

'Is there one for me too?'

'It's to both of us. Don't let's stay by the road. Come back out of sight.'

In the shelter of the hazels where nobody on the road could see them, they read the letter together.

My very dear Dot and Dick,

We were glad to hear that you had got safely to the end of your journey. It must have been great fun doing the last bit of it by water. I expect by now you are already sailing in your own new boat. Do be careful. It would be a dreadful pity and most annoying for us if you both got drowned before you have had a chance of teaching us to sail. Father is still snowed under with examination papers, but he seems to spend quite a lot of time looking at a catalogue of boats for hire on the Broads, and the red and blue pencils he uses for marking the examination papers are quite useful for putting crosses against the boats the look of which he likes. I think something may come of it. I have had a very nice letter from your friend Mrs Barrable who is at Horning and says her brother will be there and sailing with her some time in September. She asked me to give the Coot Club's best wishes as well as her own. Now about your Picts. Your father says that in a way you are right and in a way you are wrong. There used to be a theory among folklorists that the origin of the belief in fairies and such was the half secret presence in remote places of the original inhabitants of the country who had been for the most part driven out by conquering tribes. I think I have remembered his exact words. He says it is an exploded theory, but he also says that most theories get exploded sooner or later. While father is doing his examination papers, with the help of a red and blue pencil and the catalogue with pictures of boats, I have been turning out the whole house . . . '*Oh, I say, not my room,*' exclaimed Dick . . . I am not touching Dick's Museum . . . '*That's all right,*' said Dick *with a sigh of relief* . . . It must be great fun having a house of your own. Have Peggy and Nancy got one too? Remember to give my love to Mrs Dixon if you see her. Good-bye for now. Love from both of us to both of you.

Mother

P.S. Mind! No getting drowned. We want to learn to sail.

'It's no good trying to explain about Nancy and Peggy and the Great Aunt in a letter,' said Dorothea. 'Anyhow, we're doing the best we can to make sure Mrs Blackett isn't sorry she invited us. What does it mean when a theory's exploded?'

'Just that somebody's invented another,' said Dick. 'Like in chemistry. Once people all believed in stuff called phlogiston, and then in atoms, and now it's all mixed up with radium and electricity.'

'So the Picts are all right.'

'Until we can think of something better,' said Dick.

'We're going on being Picts,' said Dorothea.

'With us the theory won't really be exploded unless the Great Aunt finds out.'

'She mustn't,' said Dorothea.

After the disappointment of the day before, Dick hardly dared to let himself believe that nothing would stop them from fetching *Scarab*.

'I'm going to stop here and keep a look out,' he said. 'Just in case one of them brings a message. Anything may have happened since last night.'

'All right,' said Dorothea. 'I've a lot to do about the house.'

Two hours, three hours went by. Dick lay in hiding, looking down from the hazel bushes, watching the road through the rough scaled trunks of the larches. He had Knight's *Sailing* with him, and he caught a glimpse of a woodpecker and had a good view of three kinds of tits, a jay and a couple of magpies. A red squirrel came leaping and swinging through the feathery branches of larch trees, saw Dick, and kept taking a look at him first round one side of the trunk and then round the other, and then chattered at him as if asking what business he had in the wood. Any one of these things on ordinary days would have been enough to make Dick forget the time and everything else. Today he kept looking at his watch, and at last began to worry not because time was going too slowly but because it was going too fast. How long did it take to cook a rabbit? Hadn't he better remind Dot that whatever happened they must be ready and waiting on the promontory the moment Nancy and Peggy managed to get away?

He found Dorothea outside the hut, looking at the rabbit still hanging from its peg in the wall.

'How long does it take to cook?' he asked. .

'It looks awfully dead,' said Dorothea.

'But it *is*,' said Dick.

'I wonder how I ought to begin.'

'There's probably a scientific way,' said Dick. 'Of getting the skin off, I mean.'

Dorothea took the rabbit from the peg. Its eyes were dull, and its fur felt cold to her unwilling touch.

'They're a lot nicer running about.'

'I know,' said Dick. 'So is everything. Even tinned pemmican was running about once, and sardines were swimming and bananas were growing on trees. But we eat them just the same.'

'Picts wouldn't think twice about it. Jacky didn't. Look at those trout. And we ate them. And they were very good. I know it's no good thinking about it . . . But I wish I'd asked Jacky how to take the skin off.'

'Ask him tomorrow,' said Dick. 'Don't bother about it now. Let's have something that's ready to eat as it is. We ought to be down on the promontory early in case they get an extra minute.'

'Perhaps I'll be able to get a cookery book in Rio,' said Dorothea. 'Yes. I'll do that. We oughtn't to have to ask people everything. Can you do for now with pemmican and bread and cheese and oranges and some of the Beckfoot grog?'

'It doesn't matter what we have,' said Dick. 'So long as we're not late.'

'We'll cook the rabbit for supper tonight,' said Dorothea. 'Or dinner tomorrow. If I can get a cookery book it's sure to tell us all about it.'

Half an hour later, after a meal a good deal easier to make ready than the rabbit stew she had been thinking of, Dorothea had tidied up, Dick had put the plates to rinse under the waterfall, and the two of them were on the way, Dick with telescope and Knight, Dorothea with the scarab flag for the new boat. They were very early, and for fear luncheon might not have begun at Beckfoot, they worked their way round through the wood till they came down on the road well beyond the house, crossed it after careful scouting, and were presently looking down from the ridge on Beckfoot lawn.

'It's going to be all right today, I know it is,' said Dorothea at last.

'Two and a half more minutes to two o'clock,' said Dick.

Suddenly their hearts fell, as two prim figures came out of the house.

'Something's gone wrong again,' whispered Dorothea.

'They can't be going to sail after all,' said Dick.

'Not dressed like that,' said Dorothea.

White frocks, pink sashes, shady white hats ... if they had not known who was wearing these things, they never would have guessed.

'They're coming across the lawn,' said Dick. 'Perhaps it's to tell us it's no go again.'

'Don't shout,' whispered Dorothea. 'She may be watching from her bedroom window and if she saw them look up ...'

'Quick. Quick,' said Dick, wriggling backwards. 'We'll have to hurry to get down there or they may think we haven't come.'

Safely below the skyline they stood up and raced down the ridge. They waited at the edge of the river. They could see the roof of the boathouse over the reeds, and through a gap in the reed-beds they could see the smooth waters of the Amazon flowing out into the lake.

For some minutes nothing happened. Then they heard the noise of oars working in rowlocks. Then, close by, the loud impatient quacking of a duck. A moment later the boat was in sight. A miracle had happened. White frocks and shady hats were gone. Two sturdy pirates in shirts and shorts, with red stocking caps on their heads, were in the boat, Nancy at the oars, Peggy standing in the stern, anxiously searching the banks. She quacked again, and the same instant saw them.

Nancy backwatered with her left, pulled with her right, and swung the boat's nose round into the gap between the reed-beds.

'Giminy,' she said. 'We were afraid you never got my dispatch. We thought you hadn't come. Hop in. Have you been waiting long?'

'We saw you come across the lawn,' said Dorothea. 'We thought it meant "No Go" again.'

Nancy laughed. 'We've left all that in the boathouse. Peggy nipped out last night with our comfortables hidden in a watering can while I held the G.A. in polite talk. Get right down in the bottom of the boat. Under the sail as much as you can. She was in her bedroom when we left but you can't count on her to stay there. I thought of locking her in, but it seemed better not. If she does come out she's as likely to mouch along the lake road as anywhere. So jolly well keep your heads below the gunwale. We'll be in full view from the road till we get to Rio Bay.'

'But won't she see your red caps.'

'We could explain them' said Nancy. 'But we couldn't explain you. She probably isn't there. She went to lie down all right. But we won't take any risks. Here, Peggy. You take one oar and I'll take the other and we'll fairly bucket across.'

'Aren't you going to sail?' asked Dick.

'We'd have to tack,' said Nancy. 'Rowing's faster when there's so little wind. And we want every minute we can with the new boat. And don't shout too loud. Sound carries like anything over water. No. We're going to row there, and then we'll have a bit of time to watch you sailing.'

Dick, lying in the bottom of the *Amazon*, took off his spectacles and wiped them.

Dorothea knew the signs. 'It'll be all right,' she whispered. 'You've sailed *Titmouse*. And *Teasel*. It'll be just the same.'

'I know,' said Dick, putting his spectacles on again, and thinking of the diagrams in his book. Privately he wished very much that he and Dorothea were going to sail their new boat for the first time without anybody to look on.

'What's all that?' said Nancy, but rowing hard, did not wait for an answer. 'Trim the boat, Dot. Shift your weight a bit nearer the side. No. Not you, Dick. I say, are you getting your milk all right?'

'Yes,' said Dorothea. 'And Jacky's given us a rabbit. And yesterday while you were being prisoners he taught us how to catch trout with our fingers.'

'Good for Jacky,' said Nancy.

'But that's not all,' said Dorothea. 'It's his hut we've taken.'

'Jacky's?'

'We never knew that,' said Peggy.

'He says nobody knew. He's a better Pict than we are,' said Dorothea. 'He's got his own cupboard there, and cooking things. And that was his saw we found. And his knife.'

'I say,' said Nancy ... 'If he talks too much.'

'He won't,' said Dorothea. 'He's lent us everything, and he says he doesn't want it just now because he's too busy.'

'Well done, Jacky,' said Nancy. 'Think of him being up there and us not having the slightest idea.'

'Do you think I'll be able to get a cookery book in Rio?'

'I expect so,' said Nancy. 'What do you want it for?'

'That rabbit,' said Dorothea.

'Smuggle it down to us and we'll get old Cooky to do it.'

'I think I ought to learn,' said Dorothea.

'Jolly useful,' said Nancy. 'Keep time, Peggy. In ... out ... in ...'

'I say,' said Dick. 'What do we do about bringing *Scarab* home?'

'You'll manage all right,' said Nancy. 'Only put it off till pretty late. Don't come back with us. She mustn't see two boats arriving together. And don't try sailing up the river. It isn't deep enough to use the centreboard, and if you got blown into the bank just in front of the house ... Get the centreboard up outside. Lower sail and row quietly up ...'

'Without even looking at the house.'

'That's the idea,' said Nancy. 'Just row right past, and when you get to the lagoon and work her into the harbour she'll be as snug as anything and you can sneak away. What are you going to call the harbour?'

'Picthaven,' said Dorothea.

'Right. What's the matter, Dick?'

'Only a crick in my neck.'

'You can come up now. Easy, Peggy.'

The two pirates stopped rowing, and the boat slid on while the stowaways put their heads above the gunwale, scrambled up, one at a time, took their places in the stern and looked about them.

Already the Beckfoot promontory was far astern. Close ahead was Rio Bay with its crowds of rowing boats, its moored yachts, its boat landings, the steamer pier and, beyond it, the big sheds of the boatbuilders.

The pirates rowed on.

'Hen and chicken,' said Peggy, nodding as they passed at the two big buoys that marked the rocks that the steamers had to avoid.

'I remember,' said Dorothea, thinking of Rio Bay all ice and thick with skating Eskimos on that winter day when she and Dick had sailed a sledge in a blizzard and found the North Pole. That had been one kind of adventure. This, she thought, was quite another. Riskier, too. Rather like it in a way ... like skating on thin ice that might break at any moment. She looked at the visitors, using their oars like windmills and splashing noisily to and fro in the hired boats. They were not, like Dick and herself, outlaws whose very existence was a secret. She thought of her old story of the Outlaw of the Broads, always in flight from his enemies. At least his enemies knew he existed. That was almost homely and comfortable. This was much more difficult. She planned that her next story should be about a Pict, the very last of his race, living his life out to the end in a country whose people never even knew that he was there. Her father would be able to tell her all about Picts. Were there rabbits in England then?

Did the last of the Picts catch them and cook them? Did he, like a fox, come creeping to his neighbours' farmyards, and race back to his hills in the moonlight with a fat duck clutched in his sinewy hands? Her mind was far away when Nancy called, 'Easy, Peggy! . . . Good. They've got her in the water. There she is. By the third boatshed . . .'

CHAPTER 15

LAUNCHING THE *SCARAB*

A NARROW landing stage ran down into the water from the big grey shed. Beside it, Dick and Dorothea could see the golden flash of newly varnished wood. *Scarab* was waiting for them, tied to the stage.

Nancy, who had taken both oars, was bringing *Amazon* in. Peggy, painter in hand, was ready in the bows. With every moment Dick and Dorothea could see more of the first ship they had ever owned. She was right way up now and floating, alive, no longer a mere piece of carpentry as she had been when they had seen her upside down on trestles in the shed. Her mast, pale yellow, was lying in her, with two oars also bright with varnish, and a new red sail, neatly stowed along its spars.

'SIT DOWN, Dick,' said Nancy, startling Dick, who had not known that he was standing up.

'The sail's a lovely colour,' said Dorothea.

'It won't mildew anyhow,' said Nancy, 'Another thing is that our sail's white, and *Swallow*'s is brown and with yours red, when we're all sailing we'll be able to tell which is which a hundred miles away.'

The boatbuilder, working in the shed, had seen them through the open doors. He came out on the stage to meet them and put a hand down to *Amazon*'s gunwale, though, with Nancy at the oars, there was no need to save a bump.

'So you've come for her,' he said. 'We had her ready for you yesterday.'

'Something happened and we couldn't come,' said Nancy.

'We were thinking of bringing her across to Beckfoot this morning but summat got in t'road and we were kept busy till dinner-time.'

Nancy gasped. Dorothea's face whitened. What would have happened if the boatbuilder had turned up at Beckfoot with a boat for the people who did not exist? Again she had that dreadful feeling that they were all skating on thin and cracking ice. The danger was as much from those who did not know what was going on as from those who had become allies in the cause. But the boatbuilder did not notice and Dick and Peggy, already on the stage, were looking down into the new boat.

Nancy pulled herself together. 'Glad you didn't,' she said. 'We wanted to fetch her ourselves.' The next moment she was in *Scarab* and busy stepping the mast.

'Better let me,' she said. 'Just to save time.' The mast went up, and she cast loose the halliards. 'Good. Flag halliards ready too. Where's that flag Dot? Let Dick have it. Two clove hitches, one half way up the flagstaff and one at the very bottom. . . . Look here. Never forget to mouse the sister-hooks when you fasten the main halliard to the yard . . . Like this . . . They always shake loose if you don't . . . No. Don't hoist the flag yet. Half a minute . . . Giminy! (She slapped a pocket of her shorts.) No, it's all right. I thought I'd forgotten it . . . Now . . .'

'Forgotten what?' Dick's mind was in a whirl. Things were going too fast. Peggy was fitting the rudder. Nancy was busy with half a dozen things at once. Would he ever remember how to do everything when he and Dot had their boat to themselves?

Nancy had a quick look round. 'Sure you've got them both in, Peggy?'

'It's an easier rudder to fit than ours,' said Peggy, who had been kneeling in the stern trying to get both gudgeon pins in at once. She moved the tiller first one way and then the other. 'Ready,' she said.

'Now then, Dot. Let *Amazon* out at the full length of her painter. Then there'll be room for *Scarab* to come to the end of the stage and lie head to wind while we hoist the sail. Then we'll get her right off on port tack. You don't want to use oars if you can help it, specially on her first voyage. It'd be beastly bad luck . . .'

The old boatbuilder watched, smiling.

'Knows what she's about,' he said.

'Half a second while I fix the tackle for the boom,' said Nancy. 'All right. You can be shifting her round.'

Dick, the little flag in his hand, watched Nancy's fingers flickering at her work. Nancy's red-capped head kept getting in the way. Would he ever know how to do it? And *Scarab* was moving. Dot had let out *Amazon*'s painter and the boatbuilder was carefully working the new boat round to the end of the stage to lie where *Amazon* had been.

'Now,' said Nancy, standing up, hot and red-faced from crouching over the tackle in the bottom of the boat. 'She's ready.'

'Shall I hoist the flag?' said Dick. It was the only bit of work that had been left to him.

'Not yet,' said Nancy and pulled a small medicine bottle from her pocket. 'Ginger wine. The Great Aunt had some with her supper last night and I swiped a drop afterwards. Beastly stuff, but *Scarab* won't mind. Here you are, Dot. Your job. Wrap you hand in a handkerchief so as not to get cut. Whang the bottle hard on her stem so that it busts, and christen her . . .'

'What do I say?' asked Dorothea.

'Oh, just tell her what her name is and give her best wishes for fair winds and then Dick hauls up the flag.'

Dorothea, wrapping her fingers in her handkerchief, took the little bottle and made ready.

'Don't drop it,' said Peggy.

'It's bad luck if you don't bust it first time,' said Nancy. 'Now then . . .'

Crash!

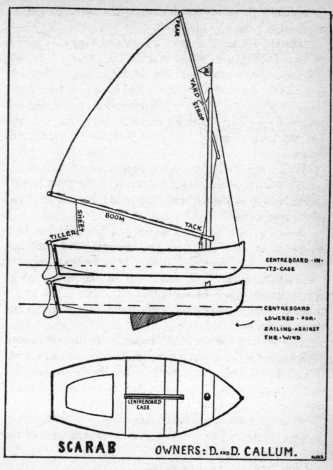

SCARAB

The little bottle smashed to bits on *Scarab*'s sharp prow. Brown wine trickled down into the water.

'I name you SCARAB!' said Dorothea. 'And best wishes for fair winds!'

'Hurrah!' The old boatbuilder, who had been gravely watching, let out a sturdy shout.

'Hurrah! Hurrah!' shouted Nancy and Peggy. 'Up with the flag, Dick. Go on. Hand over hand . . . *Scarab* for ever!'

Dick and Dorothea somehow forgot to shout. Dorothea decided afterwards that it did not really matter. The three-cornered white flag with the green beetle in the middle of it quavered up to the masthead, steadied there with the little flag staff straight up and down, and fluttered in a sudden puff of wind.

'What's the insect?' asked the boatbuilder.

'It's a scarab,' said Dick. 'It's a sort of Egyptian beetle.'

'Ah,' said the boatbuilder. 'Egyptian? I thought it was a new one for me.'

'And now,' said Nancy. 'Out you get, Peggy. Hop in Dot. I'll just hoist the sail for you. You take the halliard through the ring in the bows and it acts as a forestay. Up she goes. Sorry, Dick. Your head was in the wrong place. Spectacles all right? Make fast to this cleat. Then bowse down the tackle to cock the yard. Just till there are up and down ripples in the sail.'

'Easy with that while it's a new sail,' said the boatbuilder.

'That's so as not to pull it out of shape before it's stretched,' said Nancy. 'There you are. She's ready.' She too climbed back on the landing stage. The boatbuilder had cast off the painter and was coiling it, ready to drop it in the bows.

'Better put the centreboard down now,' he said. 'Deep enough off the end of this stage, but keep well clear of the shores once you're sailing.'

Dick lowered the centreboard.

There was a little more wind and the boom swung gently to and fro over Dorothea's head as she sat waiting in the stern.

'You'd better take the tiller, Dick,' she said.

'Cast off!' cried Nancy. 'There you go. Main sheet in a bit. Tiller to port.'

The boatman had dropped the coiled painter in the bows and, with a sudden hard push, had sent the *Scarab* sliding out into the lake.

The wind filled the red sail. Dick, watching it, went on holding the tiller to port.

'Let her come up a bit . . . Let her come up a bit . . . She's sailing,' called Nancy.

'Sure they're all right in a boat?' Dorothea heard the boat-builder ask Nancy.

'Of course they are,' she heard Nancy answer. 'They've been able seamen for over a year. They've sailed here before and on the Broads.'

Dick heard that too, but it made no difference. For the first time in his life he was sailing a boat of his own and a boat that neither he nor anybody else had ever sailed before. Main sheet in one hand, tiller in the other, he could not wipe his spectacles, but that was what he would have liked to do.

'Look out there! Where are you going?' Some men in a rowing boat shouted at him, and he luffed desperately to keep out of their way. 'Steam gives way to sail,' he had read in his book, but it said nothing about people windmilling about in hired rowing boats. Did they count as steam or sail?

'It's all right,' said Dorothea. 'She's moving beautifully.'

'But she isn't,' said Dick. In luffing to avoid the rowing boat he had brought the *Scarab* head to wind. She had lost way. The sail was flapping. It seemed to make no difference how he steered. She was drifting backwards.

He wagged the tiller violently, trying to get her back on her old course. Her head did come round at last, but the wrong way. The sail filled again and she was moving, but he would have to bring her about quick or he would be in among the landing stages. No good trying till she was sailing pretty fast . . . Now . . . 'Ready about, Dot,' he said, and put the tiller across. Would she come round or wouldn't she? She did, and once more they were heading away from the shore. Dick looked anxiously over his shoulder.

'They didn't see,' said Dorothea. 'They were getting up their sail and the boatbuilder was talking to them. 'Nobody saw, and it might happen to anybody, a rowing boat charging right across like that.'

'Just coming!' They heard Nancy's ringing call.

There was nothing in the way now, and after those first awful minutes, Dick was already feeling better. His arms no longer felt as if they had been frozen stiff. He was finding that he could watch the flag and the sail and yet keep a look out. No other rowing boat was going to be close in front of him before he saw it. Things were all right after all. *Scarab* was no harder to sail than *Titmouse*, and faster, lots faster.

'Listen to her,' said Dorothea. 'She's enjoying it.'

It was as if the wind had heard Dorothea giving *Scarab* good wishes. Fair it was not, just at the moment, but from the light puffs of the morning it had settled to a gentle breeze, such a breeze as anyone would like to have when sailing a new boat. And now, for the first time, they were hearing the quick, laughing gurgle of water under the forefoot of a boat of their own.

'The others have started,' said Dorothea quietly. 'Don't look round. You're sailing her beautifully. They'll never catch us up.'

'Ready about,' said Dick as they came near the shore of Long Island.

'What ought I to say?' asked Dorothea.

'It doesn't matter,' said Dick. 'Just be ready to shift your weight across, and keep clear of the boom. I say, they're going much nearer the shore than we did.'

'They probably know just where it's shallow and where it isn't.'

'He said we'd better keep well off the shores,' murmured Dick. 'So there must be shallows somewhere. I'm not going to take any risks. It doesn't matter if they do catch us up . . . not this time.'

'How *do* they manage to keep her going so fast?' said Dorothea.

Amazon, with her experienced crew, Peggy at the tiller, Nancy amidships, was coming on at a tremendous pace. Round she swung, close to the overhanging trees of the island, her crew shifting neatly as she turned. Back towards the mainland. Round again and, somehow, unlike *Scarab*, not losing way as she came about but getting a flying start on every tack. Dick could not help looking over his shoulder to watch her.

'How will they manage to pass us?' asked Dorothea, when it was clear that there was no hope of keeping ahead.

'The overtaking boat has to keep out of the way of the overtaken,' said Dick, remembering his book. 'We've just got to go on sailing as if they weren't there.'

'You're not doing half badly.' Nancy's voice came from much nearer. *Amazon* was not a dozen yards away, sailing side by side with them. 'Don't hold your tiller too tight. Fingers! Fingers! Don't grip it.'

'She's turning,' whispered Dorothea a moment later.

'I'm going straight on,' said Dick.

He sailed on till he was close to the trees, went about this time without losing so much way, and found to his horror that *Amazon* had turned and was coming to meet him.

'Port gives way to starboard,' he murmured to himself. 'Or is it the other way about? We're on starboard tack . . . or . . .'

He sailed on. It looked as if there would be a collision. Dick gripped his tiller and looked up at his sail as if *Amazon* were nowhere near.

'Well done, Dick!' called Nancy. 'You've got the right of way. It'll be ours on the next tack.'

Amazon had changed her course to miss them and the two boats passed within a couple of yards.

'She's turned again,' said Dorothea.

'I'm going right on,' said Dick, and Dorothea sat, watching *Amazon* foaming after them directly in their wake.

'She's turning again' whispered Dorothea, just as Dick, coming near the mainland shore, called 'Ready about.'

Scarab swung round to find herself on the same tack as *Amazon* with *Amazon* a dozen yards ahead.

'They've done it,' said Dick. 'She passed us. She'll be clear ahead of us when she goes about again.'

'They've been sailing her a long time,' said Dorothea, as *Amazon* came about under the trees and they saw that now they would not be able to touch her even if they tried.

'We'll go round the island,' called Peggy.

'Go outside the little rock with a bush on it at this end,' said Nancy. 'It looks deep enough between the rock and the island but it isn't.'

'All right,' said Dick.

'That isn't what they say to each other,' said Dorothea.

'She knows what I mean,' said Dick. 'Ready about!'

'Aye, aye, Sir,' said Dorothea, remembering the words.

Amazon swung round the little rock a dozen yards ahead of *Scarab*. Dick noticed how Peggy let out the main sheet as she turned. He did the same as he too rounded the rock. The little boats had a fair wind now and were running before it between Long Island and the islets to the west of it.

'Centreboard!' shouted Nancy, looking back to see how they were doing. 'Yank it up. You don't want it with the wind aft.'

'I ought to have thought of it,' said Dick.

Dorothea hauled it up and held it up by its jointed handle.

'Put the peg in to hold it,' said Dick hurriedly.

And then the miracle happened. *Amazon* had been twenty yards ahead and gaining. But was she? It couldn't be true. Yes. She was not gaining any more. She was not so far ahead as she had been.

'Dick, Dick,' whispered Dorothea, not daring to say it aloud. 'We're catching up.'

Bit by bit, foot by foot, there could be no doubt about it, *Scarab* was creeping up. Dick thought of nothing in the world but of keeping a straight wake. Nancy never took her eyes off them. Peggy kept glancing over her shoulder, letting out her sail a little, hauling it in and glancing over her shoulder again. And still *Scarab* crept closer and closer.

They neared the end of the island. Another forty yards and they would be out once more in the open lake. Nancy spoke to Peggy. *Amazon* turned suddenly towards the wind, spilling the air from her sail, lost speed, and then filled her sail again. *Scarab* was close beside her.

'You'd have caught us anyhow in another minute,' said Nancy. 'New boat. Dry. Clean bottom. She'd run away from us with the wind aft. Jolly good boat. When you've had her a bit you'll beat us at tacking as well . . . not always, of course. Giminy, when the G.A. goes and the Swallows come and we have three boats we'll have a race to both ends of the lake and back. Now look here. We've got to get home now. You hang about till we're out of sight. Then take her for a real spin. You're doing splendidly.'

'What did I do wrong, tacking?' asked Dick.

'You were shoving the tiller across too suddenly . . . Stops her . . . Go about when she's really moving, and let her almost do it herself . . . Just ease her round till she's head to wind and then put the tiller a bit farther over. She'll shoot quite a bit straight into the wind.'

'I thought it must be something like that,' said Dick.

'Watch your wake,' said Nancy. 'When you go about properly there isn't any swirl, or hardly any, and what there is you leave to leeward. You can see at once if you've been using the tiller too hard. Good-bye. We're going straight home. You turn back here. Go round the island again or something. Just in case she's mouching about. She mustn't see the two boats coming along together or she'll start asking questions.'

Dick hauled in his main sheet and brought *Scarab* swinging round till she was sailing close hauled. But something seemed wrong. She was not sailing as she had been but was slipping sideways.

'Centreboard, Dot,' called Nancy. 'Good-bye.'

'Good-bye.'

'Get the peg out Dot,' said Dick. 'That's what's holding it.'

By the time the peg was pulled out, the centreboard lowered, and *Scarab* once more sailing as she should, *Amazon*, still running with her boom well out, was already clear of the islands and heading for home.

'What are we going to do now?' asked Dorothea.

'Anchor,' said Dick firmly. 'Lower sail. Get the mast down, and start everything from the very beginning. That time they did everything for us. We've got to be able to do it ourselves.'

CHAPTER 16

ON THEIR OWN

Even putting an anchor down is something that has to be learnt. Dick sailed back till one of the smaller islands hid him from *Amazon*'s crew. He did not want Nancy to see what he was going to do. If she were to look back and see *Scarab* with her sail and mast down she might easily think that something had gone wrong. She might even come back to help. He wanted to be safe from help of any kind.

'You take the tiller, Dot, and head straight into the wind. I'll put the anchor over and get the sail down afterwards.'

It sounded easy. Dorothea headed *Scarab* into the wind and Dick dropped the anchor overboard. But *Scarab*, though her sail was flapping, slid on and on, till the anchor plucked at her bows and pulled her round. Then, of course, the wind filled the sail and she was off again. She was brought up with another jerk. As if to make things difficult, the wind freshened. *Scarab* was like a tethered goat, pulling all ways. When, at last, Dick cast off the halliard, the sail came down on the top of him and the peak splashed into the water.

He scrambled out from under.

'My fault,' he said. 'I ought to have waited till she stopped moving. And now I've gone and got the sail wet.'

'They couldn't see,' said Dorothea. 'It'll be all right next time.'

'I oughtn't to have let it happen,' said Dick. 'Oh! And I oughtn't have let that rope go.' He was gathering the sail into the boat and saw that the end of the halliard was flying loose above his head. He grabbed at it, too late. Already it was working through the sheave at the masthead and was out of reach. 'Oh well,' he said, 'I'd meant to take the mast down anyhow.'

'Don't let's hurry,' said Dorothea.

After that things went easier, and presently *Scarab* was lying at anchor, much as they had first seen her at the boat-builder's landing stage, with her mast down and lying in her, with the oars and the sail beside it.

Dick took breath, sat still for a moment, and cleaned his spectacles. Then, trying to remember what Nancy had done, they set to work to rig their boat for themselves. It took them a good deal longer than it had taken Nancy. One or two things were done out of turn and had to be undone and done again, but at last all was ready, the sail was set, Dorothea was at the tiller and Dick had the anchor rope in his hand.

'It looks just right,' said Dorothea.

'Don't pull at the sheet just yet,' said Dick. 'Let it go free till I get the anchor off the bottom. Then steer to port, shorten the sheet till the wind fills the sail and I'll get the anchor in as quick as I can.'

'You can always put it down again if anything goes really wrong,' said Dorothea.

Dick looked at Dorothea and nodded. He hauled in on the anchor rope. *Scarab* headed to port, the sail began to pull, up came the anchor and they were off. Dick hurriedly crammed rope and anchor in before the mast and went aft to take the tiller.

'There was nobody to do any helping that time,' said Dorothea.

They took a turn or two against the wind, beating back between the islands. Yes, everything was all right. *Scarab* was sailing just as well as when she had been rigged and had her sail set by the experts.

'Where shall we go?' said Dorothea.

'Houseboat,' said Dick. 'Timothy may be waiting to start work.'

HOW *NOT* TO LOWER SAIL

'He hadn't sent a message when they left Beckfoot.'

'He may have sent one now,' said Dick. 'Or he may have been bothered with the pigeons with nobody to show him how to fit the messages on. Anyway, we ought to go there to let him know we've got *Scarab* and can come as soon as he wants me.'

They worked their way out past the foot of Long Island, gave a good berth to the little rock with a bush on it, and headed for Houseboat Bay. They failed to fetch it in one tack, but with the second they came sailing in towards the old blue boat that had had its share in so many adventures. Dorothea knelt amidships, steadying her elbows on the thwart, while she looked at the houseboat through the telescope.

'It doesn't look as if anybody's there,' she said.

Dick said nothing. He was trying to get well to windward of the houseboat and for the moment had to keep his whole mind on sail and tiller.

He cleared the houseboat's bows with a dozen yards to spare and, at the first glance, saw that there was nobody aboard. No rowing boat was lying against the fenders.

'He may have gone to the mine,' said Dick.

'Or shopping,' said Dorothea.

'He can't have sent a message for me, or he'd be here,' said Dick.

'Then we can go anywhere,' said Dorothea.

'Look out,' said Dick. 'I've got to gybe. Keep your head down while the boom flies across ... Now ...' There was a moment of flurry, as he was not quite quick enough with the tiller and *Scarab* tried to come right round into the wind. He steadied her, brought the wind abeam and passed comfortably under the empty houseboat's stern.

'Let's go to Rio,' said Dorothea. 'I want to get a cookery book. And I didn't think about bringing any food.'

But one glance towards the crowded bay, with its trippers windmilling about in rowing boats, and a big steamer just leaving the pier, decided Dick. Once in there was enough for one day.

'Never mind about food,' he said. 'Let's take her for a real voyage.'

'North Pole?' suggested Dorothea. 'There's sure to be a

bookshop at the head of the lake. Have we got time to go the whole way?'

'It's a fair wind,' said Dick. 'We ought to have that centre-board up.'

Dorothea pulled it up and put the peg in to hold it. With the wind aft and the sail well out, *Scarab* slipped along the island shore and out into open water. Rio Bay was left astern. They were off, past Cache Island to the head of the lake that they had visited only once when, sailing a sledge in blinding snow, they had been the first to reach the North Pole.

It was very different on this warm August afternoon, with the hills purple with heather and the woods green, blue water before them instead of ice and a blue sky over all. There seemed, because they were running before it, to be very little wind, though the beetle flag blew out bravely from the mast-head and the sail pulled, and the little ship, their own at last, was slipping along, as they could see by the trees on shore moving fast against the hills. They took turns at keeping a straight wake and Dick at least, free now from the fear that he might be missing his share of the chemical work with Timothy, was ready to forget everything else in the pleasure of sailing. Even Dorothea, once they had passed the Beckfoot promontory and she could take her mind off the martyrs now back in the arena and doing their best to keep the Great Aunt purring, was thinking of her house and her housekeeping and the cookery book she wanted and not at all of the queer secrecy of the life into which they had been pushed.

She was reminded of it in the oddest way. She was at the tiller when some people in a big yacht, swooping past, gave them a cheerful wave.

'They don't know we don't exist,' she said.

'But we do,' said Dick.

'Not for the Great Aunt,' said Dorothea. 'It's like having a cap of invisibility and nobody except one person knowing you're invisible.'

This was too much for the scientific Dick.

'But she doesn't know we exist,' he said. 'So she can't know that we don't exist. She just doesn't know anything about us.'

'Well it makes it seem very funny when people wave to us as if we were like everybody else.'

'It isn't queer really,' said Dick. 'I say. I'd better steer for a bit, hadn't I?' He glanced back at their wake that showed by a big curve that Dorothea had been thinking of something other than sailing.

On and on *Scarab* ran, as if she herself were delighting in being afloat on rippled water with a fair wind to keep her moving. Sooner than had seemed possible when they had looked up at the lake from off Rio, they were nearing the big hills at the head of it. Specks that they had seen from far away were turning into houses. Bay after bay opened up in the long wooded line of the shore and closed and disappeared as they sailed on.

'We needn't go near the steamer pier,' said Dick. 'There's a river on the map.'

'Could we go up it?'

'We might try,' said Dick, who did not want to go into a crowd of other boats if he could help it.

'If we can,' said Dorothea, 'we'll be nearer to where we saw all those lights when we were at the North Pole. You can see houses there now, a regular settlement. That's where the bookshop will be.'

Dick steered away towards the other side of the lake, searching the shore for the mouth of the river.

'There's the North Pole anyway,' said Dorothea, pointing to the little summerhouse with its flag staff.

'The river must be close here,' said Dick. 'Bother those reeds.'

'There it is,' cried Dorothea.

Through an opening in the reeds they could see a long lane of smooth water.

'We'll try it,' said Dick. 'But I say, Dot. There may not be room to turn. We'd better be ready to get the sail down quick. . . .'

Dorothea took all turns but one of the halliard off its cleats, kept a firm grip of the rope, and crouched in the bottom of the boat, remembering how the sail had come down with a rush on Dick's head. Already they had left the lake and were sailing with tall reeds on either side.

Dick, as nearly as he could, steered up the middle of the river. The reeds came to an end. There were high earth banks now, and fields with grazing cows. The wind seemed to have strengthened just when he wanted less of it and, though the current was against them, *Scarab* seemed to be moving much too fast.

'I'm going to stop as soon as I see a good place,' he said. He found that he was gripping the tiller. 'Fingers Fingers!' Nancy had said. This was much worse than sailing in open water. He learnt what every sailor knows, that it is near land that difficulties begin. For a moment he thought of stopping *Scarab* by putting the anchor down. He even said to Dorothea, 'The anchor's all ready to go over.'

'I can't get the anchor out while I'm holding this rope.' said Dorothea.

'There ought not to be any need,' said Dick, clenching his teeth without knowing it, and looking at each foot of bank. He ought to be able to come alongside properly if only there was a good place. There . . . There was the sort of place he wanted, a clean bit of bank between two bushes . . .

'There's a bridge right ahead,' cried Dorothea.

'Let go the halliard, Dot . . . Quick!'

Down came the sail on the top of Dorothea.

'Quick! Quick! Grab that bush if you can.'

Dorothea scrambling from under the sail caught hold of a branch. It broke. She grabbed another. But *Scarab* was being swung round by the stream. Dick was only just in time to grab a branch as Dorothea had to let go of hers. Shifting his grip from bough to bough, and half out of the boat, Dick brought *Scarab* close under the bank.

'I can't let go,' he said. 'Could you get ashore while I hang on?'

Dorothea scrambled up the bank. Dick clung to a branch with one hand and held out the anchor as far as he could. Dorothea knelt on the bank and took it from him.

'Upstream,' panted Dick . . . 'And jam it well in.'

'Anchored,' called Dorothea.

Dick let go of his branch, bundled the sail together, and climbed ashore. Dorothea was stamping on the shank of the anchor to drive the fluke deeper into the ground. Dick stood, weak in the knees and hot as if he had been running a race in the sun. He took off his spectacles, but his hands shook so much that he did not try to wipe them.

'I did it all wrong,' he said.

'We're here,' said Dorothea. 'And we didn't bump. We didn't even scrape. I don't believe Nancy would have done it any better. There's a stile into the road by that bridge. And houses quite near. Let's go and look for that bookshop and something to eat.'

'We can easily do without grub till we get home,' said Dick, who wanted to get afloat again at once and forget the unseamanlike flurry of landing.

'It's that rabbit,' said Dorothea. 'I simply must get a cookery book.'

'I'll stay here,' said Dick, 'and get things ready.'

'I'll be as quick as I can,' said Dorothea. A minute later she waved to him as she crossed the bridge, smiled to herself as she saw that Dick was not looking at her but had climbed down again into the boat, and hurried off towards the village.

*

When Dorothea came back with her cookery book Dick had climbed ashore again and was waiting impatiently on the bank.

'I've got the book,' she said, 'and some buns and chocolate. Let's eat them before starting.'

'Better while we're sailing,' said Dick. 'Everything's ready. I've thought out what to do. It's going to take us a long time to get home. Not much wind. It's going to rain, too. Look at those clouds.'

'The man at the bookshop said it was going to, but not just yet.'

'I wonder if it'll mean less wind or more.'

'We'll be back before it begins anyhow,' said Dorothea, who knew when Dick had set his mind on anything. Two minutes later she was sitting in the stern and Dick was rowing *Scarab* out of the river. She did not even try to talk. She knew that until he had the sail hoisted again he would not be able to listen.

Everything went as he had planned. There was no hitch. Nothing had to be done twice, and when, outside the river, with her sail set, *Scarab* darted off on the first long tack of the voyage home, Dick was feeling a good deal better.

'It's luck Timothy wasn't ready for me,' he said. 'We're getting a lot of practice. It would have been awful to make a mess of coming alongside the houseboat. In the river it didn't matter so much.'

Tack after tack, to and fro across the lake, they beat against the wind. They ate their buns and chocolate. Dick steered while Dorothea looked at the gaudy paper cover on her cookery book that was covered with coloured pictures of joints of meat with paper frills, a pheasant with a bunch of long tail feathers, a piece of pink salmon with some bright green parsley, a jelly, a pie and a tremendously decorated cake.

'Of course, I'm not going to try anything really difficult,' said Dorothea. 'Even Susan wouldn't, not in camp. But there's a lot about rabbits in it. And about ways of cooking eggs. It says three and a half minutes or only three if you want them lightly boiled.'

'Books always help a lot,' said Dick. 'It would have been much worse if we hadn't been reading the sailing book so much.'

He was trying how lightly he could touch the tiller with his fingers and calculating how many tacks they would have to make to reach the Beckfoot promontory.

Dorothea turned to the pages about rabbits. 'Stew,' she said. 'Fricassée . . . Boiled . . . Jugged . . . There are about a dozen ways of doing it . . . forty-five to sixty minutes according to age . . . I wonder how old that rabbit was . . .'

'I say,' said Dick. 'They'll have finished supper at Beckfoot long before we get into the river.'

Sailing against a gentle wind is very different from running with it. It had seemed to take no time going to the head of the lake. It took a very long time to beat back. Dick was getting a lot of pleasure out of doing the best he could with her and seeing her slide on straight into the wind at the moment of turning, just as Nancy said she would. But wet-looking clouds had hidden the sun and supper-time was long past when at last they were coming into the mouth of the Amazon river. Dorothea took the tiller, and, at the word, hauled in on the mainsheet as Dick lowered the sail. She grabbed the sail itself as the boom came within reach. The whole sail came quietly down into the boat.

'Good,' said Dick. He pulled up the centreboard, got out the oars and began to row.

'What time is it now?' asked Dorothea.

'Eleven minutes past nine . . . I say, I couldn't help splashing with that oar when I looked at my watch.'

'Sorry.'

Dick rowed on doing his best to keep the oars from squeaking. They passed the boathouse. It was still daylight out of doors but, as the house came into sight, they saw the glimmer of a lamp or candles in the drawing-room. Someone was playing the piano.

'Nancy?' whispered Dick.

'No. That's someone who knows how to play. Nancy makes much more noise. That must be the Great Aunt herself.'

They were half-way between the boathouse and the coppice, Dick rowing, Dorothea watching that lighted window, when they were startled by the ringing of a bell. There was the long 'Brrrrrr . . .' of the bell, but there was more than that. It was as if someone were rattling tin plates. They knew at once what it was. The piano-playing stopped short. The bell rang on and on.

'He's sent a message,' exclaimed Dick. 'That's a pigeon gone into the loft. I ought to have reminded Nancy to take the tin tray off the bell to make it not so loud.'

A door slammed in the house.

'Don't stop rowing,' urged Dorothea.

They were slipping into the shelter of the trees when that loud, insistent ringing came suddenly to an end.

'Nancy's run out and cut it off,' said Dick.

'However will she explain it to the Great Aunt?' said Dorothea. 'That terrific noise, I mean.'

'We ought to have cut the bell out altogether,' said Dick. 'Last year we wanted it to make as much noise as possible, but this year there was no need for it to make a noise at all. They had only to keep on looking to see if a pigeon had come home.'

'It isn't your fault,' said Dorothea. 'Nobody can think of everything.'

'We'd better get home quick,' said Dick. 'Nancy's got the message and she's sure to get out and let us know what it is.'

A minute or two later they were working *Scarab* through

the channel cut in the waterlilies and through the narrow lane between the reeds. They hauled down the flag, made a rough stow of the sail, took a turn with the rope round a tree trunk before planting the anchor in the ground, dodged through the trees along the edge of the wood, climbed into the road, and hurried up the path in the dusk.

It was twilight out of doors but much darker in the hut, and Dorothea had lit the lantern before she saw that they had had a visitor.

'Cook,' said Dorothea, reading a scrap of paper by the flickering light. 'And I've gone and missed her.' She gave Dick the scrap of paper and he read

Hope your makin do. If owts wanting you can tell Jacky.
M. Braithwaite.

'Look what she's brought us,' said Dorothea.

There was hardly room for the lantern on the top of the packing case. There was a cardboard box with a dozen eggs in it, a blue paper bag of sugar, a basket of peas, a large loaf of brown bread, and two chops, ready cooked.

Dorothea sighed with relief. 'I won't have to cook the rabbit tonight,' she said. 'No need with those chops. And we'd better not wait to do potatoes.'

'Let's get supper over quick,' said Dick.

They lit the fire and made a hurried meal. All the time Dick was listening for footsteps, hoping to hear someone racing up the wood with Timothy's message. Would it say 'Come in the morning' or 'Come in the afternoon'? Well, *Scarab* was ready now and he could start at any time. Pretty awful it would have been if Timothy had sent for him the day before. But no messenger came. After supper, Dick waited in the doorway, and Dorothea read about the cooking of rabbits by the light of the dancing flames. They made up their minds at last that the martyrs would hardly escape from Beckfoot before the morning. Tired after their long voyage, they made up the hammocks and went to bed, planning an early break-fast.

It must have been about midnight when the rain began. Dorothea was the first to hear a steady drip, drip somewhere close to her. Then she heard the pattering on the roof and then rain-drops that had come down the chimney hissing on the hot embers of the fire.

'Dick!'

'Yes.'

'Is it dripping on you?'

'I was sure it was going to rain,' said Dick with the happiness of the successful weather prophet.

'But is it dripping on you?'

Dick sat up in his hammock.

'No,' he said. 'I can feel the drips if I stretch out far enough. There'll be a puddle on the floor. Are you dry, too?'

'Yes,' said Dorothea. 'Hadn't we better put a saucepan under the drips?'

'It'll make more noise,' said Dick. 'And the floor's only earth. We can't do anything now. I'll drain it in the morning and mend the roof if there's time. But look here, Dot, we ought to go to sleep. The rain won't make any difference. We've got mackintoshes. We'll be able to get to the houseboat just the same.'

CHAPTER 17

WAITING FOR THE MESSAGE

DICK woke first, and almost before his eyes were open, reached up for his watch and his spectacles that he had put for the night on the top of the beam above his head. It was still raining. The drips from the roof were splashing as they fell in a lake that was widening over the floor of the hut, but he hardly noticed them. 'Dot,' he called. 'Quick. We've overslept. It's long after time to get up.'

Dorothea woke to a very different worry. 'I wonder what we ought to do,' she said, watching the steady drip and listening to the beating of the rain on the roof.

'We've got to be ready for them as soon as they come,' said Dick. 'And I've got to bale *Scarab*. She's sure to be half full of water after last night.'

'What would Susan do?' said Dorothea.

'She couldn't do anything till she knew exactly what message he's sent. He's probably said "Come at once." But we don't know.'

'I don't mean that,' said Dorothea. 'Just look at the floor. If it goes on raining we may be forced to go back to Beckfoot. Oh, I say, and I left a loaf of bread on the table and there's water splashing on it now.'

Dick looked down at the floor. 'Drainage,' he said. 'That's all it needs. I'll do it in a minute. If I make a gutter, it'll all run out of the door.'

He rolled out of his hammock, came down with one foot in the puddle and set to work with his knife to make a narrow drain between the puddle and the door. 'It doesn't need a deep one,' he said. 'Just big enough to let the water trickle along it.' He rolled his pyjamas well above his ankles, and went on digging and scraping till the drain reached the edge of the puddle. 'I thought it would,' he said, as the water poured along it in a dusty stream. 'Go back to Beckfoot?' They couldn't let Nancy down, least of all now, when they had only to keep hidden for a few more days, when everything had gone so well, when *Scarab* was ready, and the message had come that was almost sure to say that Timothy was wanting him for the work they had to do. He scraped along the bottom of the drain to hurry the water on its way, and, as the puddle shrank into no more than a big damp place on the floor he knew without her saying so that Dorothea was feeling better.

'We've got milk left from yesterday,' she said. 'Skip along to the pool and get it, and we can have breakfast without waiting for Jacky.'

'Good,' said Dick, leaving his drain, grabbing some handfuls of dry leaves and twigs and putting a match to them.

'I'll see to that,' said Dorothea. 'You get the milk and fill the kettle at the same time.'

Dorothea was herself again. Dick put his feet into his sandshoes, put a mackintosh over his pyjamas and bolted joyfully to the beck which, no longer a mere trickle, was already overflowing at the place where it crossed the path. He lifted the stone from the hole in the bank of moss and found that water had risen in the hole half-way up the neck of the milk bottle. He filled the kettle and came hurrying back to find the sticks crackling and the fire burning up and Dorothea dressed more or less and cutting bread and butter from the dryer end of the loaf, which really was not as wet as it had seemed at first sight. 'One end of it's not wet at all, and I've got another loaf we haven't begun.' By the time they had had their milk and cornflakes, the kettle was boiling. Dick crammed in some potted meat and bread and butter, dressed while his tea was cooling, burnt his throat with it all the same, took an apple to eat on the way, grabbed the empty milk bottle and was off.

'There may be a message in the letter-box by now,' he said. 'And if only I can catch Jacky before he goes to Beckfoot, I'll be able to send an answer.'

Dorothea, ashamed of her moment of weakness at the sight of the water on the floor, and the rain coming down outside and inside as well, set seriously to the business of housekeeping. Housekeeping for Picts was easy enough in fine weather, but not when everything was damp. The first thing to do was to get things dry. She had another worry ahead of her. Today was the day for the cooking of Jacky's rabbit. She could not any longer put it off. And that rabbit, in the mind of an inexperienced cook, was bulking bigger than an elephant. It had to be skinned ... and worse ... and on these vital subjects her cookery book said nothing at all.

*

The rain had turned to a steady drizzle as Dick dodged through the trees beside the path that was now a lot of waterfalls. There was no letter in the hole in the wall. Dick had just had time to see that the hole was empty when Jacky, with a sack over his shoulders to keep off the rain, came bicycling along the road. Too late. He had already been to Beckfoot. He got carefully off his bicycle, took a bottle of milk from the basket in front of his handlebars and gave it to Dick in exchange for the empty one.

'Thank you very much,' said Dick, and hesitated. Ought he or ought he not to ask Jacky to go back to Beckfoot to find out what message had been brought by the pigeon that had rung the bell last night? How much did Jacky know about the pigeons? How much would Nancy want him to know? He decided he had better not mention pigeons at all. 'They didn't send a message for me?' he asked.

'Nay,' said Jacky.

'Oh,' said Dick. 'I thought perhaps they might.'

'It's nobbut a step. Shall I bike back and ask?'

'No, no,' stammered Dick. Jacky, meaning to be helpful, might so easily be just the opposite. What if he were to ask Cook that question just when the Great Aunt was in the kitchen ordering meals?

'Me time's me own,' said Jacky. 'Now I'm done wi' t'milk.'

'There's no need,' said Dick. 'I'd rather you didn't.'

'Right-o,' said Jacky, and rode off.

For a moment Dick thought of waiting for the postman. Then he remembered that after all that rain *Scarab* would need baling. If he could get her baled now, there would be so much time saved if Timothy's message had been to say that he wanted him to come to the houseboat at once. And Dot was at the hut in case Nancy or Peggy came up with it. So he hid the milk behind the wall, hurried along the wet, shining road, climbed the gate into the field and, with squelching sand-shoes, raced over the grass, pushed through the trees and came to *Scarab* in her secret harbour.

There was a lot of water in her, more even than he had expected. He climbed aboard, caught the baler that was floating about in her, and began to bale. Scoop ... splash. Scoop ... splash. He remembered the quick swinging motion with which he had seen Tom Dudgeon bale his punt. It was a small baler and for a long time the baling seemed to make very little difference. He baled kneeling on the thwart, shifting every minute or two, to get his weight on the other knee. His arms ached. His back ached. The odd thing was that he enjoyed it. The more work he put in, the more *Scarab* seemed to be his own. Yesterday when he had been sailing her, trying not to make mistakes, she might have been any strange boat. But now, while his back felt as if it would never be straight again and drops of sweat kept falling on his spectacles, dim already with the rain, she was his own boat and no one else's. He rested, wiped his spectacles so that until the drizzle covered them again he could get a better look at her, and wished the rain would stop, so that he could dry her wet sail for her and make her really comfortable.

He set to work again, baling first with one hand and then with the other until, as he scooped, he could no longer fill the baler. At last she was as dry as he could get her without a sponge. He worked the bottomboards back into place and stood on them, looking round to see what else he could do for her. He looked up and, through the drizzle, saw a patch of blue sky. It would do no harm just to hoist her sail for a minute. In Picthaven, sheltered by the Beckfoot coppice, there was hardly any wind. So he clipped the halliard to the strop on the yard, hoisted away and, as the red sail went up, was suddenly soused with the water that had collected in its folds. Never mind. Another thing learnt. But it was a pity so much water had got inside his waterproof. He stood there holding the halliard, watching the trickles of water running down the red sail, along the boom, and dripping about his feet.

Suddenly the rain came down again really hard. Big bubbles showed on the still water in the channel between the reeds. Big drops splashed on the wet thwarts. Dick lowered the sail and bundled it loosely along the gaff. With rain coming down like this, there would be more baling to do when the time came to sail. With that, he remembered that he did not yet know what the message was. Perhaps by now Nancy was already at the hut. He looked at his watch, found that the morning was gone as if by magic, leapt ashore and raced for home.

It was not a lucky day. He had just crossed the gate into the road when a motor car pulled up beside him.

'You're a drowned rat all right,' said a voice, and he saw the doctor looking out of the driver's window.

He could not very well tell the doctor that he was in a hurry and could not stop. So he had to wait while the doctor asked about the hut, told him to take his wet things off and get them dry, threatened that if he or Dorothea caught a cold they would have to come back to Beckfoot no matter how much Nancy wanted to keep them away, and chuckled at what he had just seen there. 'One thing about it,' he said. 'Nancy's having to pay for her games. It did my heart good to see that young pirate sitting on the edge of a chair with her arms spreading a skein of wool, and Young Peggy winding away and the old lady telling her to be sure not to pull the wool too tight.'

'Did Nancy send a message for me?' Dick put in.

'I didn't give her a chance,' said the doctor. 'I've enough on my conscience already, so when I saw Nancy trying to catch my eye, I got away quick.'

This was dreadful. And still the doctor went on talking. At last he said he must be getting on to see another patient. He put in his clutch and drove off. A gloved hand waved out of the window. Dick did not see it. He was already racing full tilt along the road.

If he had been one minute sooner he would have been in time to catch Nancy at the letter-box. As it was, he saw something brown with a flash of white disappear over the Beckfoot wall at the bend in the road. He could not be sure what it was and dared not shout. If it was one of the martyrs and she had been to the hut, Dorothea already had the news. He nearly forgot the milk, but remembered it just in time, and then, in case the postman had brought a letter, looked hurriedly into the hole in the wall. No letter, but a scrap of paper. Nancy's writing and done in a hurry. There was no skull and crossbones. There was nothing but a few pencilled words.

'URGENT NEWS. MUST SEE YOU. DON'T STIR FROM THE HUT. COMING AS SOON AS I CAN GET AWAY.'

There was no signature. Dick read it twice and then hurried up the path. Water was pouring down it, but his sandshoes were so wet that they could get no wetter and it was quicker than pushing through the trees.

Dick charged into the hut to find Dorothea sitting on the

three-legged stool with the cookery book open before her on the packing case. A roaring fire was burning. The hammocks had been stowed and the rugs had been tossed over the beams and hung there airing. Dorothea had done everything she could think of that Susan would have done if living in a hut with a leaky roof with rain dripping on the floor.

Dick noticed nothing of this. 'Dot,' he panted. 'Has one of them been here? Look what I found in the letter-box.'

'Nobody's been here, not even Jacky.'

'I met Jacky,' said Dick, 'and I've got the milk, but do look what Nancy says. I saw the doctor and he told me Nancy wanted to give him a message but he wouldn't let her. She must have got out just after he'd gone. I saw someone going back over their wall. And then I found this in the box.'

'It's all right,' said Dorothea, reading the message. 'It only means they're coming here and don't want us to be somewhere else.'

'It means they've got the message. I was sure they had. But if Timothy wants me now why didn't Nancy say so? I've baled *Scarab*. I could start at once.'

'What did the doctor say?'

'He was a bit bothered about us and everything, like he was the other day. And he said Nancy and Peggy were winding wool.'

'It's their lunch time now,' said Dorothea. 'It's a good thing I haven't started doing the rabbit. It'll take too long. They'll be up here as soon as the Great Aunt lies down to plan new tortures. Just think of her making Captain Nancy wind wool. I say, Dick, you've got sopping wet.'

'I forgot there'd be a lot of water in the sail.'

'You haven't been sailing?'

'No. Only hoisted it and lowered it again. I've baled her out. I'm ready to start any minute.'

'You won't be able to go with your things all wet. You'd

better get into pyjamas while we get your clothes dry. And I'll hot up some soup out of one of the tins.'

Dick was out of his clothes and into his pyjamas in two minutes. Dorothea, with the cooking of the rabbit put off once more, closed the cookery book with relief. The rabbit, its fur sodden with rain, had been very daunting. She had brought it in and hung it from a peg in the hut to dry. Any Pict, of course, would be glad to have a rabbit to cook, but this was not the time to start skinning it when at any minute Nancy might come racing up with something urgent for them to do. She made a simpler meal, opening a tin of tomato soup which she heated in the saucepan, and followed that with buttered eggs and sardines. While these things were being made ready, Dick's clothes steamed before the fire, and Dick turned them first one way and then another to hurry their drying.

'Two o'clock,' he said, as they bit into their apples after the meal. He went and stood in the doorway to listen.

Time went on. Twice he thought he heard footsteps. Twice he was disappointed. There was only the noise of the beck, swollen with rain, and the steady drip from the roof which, thanks to his draining, made only a small puddle that no longer spread into a lake but trickled away through the open door.

Every now and then the drizzle eased and there were gleams of sunshine through the wet trees, though more cloud was drifting from the south and the patches of blue sky showed only for a moment. Dick could settle to nothing. He tried to read the sailing book but could not keep his mind on it. Even a woodpecker, tapping at a tree close by, could not stop him from thinking that if only he had known in the morning what the message was he might by now be already in the houseboat doing work that really mattered.

'It won't take me a minute,' he said at last, looking up at

the holes in the roof. He rolled his pyjamas to his knees, put on his waterproof, went out, filled the pockets of the waterproof with moss, and climbed up on the roof at the back of the hut where the steeply sloping ground made it easy. He pushed moss into the holes he could see and, better still, found that one of the big slates had stirred near the top of the roof. He was able to work it back into its place. Just then the rain came on again. Dick slid down and came back into the hut. The rain rattled on the roof but no longer found its way in. He was able to put the chair exactly where the drip had been and to sit there without a single drop falling on his head.

'Well, that's one good thing,' said Dorothea. 'We'll be able to get things really dry.'

But all this time there was no sign of a prisoner escaping from Beckfoot. Four o'clock came. At half past Dorothea said, 'Whatever they've been doing, they'll be having tea with her now. They won't come till after tea. Perhaps they aren't going to be able to escape at all. We'll have tea anyhow, and then, whatever happens, we must skin Jacky's rabbit.'

'Not yet,' said Dick. 'It's light till pretty late, and it would be awful if we had to leave it in the middle.'

Five o'clock passed, six and seven. Dick, more and more gloomy, was back in his clothes which were singed only in one or two small places. The hut, now that the leaks had been stopped, was no longer steamy. The rugs hanging on the beams felt warm and dry. Dorothea made up her mind. 'No one will come now,' she said. 'There'll be their supper and then she'll make them play the piano. We shan't know what the message is till tomorrow. I can't put it off any longer. I'm going to cook that rabbit.'

Dick had been looking through the bird book with eyes that saw neither print nor pictures. Perhaps he ought to have been working in the houseboat all afternoon. It was simply impossible that Timothy should have sent a message just to tell him to keep away. A whole day wasted. But Dot was right. Nothing could happen now. He shut the book, and brought his mind to the problem of the rabbit. Dorothea had seen that problem clearly.

'In the cookery book,' she said, 'the rabbits and things all seem to be born naked and ready for cooking. How on earth are we going to skin it? Picts don't buy rabbits ready trussed like the picture. What do they do? What does Jacky do?'

'A Pict would skin it with a flint knife,' said Dick. 'No. Bronze, I should think.'

'Well, let's skin it,' said Dorothea.

'We'll have to take its insides out,' said Dick.

'I know,' said Dorothea. 'But how, and do we skin it first or afterwards?'

'Afterwards,' said Dick. 'I've seen rabbits and hares hanging up in shops, and they're in their skins but they've always got no inside.'

Dorothea shuddered. 'I wish we'd asked Jacky to do it,' she said.

'Scientifically,' said Dick, 'it ought to be easy ... In my biology book there's a picture ...'

'Never mind that,' said Dorothea. 'Will you do it?'

'I'll try,' said Dick. 'It's sure to come out somehow.' He pulled out his knife and opened it.

'Not here,' said Dorothea. 'Not here ... It'll make an awful mess ... Somewhere in the wood ... Quick, before it starts raining again.'

Dick took the rabbit by its hind legs and went out. Dorothea read feverishly in the cookery book. Minute after minute passed. Dick came back. He was looking very green.

'Dick?' said Dorothea, and he knew it was a question.

'No, I wasn't ... But very nearly ... It was much worse than I thought it would be.'

He laid the rabbit on the packing case.

'Things inside it,' he said. 'I threw away most of it, but

not everything. Three things like hearts. Two of them kidneys, I think, and some loose dark flaps . . .'

'I'm a pig, Dick,' said Dorothea. 'I oughtn't to have let you do it all by yourself.'

'Let's do the skinning,' said Dick. 'I tried, but I couldn't. It'll take two to do it properly.'

No one who has not tried to take it off can know how firmly a rabbit's skin sticks to a rabbit. Part of it can be freed easily enough but the four legs and the head of the rabbit must have puzzled many a Pict. Dick began, naturally in the middle where he had cut the skin already. It was a messy business but so difficult that after the first few moments Dorothea forgot its messiness, and clawed and tugged at skin and body as if nothing mattered in the world except to get them apart.

'If we could only turn it inside out,' she said. 'But it's like a glove with fingers at both ends.'

'Lets have a look at the picture in your book,' said Dick.

'But that one's already trussed,' said Dorothea.

'It hasn't got any feet,' said Dick a moment later. 'We'd better take them off first.'

Then came the idea of skinning the legs separately, and after they had got the skin off the hind legs, things began to look more hopeful. It became a sort of tug of war, Dorothea hanging on to the hind legs while Dick pulled at the skin.

'It's coming. It's coming,' said Dick. 'Just like you said, now that we've got rid of one pair of fingers.' The skin was peeling off, inside out, like a football sweater. It stuck, as sweaters often stick, with the head still inside. Here, desperate work with a knife helped.

'We've done it,' said Dick. 'Do you want to truss it like the one in the book?'

'No,' said Dorothea. 'No need. But we'd better cut it up first. It won't be exactly boiled rabbit and it won't be exactly stew, but it ought to be all right. If you can get its legs off, I'll be chopping up the onion. The book talks about peppercorns and onion sauce when you boil it and cloves and claret and bacon when you stew. But I don't suppose Picts would bother about half those things.'

'Jacky wouldn't,' said Dick. 'He said his mother says an onion is the thing that matters.'

It was nine o'clock by the time they had the rabbit jointed and in the saucepan with water covering it, and the chopped onion, and some salt, and a little milk, and a couple of potatoes, and a tin of peas. Lack of this and lack of that made it impossible to follow exactly any single one of the recipes in the cookery book, so Dorothea took hints from all, put the lid on the saucepan and pushed it in at the side of the fire.

'Now,' she said. '"45 to 60 minutes according to age and size." . . . That's boiling. "About one and a half hours." . . . That's stewing . . . We'd better let it cook till it feels all right when we prod it . . . "Sufficient for three or four persons." I wish the others were here. Or Jacky.'

It had not been raining when Dick went out to fill the saucepan and the kettle at the beck, but black clouds with hard edges were moving from the south, and it felt as if thunder was about. As dark fell they heard once more the patter on the roof.

'If it only thunders and comes down properly,' said Dick, 'it'll clear up by morning. Do you think one of them will get out and come up before breakfast? Nancy said it was urgent.'

'It's no good thinking about it,' said Dorothea. 'They'll come as soon as they can, but it's no good thinking about it now. We've got to wait till tomorrow.'

They made up the hammocks with the warm, dry rugs, lit the hurricane lantern, fed the fire with sticks from the dwindling pile, and watched the simmering saucepan. Water bubbled over between the lid and the pan, and sizzled in the fire. Dorothea looked at the rabbit and prodded it with a fork, remembered that they ought both to be in bed, but decided that they must have supper first and that the rabbit was a good enough excuse for staying up. After all the trouble they had taken over it, it would be silly to spoil it for the sake of a few minutes.

It was half past ten when Dorothea after a last careful prod decided that the rabbit was ready and pulled the sauce-pan from the fire. Squelching footsteps sounded outside. The next moment there was someone in the doorway, wet and piebald, in bathing things that glistened in the flickering light of the lantern and the fire.

'Shiver my timbers,' said Nancy. 'You're warm in here. Gosh! What a lovely smell.'

CHAPTER 18

VISITING SEAL

'Now, look here, Peggy. Don't be a tame galoot. All you've got to do is to keep quiet.' In the darkness of their bedroom, Nancy spoke in a fierce whisper.

'But you can't go out in bathing things.'

'I can't go out in anything else and come back with a lot of sopping clothes to explain. It's raining again like fun.'

'But what if she hears you get out?'

'She won't. She's asleep by now. And I've locked the door. All you've got to do is to be asleep. If you hear her moving, do a grunt and snore.'

'But . . .'

'I've got to see Dick. You know I have.'

Nancy finished making ready. She pulled a bathing cap over her hair. She put on her sandshoes. Her pyjamas were in her bed. Her clothes were neatly piled on a chair, ready for any inspection. She slipped across to the window and looked out. It was dark, but not black dark. She could hear the rain dripping from the gutter. That rain had cost them a whole day. Timothy's message had been at Beckfoot for twenty-four hours and more, and she had never had a chance of seeing the Picts. It had been a very narrow squeak getting to their letter-box and back, when the doctor had been blind to her signals so that she had not been able to ask him to carry a dispatch. She put Timothy's message between her lips so as to have both hands free. She sat on the window-sill and felt the rain with an outstretched foot.

'Go back to bed, Peggy,' she hissed. 'Jibbooms and bob-stays, it's me to shiver, not you. Go back to bed.'

She twisted round on the window-sill, felt for the rose

trellis, and found it. There was a creak or two, but nothing to matter. Two minutes later she was slipping on tiptoe round the corner of the silent house.

Once in the road, she ran. It was too dark in the wood to do anything but stick to the path, so she went straight up, stepping now on a stone and now ankle deep in a pool where the overflow from the beck was pouring down. She was as wet as if she had been in the river. That did not matter in bathing clothes. And as for waking up Dick and Dot, that did not matter either in such a case as this. She came squelching out from under the trees into the clearing, saw the red glow of the fire through the window and the open door and knew that she would not have to wake them.

*

'I've never had one single chance of getting up here all day. I say, what *is* that smell?'

'Supper,' said Dorothea. 'It's Jacky's rabbit. You're just in time.'

'Has Timothy sent to say he's ready?' asked Dick.

'Is Peggy coming too?' asked Dorothea.

'Yes he has and no she isn't,' said Nancy, holding out a wet arm and watching the water drip from her fingers. 'Somebody had to stay in case of accidents, and there's always more danger of things going wrong with two.'

'A door banging so that the gaolers know there's an escape.' said Dorothea.

'Door!' said Nancy scornfully. 'I got out through our window. The only safe way. Just think if she'd happened to come out of her bedroom and spotted me in bathing things going downstairs. I always knew that trellis would come in useful when I saw them putting it up. But look here. Don't waste time. It isn't my getting out that matters. It's your getting in.'

'But we don't have to,' said Dorothea. 'I thought last

WET AND PIEBALD IN THE DOORWAY

night perhaps it would be the only thing to do, but Dick's
managed to stop the leaks in the roof and even when it did
drip it dripped in the right place, not on our hammocks. And
I've had a fire going all day, and everything's dry.'

'You don't know what's happened,' said Nancy. 'We

couldn't let you know. It's been an awful day. First we went and were late for breakfast and then, because of the rain pouring down, the G.A. was at her very worst. One thing after another all morning. The doctor came and I tried to catch his eye to get him to go and tell you but he was a pig and wouldn't see. We didn't really mind, because we thought we'd escape in the afternoon, and I dodged out to leave a dispatch so that there wouldn't be any danger of us missing you. And then in the afternoon the G.A. was enjoying herself too much to go to bed. It was still pouring, and she kept us reading that beastly book. . . . It's not a bad book but any book is awful when you have to read it aloud and someone keeps butting in to say you're pronouncing a word wrong or putting emphasis in the wrong place and you have to go over the same sentence half a dozen times. And then came tea and after that we had a dose of Chaminade . . . just as bad as reading . . . you know . . . getting the time wrong . . . "Please Ruth, those two bars again." . . . "Ruth, you must try to remember the difference between a minim and a semibreve." . . . "Ruth! *Andante* does not mean *Staccato* any more than *Piano* means *Fortissimo*." . . . "Ruth!" Ugh! . . . After supper, knitting. . . . And there we were, boiling to come and tell you what we've got to do. Well, it was bed-time at last, and I gave her half an hour to get to sleep, and here it is . . .'

She opened her left hand and showed a tiny screw of paper.

'It's sodden wet in spite of my keeping it in my fist. It'll fall to pieces if we don't get it dry before touching it.' She crouched before the fire, and held the screw of paper in the warmth.

'Pigeon post,' she said. 'It came last night.'

'I ought to have reminded you to cut out the bell,' said Dick. 'It was bound to make an awful noise.'

'How do you know?' said Nancy sharply.

'We heard it,' said Dick. 'We were just coming up the river.'

'But it was after supper.'

'We were pretty late,' said Dorothea. 'We'd been to the head of the lake beyond the North Pole.'

'Jolly good first voyage,' said Nancy, dropping the screw of paper from one hand into the other. 'Well, if you heard it on the river, you can guess what it was like in the house. It nearly sent the G.A. through the ceiling. I bolted like a flash and there was old Cooky gasping for breath. She knew what it was all right because of last year. Well, I tore the wire off the battery and bolted back. The G.A. was telling Peggy about an electric bell in her house at Harrogate that went wrong and couldn't be stopped. "We'll have to have a man to see to it," she said. "Did you stop it?" Well, of course, I had. She said that probably all the other bells had gone wrong too, so she rang the one in the drawing-room, and when old Cooky came bustling in she told her she didn't want anything . . . she was only making sure the bell was working. And Cooky looked at me and Peggy and I glared at Cooky, and she nobly went off without giving us away. I didn't risk going out to the pigeons after that, but I nipped out before breakfast. They'd both come back. Timothy'd put the same message on each of them. . . . Shows how important it is. He'd put them on jolly badly.'

'But what is the message?' asked Dick.

'Pretty dry now, but take care,' said Nancy. 'Giminy, I'm being cooked in my own steam.'

Dick took the scrap of paper and flattened it with trembling fingers. Steam clouded his spectacles. He dabbed at them without taking them off, and began to read.

'Read it aloud,' said Dorothea.

He read:

Ready for Dick any time he can come. But I can't get on without some things from Jim's study. Acids: hydrochloric, nitric and sulphuric. Tincture of ammonia. Test-tubes. Two small crucibles. Pipette (two if he's got them). Spirit lamp. Couldn't get one in the village, but if Jim hasn't got one I think I can manage with the primus. Filter. Filter papers. Litmus. Chemical scales. Volume II of Duncan's *Quantitative Analysis*. Dick'll know where they are. Sorry to bother you, but I promised Jim I'd have the assays done before he comes back. I'm sending both pigeons in case the message drops off one of them. T.S.

'Good,' said Dick. 'We'll take them to him first thing tomorrow morning. Will you be able to get them to *Scarab*? She's in the harbour and baled out. . . . But, of course, there'll be more water in her by now.' He read through the list again. 'There isn't really an awful lot. Only you'll have to be careful about keeping the acid bottles the right way up.'

Nancy took the paper again. 'What's a pipette?' she said. 'We don't know. And litmus? And chemical scales? And filter papers? We don't know what's in the study or what isn't. We'll never find the things. We won't know them even if we see them. And it's no good telling him to come and get them himself, after she's seen him skulking off the road when we met. It would mean explanations, and once explanations get started you can't stop them. It would mean the bust up of everything.'

'The acid bottles are on the top shelf in the cupboard with a glass door. They are all labelled,' said Dick. 'The chemical scales must be somewhere about. I haven't seen them, but they're sure to be there. The litmus paper's probably in a little book. That's how they usually sell it, and you tear out a leaf when you want it. The pipettes . . .'

'It's no good telling me,' said Nancy. 'We'll never find them without you. You'll have to come in and get them for him.'

'But that'll mean explanations, too,' said Dorothea. 'You'll have to say who Dick is.'

'Jibbooms and bobstays,' exclaimed Nancy. 'There mustn't be any explanations. They always go wrong. The G.A. mustn't know anything about it. We won't even try to take the things until she's in bed and asleep. That's what I meant when I said the difficulty was going to be getting you in. But we've thought it all out. Burglary's the only safe way.'

'Burglary.' Dorothea stared.

Dick took off his spectacles and blinked, short-sighted, at the fire. 'He's got to have those things,' he said.

'Of course he has,' said Nancy. 'I knew you'd see it. Everything else is going splendidly. She's never guessed about you, and you've got *Scarab* all right, and we've saved Timothy, and she's been having a perfect orgy of bossiness, enjoying herself like fun, and we've been angels all the time, and she's going to end up by being pleased with Mother instead of jolly sick. The only thing that would make it a failure would be for Uncle Jim to come back and find that you and Timothy haven't done those messes for him.'

Dick reached for his waterproof. 'I'm ready now,' he said.

'I'm coming, too,' said Dorothea.

'No,' said Nancy. 'You can't do a burglary while it's raining and leave lakes all over the floor to show where you've been. One day more won't matter. This rain won't go on for ever. It'll be fine tomorrow. And there'll be a moon, not like tonight. You won't have to prowl round in the dark. I'll leave the study window open. Thick curtains inside. Once you're in with the curtains closed you can use a torch. You'll just collect the things and bring them up here, and sail down to the houseboat with them next morning. Oh yes. And ask Timothy if we can all come the day before she goes. I think we've a chance of getting a day off. That'll give you two whole days for stinks. Don't try to shut the window after you. It makes an awful noise. That's why I've got to leave it open for you. I'll nip down early and get it closed before she comes down to breakfast. Nobody'll ever know you've been anywhere near the house.'

'It's an awful risk,' said Dorothea.

'It can't be helped,' said Dick.

'How high is the window from the ground?' asked Dorothea, whose mind's eye already saw the burglar climbing in.

'You can get your knee on the window-sill from the path outside ... Easy as anything ... Good ... Settled ... I knew we could count on you ... I say, that rabbit does smell good.'

'It's ready,' said Dorothea. 'We're just going to have our supper. There were some things in the cookery book I couldn't put in because we hadn't got them, but they're not the sort of things that really matter. Look here, I'll eat mine with a spoon and then you can use my fork.'

'Fingers are good enough for me,' said Nancy.

'For us too,' said Dorothea.

In the red glow of the firelight, the Picts and the Visiting Seal ate Jacky's rabbit and were sure no rabbit cooked in a kitchen had ever tasted better. Dick, who had been waiting a long time for his supper, was very hungry. Dorothea felt about the eating of the first rabbit she had ever cooked much as if she were reading the proofs of her first book. Nancy enjoyed it for its own sake and still more because the Picts were doing the real thing and she was as pleased as if she had been doing it herself.

'I don't believe even Susan's ever cooked a rabbit,' she said. 'I know we haven't. When the Swallows come and we all go exploring or something, we'll catch rabbits and cook them. It's ten times better than just digging things out of a tin.'

'The cooking's easy,' said Dorothea. 'It's the getting it ready for cooking that's rather awful.'

'We hadn't found the scientific way,' Dick explained.

'Do tell us what it's like at Beckfoot,' said Dorothea. 'Are you sure she doesn't suspect?'

'I thought yesterday she did,' said Nancy. 'But it's all right. She was on a completely wrong tack. She'd somehow

got it into her head that the Swallows were about and that we
were meeting them.'

The pattering of the rain had stopped for a few minutes.
Suddenly they were startled by the crash and roll of thunder.
Nancy jumped to her feet.

'Thunder,' she said.

'I thought it would have come sooner,' said Dick.

There was another distant rumble, and heavy raindrops
beat on the roof.

'I've got to bolt,' said Nancy. 'Peggy'll be in an awful
stew. It's the only thing she's frightened of. That and the
G.A., of course. And she can't stand being alone when there's
thunder about. I've got to bolt or there'll be trouble. Coming
down a wallop too. That means it won't last long. Fine
tomorrow. Gosh, I'm cooked all over. Now for another
bath. If she lies down tomorrow afternoon, we'll meet you
at Picthaven. If we don't get there, you know what to do.
Wait till everybody's gone to bed. You'll find the study
window open. Don't make a noise and everything'll be all
right.'

She made for the door.

A flash of lightning lit up the clearing outside. Nancy was
gone.

*

Nancy raced, splashing, down the path. There was a moon
behind the clouds, but it was very dark. She had dried in the
hut, but the heavy thunder rain soaked her again in a moment.
Bother that thunder. There was no time to lose. In thunder,
she knew, you could not count on Peggy. Another flash of
lightning lit up the dripping trees. A crash of thunder sent
her stumbling. She fell, picked herself up and raced on.

Bother that thunder. Even though it did mean that the
weather would clear. If only it could have waited till she was
back. Almost she could hear Peggy's squeak, the noise of her

bare feet on the bedroom floor. She tried to remember if the Great Aunt had ever been with them when there was thunder. Did she know about Peggy? Giminy, what if she did know, had been waked by the thunder and had come across the landing to lecture Peggy on the foolishness of being afraid of it? Foolish it was, of course, but it was Peggy's one weakness, and Nancy, even when a pirate, knew there was nothing to be done about it. The only thing was, to be there. And there she wasn't.

Down on the road she could run faster. Another flash of lightning lit up the lawn as she hurried round the corner of the house. Quietly now, on tiptoe, she slipped along the gravel path, found the trellis and began to climb. Another flash came and another roll of thunder. She thought she heard Peggy's voice. Her hand was on the window-sill. She tumbled head foremost into the room.

'Nancy! Nancy!' whispered Peggy.

'All right, you thundering galoot,' hissed Nancy, peeling off her bathing dress. She wrung it out, rolled up her bathing cap in it, and left the sodden lump on a corner of the window-sill.

At that moment she heard the opening of the door of the spare room. She pushed her wet sandshoes under a cupboard, grabbed a dressing-gown that she had left on the back of a chair, rolled it round her wet body and shot under the bedclothes.

'Nancy . . . I'm coming into your bed.'

'Shut up for a minute.'

Someone was turning the handle of the door.

'Ruth . . . Margaret.' It was the voice of Aunt Maria. They heard her trying the locked door.

'You go and let her in quick . . . I can't.'

Peggy, dithering as much because of the thunder as because of the Great Aunt, got up, unlocked the door and slipped back to bed. The great Aunt came in with a lighted candle. The flame nearly blew out in the draught from the window.

'You ought never to lock your door at night,' said the Great Aunt. 'I must take away the key. Well, Margaret, I expected to find you hiding from the thunder in Ruth's bed. Is Ruth asleep?'

'No,' said Nancy as sleepily as she could, keeping all but her nose under the bedclothes.

'When there is thunder and rain, you should always close your window,' said the Great Aunt. 'There is quite a lake on the floor.'

She went, with guttering candle, to the window. Nancy waited, moment by moment, to hear her find the bundle on the sill. If a flash of lightning were to come now. . . . But none came. She heard the window closed. She heard the Great Aunt take the key from the door.

'You should never lock your door at night. Think what might happen if there were a fire and the key jammed and you were trapped up here on the upper storey.'

Nancy stopped herself just in time from telling her that with the rose trellis outside there was no danger of that.

'Good night,' said the Great Aunt. 'I remember hearing that Margaret always had to sleep with someone else when there was thunder. I am glad to see that she is growing up. Good night!'

She was gone.

White light suddenly filled the room again. There was another crash much nearer than the last. Peggy was out of bed in a moment and burrowing in with Nancy.

'It was awful,' she whispered.

'It jolly well was,' said Nancy. 'She must have been within an inch of my wet bathing things.'

CHAPTER 19

'WE'VE NEVER BEEN BURGLARS BEFORE'

Dick and Dorothea found it hard to remember afterwards anything that had happened between Nancy's running out into the thunderstorm and the moment late next night when the rising moon told them it was time for them to start.

They went to bed soon after Nancy had gone, but lay in their hammocks thinking of what they had to do. They heard the thunder die slowly away. They heard the rain stop. They woke to find bright sunshine and Jacky grinning from the doorway with the milk. They told him they had cooked the rabbit, and he tasted a bit and told them they ought to have given it more salt. 'You've tried trout and you've tried rabbit,' said Jacky. 'What you want to be doing is putting a nightline down for eels. You come to t'bridge today and I'll show you.' They told him they couldn't, but were almost afraid to say anything at all lest they should somehow let out that something serious was planned. Dick baled *Scarab* in the morning and dried her sail in the sun. At two o'clock, after eating what was left of the rabbit, they were both down at the harbour. Nancy and Peggy joined them there, but only for a few moments, just to make sure that everything was understood. They were to wait for moonrise, so as not to have to use a torch out of doors or to risk stumbling without one. The window would be open. 'We could come down the trellis and help, but it would be silly, really. The more people are moving about the more chance there is of being heard. Nobody but Dick must come in.' 'But if he's caught?' 'We'll be lying awake ready for a rescue. But he won't be caught. You've only got to do it quietly and nothing can possibly go wrong,' said Nancy, and then she and Peggy, who were in their white frocks, not in comfortables, had gone straight back to read aloud to the Great Aunt. Dick and Dorothea had got through the afternoon somehow. Dick had tried to look at birds. Dorothea had tried to read her cookery book. Both had failed. Dorothea had thought of going to sleep in their hammocks to make up for last night and to be sure of not being sleepy later on. But it was no good. They had their supper and Dorothea made it a good one, hotting up a steak-and-kidney pie. And then, when the sun had gone down and night had come, Dick took the three-legged stool to the door of the hut, and sat there, listening to owls, and watching for the rising of the moon.

*

Ages went slowly by before at last the watcher in the doorway saw the tops of the great hills touched with a ghostly light. 'It's coming up now,' he said, looking over his shoulder into the hut where Dorothea was writing something by fire-light in the later pages of the exercise-book that had been given up to housekeeping.

'We won't start till the moon's really high,' said Dorothea.

'There won't be much here anyhow,' said Dick, because of being this side of the hill and there being all those trees. But there'll be moonlight on Beckfoot almost at once.'

'It's an awful risk,' said Dorothea. 'I wish we hadn't got to.'

'It won't take me a minute if Nancy's left the window open.'

'What if she's forgotten?'

'She won't. But even if she has we know which their bedroom is. We'll have to throw earth till we wake her.'

'But you're no good at throwing,' said Dorothea.

'I know.'

'Neither am I. And if she has to get up she's sure to wake everybody else opening the window. She said it couldn't be done without making a noise.'

'She won't have forgotten,' said Dick, who was trying the electric torches. 'Dot, I think your battery's better than mine.'

'You'd better take it. I say, Dick, there's one thing. We'll know what it feels like to be burglars.'

'It isn't burgling,' said Dick. 'Captain Flint wants Timothy to have the things.'

'It will be burgling if we get caught.'

'We can explain.'

'But that's just what we can't,' said Dorothea.

The moon was rising all the time. There was more and more light in the sky, and looking down over the trees they could see the long lines of the stone walls dividing the fields beyond the river.

'We'll do it now,' said Dick, picking up his suitcase, that had been emptied for the carrying of the booty.

'I'm ready,' said Dorothea. 'I'll just put a few more logs on, to keep the fire going till we come back.'

They set out across the clearing. Dick heard Dorothea murmur to herself ... 'Stealthily, holding his breath, alert for the dread footsteps of the law ...'

'Oh, look here, Dot. Captain Flint *asked* Timothy to use those things.'

'Real burglars wouldn't be thinking of that.'

Carefully, not for fear of the law but because it was not easy walking in the uncertain light, they went down the path through the wood. A day of hot sunshine had lowered the beck and it was no longer overflowing, but they had to watch their feet so as not to step in the little pools that were left. They came to the road. Moonlight was pouring down on Beckfoot and its sheltering trees. At the gate, they were startled by a bright gleam from a window, and were afraid that someone was still awake, till they saw that it was only the moon reflected from the glass.

They listened. There was not a sound from the house.

'Keep close under the trees this side,' said Dick, and they slipped quietly through the shadows and round to the edge of the lawn. The moon lit up the whole of that side of the house, and they saw at once that the corner window nearest to them on the ground floor was wide open at the bottom.

'She hasn't forgotten,' said Dick. 'Don't make a noise on the gravel.'

'Stop ... Stop!' whispered Dorothea. 'I'm sure I heard something.'

'They've all gone to bed long ago,' whispered Dick.

He tiptoed across from the trees and stood under the open window. He reached in, felt along the curtains till he found where they met in the middle, and pulled one of them an inch or two aside. Yes. Everything was dark behind it. He felt Dorothea's fingers on his arm.

'I'll leave the suitcase here,' he whispered. 'I'll pass the things out and you can put them in. Put them so that when we're carrying it the bottles'll be the right way up.'

'Be careful about getting in,' whispered Dorothea.

'Let me put one hand on your shoulder . . . That's right . . . Keep still . . .' The next moment he was kneeling on the window-sill. The moment after that he had swung his feet inside and was feeling for the floor. He found it and pushed through the curtains, which closed behind him. He was standing in black darkness. He felt for his torch and, breathless in spite of himself, switched it on and looked anxiously round.

Yes. Everything in Captain Flint's study was as he remembered it, the high bookshelves, the glass-fronted cases, the shelves of chemical apparatus, the savage weapons on the walls, the jawbone of a huge and long-dead fish. Even in that nervous moment, the burglar smiled as his torch lit up the big hutch they had made for Captain Flint's expected armadillo, and, seeing the name TIMOTHY, where Titty had painted it on the door, he remembered that Captain Flint was using the hutch as a boot-cupboard, and smiled again as he thought of Timothy, for whom it had been designed. Then he pulled out of his pocket the scrap of paper Timothy had sent, with the list of the things he wanted. He threw the light of his torch on it and read, though he almost knew the list by heart.

'*Acids: hydrochloric, nitric and sulphuric.*'

He knew where they were, went straight to them, ticked them off on the list, took them to the window one at a time, and handed them through to Dorothea.

'Don't show your t-t-torch,' whispered Dorothea, whose teeth were chattering, though it was a warm August night.

'Sorry,' said Dick.

'*Tincture of ammonia.*'

He found that and took it to the window, remembering this time to switch off his torch before reaching out through the curtains. Dorothea took hold of his wrist and pulled.

'There's someone awake upstairs,' she whispered. 'I'm sure I heard something.'

GETTING IN

'Probably Nancy,' whispered Dick. 'I'm being as quick as I can.'

He lit his torch again and went on, working steadily through his list, so as to be sure of missing nothing. Test-tubes. He found a rack of a dozen and decided he had better take the lot. He put them on the table. He found the little crucibles. There was only one pipette, and Timothy had asked for two. Spirit lamp. He put that on the table, too. Good. It would be an awful nuisance if they had to heat test-tubes over a primus. Filter. Filter papers. He put the little book of litmus paper in his pocket. Then, after a look round for the chemical scales, he put his torch on the table, facing towards the inside of the room, so as to give him a little light and show none outside, and one after another he took the things from the table to the window and passed them out through the curtains to Dorothea.

'Have you nearly done?' she whispered.

'I've got everything except the scales and the book.'

He went back, took up his torch and began hunting for the scales. The trouble was that he had never seen them. He knew what they would be like, of course, and he searched all through the glass case of chemical apparatus. They were not there. He looked on the shelves with the bottles. He began moving round the room, looking on the tops of the book-shelves. At this point the burglar, who had so far done so well, made his first mistake. The same misfortune might have happened to a professional. Perhaps, in a hurry, he moved too fast. Perhaps the armadillo's hutch was wider than he had thought. The toe of his shoe came hard against the end of it, and the big, almost empty packing case sounded like a drum.

'Bother,' said Dick, and moved quickly on, running the light of his torch this way and that, looking for the little brass bar, the tiny chains, the glass dishes of the scales. There would be weights too.

Suddenly the light of his torch fell on Dorothea's hand, waving between the curtains.

Dick went to the window. 'What is it?'

'Come out, quick,' whispered Dorothea. 'Someone's lit a light upstairs.'

'If it's Nancy, I wish she'd come down,' said Dick. 'I can't find the scales.'

'It's not their room. It's the spare room,' whispered Dorothea.

'All right,' said Dick. 'We've got almost everything. There's only the scales and the book about quantitative analysis. I can take them in my hands. I'll bolt if anyone comes. You get back to the trees with the suitcase. Don't let the bottles rattle. I'll come in one minute . . . Remember the gravel . . .'

He was back again, hunting for the scales, and found them at once, a little flat, polished wooden box on the corner of the mantelshelf, under a measuring glass that was full of pipe-cleaners. He was cross with himself for not thinking at first that he would find them in a box, weights and all. He put the box on the table, and began his last hunt, for the chemistry book, *Duncan's Quantitative Analysis, Vol. II.* If only Timothy had said what colour it was.

He had run his torch along three shelves and found four other books on analysis but not the right one, when he heard the stairs creak. Someone was coming down. Dorothea had been right. He must bolt. But with three shelves already searched, he was sure he could find that book in a minute. And Timothy would not have asked for it if they were not going to need it. He searched desperately on.

Suddenly he heard steps crossing the hall . . . Steps going to the kitchen . . . the dining-room . . . the drawing-room . . . they would be coming to the study next . . . Should he bolt through the curtains, wait in the garden and come back later for the book? But if someone not Nancy came into the room, and found the window open, he might come back and find himself shut out. No. He must hide in the room. Under the table? There wasn't even a tablecloth to hang down and keep him hidden. His eye fell on the armadillo's cage. He was close by it. He opened the door with TIMOTHY on it, and shone his torch in. Boots and shoes, but not very many. Quietly, quickly, he shifted some of them, sat on the floor, and worked his way in, feet first. He pulled the door to after him, switched off his torch and waited in the dark.

Someone was trying the study door. No time now to wish he had bolted through the window instead. Someone was turning the key. Someone was standing in the open doorway. Through a chink in his hiding place he could see that there was light in the room. He heard steps cross the floor. They were not Nancy's steps. He heard that small impatient noise that some people make with their tongues and the roofs of their mouths when they think that someone else is to blame for something. He heard a faint rattle of curtain rings, then a crash as the window was pulled down, then the click of its metal fastener. The steps crossed the floor once more. The light was gone. The door was shut. A key turned in the lock. The steps went off across the hall and up the creaking stairs.

Dick took a long breath, the first, it seemed to him, that he had taken for an hour. He lay, listening. There was a touch of cramp in his left leg. There was no room to stretch, and any-how he dared not move for fear of making a noise with the boots and shoes whose cupboard he was sharing. Even keeping as still as he could, lying there in the dark, he could not stop two of the boots or shoes or whatever they were rubbing against each other with the sticky scrape of leather on leather every time he breathed. He waited, clenching his teeth because of the cramp, for several minutes after the creaking of the stairs had come to an end. What a good thing it was he had sent Dorothea off with the suitcase and things. That must have been the Great Aunt herself in the room, and when she opened the curtains she would have looked straight out into Dorothea's face if she had been waiting outside the window in the moonlight.

Inch by inch he worked himself out of the hutch, stopping, breathless, when the boots shifted and made a noise that

seemed like thunder in the dark. Safely out, he sat on the floor
and rubbed hard at the calf of his leg and then at the inside of
his knee joint. That was the way to cure cramp. He stretched
out his leg and turned his toes up as far as he could. Good. The
cramp had gone, though he felt a frightening twinge of it as he
stood up. There was absolute quiet in the house once more.

He switched on his torch and looked about him. Everything was just as it had been. The little box with the scales
in it was lying on the table where he had left it. Nothing had
changed, except that he knew that behind those thick dark
curtains was a closed window instead of an open one.

Suddenly he heard voices upstairs.

'No, Ruth. I merely wished to make sure you were in bed.
Someone had carelessly left the study window open.' That
must be the Great Aunt. He heard a faint mumble ...
Nancy or Peggy. Then the Great Aunt again ... 'No. You
need not go down. I have closed it myself. I must speak to
Cook about it in the morning.'

He shut off his torch, for fear that any glint of light might
show under the study door.

He heard first one door and then another close upstairs. The
Great Aunt must be back in her bedroom. What now?
Nancy and Peggy must be thinking that the burglary was over
and that he and Dorothea were already safely away. And there
was Dorothea waiting in the garden not knowing what had
happened. And here he was still in the house with that book
to find and the window to open before he could escape. And
Nancy had said that this particular window was a beast. He
tiptoed towards it. No. He must find the book first and
open the window only at the last moment, in case it made a
noise. Whatever happened he must get that book, or the
whole burglary would have been in vain. Timothy could buy
chemicals in Rio, but not the book. That and the scales were
the most important of all.

He turned once more to the bookshelves and shone his torch

on the backs of the books. He had been through that shelf already, and the one above it. He searched along the next. Books on mining. Books on Peru. Books on the Dutch East Indies. And then, at last, he found it, pushed far in between two others, a grey book, with the lettering worn faint on its back. He took it out, made sure that it was indeed the right one, put it on the table, listened and slipped quietly across to the window.

He pushed through the curtain and found that to reach the catch he had to climb on the sill. The catch would not open. He had to take the risk of shining his torch on it to see how the thing worked. It flew open with a louder click than he would have thought possible. Now for the window. He slipped down from the sill, took hold of the handles at the bottom and tried to lift it. With a squeak and a jerk it went up about a couple of inches. He tried again. It was stuck. He gave a hard, desperate pull, and the window shot up, groaning and squeaking and coming to a standstill with a bang that seemed to shake the house. Nancy had been right when she had said that no one could open that window quietly.

He pushed quickly back through the curtains and grabbed the book and the box of the chemical scales. He was just going to get out through the window when a voice from somewhere above him called out, 'Who is there?'

He waited. He heard a door open upstairs. Was she coming down again? Dick got one leg out and then the other, thankful to find that the moon had swung farther round so that, though the lawn was still bright, there was a narrow strip of shadow along the side of the house. He slid down to the gravel path.

'Stop. I can see you. I have a gun here and I will shoot.'

'Oh, Aunt Maria, you can't!' That was Peggy's voice, shrill with horror. Then came Nancy's, almost a shout, 'But, Aunt Maria, you haven't got a gun.'

Dick raced, careless of noise now, round the corner of the house. Dorothea was waiting for him with the suitcase in the shadow of the trees. She could hardly speak. 'Dick . . . Oh, Dick!'

'She couldn't really see me in the shadow,' said Dick, though at the time he had not been sure.

'I saw her at the window,' whispered Dorothea. 'She had a lamp. What did you do? When the window shut I thought she'd got you.'

'Hurry up,' said Dick. 'We've got to get away. Everyone's awake.'

The bottles jingled in the suitcase.

'I'll take that,' said Dick. 'You take these. Whatever happens, we mustn't break the bottles.'

Looking back from the Beckfoot gateway, they saw lights in the window that lit the staircase, and this time not a reflection of the moon. A moment later light showed behind the glass of the front door.

The burglars, without another word, hurried out of the gateway, and then, as quietly as they could, tiptoed along the shadowed side of the road. They were climbing the path up into the wood before Dick spoke again.

'We're all right now,' he said.

'But where were you when she was in Captain Flint's den?'

'I had most awful cramp,' said Dick.

'But where?'

'In the calf of my left leg.'

'But where were you?'

'I got into the hutch we made for Timothy, you know, when we thought he was an armadillo.'

Dorothea, who during all that long wait under the trees while Dick was in the house and the Great Aunt prowling round had felt much more like crying, suddenly laughed, not her usual quiet laugh, but a laugh like one of those coughs that will not let you stop.

Dick grabbed her arm. 'Dot,' he said. 'Don't make such a noise.'

'Sorry,' said Dorothea.

Back at home, in the hut, Dick lit the hurricane lantern and opened the suitcase. Nothing was broken, and he put the case to lean against the wall, so that the bottles should be the right way up.

'We've got everything,' he said.

Dorothea was on her knees, blowing at the embers of the fire on which she had put some fresh sticks.

'Hadn't we better go to bed?' said Dick. 'We ought to start early in the morning.'

'Not after all that,' said Dorothea. 'I can't go to bed . . . Not just yet. I'm going to make some cocoa. I'm sure that's what Susan would do. Only Susan would never be a burglar.'

The sticks flared up. In a few minutes there was a good fire burning under the kettle, and Dorothea in the warm glow of the firelight in their own home, forgetting the horror of waiting under the trees after she had heard the study window shut with Dick inside, was herself again. What a story it would make!

'Dodging the bullets they fled with their dear-won booty. Back in their lair, safe from pursuit, the burglars feasted their eyes on diamond necklaces and golden chains . . .'

'I'd have got out before,' said Dick, 'if only I could have found the book. And I was a long time finding the scales. I ought to have looked for them first. The other things didn't matter so much.'

They made their cocoa, adding hot water little by little while they stirred.

'I'm sure they all do it,' said Dorothea.

'Do what?' said Dick, sipping his drink.

'It's burglars' wives I'm thinking about,' said Dorothea. 'I'm sure they all have hot cocoa ready when the burglars come home with their swag.'

'I do wish we'd got away without her hearing at all,' said Dick.

CHAPTER 20

POLICE!

THE burglars, who had not gone to bed till after one in the morning, woke late, but were up and dressed and had the kettle boiling for breakfast when Jacky, bursting with news, brought them their milk.

'You didn't hear owt in t'night?' he asked.

'Hear what?' asked Dorothea, who had the empty bottle ready for him.

'Old Mother Lewthwaite says there was burglars at Beckfoot.'

'What!' said Dorothea. Dick said nothing but stared at Jacky.

'She knows, with her son a policeman and all,' said Jacky. 'I asked Mrs Braithwaite at Beckfoot, but she wouldn't tell me nowt.'

'Who is Mrs Braithwaite?' asked Dick.

'That's Cook,' said Dorothea. 'Go on, Jacky. What did she say?'

'She told me to get along before she helped me,' said Jacky with a grin. 'So I knew well enough there'd been something doing. Pity you missed it being up here. And you didn't hear nowt? Reckon burglars don't make more noise than what they can't help. Wish I'd seen 'em. I'd have shot 'em dead . . . so . . .' He aimed the empty milk bottle as if it were a gun . . . 'And likely got a medal from the police.'

'D-do you think they'll catch them?' asked Dorothea.

' 'Course they will,' said Jacky. 'Why, we had sheep stolen year before last and they copped the chap as far away as Kendal. I'll be going now. I mun tell my dad to look out for 'em and load his gun.'

And Jacky hurried away.

While he had been standing in the doorway of the hut, Dorothea had kept herself from looking at the suitcase that held most of the swag, leaning against the wall where Dick had put it last night. Now that he was gone, neither she nor Dick could take their eyes off it, except to glance at the wooden box with the chemical scales, and *Duncan's Quantitative Analysis*, both in full view on the shelf above the fire.

'We ought to have hidden them,' said Dorothea.

'He didn't see them,' said Dick.

'Suppose the police come looking.'

'We've got to get them to Timothy's quick.'

'Breakfast's all ready,' said Dorothea.

Dick took the box and the book, put them in the suitcase with everything else, set the suitcase beside the other and covered them both with a rug from his hammock. 'We won't wait to wash up,' he said. 'If we'd only waked up early we could have had them at the houseboat by now.'

*

After a hurried breakfast, they shut up the hut, and went down through the trees to the road. They dared not go by the path, for fear the police might be coming up and meet them with the suitcase. They waited before climbing the wall, listening for footsteps. They heard none, crossed the road, climbed the gate into the field, slipped into the edge of the Beckfoot coppice and came to Picthaven without being seen by anybody. They set the suitcase amidships, leaning against the centreboard case, so that the bottles should be the right way up, pushed off from the willow tree and worked their way out of the reeds and through the channel in the waterlilies.

Dorothea took the oars, while Dick, leaning over the stern, was fixing the rudder in its place.

'The wind's just right,' he said, looking up, after seeing that the rudder was swinging freely on its gudgeon pins.

'What for?' said Dorothea. 'Nancy said it wasn't safe to use the centreboard in the river.'

'That's just it. We shan't want the centreboard. If we get just a bit of the sail up we'll blow right out of the river without any noise at all. Those oars squeak like anything.'

'It's because they're new,' said Dorothea, who had been desperately trying to keep them quiet.

'Let's stow them,' said Dick. 'Half a minute while I get the sail ready.'

'It'll be all right, if only the Great Aunt isn't looking out of the window,' said Dorothea. 'Be quick. We're in the river already.' The *Scarab*, caught by the current, was drifting out of Octopus Lagoon.

'Now,' said Dick, scrambling aft, and putting the halliard into Dorothea's hands on the way. 'Pull at it now. Not right up. Just to lift a bit of the sail so that it catches the wind. We'll get it up properly when we're outside.'

Dorothea pulled. The yard lifted and swung round, while the boom still rested on the gunwale.

'That'll do it,' said Dick. 'Just hold it like that, and then you can let go if anything goes wrong. She's moving very well.' They were in the river now and slipping past the trees of the coppice.

'We'll be in sight of the house in a minute,' said Dorothea.

'She isn't making any noise.'

'Don't even look at the house while we're going by,' whispered Dorothea.

But, as the house came in sight behind its new-cut lawn, neither of them could help taking just a glance at the scene of last night's burglary.

They gasped. Everybody seemed to be out in front of the house. They saw Nancy and Peggy. They saw the old Cook. They saw the Great Aunt herself, pointing at the study window with her stick and talking to a policeman. And they, the burglars, were sailing past in full view, suitcase and all.

And just then, the wind failed them. Perhaps they were a little sheltered by the wood. Instead of slipping quickly through the water, *Scarab*, moving more and more slowly, was doing little more than drift with the stream. Every moment the burglars expected the policeman or the Great Aunt to turn and see them.

'Only another few yards,' whispered Dick. 'And there's wind coming.' He had glanced upstream and seen the ripples on the water. He was steering with what little way *Scarab* still held, trying to keep her heading as she had been lest, when the wind came, it should blow the sail across with a noise that no one could help hearing.

Good. Good. There was the wind again on the back of his neck. The bit of sail was pulling. Another minute and they would be out of sight beyond the boathouse. What was happening up there in front of the house? The big policeman was on his hands and knees, looking at the ground. Gravel path, thought Dick. Lucky it wasn't a flower-bed. The others were all watching the policeman. Suddenly Peggy turned her head and saw them. Dick thought he saw her mouth open, but heard, instead of a shout, a terrific fit of coughing. Cook and the Great Aunt and the policeman took no notice, but, just as *Scarab* slipped into safety beyond the boathouse, he saw that Nancy must have seen her. Nancy was watching the Great Aunt and the policeman, but she was whirling one hand in circles behind her back. The next moment they were safe. *Scarab* had passed the boathouse and was moving faster and faster out into the lake.

'Did you see Nancy? What did she mean?' asked Dick.

'She meant we're to go ahead. She's as pleased as anything. She's guessed we've got the things in the boat. But Dick, what's going to happen if the policeman finds my footprints by the trees?'

'He may not look there,' said Dick. 'Anyway, we can't do anything except just take the things to Timothy.'

'But it isn't only the burglary,' said Dorothea. 'If we get caught, everything'll be discovered. Nancy'll have to say she left the window open for us. Timothy'll have to explain, and then the Great Aunt . . .'

'Look here, Dot. Will you come and steer while I get the sail up the whole way? No. Just hang on to the halliard till I can get hold of it.'

Nothing was forgotten this time. The centreboard was lowered, the sail hauled up, and, with Dorothea at the tiller, *Scarab* cleared the point of the Beckfoot promontory.

'I've just got to get the boom down a bit,' said Dick.

'It's quite all right,' said Dorothea, looking back over her shoulder almost as if she expected to see the policeman coming after them in the Beckfoot rowing-boat.

'A lot better now,' said Dick, after making fast the tackle. 'Head for this side of Long Island. West wind. She'll do it beautifully.'

'You come and steer,' said Dorothea. 'Anyhow, we've got the things away.'

There was no more talking. So long as *Scarab* carried that cargo, the only thing that mattered was to get her to the end of her voyage and hand it over. Every now and then one of them glanced astern to see the promontory growing smaller. There was no sign of any pursuit but they did not feel safe. What was going on behind that promontory? Had the policeman found their tracks in the soft ground under the trees? Had Nancy or Peggy made a slip? Each time she looked astern Dorothea half expected to see people standing on the promontory and the policeman looking through a telescope and tilling the Great Aunt, 'There go the thieves!' Or would he telephone to headquarters? Would they meet a rowing-boat, or a fast motor launch, coming out of Rio Bay, with a crew of police in their blue uniforms, hurrying to stop the *Scarab*? 'What is in that suitcase?' the police would ask. Would they be taken as prisoners to Rio? What would it be safe for them to say, when they did not know how much had been discovered?

'Is this the fastest she'll go?' said Dorothea.

'I don't know,' said Dick. 'It's a reach with the wind like this and the book says you must keep the whole sail pulling but not have the sheet hauled in tighter than you need. I'm trying to find the right place. She'd go faster if Nancy was sailing her, or Tom.'

Though perhaps Nancy or Tom Dudgeon would have done a little better at the tiller, Dick was doing pretty well. The water was creaming under *Scarab*'s forefoot. She was heeling over a little but not too much, and her wake (if not quite as straight as it should have been) was a long one. Rio and its crowded bay disappeared behind Long Island. Smaller islands were slipping by. A boat with a party of people fishing for perch in a little bay was hardly sighted before it was hidden again as *Scarab* hurried on her way. She came out into the open water at the far end of Long Island and Dick swung her round on her new course to Houseboat Bay.

'Sorry. Sorry,' he exclaimed. 'I say. Do see that the bottles are all right.'

He had swung her round almost at right angles to her old course and the wind had flung the sail across with an unexpected gybe. Dorothea's head had had a narrow escape from the boom, and the suitcase had been jerked over on its side. Dick very nearly let her fly right round into the wind, stopped her just in time, narrowly escaped a second gybe and then, easing out the sheet, steadied her once more.

'My fault,' he said. 'Sorry.'

Dorothea felt guilty even to look at what was in the suitcase but was glad to find that nothing had been broken.

Scarab, with the wind aft, was heading straight for the old blue houseboat.

'No flag,' said Dick. 'But there wasn't the other day either.'

'What shall we do if he isn't there?'

'He may have gone to look for us because of our not bringing the things yesterday.'

'He may have run right into the policeman. Look out, Dick, that steamer's going to run us down.'

The steamer, a big one, her decks crowded with passengers, going on her way from Rio to the foot of the lake, gave them, for the moment, plenty to think about. Dick judged her speed, decided that she would pass easily ahead of them, and held on his course. That was quite right, but he forgot the big wash that was following astern of her. The steamer crossed their bows, the passengers cheerfully waving at the little boat, and the next moment *Scarab* was being thrown all ways at once. Dick and Dorothea hung on as well as they could, helplessly watching the suitcase fall over and slide from side to side.

'Well, if they aren't broken now . . .,' said Dick as at last their tossing came to an end.

The people on the steamer were still waving handkerchiefs.

'They think we're doing it for fun,' said Dorothea bitterly.

'Do look in the suitcase,' said Dick, steadying *Scarab* on her course once more.

It was a miracle. Things had been shaken up a good deal, but nothing was broken and no stoppers had come out. By the time Dorothea had everything packed as it had been, and the suitcase once more leaning against the centreboard, they were already close to the houseboat.

With the wind blowing straight into the bay, the houseboat, lying to her mooring buoy, was heading straight out.

'He isn't here again,' said Dick, seeing no rowing-boat against the fenders at her side.

'We'll get rid of the things just the same,' said Dorothea.

Just then, as the houseboat swung a little, they saw the rowing-boat lying astern of her. 'Good. Good,' said Dick. 'It's all right. Dot, could you be getting the halliard loose? I'm not going to try sailing her alongside . . . That's right . . .

Quick . . . Don't let go of it altogether. Let it down hand over hand . . . Not yet . . . Wait till the sail flaps . . . I'll tell you when . . .'

He put the tiller down hard. *Scarab* shot round into the wind. The sail flapped. He hauled in the main sheet. 'Now . . . Dot . . . Now. Lower . . . Lower . . . Lower away, I mean.'

Down came the sail.

'That's all right,' said Dick, watching Dorothea struggle from under it. 'It doesn't matter, just a bit of it going in the water. Anyhow, it's down.' He bundled it together with the spars, and put the rowlocks ready. Out of breath but joyful, he pulled the oars free, laid them in the rowlocks and began to row. 'Oh bother,' he said. 'I forgot the centreboard.' He pulled it up, rowed with one oar, backwatered with the other, as he had seen Tom Dudgeon do when turning *Titmouse* in a hurry, and warily brought *Scarab* towards the houseboat.

'We mustn't bump,' he said aloud. 'Dot, you be ready to hold her off.'

'Hullo!'

The tall, lean Timothy, stooping to save his head, had come out of the cabin door.

'Oh, good,' said Dorothea, scrambling for *Scarab*'s painter.

'I thought I heard a bit of splashing,' said Timothy, and Dick, who had been rather ashamed of that splashing, was suddenly glad that he had made it. With Timothy on the deck of the houseboat, to use a boathook or take a painter, it was going to be much easier coming alongside.

'Here you are, Dorothea,' said Timothy. 'I'll catch that rope if you'll throw it.'

She threw the painter, but Timothy was no sailor like Captain Flint, and Dorothea had had no practice in coiling a rope and throwing it so that the weight of the coil carries it out. The rope reached the houseboat, but Timothy missed it, and they watched the end slip back into the water.

'I'll bring her a bit nearer,' said Dick, while Dorothea pulled the painter in again, glad that Nancy and Peggy were not there to see.

At the second try Timothy caught the painter, and, like all landsmen, no sooner had the rope in his hands than he began to pull.

'PLEASE don't pull,' shouted Dick. 'Fend off, Dot. Hold her off, or we'll bump after all.'

'Sorry,' said Timothy. 'You sailors'll have to tell me what to do.'

Between them they managed to get *Scarab* lying comfortably against the fenders by the little ladder that hung on the side of the houseboat.

'Has Nancy sent the things I asked for?' said Timothy.

'They're all in my suitcase,' said Dick. 'I ticked them off on your list.'

Timothy reached down and Dick passed the suitcase carefully up. Timothy opened it at once.

'Nothing broken,' he said. 'And you've got the scales. And the book. Thank you very much. I've been wanting those things badly. Come on board, won't you?'

'You haven't begun the assays?' asked Dick.

'Couldn't without these things,' said Timothy. 'And you're going to help, aren't you?'

They climbed aboard, and Timothy, suitcase in hand, led the way down into the cabin. He began to unpack at once and put the things on the table as he took them out. His visitors could hardly believe that his was the tidy cabin they had seen the year before. The mess was dreadful, worse in some ways than when the Arctic explorers had been busy there making fur hats out of sheepskins. A big sheet of the ordnance survey was pinned between two of the windows. The long seats on either side of the cabin were covered with papers. On one end of the table were the remains of what looked as if it had been breakfast and the supper and dinner of the day before, and the whole of the other end was covered with plates and saucers, each with its little pile of copper ore, and each with a bit of paper with a number on it.

'Bit of a chemist's shop,' said Timothy, happening to see Dorothea's face as he found room among everything else for the last of the contents of the suitcase. 'But, with not being able to work in Jim's study . . . By the way, did Nancy have any difficulty with the old lady about borrowing the things?'

'I got the things,' said Dick.

'And the old lady didn't mind?'

'She didn't know,' said Dick.

'But didn't she see you when you went in to get them?'

'No,' said Dick, catching a warning look from Dorothea.

'We'll be able to get ahead now,' said Timothy, who had taken the list that the pigeon had carried and was adding a tick in ink to each of Dick's pencilled ones. 'You've brought the whole lot.'

'Are you going to begin?' asked Dick.

Timothy glanced at the clock. 'May as well start right away. We'll have to dig out something to eat, though.'

'I can do that,' said Dorothea.

'Better than I can,' said Timothy. 'You'll find a lot of stuff through that door. Give us anything you like.' He took up the book on quantitative analysis and began turning the pages, looking for a formula he wanted.

Dorothea went through to the fore cabin, to find the galley in a state that would have been very shocking to Susan. She looked back, saw that Timothy was reading, caught Dick's eye and beckoned. Dick followed her through the door.

'He doesn't know it was a burglary,' she said. 'We'd better say nothing about it.'

'Anyhow,' said Dick, 'it isn't a burglary any longer. He's got the things, and Captain Flint had said he could use them.'

'I'm glad we haven't got them any longer,' said Dorothea. 'But I do wish we knew what's happening at Beckfoot.

Buttered eggs, I think,' she went on. 'He's got lots of eggs and butter and I know I can do that. But the frying pan's in an awful mess, and there isn't a single clean plate. You go back and stay with him while I get a bit tidy. Susan wouldn't begin to cook with everything like this.'

Dick went back into the main cabin, but found Timothy hard at work, copying things out of the book. He watched for a time and then came back to Dorothea. 'He isn't ready for me yet,' he said.

'You take that towel,' said Dorothea. 'I've got the primus going, and the water's fairly warm. I'll wash and you wipe.'

It was a full hour before Timothy thought of them again. Suddenly they heard the book slam, and a moment later he was stooping at the door into the fore cabin. 'I say,' he said. 'It's two o'clock. You people must be starving.' Then he saw that Dick was rubbing the last of a pile of clean plates, and that Dorothea was anxiously breaking eggs into a basin, and at the same time watching a big lump of butter dissolving in a frying pan on the stove. 'That's mighty good of you,' he said. 'Cleaning up like that. I'm afraid I've been rather letting things slide.'

'It's going to be buttered eggs,' said Dorothea. 'But there may be just a few bits of eggshell.'

'No matter,' said Timothy. 'Somebody else will have cooked it. Not me, for a change. And as soon as we've had it, Dick and I can get to work.'

Presently, sitting round the end of the table where they had made room for their plates among the samples and bottles and chemical apparatus, they were eating buttered eggs, drinking ginger-beer from the store that had been left by Captain Flint, and hearing of all that had been going on at the new copper mine that had been the result of their last summer's gold prospecting with the Swallows and Amazons. Everything had gone very well, and now there were all these samples that Timothy had meant to analyse in Captain Flint's study, before his partner came back. They had nearly finished their meal when there came another awkward moment.

'Bit of a nuisance that old lady turning up,' Timothy said. 'But it don't matter now that she's let us have the things I wanted. She can't be quite as bad as Nancy seemed to think her.'

Dick and Dorothea looked at each other, remembering last night and seeing once more the dreadful picture of the policeman searching for their tracks with the Great Aunt telling him where to look.

'It wasn't really quite like that,' began Dorothea. 'You see . . .'

She was interrupted by a cheerful shout at the very door of the cabin.

'Houseboat, ahoy!'

'Who said we'd come bumping into paint? You never even heard us come aboard.'

Nancy and Peggy, in their white frocks, came charging in.

'She's taken an aspirin and gone to bed,' said Nancy. 'Thank goodness. Did you get everything last night? Is it here? Well done. At our end, we've got the police fairly flummoxed.'

CHAPTER 21

AS OTHERS SEE US

'POLICE?' said Timothy, staring at his new visitors. 'What do you mean?'

Nancy laughed. 'It looked pretty awful at one time, but it's all right now. I say, you did manage to get everything? We looked all round but we couldn't see that anything had been taken.'

'He got everything,' said Dorothea.

'Good. Though you were a bit of a galoot to come back and open the window after she'd shut it. Whatever did you do it for? I told you that window makes a row.'

'I couldn't help it,' said Dick. 'I tried to do it quietly, but it stuck and then went up with a jerk.'

'But why on earth didn't you leave it alone?'

'There was no other way out,' said Dick.

'Great snakes and crocodiles,' exclaimed Nancy, while Timothy looked from one to the other, not understanding at all what they were talking about. 'Jibbooms and bobstays! You don't mean to say you were inside, watching her snooping round?'

'I couldn't see her,' said Dick, 'but I knew she was there.'

'But why didn't she see you?' said Nancy. 'She had a lamp.'

'I know.'

'But there's nowhere to hide except behind the curtains and she must have looked there because she shut the window.'

'I was in Timothy's . . . I mean, the armadillo's . . . You know . . . the boot cupboard.'

Nancy's mouth fell open. 'Giminy!' she gasped. 'You were in there . . . You and she were in the study together!'

'When I heard her shut the window I thought she'd got him,' said Dorothea.

'Giminy!' said Nancy again. She picked up the flat wooden box of the chemical scales. 'She was right after all. Look here. Was this one of the things you took? Was it on the table when she was in there shutting the window.'

'I think so,' said Dick. 'Yes. I'd found it just before I heard her coming downstairs. I'd put it on the table while I was hunting for the book. We'd got everything else safely away.'

'Golly, how lucky we didn't know about it. It was just that box that settled Sammy. He asked her what was in it, and she didn't know, and he asked us and of course we didn't know either.'

'Sammy is the policeman,' explained Peggy.

'But what on earth is all this?' asked Timothy.

'Burglary,' said Nancy, in a voice at the same time grim and gleeful. 'It was the only way. You see, Dick was the only one who knew all the things you wanted by sight, so he had to come in and get them. And we couldn't bring him in broad daylight without telling the G.A. about him, and of course we couldn't do that. We'd have had to tell her about you, too. So it had to be burglary. I left the window open for the burglar to get in and in he got and then something happened . . .'

'We were listening in terror,' said Peggy.

'No terror about it,' said Nancy. 'At least, not until there was a bit of a noise.'

'I kicked Timothy's . . . the boot-cupboard, by mistake,' said Dick.

'That was it, was it?' said Nancy. 'Well, the next thing we knew was the G.A. out on the landing and looking into our bedroom. We were asleep of course. Then we heard her go downstairs, and we stood by, ready to dash down and explain if the worst came to the worst. It would have been pretty awful if we'd had to do that. All our plans about being angels and keeping her happy would have gone bust.'

'Angels!' muttered Timothy to himself.

'Martyrs, really,' said Dorothea, who had heard him. 'You don't know what a dreadful time they've been having.'

'Then we heard her slam the window down. There was no talking, so we thought the burglar had got away. All we bothered about was whether he'd had time to get all the things. We heard her lock the door and come upstairs again. She came straight to our room, and we were wide awake this time, because of the noise, of course. She said somebody, meaning one of us, had carelessly left a window open. Then she stalked off to the spare room. And then ... Kerwallop, but that window did go up with a bang. We couldn't think what was happening, but after a row like that there was no point in pretending not to hear it, so I yanked Peggy out. There was a light under the spare-room door, so I thought we'd better charge in and we did, and there was the G.A. leaning out of the window and saying she was going to shoot. She said there was a man in the garden. Of course she hadn't got a gun. I said so pretty loud in case Dick was down there and thought she had. Jolly sporting of her, anyhow, even to pretend. I never would have thought she had it in her.'

'She's *your* aunt, you know,' said Timothy with a grin. 'But, look here, Nancy, I'd never have asked for those things if I'd thought for a moment it would mean anything like this.'

'Rot,' said Nancy. 'You had to have them, and burglary was the only way. Dick and Dot made a jolly good job of it. It was just a bit of bad luck kicking your hutch ... But a bit of good that it was there and that Dick nipped into it in time.'

'I'm glad it's been useful,' said Timothy. 'I've always felt it was wasted on me.'

'Well, you're too big for it,' said Nancy.

'There wasn't much room in it even for me,' said Dick.

'Weren't you in a stew when she said she'd shoot?' asked Peggy.

'I was, a bit,' said Dick. 'Specially when she said she could see me. Then I remembered that the wall was in shadow, and she couldn't see down there anyhow unless she had a neck like a giraffe . . . Or perhaps an ostrich,' he added.

'I was just waiting for the bang,' said Dorothea.

'Well, it's been a huge success,' said Nancy. 'And they're quite safe now. The only thing is, Cook's given notice. She just couldn't stand it any longer. She wanted to do it the very first day and then again about the milk.'

'But that's awful,' said Dorothea.

'It will be if she sticks to it,' said Nancy. 'We've simply got to get her to take it back, but it's no good saying anything about it till the G.A.'s safely gone.'

'But go on,' said Timothy. 'What happened next? How do the police come into it? Once they're in, you never know where they'll stop.'

'What do you know about it?' asked Nancy. 'Have you ever been wanted by them before?'

'Only in Peru,' said Timothy. 'Did your Uncle Jim never tell you about that time when he and I . . . Oh, never mind about that. Go on. What sort of a mess are we all in now?'

'No mess at all,' said Nancy. 'It all turned out very well. Thanks to the G.A. being so certain she saw the burglar.' She paused.

'Go on,' said Timothy.

'Well, if anybody's wanted by the police, it isn't Dick,' said Nancy with a grin. 'That's one thing. She said it was a tall man, thin, with a battered felt hat. She said she'd seen him before, slinking off with a very suspicious manner . . .'

'But I was nowhere near,' said Timothy. 'And I've only seen her that once.'

230

'Well, she even described your clothes. Grey trousers, baggy at the knees. Brown coat, not fitting very well, probably stolen.'

'Great Scott!' said Timothy.

'It's all right,' said Nancy. 'Sammy was quite good for a policeman. He asked her if she could be sure of the colours in the moonlight, and she had to explain that she had only seen the colours in the daytime when you were loitering . . . yes, that's the word she used . . . loitering suspiciously in the road.'

'But look here,' said Timothy.

'Then she didn't really see Dick at all,' said Dorothea.

'She couldn't have,' said Dick.

'The next thing was . . .'

'When did all this happen?'

'This morning,' said Nancy. 'She rang up the police in the middle of the night, but there was no one they could send. This morning Sammy turned up as soon as we'd finished breakfast. I suppose they sent him because he knows Beckfoot, with his mother living close by and being our mother's old nurse.'

'I hope he knows *you*,' said Timothy.

'Oh yes,' said Nancy. 'And that was simply splendid. Because he said at once that probably it was us up to some game. And then the Great Aunt fairly blew up. She asked him if he thought she was a nincompoop. She told him she'd seen us both in bed before she went downstairs and again when she came up after closing the study window. She told him that we were in bed when she heard the burglar come in the second time, and that we were in her bedroom when she saw him rushing away. And Sammy listened as solemn as an owl, and scribbled in his notebook, and said he would like to be clear about that. Had the man got in twice? And the G.A. said that of course he had and she could prove it. She jawed away about the wooden box with Uncle Jim's name on it that was lying on the study table when she closed the window and was gone when she came down the second time after the burglar had bolted. And Sammy was first rate again. He asked her what was in it, and she didn't know. She asked us, and we didn't know. Lucky we've never been interested in stinks, except of course fireworks. Actually we didn't even know the box was there. What is in it?'

'Chemical scales,' said Dick. 'For weighing things.'

'Well, the G.A. didn't know. And then he asked her to give him a list of the articles stolen. And that fairly stumped her. "Silver?" asked Sammy. "Coops and moogs? That's the stoof what they generally go for." And we all crowded into the study and hunted round, and nobody could see anything missing. We began to be a bit afraid Dick and Dot hadn't got away with it. And the G.A. went on about that box. And Sammy had written "Articles missing" in his notebook. We saw it. And under it he wrote, "Small wooden box, contents unknown." "With Mr James Turner's name on it," said the G.A. And he wrote that down too . . .'

'Botheration,' said Timothy. 'I'll have to keep that out of the way.'

'Perhaps you'd better,' said Nancy. 'The G.A. did give a pretty full description of you. But, of course, they won't come looking here.'

'You never know,' said Timothy, handling the box as if it had suddenly become dangerous. 'Look here. Does she know Jim's lent me his houseboat?'

'She's never said anything about it,' said Nancy. 'Why should she know? Uncle Jim won't have written to tell her, and we haven't given you away. It's all right. And she doesn't know you by sight, except as a tramp. And anyhow, let me finish about Sammy.'

'Go ahead,' said Timothy.

'We saw him searching in the garden,' said Dorothea.

'I know,' said Nancy. 'And weren't we glad when we saw you slipping out in *Scarab*. That was the first thing that let us think that perhaps you'd got the things after all. We were almost resigned to thinking you'd failed. Well, Sammy looked at the window from the inside and asked her if she had latched it and she said she had. Then Sammy smelt round the latch, and opened the window and looked as hard as he could, and said there were no marks of anybody forcing the latch from outside. "But I tell you the room was empty," snapped the G.A. "I shut the window and locked the door. I had to unlock it again to get in. It only shows the man was a professional. When there are suspicious characters about, why don't the police lock them up before they have a chance to break into people's houses? A clever, cunning rascal like that. I could see at a glance he was up to no good." '

'It won't be safe for me to go ashore,' said Timothy.

'Keep out of her way, that's all,' said Nancy. 'You'll be all right with Sammy. Wait till you hear what happened next. We went into the garden, and Sammy stared at the path, but it's all hard gravel and there weren't any marks. Then he found a whole lot of footprints just off the path, under the trees. We thought everything was up.'

'That was me,' said Dorothea.

'Let's have a look at your hoof,' said Nancy. 'Yes. It's just the same. Tremendous piece of luck. The moment old Sammy found those hoofmarks he went charging back to his first idea. He looked at me as if he was a judge and asked me to put my foot in one of the marks. And of course my hoof was too big. "But I tell you they were both in bed," said the G.A. Sammy didn't answer her. He asked Peggy to try her hoof and it fitted. It fitted exactly. Jolly lucky Dot's got biggish hoofs for her size. And jolly lucky we all wear the same sort of sandshoes with a criss-cross pattern on the soles. That settled Sammy. The G.A. could tell him we were in bed till she was blue in the face, but Sammy thought he knew better. He was very polite and that made her madder than ever. He said that anybody might make a mistake in moonlight but he thought that perhaps there had been no burglary at all.

And the G.A. asked if that was all we got by paying income tax and generally things were pretty hot and lively. Old Sammy was grand. He said he would report all the details and they would keep a look out for suspicious characters and he hoped that as soon as she had been able to make out a list of the things stolen she would send it to the police sergeant. And I gave him privately one tremendous wink, just to make him more sure than ever it was us. And Sammy just glared at me, but he didn't say anything. And off he went. We spent the rest of the morning with the G.A. rummaging in the study trying to find what was missing, but, of course, she never thought of anybody taking beastly chemicals, and the cups Uncle Jim got rowing were all there, and a medal or two, and the G.A. got madder and madder, but not with us, and poor old Cook kept saying she was sure the study window had never been left open, and at last we had a silent lunch and the G.A. said she had a headache and took an aspirin and went to bed. We thought it was safe to ask if we might go for a sail and she said we might if we felt up to it, but not to be late for tea. So we came here full tilt. We didn't even wait to change these loathsome frocks. And now we've got to race back and go on being angels for all we are worth. Look here. Is it all right about the day after tomorrow?'

'We forgot to ask him,' said Dorothea.

'Us coming here for the day?' said Nancy. 'It's the one thing planned we haven't done. I've been putting out feelers about our going out for the whole day, and she said we'd been remarkably good and we could take the day before she departs if it turns out fine because she'll be packing and won't be able to help us with holiday tasks. Of course, that was before the burglary. She may change her mind now, but I don't see why. I'll ask her again to make sure.'

'You can come all right,' said Timothy. 'So long as you don't bring the police on your trail. Dick and I ought to get our job done by tomorrow night.'

'Good,' said Nancy. 'I'll ask her again, and we'll get a note out to Dick and Dot, so that they can tell you when they're here tomorrow.' Nancy was already going out of the cabin door.

'Won't you have a lemonade or something?' said Timothy.

'No time,' said Nancy.

'Are you going back now?' said Dorothea.

'Got to,' said Nancy.

'We're just going to start that work,' said Dick.

'Well, why not? You can't come with us. Supper's at half-past seven. Don't try slipping up the river till then. Safe enough while she's ladling out soup or telling us not to talk with our mouths full. But if she saw anybody near the house today she might want to stop them and ask questions. Aspirin and all, I bet she's still in a bate when she wakes up. That doesn't matter, so long as she doesn't change her mind about letting us have a day off.'

In a few minutes *Amazon*'s sail was set, and Peggy and Nancy pushed off from the houseboat and began tacking out of the bay.

'Nothing for Timothy to worry about,' Nancy called out. 'Everything's been a great success.'

'It's my own fault,' said Timothy, watching the little white sail going farther away. 'Jim warned me to look out for squalls, and I ought never to have given that young woman a chance of raising them.'

'But don't you see?' said Dorothea. 'What she's been doing all the time is trying to keep Miss Turner happy and not to have any squalls at all.'

'Well, partner,' said Timothy to Dick. 'Let's get down to it. We've got to begin by weighing out equal quantities of all those samples.'

'I'll just get our plates out of the way,' said Dorothea.

CHAPTER 22

PLANS AND CHANGE OF PLANS

FOR the rest of that day and all the next the Picts had no news from Beckfoot except a short note from the martyrs that they found in the letter-box in the wall by the road. Dick and Timothy had worked all afternoon, while Dorothea looked at books, tried to clean up a bit in the kitchen, made tea for them, and hurried Dick away in time to get back to the mouth of the river by half-past seven. They brought *Scarab* up the river without seeing anybody, left her in her secret harbour and went home, finding the note from the martyrs in the letter-box. 'The day after tomorrow. We can come. Tell Timothy. With any luck we'll be able to start first thing.' They half expected a visit from Cook that night, but were rather glad she did not come, because she would have talked about the burglary and the actual burglars would have found it difficult to listen to her without giving something away. Next day, after pinning a note to the door of the hut to tell Jacky to leave the milk and to take the empty bottle, they sailed down to the houseboat after an early breakfast. All that day was spent aboard. Dick and Timothy worked in the cabin in such a powerful smell of chemicals that Dorothea left them to it and read a book on deck. Soon after tea the work was done, or at least the part in which Dick could help, and Timothy cleared them out.

'Are you sure I can't help any more?' said Dick, who had forgotten burglary, the Great Aunt and everything else in the pleasure of using test-tubes and spirit lamp, dissolving this, evaporating that, and weighing minute deposits with scales delicate enough to show the weight of a feather.

WORK IN THE HOUSEBOAT

'No,' said Timothy. 'You've been very useful and we've
got through in half the time it would have taken if I'd been
alone. What I've got to do now is to work out all our results,
and put them into a report ready for Jim. And if I can get the

237

job done tonight I'll be free tomorrow. Not much hope of working then with Nancy and Peggy skirmishing round.'

Dick and Dorothea got home again without being seen, had supper and went to bed with easy minds. No news was good news. Nancy had been right. The police had made up their minds that there had been no burglary at all. The Great Aunt had never guessed at the existence of the Picts and she must be very pleased with the martyrs, or she would never have given them leave to have a whole day to themselves. Tomorrow, they would all be sailing together, capturing the houseboat perhaps, or even going to Wild Cat Island. And the day after that the Great Aunt would be gone. Nothing could go wrong now.

*

Next morning, the third after the burglary, they woke to a day on which nothing happened as it had been planned except that Jacky brought the milk as usual. For one thing, there was not a breath of wind. That meant that *Scarab* and *Amazon* would not be able to race to the houseboat. There could be no sailing at all. Dick looked round the sky but there was not even the smallest cloud to promise that wind was coming. Dorothea sent him down to the road in time to catch the postman on his way to Beckfoot, but there were no letters for Picts. He came back to the hut to find that she had hurried through the washing up, and had made up her mind to leave everything tidy before starting. She told him to bring some more wood in, ready to light the fire when they came home in the evening.

'But Dot,' said Dick, 'we ought to be getting *Scarab* out of the river.'

'They'll never be ready as soon as this,' said Dorothea.

'They said "First thing",' said Dick.

'That was when they thought we were going to be able to sail,' said Dorothea. 'Besides, she's sure to want them to dust something, or pick flowers for the drawing-room.'

'Here they are,' said Dick. 'I told you so. They've been waiting for us. They've come up to find why we're not ready.'

But it was neither Nancy nor Peggy who was at the door of the hut.

'Can you get hold of those two?' asked Timothy, shrugging his shoulders out of the straps of a heavy knapsack.

'They'll have started,' said Dick. 'They're probably out on the lake.'

'I'm sure they're not,' said Dorothea.

'I want to stop them if I possibly can,' said Timothy.

'Has something awful happened?' asked Dorothea. For a moment she saw policemen searching the houseboat and Timothy in flight.

'No, no,' said Timothy. 'Nothing's happened. But two of the results we got yesterday seem to me a bit odd and I want to go to the mine to get some more samples. Would you mind if we went there instead of your coming to the houseboat?'

'Good,' said Dick.

'We'd love to go,' said Dorothea. 'And they won't mind either. There isn't any wind for sailing.'

'I'll go and see if I can catch them,' said Dick.

*

He climbed up to the look-out place on the top of the promontory just in time. Nancy and Peggy were already crossing the lawn towards the boathouse. They were not wearing their white frocks but were in their ordinary rig of shorts, shirts and red caps. The Great Aunt, thought Dick, must be ill and in bed, but surely it was taking rather a risk to cross the lawn like that when she might be looking from a window.

For that same reason, that the Great Aunt might be at a window, he did not dare to wave to them. What was the best way of making them look up? He remembered that owls were barred in daylight. He dared not risk a curlew without practice. Nothing for it but a duck, even though rock and heather were not a likely background. He quacked, not very loudly. He quacked again. Nancy looked up, hesitated a moment, and then walked straight on towards the boathouse.

Dick left his look-out place and ran down to the edge of the river, to catch them on their way out, where he could not be seen from the house.

He had hardly got down to the reeds when he heard them working the boat out. Then he heard a quack, much better than his own, and there was the boat coming close along the edge of the reeds, Nancy rowing and Peggy standing in the stern.

'Ahoy!' he said quietly, and the boat's nose came pushing through towards him.

'Couldn't answer,' said Nancy. 'She was standing at the drawing-room window. Where have you left *Scarab*? We never saw you pass.'

'The plan's all changed,' said Dick. 'Timothy's at our hut. We're not going to the houseboat. He's got to get some more samples from the mine. We're all going up to High Topps.'

'That's all right,' said Nancy. 'It was going to be awful waste mucking about in a dead calm. And it's no fun rowing a boat that's meant to sail.'

'Those sandwiches'll come in handy after all,' said Peggy.

Nancy laughed. 'The G.A. told Cook to make us sandwiches and we couldn't say we didn't want them. She'd have wanted to know where we were going to get any grub.'

'Timothy's got an enormous knapsack,' said Dick.

'We'll be pretty hungry if we're going up to the mine,' said Nancy. 'But look here. What are we going to do about *Amazon*? We can't take her back to the boathouse or she might see us coming away. The boathouse door's in full view of the house. We'll have to haul her up here.'

Dick, eager to see the mine again, and thankful that the

others did not mind the change of plan, helped them to haul her up. They made a wary crossing of the road, and instead of passing Beckfoot and going up the path, they cut straight up into the wood and worked their way round to the hut. Dick ran in first.

'I've got them all right,' he said. 'And they don't mind a bit, because of its being a calm.'

'Good work,' said Timothy. 'Hullo, you two. The old lady didn't change her mind about letting you go?'

'That's the rum thing,' said Nancy. 'I thought she'd be humming and hawing at the last minute, but she wasn't. She was full of beans because we were clearing out. Anybody could see it. You might have thought she was up to something on her own and wanted us out of the way. But she can't be, of course. Only packing.'

'Any more trouble with the police?' asked Timothy.

'Oh no,' said Nancy. 'It's quite all right with the police. Sammy came yesterday morning and asked her if she had made up a list of the things missing, and of course she hadn't, so she just bit his head off and described you all over again.'

'I shall be jolly glad when tomorrow's over and she's gone,' said Timothy.

'She's started a new idea now,' said Peggy.

'Good,' said Timothy.

'She's started being a detective herself,' said Nancy. 'No. It's all right. She doesn't know anything about the Picts. She spent all yesterday morning snooping round for clues. With us to help. We helped like anything. She's been through Uncle Jim's den like a tornado. And she was booming away about the police and what asses they were for thinking we had anything to do with it when she'd told them she'd seen us both in bed. Then in the afternoon she went out and had another look at those footprints.'

'She'll find out about us,' said Dorothea.

'Not she,' said Nancy. 'But she's a wee bit warmer than

241

she was. You remember I told you she'd got it into her head that the Swallows were about and that we were meeting them? Well, she's at the same idea again. It's a bit awkward for her when she had made up her mind she'd seen the burglar and even described him to Sammy, but it came out good and clear after tea. She thinks now that the Swallows are somewhere near and that John and Susan did the burglary. We couldn't think why she kept harking back to them after we'd had a bit of a row about them already . . .'

'Hullo,' said Timothy. 'A row? I thought you didn't mean to have any.'

'It wasn't Nancy's fault,' said Peggy. 'The G.A. simply asked for it.'

'It wasn't really a row,' said Nancy. 'It was like this. She'd said, just out of the blue, while we were sleuthing round, that we had improved a lot, and we were a bit bucked because that was just what we've been working to make her think. What's the good of being angels for days on end all for nothing? But then she asked what was the name of those children who were camping near the low end of the lake last time she was here in the summer, and of course I had to tell her it was the Walkers, and she said she thought they must have had a very bad influence on us and that it was a good thing they weren't here . . . Well, I ask you? Who wouldn't blow up? Think of Susan, or John, or Titty, or even Roger being a bad influence on anybody! And of course when I blew up and said they were our friends she blew up too, and said they were always making us late for meals and that sort of rubbish, and that she'd told Mother we'd be better without them. "And so you are," she said with a would-be loving leer. And I said that Mother likes them too, and that anybody who knew them would say the same. Well, she calmed down and there was no more about them for a bit. And then last night, after she'd been having another look at what's left of Dot's hoofmarks under that tree (we've done a bit of careless trampling) she started again.

All of a sudden she said, "I suppose those Walker children are not staying in the neighbourhood now?" And I said, "I wish they were but they aren't coming for another week." And later on, when we were having supper, she had another go. She said, "You are quite sure those children have not come yet?" and looked gimletty at me, and I said, "Not for another week, Aunt Maria." And she said "Ah!"'

'You mean she didn't believe you?' Dorothea was indignant.

'She didn't say she didn't but it sounded like it,' said Peggy.

'She wouldn't dare,' said Nancy. 'But you know how natives are when they get an idea in their heads. And she's got two now, and there's a sort of civil war going on inside her. You see, she rubbed it hard into Sammy about the suspicious character and she'd about persuaded herself that she'd actually seen him in the moonlight. And now she's got this other idea about the Swallows. All the better. The more she tries to get Timothy in jail and the more she worries about the Swallows, the less likely she is to find out about our Picts.'

'Those Walker children are safely out of the way,' said Timothy, 'and I'm not. Another thing is, if she starts making inquiries about children somebody may put her on the track of the right ones.'

'There isn't a traitor in the place,' said Nancy. 'And it's all right anyway. Her train goes at two o'clock tomorrow. She's packing this morning. And after all yesterday's sleuthing, she's sure to lie down in the afternoon. She isn't going to have time to ask anybody anything.'

'I say,' said Dick, 'if she was at the window she must have seen you come across the lawn in those clothes.'

'She told us we might. She was agreeing to everything we asked. I told her Mother always lets us wear comfortables on holiday, and she said, "I don't like to see you in them. Most unsuitable," and I said she wouldn't be seeing us in them once we were out, and she said, "All right. Wear whatever you like." And then, at the very last minute, she was back at the Swallows again. She said, "You are quite sure you will not be seeing those Walker children?" and I said, "But I told you they won't be here for another week." And that was that. She didn't even ask where we were going.'

'What would you have said if she had?' asked Timothy.

'We'd have told her we were sailing down the lake to Uncle Jim's houseboat. And so we were.'

'Glad I was in time to stop you,' said Timothy.

'Hey,' said Nancy. 'What would have happened if you'd missed us?'

'I left a note on the cabin door,' said Timothy, 'and I'd have got back from the mine in the afternoon.'

'Giminy,' said Nancy. 'Natives have no consciences at all. You'd invited us . . . At least you'd said we could come.'

'He couldn't help it,' said Dick, 'if he had to go to the mine.'

'That's the spirit,' said Timothy. 'Work first. What about getting going?' He hove his enormous knapsack off the ground.

'What have you got in that?' asked Nancy.

'Rations for the party.'

'You can't carry the lot,' said Nancy. 'There's nothing in our knapsacks except a few sandwiches.'

'We've got knapsacks, too,' said Dorothea.

'Everybody carries her own grub or his,' said Nancy. 'And if it gets too heavy they've only got to eat it and have nothing to carry at all. Go on. Empty it out and let's see what there is.'

'We'll never eat all that,' said Dorothea.

'Of course we will,' said Nancy.

'None too much, I expect,' said Timothy. 'But I'll tell you what I haven't got and that's matches. I've run right out. I'd meant to have gone to the village on the way here, but I was afraid you might have started.'

Dorothea went to her store and gave him a full box.

Timothy took a pipe from his pocket. It was already filled with tobacco. He lit it and puffed at it, while the provisions were being divided among the different knapsacks. 'First pipe since yesterday,' he said. 'I used the last match getting the primus going for supper.'

'Come on,' said Nancy. 'Mining expedition. Trek to the goldfields. As good as last year. Except that the Swallows aren't here, and Timothy's a partner instead of a hated rival.'

They set out, going up to the top of the wood, and along the fell, to cross the valley of the Amazon higher up and climb into the mining country.

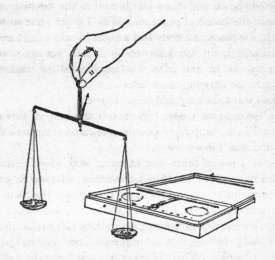

CHAPTER 23

THE GREAT AUNT GOES TO SEE
FOR HERSELF

COOK was leaning back in her chair, having a sit-down, with her hands crossed and her head already nodding, when the drawing-room bell rang. She hardly heard it. She had had a difficult morning helping Miss Turner to pack and keeping her temper as well as she could. Nancy and Peggy were out and away with their packets of sandwiches. She had given Miss Turner her lunch and had a bite herself in the kitchen, and now, with the house at peace and Miss Turner gone to her bedroom, she thought a body had a right to take things easy. The bell rang again. Cook started up. It rang yet again, and she hurried out to find Miss Turner, dressed for walking, standing at the drawing-room door.

'I shall want the car,' said Miss Turner.

'But,' stammered Cook, 'you aren't thinking of driving it, Miss? There's only Billy Lewthwaite can do that with the Missis and Mr Turner away.'

'You will please fetch him at once,' said Miss Turner, and Cook went out to find Billy Lewthwaite, who was digging in the potato patch behind his mother's cottage. His mother, Mrs Lewthwaite, Mrs Blackett's old nurse, had heard all about the burglary from Sammy, her elder son, the policeman, and was glad to have a crack about it with Cook. She had been told some of the things Miss Turner had said about the police, and, as a policeman's mother, she had a good deal to say herself, about Miss Turner. But Billy, her son, was glad to have a chance of driving old Rattletrap as a change from digging potatoes. He put on his coat, took the old yachting cap that he liked to wear when he was being a chauffeur, and hurried off to Beckfoot. By the time Cook came back he had got Rattletrap going, and Cook met him, driving out of the Beckfoot gateway, changing gears only a little less noisily than Mrs Blackett. Sitting very straight in the back of the car was Miss Turner.

'Wouldn't look at me,' said Cook to herself. 'Thinks I should have come back on the run, likely. What's she doing, driving that way along?' Puzzled, she stood and watched the car, with its wobbly back wheel, sway round the corner. She listened to it rattling and clattering up the little rise, down the other side and away on the road to the foot of the lake. She went back to her kitchen, settled down and had slipped off again into the pleasant afternoon nap that Miss Turner had interrupted when she was waked once more, this time by a bang on the door that opened into the kitchen from the yard.

'What's ado now?' she asked herself. 'Can't folk leave a body alone?'

'Where at's Mr Turner's petrol?' panted Billy Lewthwaite, scratching his head with a finger under his yachting cap. 'Every can in t'garage is empty.'

'Have you run short?' said Cook. 'Where's the car?'

'Happen a mile down t'road,' said Billy. 'She was running right enough, and then the engine started hop and go lucky and then it packed up. I'd all t'plugs out and back before I thought me to look in t'tank.'

'But where's Miss Turner?'

'Sitting up in t'owd car looking like thunder and waiting whiles I get back. I pushed her to t'side of t'road and left her. But where at's Mr Turner's petrol?'

'If them cans is empty you won't find none nearer than head o' t' lake.'

Billy looked wildly round. 'It ain't what she says. It's how she looks,' he muttered.

Cook suddenly laughed. 'Sitting up there,' she laughed.

'Eh, I'd give summat to see her.' And then, seriously, 'You'd best be off, Billy, lad.'

'And my bike's wanting a back wheel,' groaned Billy. 'I put my foot through t'spokes Saturday night.'

'You'd best take Miss Nancy's,' said Cook. 'I'll make it right with her. Don't you waste a minute, with Miss Turner left at t'side o' t'road. And me and all of us killing ourselves all these days keeping things easy.'

They went across the yard and Billy took Nancy's bicycle from the shed under the pigeon loft.

'It *would* have tyres flat,' he growled, tore the pump from it and pumped them up. Then with a petrol can in one hand, and his knees nearly hitting the handlebars as they came up, he rode desperately off.

*

A butcher's man was driving home to the town a dozen miles beyond the foot of the lake. His van was almost empty after delivering joints of meat, steaks, saddles, sirloins and what not at houses all through the district. He had only a few more houses at which to call. That evening he was to play as one of a team in an important darts match, and, as he drove, he was seeing the darts-board before him. In his mind's eye, he saw himself score a double top, a twenty and a sixty with his first three darts. Ah, if he could only do that when the time came. He could almost hear the stamping of applauding feet on the tavern floor. He was smiling to himself as he swung his van round a corner and saw an ancient motor car, with an elderly lady sitting in the back of it, drawn up at the side of the narrow road, giving him hardly room to pass.

He put his foot on the brake and slowed down, saw that he could get through with about an inch to spare, wondered what had become of the driver of the old car, was sorry that he had no chance of telling him what he thought of him for leaving his car in such a place, and was just squeezing through with the brackens at the side of the road brushing the dust from his mudguards, when a closed parasol suddenly waved in front of him. He stopped.

'How far are you going along this road?' the old lady asked him.

No business of hers, of course, but he told her.

'You will pass Swainson's farm?'

'Aye.'

'I shall be obliged to you if you will convey me so far.'

'That's all right, Ma'am,' he said. 'Just you hop in. Puncture, is it?'

'No, said the old lady. 'Not a puncture.'

She got out of the car, and the butcher's man saw that hopping in was not going to be easy for her. He moved his van forward a yard or two, hopped out himself, and opened the door on the other side.

'Now, Ma'am,' he said. 'You leave your umbrella to me. Just you take hold and I'll give you a boost behind.'

'I am sorry to trouble you,' said the old lady, did as she was told, and was presently seated in the front of the butcher's van.

'Fine weather we're having,' said the butcher's man, as he got in and put his engine into gear. 'For the time of year,' he added.

He wondered what was wrong with her. She sat there saying nothing, and, as he glanced sideways, he saw that her lips were tight together. 'Taking trouble to somebody,' he said to himself.

He drove on along the winding road, sometimes close to the side of the lake, sometimes separated from it by a patch of coppice or by fields sloping down to the water, passing a house or a cottage here and there. The old lady did not seem to want to talk. Something on her mind, he thought. He had a try again about rain and visitors coming together in August, but it was no good. So he shrugged his shoulders and drove on in silence. He turned suddenly off the road through a big open gate and up a drive between trees.

'But this is Crag Gill,' said the old lady.

'Aye,' he said. 'Leg o' mutton to leave here.'

'I think I will get down,' said the old lady. 'I must ask you to stop.'

'Do you know Miss Thornton of Crag Gill?' he asked.

'I will get down now,' said the old lady.

'It's nobbut a step to Swainson's from here,' he said, guessing that his old lady had no wish to be seen driving up to the back door of Crag Gill in the front seat of a butcher's van. 'It's nobbut a step. But if you don't feel like walking it, I'll pick you up again when I've left my leg o' mutton.'

'Thank you,' said the old lady, and he got down and helped her to the ground.

'Thank you,' she said again, and set off, walking back to the gate.

'Rum old girl,' thought the butcher's man, climbed into his seat and drove up to the house. At the house there was a bit of an argument about the last week's joint and, in proving to the cook that you couldn't have meat without bone, he did not mention his passenger. He was rather longer than he had expected, and was glad that the old lady had not been there to hear what the Craig Gill cook had to say about him. But when he left, he hurried, thinking to pick her up again. There might be a tip coming or there might not. At least he could give her a chance. Even if it was only a sixpence, there was no harm in a glass of beer on a hot day.

But his passenger was not waiting for him by the Crag Gill gate. Nor did he find her on the road between that gate and Swainson's farm. 'Quicker on her pins than you'd have thought,' he said to himself. He did not mind. After all, he had not thought of the sixpence when he had taken her up. He drove on, thinking of his imaginary dart-board, left his last parcels in the village at the foot of the lake, and never thought of the old lady again.

*

Mary Swainson, old Mr Swainson's grand-daughter, had been told by her grandfather that she was looking as pretty as a picture, had been reminded by her grandmother of the messages she was to give to her aunt, had said 'Good-bye' to both of them, and had set out from the farm in her best clothes, carrying a wicker basket. Once a year she went to spend a week with her aunt, who had married a farmer down Preston way. The old people were always in a stew lest she should miss her train, so she had set out in plenty of time to row comfortably up the lake to the village on the opposite side, leave her boat with a friendly boatman, and take the bus from the steamer pier up to the railway station. Going that way she had a quick journey with no changes, instead of having to change twice and travel all round the estuary as she would have had to do if she had gone from the railway station at the foot of the lake. She walked through the wood by the cart track, stopping for a moment to make sure that she had her spending money safe in her purse. She thought of her Jack, who always fussed about her going away. Good for him to miss her for a week. Mary Swainson was smiling happily when she came to the road and saw old Miss Turner, Mrs Blackett's aunt, walking towards her.

Mary Swainson knew her at once. As a child she had been very much in awe of her. She reminded herself that she was now grown up and was going to marry Jack, the woodman, as soon as she thought fit, while Miss Turner, poor old thing, had never married at all. Crossing the road, to go through the coppice down to her boat, she smiled at Miss Turner with a queer mixture of kindness, pity and fear.

'Mary! Mary Swainson,' said Miss Turner.

'Yes, Miss Turner,' said Mary.

'You have some children staying at the farm, I think?'

'Nay, we've no one this year,' said Mary. 'What with Grandmother getting old and Granddad not able to get about, we've not been taking visitors latterly.'

Miss Turner prodded the ground with her parasol. 'Not staying in the house, perhaps, but camping in tents quite near. You know the children I mean. They were for ever making my nieces late for meals when I was staying at Beckfoot the summer before last. Walker, I think their name is.'

'Oh, them,' said Mary. 'No. We've seen nothing of them this year.'

'My nieces did not come here this morning?'

'No, Miss Turner. If the Walker children are back again, they'll be on the island most likely. They stay at Holly Howe on the other side. They had trouble with their boat that year. That was how they came camping up on the fell behind our house.'

'On the island?' said Miss Turner, looking towards the lake, which she could not see because of the thick coppice between the road and the water.

'If they're here, that's where they'll be,' said Mary. 'And Mrs Blackett's two'll likely be with them. They generally what make for the island, unless they're going to Mr Turner's houseboat. I could put you across, Miss Turner, if you want to join them. Or I'll give them a shout as I go by and they'll bring a boat over to fetch you.'

'Are you going up the lake?'

'I've plenty of time,' said Mary. 'I'm going on my holiday,' she explained. 'It won't take me more than a minute or two to put you across to the island.'

'I shall be glad if you will,' said Miss Turner, so grimly that Mary wondered for a moment if she had done right and if Miss Turner's nieces would be glad to see Miss Turner.

She led the way along the path through the coppice. Who

would have thought of old Miss Turner walking all this way by herself? Mary decided that it was much better for her to go home in one of the children's boats instead of traipsing that long road a second time in one day.

They came to the edge of the lake, and Mary unfastened the chain of her boat, put her basket in the bottom, helped Miss Turner in, pushed off and was presently rowing sturdily for the island.

'It's not like them to be without a fire,' she said, when they were half-way across.

Miss Turner, watching the island, said nothing.

Mary rowed to the south end of the island, to look in through the rocks to the little harbour that was used by Nancy and Peggy and their friends. The harbour was empty. She rowed on. 'There's a place on the other side,' she said, but, as she rowed along the farther shore of the island it was soon clear that no boats were there at all.

'Nay, if there are no boats, they can't be here,' she said. 'They'll be on the houseboat.'

'But my nephew is away,' said Miss Turner.

'There'll be his friend,' said Mary. 'There was somebody on the deck when I went by the other day.'

'Someone living there now?'

'I did hear it was Mr Stedding, who's working with Mr Turner away mining up at High Topps. But I'll take you there, Miss Turner. It's nobbut a yard or two out of my way, and if they're not there you can come on with me, and one of the boatmen from the village'll put you across to Beckfoot. It's a hot day and all to be walking.'

'I shall be glad if you will,' said Miss Turner, and Mary stretched to her oars again and rowed steadily on with the easy, quiet stroke that comes natural to lake-country folk who have used the water all their lives. Miss Turner sat very straight in the stern of the boat, looking this way and that along the shores.

'Nay, there's nobody on the houseboat neither,' said Mary, as she turned into the bay where the old blue houseboat lay to its mooring buoy. 'No bairns, anyway. They've a flag they have up when any of them are there. Mr Turner puts it up when he's expecting them, and likely the other gentleman would do the same.'

'I think we will go and see,' said Miss Turner.

'Yes, Miss Turner,' said Mary, and, beginning now to be afraid of missing her bus to the station, rowed a little faster and soon brought her boat alongside.

'Nay, there's nobody here,' she said, standing up and looking in through the cabin windows.

'Very strange,' said Miss Turner. 'Perhaps I was mistaken.'

Mary had worked her boat towards the houseboat's stern, and was just going to sit down and take to her oars again when she saw something white.

'There's a bit of paper on the cabin door, Miss Turner,' she said. 'Maybe they've left a message for you.'

'Will you see what it is,' said Miss Turner, and Mary, taking her painter in one hand, climbed up the little ladder, looked at the paper and read it aloud to Miss Turner, who was still sitting in the boat.

'*Make yourselves at home till I get back. Timothy.*'

'They're expected anyhow,' said Mary. 'He's left t'key in t'door.'

Miss Turner thrust her parasol towards Mary, who took it and gave her a hand as she climbed aboard.

'I will wait for them.'

'Aye, that'll be best. You might easy miss them coming past the islands, and they'd be sorry for that.'

'I am much obliged to you, Mary,' said Miss Turner.

'That's all right,' said Mary, 'I'd best be going now.'

'Not late, I hope,' said Miss Turner.

'Nay, I'll do it right enough,' said Mary, but for all that

knew she had now no time to spare, and rowed fast out of the bay. For some minutes, she saw Miss Turner standing on the deck. She saw her disappear into the cabin. The houseboat looked as deserted as before. 'Gone in to have a good sit down,' thought Mary. 'And no wonder, poor old body,' and with that she saw the steamer coming from the foot of the lake, and knew that if she did not get to the pier before it she would miss her bus, which was timed to meet the steamer and take its passengers to the station.

It was a near thing and Mary was hotter than she liked as she came to the landing-stage. The steamer, with a great flurry of reversed propellers, was coming alongside the pier. There was the bus, ready to start. Mary pushed her painter into the hand of the old boatman who knew her well, asked him to mind her boat for her, told him she would be back in a week's time, ran along the pier with her basket and took her seat in the bus just as it moved off. That was all right. It would have been a bad beginning to her holiday to miss the bus and miss the train. Then, at the station, there was her ticket to buy and a place to find in one of the through carriages. And Mary was off for her holiday and never thought of Miss Turner again until she came back a week later.

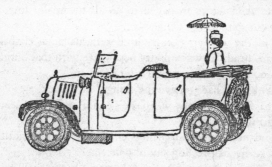

CHAPTER 24

CARE-FREE HOLIDAY

'IT's almost too good to be true,' said Nancy, taking a long breath and looking back down the valley from half-way up the steep slope of Greenbanks, where the expedition had halted for a rest.

'What is?' asked Peggy.

'This, of course. Don't you realize it's still morning? And we're not doing holiday tasks. We're not mowing the lawn. We're not weeding. We're not winding wool. We're not arranging flowers. We're not dusting the drawing-room ornaments. We're not thumping the beastly piano. We're not reciting sloppy poems. We can shiver our timbers without catching a glassy eye. And we haven't got to be back till supper-time. It's as good as if she didn't exist at all.'

'Let's pretend she's a Pict,' said Dorothea, 'for a change.'

'And tomorrow she goes, and if she isn't pleased with us she ought to be. Nine days. Ten counting tomorrow. And there hasn't been a single real row, except for Cook giving notice. And we've managed to do all the really important things in spite of her being here.'

Timothy was lying on his back with his hands clasped behind his head. 'It was a pretty near shave with that burglary,' he said, 'but I blame myself a bit for that.'

'Well, you had to have the things,' said Dick.

'It'll feel very funny when she's gone,' said Dorothea, 'not being Picts any more.'

'And not being a suspicious character,' said Timothy. 'I don't really like feeling shy of policemen.'

'And not being angels,' said Nancy. 'It's been jolly hard work being angels for nine whole days on end.'

Timothy looked queerly at Nancy. He sat up. 'Let's look at your shoulders,' he said. 'You've had Dick and Dorothea in hiding for all this time. You've roped in the postman and the milkboy and the cook and me and the police and the doctor and tied us all up into knots, and . . . let's see those shoulders.'

'What's the matter with them?' said Nancy.

'I can't see any wings on them anyhow,' said Timothy, 'but I wouldn't be surprised to find you had hoofs and a tail. Jim warned me. He told me to keep an eye on you and look out for squalls. I asked him what you were likely to do and he said it was no good telling me what you'd done already because the thing you'd do next would be sure to be different and worse.'

'Uncle Jim's a pig,' said Nancy. 'What is it, Dot?'

'I was wondering what's happening at Beckfoot now.'

'She's solemnly packing,' said Nancy. ' "Cook, my black dress, please. Cook, that's not quite the way to fold it. Now my shoes. No. No. Heel to toe. No, Cook, I think it will be better if the dresses lie flat on the top. And, Cook, I shall need those shoes this evening." And poor old Cook's holding in and holding in until she's fit to bust. She's given notice, so she doesn't see why she shouldn't let fly. I told her she's simply got to hold in just for one more day.'

'I expect that's where the wings are,' said Timothy.

Dick stared at him, and then suddenly laughed, at the thought of a fluttering cook.

'I don't care what you say,' said Nancy. 'We've never been so good for so long at a time, in all our lives.'

'Let's try to forget her just for a bit,' said Dorothea.

'Good idea,' said Nancy. 'Forgotten. Wiped it out. Done with. Gone . . . Shiver my timbers. Let's get on. The S.A. and D. Mining Expedition treks to the Gulch.'

*

They climbed on and came to the edge of High Topps.

Green was showing here and there on the earth that had been blackened by the great fire. They reminded each other of that dreadful day, and of how Nancy, Peggy, John and Susan had sheltered with Timothy in the mine while the fire raged past, and then had raced over the ashes to the rescue of the others. They looked away to the right to Kanchenjunga. They spoke of the moles finding their way through the old working to Slater Bob's quarry. They laughed over the way they had fended off Timothy when as 'Squashy Hat' he had seemed to be a rival prospector. They told him how, secretly, at night, they had watched him through the farmhouse window.

Dick, alone, had other things to think of. 'I'd forgotten there'd be no heather,' he said. 'I'll have to climb up on the other side where it didn't get burnt.'

'What for?' asked Timothy.

'Fox-moth caterpillar,' said Dick.

'What do you want it for?'

'It's not quite as interesting as the Vapourer,' said Dick. 'But I've never had one. It feeds on heather and then goes to sleep for the winter and doesn't turn into a chrysalis till next spring.'

'What does it look like?' asked Nancy.

'Brown and black velvet,' said Dick.

'Right,' said Nancy, 'we'll all hunt.'

'Thank you very much,' said Dick. 'I've brought a box for it.'

'Good,' said Nancy. 'Burglar one day, professor the next.'

'And wasn't it you who found the mine?' said Timothy.

'It was Roger,' said Dick.

'Thanks to being a lazy little beast,' said Nancy. 'Giminy, I wish the Great Aunt was right and the Swallows were here now.'

'Good thing they're not,' said Timothy.

'You couldn't have turned them all into Picts,' said Dorothea. 'Not Roger anyway.'

THEIR OWN MINE

'We couldn't have done it if there'd been more of us,' said
Dick. 'With Picts all over the place, somebody would have
been sure to get caught.'

'Oh well,' said Nancy, 'they'll be here soon, and something's sure to happen. It always does. It won't be like this when the main object is for nothing to happen at all.'

'Only burglary,' said Timothy quietly.

'That couldn't be helped,' said Nancy. 'And nobody was caught. And nobody's going to be.'

'She hasn't gone yet,' said Timothy.

'She's packing,' said Nancy.

'Do let's try to forget her,' said Dorothea.

*

After that, for quite a long time, no one mentioned the Great Aunt. No one mentioned Picts. Martyrs and Picts alike were prospectors again, crossing the blackened desert of High Topps to the mine they had themselves discovered.

'You've never seen the mine since Slater Bob and Timothy and Captain Flint really got working at it,' said Peggy. 'We haven't seen it ourselves since the Easter holidays.'

'It's come on a lot since then,' said Timothy. 'That old man's a demon for work.'

They came at last to the edge of the Gulch. It was no longer the ravine of last summer that, but for the old working half hidden by heather so that anybody might miss it if he did not know where it was, had looked as if no human being had ever explored it. The heather had been burnt by the fire, of course. But the entry was hidden now by huge piles of broken stones. Other smaller heaps of stone lay about. There were well-trodden paths from heap to heap. There was a wheelbarrow and some sort of a stone-crusher.

'Have you got all that out of it?' exclaimed Dick.

'There'll be a lot more to come,' said Timothy. 'And we've begun driving shafts down from above.'

Up on the hillside, where last summer had been Timothy's white spots painted on the rocks, were small grey piles of broken stone.

An old man, with very long arms, came out from between

the heaps in front of the entry, and blinked in the sunshine.

'Hullo!' shouted Nancy, 'there's Slater Bob.' The prospectors charged down into the Gulch.

The old man waved them back. 'You can't go in now,' he said. 'I'm firing.'

'Hang on a minute,' said Timothy.

Perhaps twenty seconds later there was a loud boom from the inside of the hill and a cloud of smoke and grey dust, stirred by the explosion, blew out of the entry to the mine.

'Blasting,' said Dick. 'Can we go in now?'

'Best let it settle,' said Slater Bob.

'What about food?' said Timothy. 'I don't want to mix copper ore with my grub and I'll be wanting to use my knapsack.'

'Let's get it over and then go in,' said Nancy.

'Have you had your dinner, Bob?' Timothy asked the old man.

'I was coming out for it now.'

'I've a bottle of beer to help it,' said Timothy.

'I generally what drink cold tea,' said the old man, 'but I don't mind a sup o' beer.'

'He means he jolly well likes it,' Nancy explained privately to Dorothea.

Knapsacks were emptied and parcels opened. There were the sandwiches Cook had made for Nancy and Peggy and an astonishing lot of food brought by Timothy . . . a parcel of cherry pies, a cold chicken, a bag of oranges, four bottles of lemonade, two bottles of beer and a cake. When the knapsacks were emptied and everything spread on the ground, it looked a feast almost too good for miners and prospectors.

'But you didn't cook that chicken in the houseboat, or those pies,' said Dorothea, remembering the state of the galley even after she had done her best with it.

'I didn't,' said Timothy. 'Eggs and bacon are my line. I ordered a few things the day I sent off those pigeons, thinking I'd be having visitors. I've a friend in the hotel by the pier. You'd have had some of these things yesterday but they didn't turn up till late last night, and I very nearly didn't get them even then. I was working, you know, and the boy who brought them said he'd been shouting from the shore for half an hour.'

'Good thing you heard him in the end,' said Nancy.

Timothy was opening the outer pocket of his knapsack. He brought out two big slabs of chocolate. 'I was forgetting Roger wasn't with us,' he said.

'We won't bother to save it for him,' said Nancy, and Dorothea thought that Nancy's way of saying 'Thank you' was not very different from old Slater Bob's.

Old Slater Bob drank his beer, but he would have none of the food the expedition had brought with them. Bread and cheese was what he had and bread and cheese was what he liked. 'I've quarried and mined for fifty years on a bit of cheese to my dinner and I don't fancy nowt else.'

They were hungry enough after the long trek, and there was nothing left of the provisions when at last Timothy and the old man, who had been talking of mining all the time, got to their feet.

'Are you going in now?' asked Dick. 'Can we come?'

'And welcome,' said the old man.

'Who's got torches?' said Timothy.

'We both have,' said Dorothea.

'The batteries are rather run down,' said Dick, and just for a moment his mind shot back to the night of the burglary.

'They'll do,' said Timothy. 'Bob's got a pretty good light.'

The old man was carrying an acetylene lantern. He turned it up, so that a bright white flame nearly dazzled them, and led the way into the old cave where Roger had found the copper.

'What's that hissing?' said Peggy.

'Water on the carbide,' said Dick, and caught Nancy's

eye, and knew that she was thinking of saying the word, 'Professor'. He did not wait to hear it, but followed Timothy and the old man into the cave. The cave was twice the size it had been when he had known it. It was as if the whole back of it had been moved farther into the hill, and in the middle of that new wall of raw stone was the opening of a tunnel four feet wide. In the cave the bright light of the lantern was answered by reflected sparks from lumps of copper ore. He heard the old man talking to Timothy, saying that he didn't think much of No. 3, but 4 and 5 were promising well. 'If some of that's not right good stuff, I don't know nowt about copper.'

'What are the numbers?' Dick asked when he got a chance. 'Are they the same as the numbers on the different lots we were working at in the houseboat?'

'That's it,' said Timothy. 'Jim numbered the sections, and what we're doing is checking up on probable yield. The stuff varies a lot. That's why I want fresh samples. Two of our results seem a bit queer.'

'Let's go on and see the place where you were blasting,' said Nancy.

'Nowt to see,' said the old man. 'Not till I've cleared the muck away.'

'Well, let's see what there is,' said Nancy.

They went on through a dark tunnel, following the lantern, most of the light from which was hidden by old Bob himself.

'There isn't any shoring,' said Dick, remembering the tunnel under Ling Scar and the wooden walls that had collapsed behind them so that they could not get back.

'Rock,' said old Bob. 'There's no soft stuff here.'

Dorothea, torch in hand, came last, throwing her light on the rough walls of rock, the roof, and the uneven floor. There was not much to see, she thought, but if old Bob and Timothy and Captain Flint had put such a lot of work into it, that prospecting of last summer must really have been a success.

Somehow, she had never believed that it would end in the working of a real mine. Even the samples on the table in the houseboat had not meant much to her, though they had to Dick. But now, walking gingerly along, not in an old abandoned passage but in a new-cut tunnel, and listening to the talk that was going on between the old man and Timothy, she knew that last summer's triumph was real and not pretence.

'Peggy,' she said, 'the Swallows'll be most awfully pleased.'

'Roger will anyway,' said Peggy. 'We'll all be sick of hearing how he found it.'

Presently they could go no farther. The tunnel was blocked by a heap of stone debris. The old man held the lantern up to let them see it. 'That's all there is to see,' he said. 'Good firing that. It's brought a gey lot down for me to clear. You mun gang out now and up the fell, if you want to see our new shafts.'

'But how is it done?' asked Dick, and a yard or two farther back in the tunnel the old man took Dick's finger and rubbed it along a narrow groove in the rock. 'That's how,' he said. 'Yon's what's left of a boring. You bore a hole to take your cartridge. You bung him in, with a long fuse to him. You set a match to the fuse and leg it for the open. Eh, I need longer fuses these days than I did when I was a lad.'

They went back through the tunnel, through the half light of the outer chamber, and so into the blazing sunshine.

'Well, we've seen our mine,' said Nancy. 'Not much to see, but Uncle Jim's as pleased as anything, so it must be all right.'

'Most awfully interesting.' said Dick, and meant it. 'Thank you very much.'

Timothy laughed. ' Better come up and see the shafts,' he said.

They climbed up out of the Gulch and up the fell, to see

that where once upon a time there had been white spots, painted by Timothy, there were now holes going down into the hill. Dick, listening to Timothy and old Bob talking of gosson and pyrites, found what he wanted without even looking for it. He had been listening, with his eyes hardly seeing a clump of heather at his feet, when something moved among the tiny purple flowers.

'Got it,' he cried.

'What is it?' said Timothy, startled, and he and the old man turned to see.

'Fox Moth caterpillar,' said Dick joyfully.

'One of they Woolly Bears,' said the old man.

'It's not really a Woolly Bear,' said Dick seriously. 'The woolly bear's a Tiger Moth.' He took his box out of his knapsack, cut some heather with his knife and put it in, carefully lifted the caterpillar from the heather, dropped it in the box, and wiped his hands on the ground.

'Why do you do that?' said Nancy.

'It's the hairs,' said Dick. 'If you touch one and then touch the back of your other hand or your cheek, it starts itching like anything.'

'Good old Professor,' said Nancy.

'How many do you want?' asked Peggy. 'Here are two more close together.'

'Three's enough,' said Dick. 'It's no good getting more. They eat a lot of heather. I say, I'm awfully glad we found them. I promised one to another chap at school, and he's getting me a Poplar Hawk in exchange. There are some where he lives.'

Collecting caterpillars, looking at the mine, listening to Timothy and Slater Bob, seeing far away buzzards floating round the distant crags, fairly cleared the Great Aunt out of all their minds. Picts forgot that their existence was a secret. Martyrs forgot their hardships. Once more, they were prospectors, pirates, explorers, naturalists and what not, looking out over the hills and afraid of nothing in the world that stretched below them in the sunshine.

There was still much of the day before them, and when Timothy had stowed away his samples in two little canvas bags and put them in his knapsack, they said 'Good-bye' to the old miner and went off across High Topps to visit last year's camp. They found Titty's well, with water still bubbling up into it, tidied the stones round its edge, one or two of which had fallen in, and then went down through the wood to Mrs Tyson's.

Here, of course, there was great talk about the fire on the fell, and of how the pigeon had carried a message in time to bring Colonel Jolys and his firefighters. Mrs Tyson would not hear of their going on without a cup of tea. 'Aye,' she said. 'You did us a good turn that day, you and your pigeons, and me going on at you for setting the Topps afire. I was right ashamed after, and I said so to your mother. And how is Mrs Blackett? Poorly she's been by what I hear.'

'She's all right now,' said Nancy. 'And she's coming home the day after tomorrow.'

'I've a pot of honey for her,' said Mrs Tyson. 'Happen you'll take it.'

'Thank you very much,' said Peggy.

'And where are all the others?' asked Mrs Tyson. 'We'll be glad to see you all again.'

'They'll be here next week,' said Nancy.

'Let's hope the weather'll hold for them. This summer's not like yon. Eh, that was a summer for fires. It was a lucky thing for us, you getting Colonel Jolys here so quick. When I heard his horns blowing I couldn't believe it, and me thinking they were far side o' t'lake, and no one to know owt was doing till all was burnt.'

At last they set out on the long trek home. Unwilling to separate, but thinking that it would hardly be wise for Martyrs, Picts and a Suspicious Character to risk being seen together on the road, they left it and came back, as they had gone, along the top of the wood that hid the Picts' hut. They went beyond the hut, because Nancy and Peggy had to get round to the river to bring *Amazon* back into the boathouse. Then they came slowly down the wood together.

'Go ahead, you two,' said Timothy to Nancy and Peggy. 'I'll give you a minute or two to get clear across the road.'

'It's been a lovely day,' said Dorothea.

'Only one more night,' said Nancy, 'and then we'll have one good day after another. Come on, Peg. We've got to get into pretties for supper. It's the last time, and, remember, when she says she would like a little music, you've got to look eager. Tonight, we've got to be better than perfect.'

'Good luck to you,' said Timothy with a smile.

And at that moment they heard someone talking on the road below them.

'Careful scouting,' said Nancy, and began going quickly down, dodging from tree to tree.

'Better sit tight,' said Timothy, but Peggy was already creeping down after Nancy.

'They're much better at it than we are,' said Dorothea.

'Nancy's slipped,' said Dick, as a sudden noise of breaking twigs came from below.

And then they heard Cook calling out, 'Miss Turner! Miss Turner! Is that you?' Dick and Dorothea looked at each other and then at Timothy. All three had heard the note of panic in Cook's voice.

CHAPTER 25

TOTALLY DISAPPEARED

'SOMETHING's happened,' said Dorothea.

Timothy was already hurrying down. Dick and Dorothea hurried after him. They were in time to see Nancy and Peggy scramble over the wall into the road, where Cook was standing wringing her hands. A young man in gardening clothes was standing beside her scratching his head with one hand and twiddling an old yachting cap with the other.

'Eh, thank goodness you've come back,' they heard Cook say. 'Isn't you aunt with you?'

'Of course she isn't. We've been to High Topps.'

'She's gone,' said Cook.

'But where? When? How?'

'Nay, if I knew that I wouldn't be in such a scrow. Two o'clock she was away and it's seven now, and Billy here was the last to see her in this world. . . .'

'Hey, Timothy!' called Nancy. 'Oh good, you're here . . .'

'Mr Stedding'll know what best to do,' said Cook.

'But what's all this?' said Timothy.

'It's me to blame,' said Billy Lewthwaite, putting on his yachting cap and touching it as he spoke and then desperately scratching his head again. 'Forgetting about looking in tank what with Miss Turner waiting to be off.'

'But off where?' said Nancy. 'What happened?'

'She had her lunch,' said Cook. 'And then she sent me for Billy to drive the car for her. She was in a tearing scrow to be off. Stiff as a poker she was and waiting with her blue parasol and all, while I run to Mrs Lewthwaite's. And by the time I come back Billy'd fetched the car out and away with her. Little I thought I'd never see her again when she passed me by the gate, sitting up there looking neither right nor left.'

'But where was she going? Billy must know where he took her.'

'She told me to take t'lake road and go along for Swainson's,' said Billy. 'And I was in a fair muzz with her being at me because I'd only me chauffeur's cap and hadn't thought for to take me blue coat what with being in a hurry like. We'd not gone above a mile likely when the engine went funny, and then it stopped, and with her asking questions and all, I was a bit before I found what was gone with it. All t'plugs out and back. Tank was empty. That was all. And she sent me running back to fetch some petrol, and there wasn't a drop in t'garage.'

'And Billy went off on your bike,' said Cook, 'and fetched a can from head o' t'lake.'

'Bother the petrol,' said Nancy. 'Where did you take her?'

'I come back,' said Billy, 'and there was t'owd car where I'd left it at t'side o' t'road, and nobody in it. She was gone. I'd left her sitting in it looking like as if she'd be glad to take a spanner to me. And when I come back she was clean gone.'

Dorothea was watching Billy with interest. Funny to be making such a fuss just because an old lady had grown tired of waiting in the car and had gone for a walk. But nothing that had to do with the Great Aunt was really funny. Billy Lewthwaite looked ... How did he look? Dorothea asked herself. She knew he must be the policeman's brother, but he looked almost as if he were a nephew of the Great Aunt. Worried. And anybody could see that Cook was really frightened.

'What did you do?' asked Timothy quietly.

Dorothea saw Nancy give him a queer look. She did not know that Nancy had suddenly been reminded of the time of the fire, when the shy Timothy had stopped being shy altogether and had taken charge and led the rescue party that had dashed across the smouldering heather.

'I didn't do nowt,' said Billy. 'I emped the petrol in, and I sat there waiting for her. I thought, maybe, she'd gone for a bit of a walk like.'

'And then?'

'She didn't come and she didn't come, and I thought, maybe she's wanting me to come after her. So I went along in the car, watching out to see her in t'road. Matter of two mile I went. And then it come over me that happen she'd walked t'other way, and gone back to Beckfoot to her tea, and likely been sitting there when I left the bike and went running on wi' t'petrol. I thought, by gum, she'll give me a proper blacking, but best get it over soon as late, so I turned t'owd car round and brought it back. It's in t'yard now.' And Billy turned to take them to the yard as if the sight of old Rattletrap would help them to understand.

Nobody seemed to remember now that it was unsafe for the Picts or for Timothy to go through the Beckfoot gateway. They all went through and into the yard, and stared at the old car as if they, too, were thinking like Billy.

'Where was she sitting?' asked Dick.

'Back seat, off side,' said Billy.

Dick opened the door and looked carefully about. But there were no clues to be seen.

'What was that place she mentioned?' asked Timothy.

'Swainson's.'

'What is it?'

'It's a farmhouse,' said Nancy. 'Friends. Old Mr Swainson used to be the best huntsman years ago and Mrs Swainson makes patchwork quilts. The G.A. knows them very well. That's where the Swallows stayed one year. At least they didn't stay there, but they camped up above.'

'Did you go and ask there?' said Timothy to Billy.

'Nay. I'd turned back before that.'

'It's worth trying,' said Timothy. 'Hop in, and we'll

go there now and ask. You'd better come too, Nancy. If she's there, I'll just fade away and walk back.'

'She's been away a long time now,' said Cook. 'Nay, there's worse than that gone wrong. You'll not find her at Swainson's. Loss of memory, that's what it is. Wandering. Up on t'fells likely enough. And dark coming on.'

'Shut up, Cook,' said Nancy, with a glance at Peggy and Dorothea.

'I've a feeling in my bones,' said Cook.

'She'll be back here in half an hour,' said Timothy, as Billy, whirling the rusty crank, stirred old Rattletrap to life. Timothy was already sitting where the Great Aunt had sat. Nancy, looking grave, climbed in beside him. Billy Lewthwaite slipped into his place in front, straightened his cap, and drove out of the yard.

*

'I say,' said Dick, 'do you think we ought to be here?'

'Pretty awful if she were to come in and find you,' said Peggy. 'I'll come up to the hut with you and we'll wait there.'

'You don't stir out of Beckfoot, Miss Peggy,' said Cook. 'Not till we know what's gone with her. Eh, for this to happen, with the mistress away and all.'

'We'd better go,' said Dorothea.

'You bide where you are,' said Cook. 'You come into my kitchen.'

'Yes, do,' said Peggy. 'We'll see from the window when they bring her back. We can easily get you out. And there's the larder to hide in. And the pantry.'

'There's nowt for you to fear now,' said Cook. 'They'll be bringing her back feet foremost.'

'Steady on, Cooky darling,' said Peggy. 'She's probably sitting with old Mrs Swainson telling her there's something wrong about something.'

Cook laughed in spite of herself. 'Telling her she's setting the wrong way about making patchwork quilts, likely. Mrs Swainson'll give her a flea in her ear.' The thought seemed to cheer her.

'We really ought to go back to our house,' said Dorothea. 'I've got supper to get ready.'

'You bide where you are,' said Cook again. 'I'll have supper for you. You can eat it in my kitchen. Not but what you've a right to eat it anywhere. Didn't Mrs Blackett invite you? Eh, you should never have gone out to that old ruin, nor shouldn't if Miss Nancy hadn't fair rushed me off my feet, and me in a scow with Miss Turner coming where she wasn't invited nor yet wanted.'

'I'd better go up to the hut anyway,' said Dick. 'Just to look.'

'Why?' asked Peggy.

'Just to make sure she isn't there,' said Dick. 'Supposing she's found out about us? Supposing she's sitting in the hut, waiting to catch us when we come back?'

'Rot,' said Peggy. 'Why did she take Rattletrap the other way?'

'She didn't stay in the car,' said Dick. 'I think I'd better go and see.'

'I wouldn't put it past her,' said Cook suddenly. 'And if she's there, as good find her now as later.'

Dorothea, looking at Cook, knew that if she was jumping at straws like this, she must be really worried lest something much more serious had happened.

'We'll all go,' she said.

Peggy who, now that Nancy was away, was doing her best to fill her place, put her foot down firmly. 'Jibbooms and bobstays,' she said, in quite the Nancy manner, 'if she's there it's all the more reason why you shouldn't walk straight into her jaws. I'll go. You stay here. I'll scout round pretty carefully and if she's there I'll come back and we'll wait for Nancy. Nancy'll know what we'd better do.'

'But if she sees you?' said Dick.

'I've come to look for her,' said Peggy. 'It'll be all right her seeing me. Better if she doesn't, of course. But it would be ten million times worse if she saw you.'

'Eh, but I hope you find her,' said Cook. 'But come back quick. I don't want another lost. And if she comes back with Miss Nancy, she'll be asking for you. Not that it's likely. It's in my bones there's more than that amiss. Just as I was thinking we were through the worst, with her going to-morrow. She was bad enough before, but what with her burglary and police and all ... eh, I'd have done better to walk out the day she come, and so I would if it hadn't been for thinking of Mrs Blackett. Now you come in, you two, and sit you down out of sight from the door ... though she isn't one to be coming in by any door but the front.'

'Back in ten minutes,' said Peggy and hurried away.

Dorothea and Dick followed Cook up the steps out of the yard and into the kitchen. They hung about watching her bustling round, muttering to herself, slamming knives and forks on the kitchen table, fetching cold meat from the larder, popping potatoes in a saucepan, and stopping every now and then to listen, as if at any moment she thought she might hear Miss Turner's footsteps somewhere in the house.

'She might have seen a bird while she was waiting,' said Dick, 'and got out of the car to have a better view, and sat down to watch it and fallen asleep.'

'She can't have gone far from the road,' said Dorothea. 'But she's not the sort of person to be interested in birds.'

They heard footsteps in the yard, but it was only Peggy coming back.

'Nobody there,' she said. 'I've been right into the hut.'

'Hadn't we better go then?' said Dorothea.

'Wait for Nancy,' said Peggy.

'But if the Great Aunt comes home with her?'

Peggy said nothing. She was listening, and they knew that Peggy, like Cook, was feeling in her bones that something had gone seriously wrong.

'They're gone a gey long time,' said Cook.

It was growing dusk when at last they heard the tinny hooting of Rattletrap's horn and then the noise of the old car turning in at the Beckfoot gate.

'You bide still,' said Cook, as Dick and Dorothea jumped to their feet, looking round for a hiding place. 'They'll stop at the front door if they've found her. . . . Nay, I knew they hadn't.' With a rattle and a squawk of the brakes the old car had pulled up in the yard. Billy Lewthwaite, Timothy and Nancy were getting out. All three were looking grave.

'She's not been to Swainson's,' said Nancy.

'You don't think she's found out about us and gone off in a rage?' said Dorothea.

'We've been right down to the foot of the lake and asked,' said Timothy.

'We thought of that,' said Nancy, 'but I knew she'd never go from that station anyway, because of all the changes. She never does. We saw old Carrotty, the porter, and he said he hadn't seen her for three or four years.'

'He knows her,' Peggy explained to Dorothea. 'He used to work here years ago.'

'If only I'd ha' looked in yon tank,' said Billy. 'Everybody'll be on to me about it.'

'She was all right when you left her,' said Timothy. 'You're not to blame.'

'Supper's waiting when all's said and done,' said Cook. 'You slip along to your mother's, Billy. She'll be wondering what's gone with you.'

'Shall I say owt to Sammy if he's at home?'

Police again. Nancy, Peggy, the Picts and Timothy looked at each other.

'If she doesn't turn up soon, I shall have to ring up the sergeant myself,' said Timothy.

*

Supper at the table in the kitchen was a grim meal. Having it there at all showed how wrong things were. Dick and Dorothea were feeling they had no right to be in the house. Timothy, of course, had even less, but he had told Cook that he did not mean to leave until Miss Turner had been found. Nancy and Peggy were feeling that a Great Aunt spending all her time in trying to improve them was better than a Great Aunt who had disappeared.

'If she wanted to vanish,' said Nancy, 'she might have waited another two days. If she disappeared at Harrogate or somewhere people would simply say "Three Cheers" or "R.I.P." and have a celebration. But disappearing here, when we've kept her happy all the time, and only one day to go before she clears out properly . . . Oh, Giminy, Giminy! What will Mother say?'

'She'll turn up all right,' said Timothy.

'She may be doing it on purpose,' said Dorothea.

'Better tell the police,' said Cook, putting a treacle tart on the table in front of Timothy. 'They'll drag for her.'

Timothy frowned. 'Nothing like that,' he said.

'Of course, she might have tumbled in the lake,' said Dick.

'But it's quite shallow at the edges,' said Nancy.

'Much more likely she went for a stroll while waiting for that petrol,' said Timothy. 'She may have sat down and fallen asleep. . . .'

'She always did sleep in the afternoons,' said Nancy hopefully. 'Or nearly always.'

'The doctor told her to,' said Peggy.

'We'll ring up that doctor if she doesn't turn up soon,' said Timothy.

'She isn't one subject to fits,' said Cook.

*

'No good your waiting,' said Timothy when supper was over. 'You two had better clear off to your house in the wood.'

'What are you going to do?' asked Nancy.

'Stay here,' said Timothy. 'With Jim and your mother away, I'd better be on hand in case something needs doing. There wasn't a sign of her all along the road. If she doesn't walk in soon, I'll have to telephone to the police.'

'But you'll be getting arrested for burglary,' said Dorothea.

'Who cares?' said Timothy. 'We'll have to have a regular search and the more men they can send the better. The police are the only people for a job like that with thick woods all over the place.

Nancy's face suddenly lit up.

'Colonel Jolys,' she exclaimed. 'I'll go and ring him up at once. He'll be lots better than the police. There hasn't been a fell fire for ages and there won't be after all that rain. They'll be delighted at the chance of really doing something, and there are hundreds of them.'

'Hundreds of what?' asked Timothy.

'Firefighters,' said Nancy. 'You saw them last year. Colonel Jolys has them all trained. They sound horns and everybody who's got a motor car loads up as many as he can carry and they go wherever they're wanted. They'll search the whole of the woods in no time while the police are just mooning about taking notes.'

'It's not a bad idea,' said Timothy. 'But we'll talk to the police first. Here. Clear out, all four of you. You take these two home and come back.'

*

Picts and Martyrs groped their way up the wood together.
Dick lit the hurricane lantern in the hut. Dorothea set about
lighting the fire.

'Aren't you going to bed?' said Peggy.

'Not just yet,' said Dorothea. 'We simply can't. I know
why Timothy wanted to get rid of us.'

'Why?' asked Nancy.

'He thinks something really awful's happened and he
didn't want us to hear what he was going to say to the police.'

'I wish we'd never gone out today,' said Peggy.

'So do I,' said Nancy. 'I ought to have guessed something awful was going to happen when she was so jolly
ready to let us go. It wasn't natural. It was almost as if she
wanted to be alone.'

'You don't think she'd found out about us?' said Dorothea.

'Of course not,' said Nancy. 'If she had, she'd have been
up here first thing, instead of doing her packing. She's
never guessed a thing about you or she wouldn't have been
keeping on so about the Swallows. No. It's something else
altogether.'

'We'd better go back,' said Peggy. 'In case she's come.'

'If she has,' said Dorothea, 'do you think you could . . .?'

'If there's any news, we'll come up and tell you at once,'
said Nancy, 'even if it means breaking out by force.' And
with that she and Peggy hurried off in the dark, and left Dick
and Dorothea to themselves.

*

Dick and Dorothea sat by their fire. There was nothing
they could do to help but going to bed seemed impossible.
Dick looked at his caterpillars, put his box in a cool place,
came back to the fire and tried to read about Fox Moths in
Common Objects of the Country. There was a good picture of
them but it was blurred for him by pictures of the Great Aunt
talking on the lawn, of the Great Aunt lying with a broken

ankle, waiting to be found, of the Great Aunt hearing Timothy, Nancy and Billy pass close by in the motor car and being somehow unable to call out to them, pictures that he could not help seeing.

'They ought to be able to find her,' he said suddenly.

'They could,' said Dorothea, 'if only they could get into her mind. But nobody knows why she went out at all. It was after her lunch. It was when she's supposed to lie down. Why did she go out instead? And with the motor car? If we only knew that there would be somewhere to start.'

'I don't believe they properly looked for tracks,' said Dick.

'There wouldn't be any in the road.'

'But she must have gone off the road and there'd be tracks in the grass. They'll have to look for them tomorrow.'

'It may be too late,' said Dorothea.

'I know,' said Dick.

It was long after midnight when they heard footsteps outside. Nancy and Peggy had come up again from Beckfoot.

'I knew you'd be still up,' said Nancy. 'Timothy said you'd be asleep.'

'Has she come back?' asked Dorothea.

'No,' said Nancy. 'Cook's sitting in the kitchen with the door open. Timothy's just gone for another walk along the lake road. Cook wanted us to go to bed, but I thought we'd just come up and tell you. The police'll be here first thing in the morning. And I did telephone to Colonel Jolys. He was as pleased as Punch. I knew he would be. Not about her being lost, of course, though Mother says he hated her when he was young, but because of being able to have a go at finding her. He's coming with all his men. He says they'll comb the whole place. He's coming with everyone he can get unless she turns up during the night. Timothy says the police think she probably will.'

'If she's lost her memory she may be anywhere,' said Dorothea, 'and probably thinking she's somebody else.'

'She isn't like that,' said Nancy.

'She may be awfully ill,' said Peggy, 'or even dead.'

'No,' said Nancy.

'You don't think she's run away on purpose?' said Dick.

'What from?' said Nancy. 'She's been having the time of her life. One long orgy of bossiness. We've made her jolly happy.'

'It can't be that,' said Peggy. 'She'd done all her packing ready for going away, and Cook heard her telephoning to arrange with somebody to come at one o'clock to take her to the train, and she told Cook she'd be wanting sandwiches to take with her.'

'Something simply must have happened to her,' said Dorothea.

'And the very last day,' said Nancy. 'And we'd managed so jolly well. We'd almost got accustomed to her ourselves. And . . . And she really was pretty sporting when she thought that Dick was a full-sized burglar.'

The Great Aunt lost was beginning to seem a very different character from the Great Aunt invading Beckfoot in holiday time and having her own way about everything.

'Well,' said Nancy at last, 'you'd better go to bed now. We all will, or we'll be no use in hunting for her tomorrow. Come on, Peggy. Good night. Jibbooms and bobstays! It'll be daylight in a few more hours. Good night . . .'

'She's quite right,' said Dick, when they could no longer hear the footsteps going down the moonlit wood. 'I'm going to bed. I'm going to sleep thinking about the Great Aunt. It often works with mathematics. I've often done it. You go to sleep thinking about a sum and wake up to find you know what you've done wrong.'

Dorothea, before climbing into her hammock, looked out at the ghostly trees.

'It's a warm night,' she said. 'That's one good thing.'

CHAPTER 26

THE HUNT IS UP

THE sound of a coach-horn waked them in the morning. Another horn sounded and then another, making the cheerful noise that used in coaching days to echo through these hills. The sounds came from far away, towards the head of the lake.

'It's the firefighters. They're coming,' said Dorothea, rolling out of her hammock and going to the door of the hut. Already the sun was high in the sky and the clearing was dappled with shadows from the trees.

Dick reached up for his spectacles from the beam above his head, slid down and joined Dorothea. He was remembering the day last summer when High Topps was ablaze and the fire was sweeping across heather and bracken towards the woods and the farms below. The sound of the horns had meant help then, and help just before it was too late. This time . . .

'She hasn't come back or Nancy'd have telephoned to stop them,' he said.

'She'd been out all night,' said Dorothea. 'Lying with a broken leg, too weak to shout or even move. It's a good thing they make such a noise. She'll hear them, too, and know that help is coming.'

Again the horns sounded.

'They're nearer now,' said Dick. 'They must be close to the bridge. They'll be coming along the road in a minute. Let's go down.'

'We'd better not,' said Dorothea. 'Not till Nancy or Peggy comes up from Beckfoot.'

'If there are hundreds of people looking for her, it'll be safe for us to look, too. We ought to have a try for footprints along the edge of the road where they found the empty car.'

'It would be lovely if you did find them,' said Dorothea. 'And then the rescuer would have to slip away without giving his name . . . I could make a story like that, where the one who does the rescue simply can't give his name because he's wanted by the police.'

'There go the firefighters,' said Dick, as the horns sounded from the road below them. 'Four motor cars at least. And listen. There are lots more coming . . .'

More and more coach-horns were sounding far away.

'We'd better get dressed at once and have breakfast. You go and get the mugs. They've been rinsing in the beck since breakfast yesterday. And get washed at the same time. And fill the kettle. What's that?' A deep, booming bark from the direction of Beckfoot startled them both.

'It's not an ordinary sheep-dog,' said Dick. 'And it's not . . .'

'It's the police,' said Dorothea. 'They've brought a bloodhound. I suppose they always do when anybody gets lost.'

*

They were washed, dressed and ready for anything, but there was still no sign of Peggy or Nancy. The kettle was boiling, the cornflakes had been waiting for some time, and Dorothea had filled the saucepan and pushed it in at the side of the fire to be ready for the eggs, when, at last, Jacky came up with the milk.

'Have you heard what's oop?' he panted. 'You should be down at Beckfoot. They've the firefighters out and the police and all. Sergeant's brought his bloodhound. And my dad's coming with our Bess. She's a right clever dog. Hasn't nobody told you? There's owd Miss Turner made away wi' herself, that's what my mother says. They're going to hunt the woods for her, and if they don't find her they'll be dragging t'lake. Eh, but I hope they'll let me go in t'boat.'

'I'm sure she hasn't killed herself,' said Dorothea.

'That's what my dad says. He says she'll have got herself cragfast or brambled like, so's she can't move, same's a sheep.'

'Just lying and waiting to be found,' said Dorothea.

'Happen they'll find her, happen they won't,' said Jacky. 'I'se off to see.' And with that Jacky, forgetting in his hurry even to take the empty milk bottle, dashed off to join the hunt.

They ate their breakfast and then could wait no longer, but slipped cautiously down the path towards the road. They were nearing the bottom of the wood when they heard footsteps coming up. It was the postman, with a letter addressed to Dorothea. 'I didn't leave it in the wall,' he said. 'I wanted a word with you. You haven't seen owt of Miss Turner?'

'No,' said Dorothea.

'She's not up with you in yon hut?' said the postman. 'I thought I'd make sure. I wouldn't put it past them two lasses of Mrs Blackett's to be hiding her away. With their skulls and crossbones and all. Kidnapping. Prisoner or summat. With them two limbs you never know.'

'They didn't have anything to do with it,' said Dorothea.

'So you think,' said the postman. 'And what about that man breaking into Beckfoot? Sammy tells me there wasn't a man about the place at all, just them two limbs at their games. And a nice trouble they'll have made for me if it comes out about my bringing your letters and keeping all dark about Miss Turner saying you wasn't known.'

'But they were our letters,' said Dorothea. 'And nobody'll ever find out about them.'

'Poor lookout for me if they do,' said the postman. 'I've told myself a dozen times I should have out right away and told Miss Turner that you two and them two were up to game. But Miss Nancy's too quick. She has you in trouble with one foot, and before you can lift out you're opp to t'neck.

And then for this to happen. The sergeant's over on this side, and the firefighters and all. They'll be asking one question after another and if one thing don't come out another will.'

'It'll be all right if they find her,' said Dorothea. 'She's going today.'

'Ay, but will they? And there's Mrs Blackett coming back tomorrow. I saw the postcard. And what'll she say? It's a sad trouble for her to come back to and all. Well, I've kept my mouth shut so far . . .'

'You mustn't let out about the letters now,' said Dorothea urgently.

'I can't do nowt else but keep quiet. It's other folk's tongues I'm fearing. There's too many folk know too much. There's the folk at Watersmeet for one. There's young Jacky with a tongue that'd talk the hind leg off a Herdwick sheep. And Mrs Lewthwaite's been cracking away with Mrs Braithwaite. She knows, and her Billy, and Sammy by now like enough. They're all in it, but there's only got to be one word said and they'll all be talking to save theirselves and let other folk take the blame. And there was I thinking all was right, with Miss Turner going away today and Mrs Blackett coming back.'

And the postman, gloomily shaking his head, stumped off again down the path to his bicycle in the road.

'We've just not got to be seen,' said Dorothea.

'But if we can't be seen, how can I look for those tracks?' said Dick.

'It can't be helped,' said Dorothea.

She opened her letter. It was just an ordinary pleasant, happy letter from their mother, telling them that their father was nearly through with his examination papers and looking forward to coming north and being given sailing lessons by the captain and mate of the *Scarab*. It hoped that Mrs Blackett would come back all the better for her holiday, and that everything had gone perfectly so that she would feel glad she had invited them. It said there were more underclothes coming for both of them.

'If she only knew,' said Dorothea, 'how dreadful everything's going to be.'

More motor cars passed on the road below them.

'I simply must go down and see what's happening,' said Dick.

'We won't go out on the road at all,' said Dorothea. 'We'll go along through the trees, so that we can keep out of sight, and be near enough to the road to catch Nancy or Peggy if they're on their way to our house.'

Twenty yards above the road they dodged through the hazel bushes and young birches. Below them was the fringe of larches and pines at the bottom of the wood. It would have been easier walking on the smooth carpet of brown needles, but not so safe. At the edge of the coppice, though all the time they had to be pushing branches out of their way, they had only to sit down and stay still to be invisible, while they themselves could see down between the tree trunks to the low wall and the road beyond it.

There was a tremendous noise of people talking near the Beckfoot gate, and every few minutes yet another car came along the road. Presently they could see a whole row of cars waiting.

'I'm not going any nearer,' said Dorothea.

Lurking low and looking down through the larches opposite the house they saw a shortish, stout man, with a hunting-horn on a sling about his shoulders, get into an open motor car and stand up on the seat. There was a sudden silence.

'That's Colonel Jolys himself,' said Dorothea.

'I expect all those men are firefighters,' said Dick. 'Or most of them. There's Jacky, close to Colonel Jolys's car.'

'Shut up, Dick. Listen. What's he saying?'

284

AT THE BECKFOOT GATE

The Colonel, for all that he was a smallish man, had a big, carrying voice.

'Now, men,' he boomed. 'We want one chap to every fifty yards. Ten to a team. That's five hundred yards a team. We start at the lake shore, and work up the woods to the fell.

Each team leader sounds his horn from time to time so that we can keep in touch, and the moment she's found the nearest leader gives a single, long blast, as long as he can blow. Understand? Our usual coach calls to each other, and a single, long blast when she's found . . . like this . . .' He reached down into the car and took up a long, straight coach-horn, not like the curved hunting-horn he carried to signal to his men. He put it to his lips and blew . . . on . . . and on . . . and on.

'He'll burst,' said Dick at last.

But the Colonel only got very red. He did not burst and even from where they were crouching, Dick and Dorothea could see that he was thinking he could still blow a good blast for his age.

'Off you go,' he shouted, after waiting a moment to get his breath. 'Drop your men by numbers, fifty yards apart.'

There was a great noise of starting engines. One or two of the leaders blew their horns to call their teams together. Men were piling into the cars, and one after another the cars moved off.

'There's Nancy,' said Dick. 'And look how she's dressed!'

'That's to please the Great Aunt if they find her . . . She's getting into Colonel Jolys's car . . . Peggy too . . . They aren't coming up for us at all. We'd better go back . . .'

'That blue car's police,' said Dick. 'I say, just look at the bloodhound. They'll take it to the place where the car was left and start from there. There won't be any need to look for tracks. Look. That policeman's got a cloak or something. Hers, to give the bloodhound a taste of the right scent.'

'There's Timothy, just come out of the gate. He's talking to Colonel Jolys. He's going, too.'

'No, he isn't. They're off. Timothy's stopping behind. For fear of meeting her. It would be pretty awful if he did.'

Colonel Jolys's car, with Nancy and Peggy sitting beside the Colonel, four men crammed into the back and two more standing on the running-boards, moved off after the blue police car with the bloodhound. Another car, crowded with men, followed the Colonel's. Carload after carload of men was getting under way. They saw that Jacky had managed to find a place.

'Why is Cook crying?' said Dick, seeing her standing at the Beckfoot gate, looking down the road and mopping her eyes with her apron.

Dorothea did not answer. Somehow seeing all those cars moving off to hunt for the Great Aunt had made her own eyes inclined to blink ... not for any reason, she told herself angrily, but she could not help it.

'I say,' said Dick, 'I never saw Rattletrap.'

'Timothy'll be going in that,' said Dorothea.

The last car was gone. They saw Timothy, talking to Cook, who turned and went in through the gate. Timothy, alone in the road, set off, almost at a run, in the opposite direction to that taken by the hunt.

'He's going to our house,' said Dorothea. 'Stop him.'

Dick plunged out of the hazels and raced along through the larches.

'Hullo!' he called quietly, and then again, a little louder.

Timothy stopped short, looked up and down the road, caught sight of Dick, jumped over the wall and came up into the wood to meet them. His eyes were tired. He had not shaved. He looked as if he had been up all night, as indeed he had, except for a few minutes when he had fallen asleep in a chair by the kitchen fire.

'Good,' he said. 'No one's seen you? I was just coming up to tell you what we think you'd better do. It's like this. If we don't find her where we think she is, in the wood at the side of the road, those lads will be hunting here, there and everywhere, and if they come on you, they'll be asking questions. We don't want to have to do any explaining to anybody if we can help it. I wish to goodness Nancy hadn't ... but it's no good talking about that. I'm to blame, too ...' He brushed a hand across his forehead. 'Nancy meant well, and so did you, and it wouldn't have mattered if nothing had gone wrong. But when there's trouble it always means a whole lot of questions that otherwise wouldn't be asked. You're best out of the way. Yes. Yes. Nancy agrees.'

'Do you think Miss Turner's all right?' asked Dorothea.

'Sure she is,' said Timothy. 'Broken ankle, perhaps. Anything. That doctor says there's nothing wrong with her heart. That was what I was afraid of. She may have called on a friend and stayed the night. She may turn up at any minute. Don't you worry about that. The main thing is we've got to keep you out of her way. Out of everybody's way. There really might be a bit to explain if she met you.'

'But where can we go?' asked Dorothea.

'There's only one place where you'll be sure of meeting nobody. You can slip down to your boat now. They've all gone the other way. Nobody about. Off you go. Get your boat and go and wait for me on Jim's houseboat. Plenty of grub there. Everything but matches. Take a box with you. Key's in the door. You slip out and away. Once you're on the lake there'll be no one to ask questions. Go along to the houseboat. . . . Take what you can put in a knapsack, so that you can doss down there if you have to. But go now. I'll be along as soon as I can. I'll see that anything you leave in that hut's all right. Understand?'

'Yes,' said Dick.

'Yes,' said Dorothea.

'You see the one thing that mustn't happen is for you to meet the old lady.'

CHAPTER 27

THE ONE THING THAT MUSTN'T HAPPEN

THEY did exactly what they had been told. Dorothea packed their pyjamas and washing things and two boxes of matches into her knapsack, adding at the last moment one of her exercise books. Dick, in case they might not come back for some days, took his collecting box with the caterpillars in it, as well as the telescope, and *Scarab*'s flag, and Knight's *Sailing*. Other things were hurriedly stowed in their suitcases. These they locked. Now and then, while they were packing, they heard the sound of distant horns. The hunt had begun. They took a last glance round to see if there was anything they had forgotten. They went out with the odd feeling of deserting an old home. Dick tied up the door with a bit of string, as it had been on the day they had first seen it.

'Of course anybody could get in at the window if they wanted,' said Dorothea.

'Or untie the string,' said Dick.

Not another word was said as the Picts left what had been their home for ten days, and hurried down the wood, and so to *Scarab* lying in her reedy harbour.

They poled her out into the lagoon, where Dick took the oars and rowed fast down the river. As they left the shelter of the trees and looked up across the lawn, Beckfoot might have been an empty house but for the curtains in the windows. They saw no one.

'Timothy's gone after the others,' said Dick.

'Cook's sobbing in the kitchen,' said Dorothea. 'She's thinking of Mrs Blackett and having to tell her what's happened.'

'I think I could have got out of that window,' said Dick, 'and she wouldn't have seen me. But if I had I couldn't have got in again after she shut it and we wouldn't have had the things he wanted most.'

'Nothing's going to matter now,' said Dorothea.

'If only she'd waited till she got to Harrogate,' said Dick.

'If she's broken her ankle,' said Dorothea, 'she'll be here for ages, waiting till it mends.'

They passed the Beckfoot boathouse, with the faded skull and crossbones, and thirty yards farther down the river saw *Amazon*, pulled up, where she had been left the day before.

'Nancy must be in an awful stew,' said Dick, 'not to have come down and put her away.'

He rowed gloomily on until, out in the lake, with the sail to set, they forgot for a moment the troubles that were closing down on Picts and Martyrs alike. Dorothea fitted the rudder in its place and waited, ready to steer, while Dick pulled *Scarab* round till she was heading straight into the southerly wind. He had made everything ready before leaving harbour. He stowed his oars and seized the halliard. 'Now,' he said, and hauled up the sail. 'Keep her going on the port . . . no . . . the starboard tack. Slack out just a bit while I haul down the boom. Tighten it in again. She's off.' He lowered the centreboard. 'Good. That's the best we've done yet. Now for the flag . . . I ought to have had it up before . . .'

'Do you think we ought to have a flag?' said Dorothea, her mind flying back to what was happening on shore, and thinking, if they had a flag at all, that perhaps they ought to hoist it to half-mast.

'It'll be awfully hard to sail without it,' said Dick. 'The book says you ought to sail by the feel of the wind on your cheek, but I'm sure I can't . . . not yet. And you can't either.'

'We'll have the flag,' said Dorothea. 'Of course we can

have it. We're not supposed to have anything to do with Beckfoot. We're just a boat, sailing on the lake.'

'Good,' said Dick, and set about bending the little flagstaff to the flag halliards. This was the only thing that did not go like clockwork. Somehow, while he was hauling it up, the flagstaff turned upside down, and then entangled itself at the masthead. He hauled it down again. 'I ought to keep just a little strain downwards even while hauling it up,' he said to himself. 'And it ought to go up steadily, not in jerks.' The second try came off all right, and the green beetle on its white ground blew merrily out above the top of the mast as if nothing was the matter anywhere in the world. Dick made a neat coil of the end of the main halliard, arranged the oars one each side, with their blades meeting in the bows, and turned to take the tiller.

At the sight of Dorothea's earnest face, watching the sail to see that it was full, watching the flag to see that she was not sailing farther off the wind than she needed, he changed his mind and sat down on the middle thwart on the windward side of the boat. Dorothea was doing very well, and the mate ought to be able to handle the ship as well as the captain.

The faraway noise of a horn startled them both. For some time they had heard nothing of the hunt. For a moment they thought the Great Aunt had been found. But they remembered there was to be a long blast for that, and this was a regular coach call. It was answered by another and yet another a long way down the lake, the firefighters signalling to each other. Then there was silence again.

'Look out, Dot. She's right off the wind.'

'Sorry. Let's go round.'

'All right.'

Dick looked critically at the swirl in the water where *Scarab* had come about, but he did not say anything.

That first tack had taken them across the lake to the opposite shore. With Dorothea steering, and thinking not only of the wind in the sail but also of the search for the Great Aunt, *Scarab* had not done as well as she might, and when they crossed the lake again they found themselves still quite near the Beckfoot promontory.

'You'd better take her for a bit,' said Dorothea.

Dick changed places with her.

'I'll take fairly short tacks,' he said, 'and we'll keep along this side.'

'Not too near,' said Dorothea. 'But let's go near enough to see. There are lots of other boats about. We're just one of them. There's no reason why we shouldn't go anywhere.'

So, zigzagging down the lake in the sunshine against an easy wind from the south, they watched for signs of the hunt. There was very little to be seen. Here and there, they saw men on the shore below the woods. Here and there, where the road ran close to the lake, they could see a waiting motor car. Sometimes they heard coach calls answering each other. But, if they had not known what was going on, they would never have guessed that anything out of the ordinary was happening. People in rowing-boats, people in sailing yachts, were moving about the lake and hearing the horns on shore without dreaming that close by them men were searching, combing the countryside for a human being.

For a few moments they heard the barking of the bloodhound, but it stopped almost at once.

'Do bloodhounds bay when they're following a scent?' asked Dorothea.

'I don't see how they can when they're sniffing,' said Dick.

'They probably do when they get excited,' said Dorothea. They were between Long Island and the western shore when they heard the bloodhound again, much farther down the lake.

'That's not really baying,' said Dorothea. 'Just barking. He hasn't found anything.'

A horn sounded high up in the woods.

'She'll never have gone right up there,' said Dick. 'I'm sure they ought to have looked for footprints close to where they found the car. They must have started the bloodhound in the wrong place. I wish they'd let us come, too.'

'They couldn't,' said Dorothea. 'You heard what Timothy said. If we were with them when they found her, and she saw us talking to them, they'd have to explain, and they'd be done for, and she'd be horrible to Mrs Blackett, and the postman would get in a row, and Cook, and Jacky, and Timothy, and the doctor. But, oh, I do wish she was safely found.'

'She can't have gone far,' said Dick.

'Jacky said they were going to drag the lake,' said Dorothea.

They came out on the farther side of Long Island and, looking across the lake, could see the old blue houseboat lying in its sheltered bay.

'Don't let's go there just yet,' said Dick. Somehow, while sailing, things did not seem so bad. The moment they stopped, there would be nothing to do but think.

'There isn't really any hurry,' said Dorothea, 'now we're on the lake. All that matters is for us to keep out of the way.'

They sailed on, tacking this way and that, now and again hearing horn answering horn in the steep woods below the fells.

'Dick,' said Dorothea at last, 'perhaps we'd better go there and get unpacked. And I ought to get some food ready. He said we were to take anything we wanted.'

'We'll sail again later,' said Dick.

'If she's all right when they find her, Timothy's sure to come straight home. He won't want her to see him. We'd better have everything ready.'

Dick swung *Scarab* round, eased out the sheet, and set his course for Houseboat Bay and their new hiding place.

'We haven't slept in a boat since we were sailing in *Teasel*,' said Dick.

'No,' said Dorothea, but not as if she were looking forward

to it. Sleeping in a boat for fun was one thing, but sleeping in a boat because everything had gone wrong was quite another. While Dick was steering *Scarab* across the lake to Houseboat Bay, Dorothea was looking back at the opposite shore, and listening, listening for the long-drawn blast that was to be the signal that the hunt was ended and the Great Aunt found. She wondered if anybody had thought of having a stretcher ready.

Dick, doing his best to remember not to grip the tiller but to steer with his fingers, doing his best to find exactly how far to ease out the sheet, to have *Scarab* making the most of the wind, for a few happy minutes forgot the Great Aunt altogether. He did not speak till *Scarab* was coming into Houseboat Bay, and, sheltered a little by the southern point, was heeling less and moving slower. Then he said, 'Dot, I'm going to try coming alongside like Nancy, without lowering the sail first.'

'Do you think you can do it without bumping?'

'I shall steer as if I was going under her stern,' said Dick, 'and then turn into the wind till the sail flaps. She ought to stop right alongside. Will you be ready to fend off and catch hold of the ladder? Look out for the boom. It'll swing in when we come head to wind.'

'All right,' said Dorothea.

'The thing is to know just when to turn,' said Dick, not to Dorothea but to himself.

It takes practice and a lot of confidence to sail a small boat straight at the stern of a big one and then turn at the last minute and come sliding up alongside within reach but without touching. Dick turned too soon.

'Never mind,' he said, 'I'll come round again and do it next shot.'

He sailed off to windward, brought *Scarab* round with a most successful gybe and headed for the houseboat to try again.

THEY WERE STARTLED BY A SPLASH

'Dick,' said Dorothea, 'there's someone on board.'

'There can't be, or there'd be a boat against the ladder. He's got his own boat over on the other shore.'

'It looked just as if there was something moving behind the cabin windows,' said Dorothea.

Dick, in spite of thinking that Dorothea was wrong, had turned *Scarab* sharply as she spoke. Her sail filled on the port tack. They were moving away from the houseboat again when they were both startled by a splash. They looked back and saw a newspaper being shaken out over the water from the houseboat's afterdeck.

'Boy!'

The shaking out of the newspaper stopped. Someone wearing what looked like a large white turban was beckoning to them.

'Boy!'

'I'll come round in a minute,' called Dick. 'Got to gybe again. Look out, Dot!' Round came *Scarab*, the boom swung across, and for a third time he was heading for the houseboat to come alongside as Nancy would have done.

'I knew there was someone,' whispered Dorothea.

'Why didn't Timothy tell us?' said Dick. 'Don't talk, just for a minute. I'll do it this time. Look out for the boom.'

He aimed again straight for the houseboat's stern, kept on just a little longer, and then swung his little ship up into the wind. For one dreadful moment he thought there was going to be a bump. There were not many inches to spare, but round she came without touching.

'Grab the ladder, Dot. She's hardly moving. We've done it.'

Dorothea grabbed the ladder, but did not speak. She could not. She had seen what Dick now saw as he looked up. The stranger on the houseboat was unwinding the towel she had put round her hair, and, though neither of them had ever had a close view of her, they had watched her from a distance, and knew at once who she was.

For a moment Dorothea, in her horror, thought of pushing off from the ladder and getting away from the houseboat as fast as *Scarab* could take them. But that was impossible. The Great Aunt was speaking to Dick.

'Boy,' she said again. 'Are you a local boy or are you a visitor?'

'A visitor really,' said Dick ... 'Hang on, Dot, or she'll start sailing again.'

'Do you know the lake well?'

'Not very.'

'Do you know a house called Beckfoot, on the other side, beyond the island? ... There is a small river ...'

'I know it,' said Dick.

'I shall be very much obliged to you if you will take me there. I have to go there before catching a train. Will you be so good?'

'Yes,' said Dick.

'You will excuse me a moment,' said the Great Aunt and went down into the cabin.

'Dick,' gasped Dorothea, 'you know who it is?'

'It's her,' said Dick wretchedly. 'But what could I say? I couldn't say anything else.'

'What are we to do?'

There was no time to say more. The Great Aunt had put on her hat and was coming out of the cabin. They saw her turn. They heard the sharp click as she turned the key in the lock. They saw her take the key out, change her mind and put it back. They heard her sniff as she glanced at a bit of paper pinned to the door. She bent down and handed her parasol to Dick. Dick took it without looking at it and laid it down in the boat. His eyes were on something she was still holding, a flat oblong wooden box, with a name on it. She had found the box with the chemical scales.

'Will you take this, please?'

Dick took it with shaky fingers and put it by the side of his box of caterpillars.

'And now, perhaps, if you will lend me your hand ...'

'It's easier to turn round and come down backwards,' said

Dorothea, seeing the Great Aunt hesitate. 'At least,' she added hurriedly, 'I should think it would be.'

The Great Aunt came down backwards. Dorothea timidly took hold of one of the Great Aunt's ankles and guided her foot to a thwart. The Great Aunt came down into the boat and took her seat in the stern.

Dick did not know what to do, because while she was sitting where she was he could not use the tiller.

'Do you happen to know what time it is?' she asked.

Dick pulled himself together and looked at his watch. 'Twenty-nine minutes past eleven,' he said.

'How long will it take you?' asked the Great Aunt.

'Not very long if the wind keeps like this,' said Dorothea.

'I have a conveyance ordered to call for me at Beckfoot at one o'clock,' said the Great Aunt.

A new horror swept into Dorothea's mind. What if Nancy, or Peggy , or Cook, or Timothy, had thought of telephoning to the station to say the motor car was not needed because of the Great Aunt being lost? But she could not speak of that. She saw Dick looking helpless.

'Please,' she said. 'You'll have to move just a bit because of the steering.'

'I am not accustomed to sailing-boats,' said the Great Aunt, 'though I have two nieces who sail quite a lot. You will have to tell me what to do.'

'If you sit just there,' said Dick, 'just a little farther forward, I can manage sitting here, and D—. . . (he pulled himself up, thinking that it might be better to mention no names) . . . my sister can keep the weight right by coming on this side. Push her nose off . . .'

Dorothea pushed off from the ladder.

'I'm awfully sorry,' said Dick. 'You have to look out for that boom. It won't do it again. At least, I'll tell you if it's going to.'

'My own fault,' said the Great Aunt.

Scarab's sail filled and they were off.

Just then horns sounded again on the far side of the lake.

'Curious,' said the Great Aunt. 'This is not the hunting season, and there are no coaches now as there used to be, but I think I have heard horns again and again during the last two hours.'

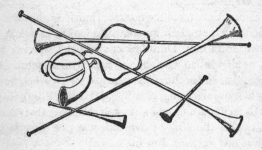

CHAPTER 28

THREE IN A BOAT

'WHAT *are* those horns?'

The Great Aunt asked the question, but Dorothea was not sure that she expected an answer. She looked at Dick, but got no help from him. Dorothea knew Dick's steering face, the look he always had when he was busy with something and thinking of that and nothing else. She had seen it when he was thinking of stars, of mining, of sailing, of birds or even of caterpillars. His face was different now, and she knew that he was, very unhappily, thinking of two things at one. Steering, of course, was one of them. But the other?

Dorothea looked at the Great Aunt, sitting in the stern, just far enough forward to give Dick room to use the tiller. She looked at Dick and saw his eyes glancing again and again at the wooden box with James Turner's name on it. 'Whatever happens, you must not run into her now,' Timothy had said. And here they were, with the Great Aunt in their own boat, taking her to Beckfoot with evidence of the burglary beside her. No wonder Dick was finding it hard to keep his mind on his steering. Just for a moment Dorothea caught herself thinking it would have been better if Jacky had been right and the Great Aunt was drowned and done with. But she thought that only for a moment. That would have been far worse. Still, if it had been a sprained ankle, or even a broken one, it would not have been so bad. She would have been found by now, and found by someone else. That was what mattered. If only somebody else had found her.

Then another thought startled her. The Great Aunt did not know them. They must not let out that they knew her. Would

Dick think of that? At any moment he might call her Miss Turner, and she would ask him how he knew.

'I wonder what they are doing,' said the Great Aunt as the horns sounded again.

'They're looking for somebody's who's lost,' said Dorothea, very clearly, looking at Dick. It was no good. She could not catch his eye.

'Somebody lost?' said the Great Aunt, and a spot of red showed on each cheekbone. 'Do you know who?'

'We heard it was a Miss Turner,' said Dorothea, gripping very tightly the thwart on which she was sitting, to stop the trembling of her fingers.

'Humph!' The spots of red were spreading over the Great Aunt's cheeks, and she pressed her lips together. 'I am Miss Turner,' she said after a pause, 'and I am not lost.'

'Of course not,' said Dorothea, with great relief. It would be all right now even if Dick did call her Miss Turner without thinking.

Just then, far away down the lake, they heard a deep, echoing bark.

'That's the bloodhound, Miss Turner,' said Dick. 'It must have made a mistake.'

The Great Aunt snorted. At least, that was the only word Dorothea could find afterwards that seemed to fit the noise she made. It was certainly more than a mere sniff. 'Bloodhounds!' she said. 'What foolery! I have been spending the night in my nephew's houseboat, cleaning up the pigsty I found there. Lost! I have been working like a charwoman. Why, you saw me emptying into the lake the last of the rubbish I found there, heaps of it, even on the table in the cabin.'

Dorothea glanced anxiously at Dick, as *Scarab* made a sudden swerve. Rubbish. Heaps of it. . . . The Great Aunt had thrown overboard all the samples from the mine. Timothy's work wasted, and Captain Flint coming back tomorrow.

Dick turned white, but remembered in time that he must not say anything about it.

'Lost?' the Great Aunt went on, and Dorothea knew that she was explaining things to herself. 'There may have been a slight misunderstanding. I did expect that my nieces would be calling for me. But lost! Bloodhounds! They must indeed have gone out of their senses.'

'I think the police brought the bloodhound,' said Dick, and Dorothea trembled again. She caught Dick's eye and opened her own wide. Dick had been just going to say something else, but he saw that he had better not and bit off his sentence before it was out of his mouth.

As Dorothea said afterwards, it did not really matter, because the Great Aunt was too angry to notice. Her anger showed in a queer way. She opened her parasol with a jerk, held it over her head, sat up even straighter and looked about her as if she were a visitor being taken for a turn on the lake. She lifted her chin. Her lips were tight together. And Dorothea suddenly knew that the Great Aunt was herself afraid of something. Not exactly afraid. Defiant was the word, thought Dorothea, and remembered the picture of the stag at bay on the bedroom wall at Dixon's farm.

'It's quite all right,' said Dick earnestly. 'Only you'll have to put it down a bit if we have to gybe. It's quite all right now. If anything, it acts as an extra sail.'

The Great Aunt hardly seemed to have heard that he was speaking. She certainly did not hear what he said.

'But those horns,' she said. 'They don't belong to the police.'

'That's the firefighters,' said Dorothea. 'Colonel Jolys's firefighters.'

'Tommy Jolys!' exclaimed the Great Aunt. 'Hunting me with horns. I shall have something to say to him. He was always a noisy and ill-behaved little boy.'

Dorothea remembered the stout, white-moustached, bald-

'IT ACTS AS AN EXTRA SAIL'

headed Colonel, standing in his car and talking to his men, and found it hard to put the two pictures together. Suddenly she found herself wondering what the Great Aunt had been like as a little girl. She gave it up. The Great Aunt was one of those people who could never have been young at all. She must have been a Great Aunt, and her sort of a Great Aunt from the beginning of time.

'It is really a beautiful day, though very hot,' said the Great Aunt. 'Colonel Jolys and his friends seem to be doing a great deal of hard work for nothing.'

Dick cleared the little rock at the southern end of Long Island and turned north. That brought the wind dead aft and he had to look to his steering and watch the little flag at the masthead, for fear of a sudden gybe that would bring the boom swinging across to knock the parasol out of the Great Aunt's hand. Dorothea, without being told, pulled up the centreboard.

She sat down again and made ready for the worst. She had had a faint glimmer of a hope that they might be able to take the Great Aunt to Beckfoot, put her ashore without meeting anybody, and sail hurriedly away to safety. She had hoped that Dick had the same idea in his mind. But now, sailing not on the Rio side of the island but between the island and the western shore, they would be in full view of any of the hunters who might happen to look out over the lake, unless by good luck one of the smaller islands might happen to be in the way. Of course there were plenty of other boats about, but there was only one sailing boat with a red sail and a scarab flag, and only one with an old lady sitting in the stern, holding a blue parasol, as if on purpose to catch anybody's eye. Nancy or Peggy or Timothy might be anywhere, and any one of them was likely to look out over the lake to see whether or not *Scarab* was lying astern of the houseboat with the Picts, who had to be invisible, safely hidden in the houseboat's cabin. She looked anxiously along the shore.

Here and there she thought she could see people moving across open spaces between the trees. She looked for the flash of a white frock. If Nancy and Peggy saw *Scarab* they would shout at once, or would they think in time, and not let the other hunters know till she and Dick had got away again? There was nothing to be done about it. Sailing along, with the Great Aunt in the boat with them, they were trapped. Their only hope was to get quickly to Beckfoot and find it still deserted as it had been when they left the river.

'Do you know some children called Walker?' asked the Great Aunt, and Dorothea felt her heart trying to jump out of her throat.

'Yes,' she said. 'They stay at Holly Howe.'

'Are they here now?'

'No,' said Dorothea. 'But I believe they are coming next week or the week after.'

'Indeed,' said the Great Aunt. 'So I have been told. I fear I have done my nieces an injustice.' She said no more, and Dorothea said nothing. She had not the smallest idea what the Great Aunt meant, but she was full of dread lest the next question should be, 'Do you know my nieces?'

It was never asked. They had left the islands and were sailing along towards the Beckfoot promontory. The Great Aunt had asked again about the time. Dick, narrowly avoiding a gybe while he looked at his watch, had told her. The Great Aunt had said, 'That is very well. It would be unfortunate if I were not ready at one o'clock. I am really very much obliged to you both.' Dorothea was just thinking that things might go right after all, when she heard a sudden shout from the shore where the road ran close to the lake.

All three of them had heard it. A moment later they heard it again. Then several people were shouting together. Then came a long triumphant blast on a coach-horn, a long blast that went on and on and on and broke off with a sigh as if the horn blower had no more breath. A moment later they heard the same long blast from another horn. Horn after horn took it up, far away down the lake. From the shore a voice, that might have been Colonel Jolys's, let loose a ringing, echoing 'View Halloo!'

The Great Aunt's parasol shook a little more than could be explained by the gentle wind. She tapped impatiently with her fingers on the box with the chemical scales that was now resting on her knee.

'View hallooooooooooooooooo!'

Ten or a dozen men were shouting together.

'VIEW HALLOOOOOOOOOOOOOOOOO!'

The shout was taken up far along the shore. They could hear the old hunting cry coming from the high woods. Again and again the horns blew that long triumphant blast.

'They've seen you,' said Dorothea. 'They're awfully pleased.'

She thought to herself that only Jacky would be disappointed that there would be no dragging for the Great Aunt's corpse. She was alive. She was found. Of course everybody was pleased! And then again she remembered that the one thing had happened that ought not to have happened. They had met the Great Aunt. It was not her fault, or Dick's, but there they were in the boat with her. There was small hope now that they would find Beckfoot deserted. Nancy's plan, which had worked so well, was all going wrong at the very last minute. The martyrs had been angels all that time for nothing. The Picts had hidden in vain. And many other people were going to get into trouble as well.

Motors were hooting now, here and there, along the road by the shore. Through a gap in the trees, Dorothea saw men piling into one of the cars. Was that a white frock among them? She could not be sure. Hooting joyfully, the car was moving off towards Beckfoot. There was another, and another. She looked at Dick. Dick, too, had seen, but the wind was dead aft, and he was trying not to let himself think of anything but his steering. She saw him glance anxiously at the Great Aunt's parasol. It might be working as a mizen sail, but it would be pretty awful if there were a gybe and the boom were to come over and knock it out of her hand. He had never practised in *Scarab* picking things up when they had dropped overboard. He had done it in *Titmouse* when Tom and the Coots had been giving him lessons in sailing. He wished he had thought of trying it in *Scarab*. Tomorrow he would try it with a matchbox. Tomorrow? Dorothea did not know what he was thinking, but she saw his face change. Dick, like Dorothea, knew that disaster was ahead of them.

'Do you not think,' said the Great Aunt, 'that rowing might be a little quicker than sailing?'

'I don't think so,' said Dick. 'But it will be when we get into the river.'

'You know best, I dare say,' said the Great Aunt. 'I mention it only because it is really important that I should get back. I have a train to catch.'

Nobody knew better than Dick and Dorothea how important it was that she should catch it.

'What about trying with the oars?' said Dorothea.

'No use,' said Dick. 'We should only lose time.'

'I am sure you are doing your best,' said the Great Aunt, little knowing how very true it was.

Already it was clear that a great many people would be at Beckfoot before them. Motor car after motor car hooted along the road by the lake, carrying the hunters back. However fast a little boat sails, it is a tortoise compared with a motor car. Horns were cheerfully blowing behind the Beckfoot promontory long before *Scarab* had rounded the point and was coming into the river.

'I'll row now,' said Dick. 'Will you put the rowlocks ready?'

Dorothea, no longer daring even to look at the Great Aunt, set the rowlocks in their places.

'Shall I lower the sail?' she asked.

'No need,' said Dick, thinking of the difficulty of lowering the sail with the Great Aunt in the boat. 'We'll be on port tack going up, and the wind will keep the sail out of the way.'

The reedy banks of the river were closing in on either side.

'Ready now,' said Dorothea.

'Change places with me,' said Dick.

Dorothea sat at the tiller, and Dick put the oars out and began to row.

There was a tremendous noise in the Beckfoot garden, a noise of people talking, shouting, laughing, with now and then a coach call or a hunting call on one of the firefighters' horns. Dick did not look round. Out of the corner of his eye he saw *Amazon*'s stern in the reeds. He knew that they were coming near the boathouse. He knew, too, that Dorothea was not steering very well.

Dorothea, gripping the tiller, with the Great Aunt close beside her, could see that the Beckfoot lawn was crowded. She caught sight of Nancy and Peggy. She saw Timothy and Colonel Jolys. That was the doctor, talking to Timothy. That was the postman. And that was Jacky, working his way between larger folk to get a better view.

'If you will put me ashore here,' said the Great Aunt.

'I don't think she'll go into the boathouse with the mast up,' said Dick.

'I believe there is quite deep water at the edge of the lawn,' said the Great Aunt.

Hands were reaching from the lawn as Dick stopped rowing, and Dorothea steered towards it. There was a sudden silence. Somebody had hold of *Scarab*'s mast. Several hands were on her gunwale. Nancy's and Peggy's were not among them, though Dorothea caught a glimpse of their horrified faces in the crowd.

Colonel Jolys cleared his throat. He stood all ready to make a speech and at the same time to help the Great Aunt ashore.

'Miss Turner,' he began, 'I think I am speaking for all of us when I say . . .'

'Tommy Jolys,' the Great Aunt interrupted him, 'am I right in supposing that you are the leading spirit in all this foolery?'

CHAPTER 29

GREAT AUNT MARIA FACES HER PURSUERS

NANCY had been the one to see *Scarab* sailing towards Beckfoot, with Dick and Dorothea and a passenger with a parasol. She had shouted to Colonel Jolys who was by his car in the road, making up his mind where next to take his men after drawing blank in the wood. He had given the long-drawn blast that signalled 'FOUND' to all the others and, collecting his own half-dozen firefighters, had driven straight to Beckfoot. Peggy had been farther down the lake but came with another lot of the men a few minutes later. Nancy, watching car after car of men drive up, was waiting for her at the gate.

'It's all up,' she said. 'She's met the Picts. She's in their boat with them. They're coming round the point now.'

'What shall we do?' said Peggy. 'Bolt?'

'We can't,' said Nancy. 'There'll be the most awful row. We've just got to explain. I was a galoot to shout when I saw her. But somebody else would have seen her anyway. It's all up now. Oh! There's Timothy. Hi! We're done. It's all up. She's met them and they're bringing her home in their boat.'

'Thank goodness she's found,' said Timothy, mopping his forehead. 'Worse things might have happened.'

'Nothing could be worse than that.'

'Dragging the lake,' said Timothy. 'Come on. We've got to take what's coming to us.'

Cook, hearing the noise of the motor cars coming up one after another, ran out of the house.

'Have they found her?' she cried. 'Is she badly hurt?'

'Dick and Dorothea have found her,' said Nancy grimly.

'And she looks all right. She's in their boat. They'll be here any minute now.'

'Them two,' exclaimed Cook. 'I knew all along it would come to that.' She wrung her hands. 'She'll find out all now. And what she'll have to say to your poor mother . . . She can say what she likes to me. I've given notice already . . .'

And Cook, with Timothy, Nancy and Peggy, joined the crowd that was pouring round the house to the lawn. The doctor, who had been talking to Colonel Jolys, pushed his way towards them.

'I ought to have given you away at once,' he said, 'and this would never have happened.'

The postman did not come up and speak to them, but Nancy saw him looking at them, standing first on one leg and then on the other, as if in a mind to go, yet wanting to know the worst and get it over. Nancy could not meet his look and turned away.

'They won't be dragging t'lake after all.' They heard a shrill complaint, and saw Jacky with his father and their sheep-dog.

All the accomplices, willing and unwilling, were there, every single one who had found himself or herself doing what Nancy thought best because it was too late to do anything else, Cook, Timothy, the doctor, the postman and Jacky. And in a moment or two Dick and Dorothea would be there, with the Great Aunt herself.

'I say, Peggy,' said Nancy. 'It's all my fault anyway. I'll have to say so. You'd better leave the talking to me.'

'Where did they find her?' asked Peggy.

'I don't know,' said Nancy. 'They were bringing her up the lake when I saw them first, half-way between Long Island and our promontory. Idiots to go and pick her up if they saw her on the shore.'

'When I last saw them,' said Peggy, 'they were going the other way.'

'If only people would do what they were told,' said Nancy. 'I say, Timothy, you did jam it into their heads that they were to go to the houseboat, didn't you?'

'I did,' said Timothy. 'I told them that the one thing that mustn't happen was for them to meet her, and that they were to go along to the houseboat and sit tight.'

'Mutton-headed galoots,' said Nancy. 'If only they'd done that and left things alone. Hullo! Here they are.'

The crowd on the lawn surged towards the river as *Scarab* came into view by the boathouse. Nancy, Peggy, Timothy and Cook pressed forward with the others. More and more of the firefighters were pouring round the corner of the house.

Suddenly Nancy, seeing all these people waiting for one old lady after they had spent the morning hunting for her, felt as she would have felt if she had seen a fox cornered by a pack of hounds. For a moment she forgot her own troubles. It was going to be pretty awful for Aunt Maria to face a crowd like that.

'She doesn't look as if anything had happened at all,' said Peggy.

'Give her room to get ashore,' ordered Colonel Jolys.

'He's pretty sick he didn't find her,' said Peggy.

'He's had a good run for his money anyhow,' said Nancy.

The Colonel looked round and made an angry gesture to quiet those of his men who were welcoming the fox with triumphant blasts on their horns. There was half a second of silence. The Colonel loudly cleared his throat.

'Bless my soul,' murmured Timothy. 'He's going to make a speech.'

The Colonel was handing the Great Aunt out of the boat. He began his speech, but did not get very far with it.

'Tommy Jolys,' the Great Aunt interrupted him, 'am I right in supposing that you are the leading spirit in all this foolery?'

311

With the first words she spoke as she came ashore, the Great Aunt set the tone for all that followed.

Colonel Jolys, D.S.O., organizer of the district firefighters, leader of men, hero of many wars, became in a moment Tommy, the little boy of fifty years ago. His dignity was gone. It was as if someone had pricked a toy balloon. The speech that he had meant to deliver died on his lips. He shifted from one foot to the other without a word to say. The Great Aunt had no mercy.

'No, Tommy,' she went on slowly. 'You have really changed very little. You always liked toy trumpets . . . I remember seeing you, and hearing you, lying on the nursery floor howling with temper because your sister had trodden on the tin trumpet you had then. You lay there, howling and kicking, until your mother picked you up and very properly chastised you.'

One of the firefighting young men laughed, a laugh that broke off short as the Colonel turned to see who it was.

'But, Miss Turner,' he stammered.

'Tin trumpets, Tommy,' said the Great Aunt, and Peggy, staring at her, suddenly thought that it was very like hearing Nancy calling somebody a galoot.

'Now for it, Peggy,' said Nancy, and pushed through between Colonel Jolys and the sergeant of police from the other side of the lake.

'Aunt Maria,' she said. 'Are you all right? We've been in the most awful stew about you . . .' She broke off short. She had just seen what the Great Aunt was holding in her hand, the wooden box with the chemical scales.

'Quite all right, my dears,' said the Great Aunt. 'Do you know, Ruth, that you have torn your frock? And Margaret seems to have been rolling on the grass in hers . . .'

Cook broke in. 'And how would they not, Miss Turner? Hunting the woods looking for your corpus. There's never a white frock made to last two minutes in them brambles.'

THE GREAT AUNT STEPS ASHORE

'Ah, Cook,' said the Great Aunt. 'It is nearly one o'clock, when, as I think you know, I shall be going to the station. I hope you have remembered to prepare my sandwiches.'

'Sandwiches, Miss Turner! We was thinking more'n likely you was gone where you wouldn't want sandwiches.'

313

'I hope they will be ready,' said the Great Aunt.

The sergeant of police took his turn. 'It is Miss Turner, isn't it?' he said. 'We were informed last night that you had disappeared, leaving no trace, from a motor car left standing on the road . . .'

'I am not, so far as I know,' said the Great Aunt, 'under any obligation to keep the police informed of my where-abouts. Nor, if you will allow me to say so, have I any reason to suppose them other than disgracefully incompetent.'

The sergeant of police was not to be put down so easily. 'I should point out to you, Miss Turner, that a section of the police have been taken from their duties, and a large number of other men have had to leave their work . . .'

Nancy hesitated only a moment, and charged in to the rescue.

'She had nothing to do with it,' she said. 'It was all my fault. It was just that when Aunt Maria didn't come home, I got a bit worried and couldn't think of anything else to do, except telephone to you and to Colonel Jolys.' She glanced at the Great Aunt. Their eyes met for a moment. It was surprising, but it almost seemed that the Great Aunt was pleased.

'And madam,' said Colonel Jolys, 'I think I may say that though we did not have the good fortune to find you, my men made a pretty good job of combing the ground. If by any chance you had fallen anywhere in these woods, I think one or the other of us could hardly have failed to rescue you.'

'Tin trumpets,' said the Great Aunt as if to herself, and added, 'I hope at least that you have enjoyed yourselves, even though you were looking for somebody who was never lost.'

'Madam,' said the sergeant of police, opening his note-book, 'I have to complete my report. Have you any objection to stating where, in fact, you were?'

'None whatever, sergeant. I was in my nephew's houseboat, which I found untenanted, open and in a disgraceful condition.'

Nancy's mouth fell open. Nobody heard Peggy's stifled gasp. Timothy, very red in the face, came forward, hardly able to keep his eyes from the box with the chemical scales that the Great Aunt had in her hand, as she watched the sergeant of police writing busily in his notebook. She turned as Timothy spoke to her.

'I really must apologize,' he said. 'I fear you were misled by the note I left on the cabin door. It was meant for other visitors. If I had known you were coming, I should have done a bit of tidying.'

The Great Aunt looked him up and down. 'We have, I think, met before. Unwillingly, on your part. If you remember, you jumped over a wall and ran away into the wood. There was also another occasion, after which I found it necessary to describe you to an imbecile of a local policeman. You will, I think, recognize this box belonging to my nephew. If you needed it, and were a friend of his, do you not think it would have been simpler to ask for it, instead of breaking into this house at night? But for the obstinate stupidity of the constable, who refused to act on the information I gave him, information exact in every particular, you would have been very properly laid by the heels. I cannot say I congratulate my nephew on his choice of friends. As for the state in which I found his houseboat, to describe it as a pigsty is unjust to the brute creation. You will at least, when you go back there, be able to make a fresh start, and I hope you will try to keep it clean for the twenty-four hours before he returns. I have spent much of the morning emptying dirt into the lake. Now, if you are a friend of Jim's I will let you have this box, and I hope that you will in future remember that burglary is not usually held to be among the accomplishments of a gentleman.'

There was a moment of dreadful silence, when Nancy thought that Timothy could hardly help telling the truth to save himself. But he said nothing at all.

'Do I understand?' the sergeant of police began again.

'I hardly think so,' said the Great Aunt. 'And now, if you will excuse me, I must leave you. Bad manners are, alas, infectious, and I have yet to thank the two charming and well-behaved children but for whose unselfish action I should have been in danger of missing my train.'

The moment had come. Nancy braced herself for confession. Everybody turned to look towards the river. And there was the river flowing placidly by the edge of the lawn. But of the little boat with the red sail that had been waiting there against the bank, there was nothing to be seen.

'But they're not there,' said Peggy.

'They've gone,' exclaimed Nancy, almost shouting, as hope, that had died altogether, leapt again to life in her heart.

'I have been most remiss,' said the Great Aunt. 'I omitted to ask them their names. I dare say you will see them again on the lake. They would, I think, be most suitable friends for you. Their boat, I noticed, has a red sail, and some sort of green insect on its flag. You will tell them that the old lady to whom they were so kind is very sorry that she had no opportunity of saying how grateful she was to them. And now, Ruth, we will leave these hunters. Come, Margaret, the motor car I have ordered should be here at any minute. And I have a letter to write to your mother.'

The crowd made room for them again as the Great Aunt, with Nancy and Peggy, walked up towards the house.

Colonel Jolys, twice suppressed, took fresh courage. 'Miss Turner,' he said, 'I have a car here, and if I may offer you a lift . . .'

'Thank you, Tommy,' said the Great Aunt. 'Your triumph must be incomplete. You have had your nice, noisy hunt, but I fear you must go home without carrying your kill in your car.'

The doctor, who was beginning to think that he at least was going to escape without trouble, had the misfortune to be just in her way as she moved on across the lawn.

Nancy glared at him. The danger was not over yet. But she need not have been afraid.

'Ah, doctor,' said the Great Aunt. 'So you, too, have been amusing yourself with Tommy Jolys and his friends?'

'I thought,' stammered the doctor. 'I feared that I might be needed.'

'Indeed,' said the Great Aunt. 'Then at least I cannot accuse you like the rest of them of not minding your own business.'

'I am very happy to find that I . . . that my . . . that . . .'

The Great Aunt bowed to him and passed on. She stopped short by the door at the sight of the unlucky Sammy, the policeman, who was carrying a black silk cloak on his arm. She pointed at it with her parasol.

'Constable,' she said, 'what are you doing with that cloak?'

'We had to have something, Miss, just to give the smell to the dog.'

The great Aunt drew in her breath. 'Do you mean to say that you have had the impertinence to open my boxes. I packed that cloak yesterday.'

'We didn't touch owt else,' stammered the policeman.

'Take it from him, Margaret,' said the Great Aunt.

'It was for the bloodhound,' said Nancy.

'I know,' said the Great Aunt. 'Bloodhound, indeed! Constable. You will remember that I described to you the disreputable fellow who was responsible for breaking into this house. You were unwilling to believe me. You will find him now, talking to Colonel Jolys. No. I do not intend to prosecute. That incident is closed, but not thanks to any efficient action on the part of the police.'

'No, Miss,' said Sammy.

'You are, I think, Mrs Lewthwaite's son,' said the Great

Aunt. 'It would be useless to talk to your sergeant, but I regret that I am leaving too soon to have a few words with your mother.'

She went up the steps and into the house, followed by Peggy with her cloak.

Nancy lingered a moment.

'Cheer up, Sammy,' she said. 'I say. Did the bloodhound find anything?'

'Nowt,' said Sammy. 'He called to a scent by Crag Gill gates and ran it near to Swainson's and then down to t'lake.'

'Swainson's,' said Nancy. 'What can she have been doing there? They told us they'd never seen her.'

She hurried in, and upstairs, to find the Great Aunt in her bedroom, carefully refolding the cloak and putting it back into her box.

'Now, Margaret, just look carefully round to see if I have forgotten anything,' said the Great Aunt, going to the writing table in the bedroom. 'And, Ruth, go down and see that Cook is making my sandwiches, and ask her to let me know as soon as the motor car arrives.'

*

Outside, in the garden, the huntsmen were licking their wounds.

'My word, she is a tartar, that old lady,' said the sergeant of police.

'Flattened us out one after another,' said Colonel Jolys. 'Down with one and ready for the next.' He turned to Timothy. 'She had her knife into you properly. What did she call you? A burglar and what not? Did you do any burgling?'

'It's a long story,' said Timothy.

'If you ask me,' said the doctor, 'we've that young rip, Nancy, to thank for everything. And we're lucky it's not worse. There's . . .'

Timothy winked at the doctor. 'By the way,' he said, 'did you see where those two strangers went?'

'Well, I'm off,' said the sergeant.

'Half a minute,' said Colonel Jolys. 'We'll be the laughing stock of the whole place if we just troop back with our tails between our legs.'

'What can we do, Colonel?' said the sergeant.

'Give her a cheer when she comes out,' said Colonel Jolys.

CHAPTER 30

REWARD OF VIRTUE

DICK looked at Dorothea. Dorothea looked at Dick. The same idea had come to both of them.

Dick was holding *Scarab* close to the bank with a tight grip on a clump of grass. Dorothea was still clutching the tiller. Minute by minute, both had been waiting for somebody to say the careless word that would mean disaster. No one had said it. From the moment the Great Aunt had stepped ashore, to deal so firmly with her would-be rescuers, no one had had eyes to spare for the little boat in which she had come. As the Great Aunt, with dignity, walked up the lawn towards the house, the crowd made way for her and closed in behind her. Not one single face was turned towards the river. Dick let go his tuft of grass and pushed off from the bank. There was a chance yet.

Scarab drifted silently away from the lawn and down the river. The high ridge of the promontory sheltered them from the wind. The sail hung idle. Dorothea touched the slack main-sheet, but saw the warning in Dick's eyes and let it lie. Foot by foot they drifted away from the lawn and downstream towards the boathouse. And still nobody turned to look at them. Dick dared not use those new and squeaking oars. He had no need. For one nervous moment he thought he might have to fend off from the wall of the boathouse, but *Scarab* drifted clear. A moment later and they were out of sight from the lawn.

'We've done it,' whispered Dorothea.

Scarab drifted on along the reedy shore. In among the reeds, only a foot or two away, was the stern of *Amazon*,

320

where she had been left the day before. Dick grabbed an oar, was just able to reach her, and brought *Scarab* in beside her.

'Is it safe?' said Dorothea.

'Better than going outside,' said Dick. 'On the lake we could be seen from anywhere.'

He took *Scarab*'s painter, scrambled from one boat to the other, made the painter fast, scrambled back again and lowered sail.

'Never mind about a stow,' he said. 'Come on.'

'Where?' said Dorothea. 'We can't get back to the hut with all those people about.'

'Look-out post,' said Dick. 'We simply must know what's happening.'

They got ashore by way of *Amazon*, after letting *Scarab* out to the end of her painter so that she lay downstream against the reeds.

Quickly, quietly, they climbed to the top of the ridge, snaking the last few yards till, from among the rocks and heather, they could look down on the Beckfoot lawn.

The crowd had moved nearer to the house. They caught sight of Cook hurrying towards the garden door. The Great Aunt was talking to a policeman. The white frocks of Nancy and Peggy were close beside her.

'Has she found out or hasn't she?' said Dorothea.

'She's going indoors,' said Dick. 'What's Peggy carrying?'

'Nancy's gone in, too.'

'Timothy's talking to Colonel Jolys,' said Dick.

'And the doctor,' said Dorothea. 'If she asked him questions he'll have told her everything. He said he would.'

Dick looked at his watch.

'What time is it?' asked Dorothea.

'Fourteen and a half minutes to one.'

*

No fourteen and a half minutes ever went so slowly.

The crowd on the lawn was thinning. Firefighters and their helpers were pouring back towards the road. Groups lingered talking, but all kept moving in the same direction. Presently there was no one left. The new-cut grass looked like a football field after the players have all gone home. But the watchers on the ridge knew that the players had not gone far. They could hear the noise of many people talking.

'What are they waiting for?' said Dorothea. 'They know now she isn't lost. Why don't they go away?'

Minute after minute went by. The Picts, lying on the top of the ridge, looked down on the trodden, deserted lawn, and on the silent grey house. No one showed at any of the windows they could see. Somewhere inside the house were Nancy, Peggy and the Great Aunt . . . not a Great Aunt who did not know the Picts existed, but a Great Aunt who had been in the boat with them, who had talked with them, whom they themselves had brought back to Beckfoot.

'I believe the theory's exploded already,' said Dick, half getting to his feet. 'Somebody must have said something, and they're getting in a row now. We'd better go down and tell her it was our fault, too.'

'We don't know,' said Dorothea. 'Her having seen us doesn't matter so long as she doesn't know who we are. If she doesn't know we're Picts, we still are. Wait till one o'clock and see if she goes. What time is it now?'

'A quarter of a minute to one.'

'There's a car coming now,' said Dorothea, only just stopping herself from jumping up.

'Firefighters going away,' said Dick.

'It's coming from the head of the lake,' said Dorothea.

They heard it coming nearer and nearer, hooting at the bends in the narrow road.

'It's stopped,' said Dorothea.

A coach horn sounded for a second, but stopped short as if

its owner had been ordered to shut up. The noise of talking grew louder. But there was no sound of cars moving off.

'Why don't they go?' said Dorothea.

The noise of talking grew louder yet and then came suddenly to an end.

'What *is* happening?' said Dorothea.

A minute went by without a sound.

Then, from behind the house came Colonel Jolys's voice, shouting, 'Now lads! Miss Turner! Hip, hip, hurrah!', the last words drowned in a burst of cheering, and a tremendous fanfare of trumpets. Coach calls and hunting calls fought with each other. Every man who had a horn was blowing it as hard as he could.

There was silence once again, then a single short hoot from a motor horn.

'She's going,' whispered Dorothea. 'She *must* be going. She must be going now. That was her car hooting as it went out of the gate.'

They heard it again, farther away.

Behind the house there was talking and shouting again, and the noise of engines being started and cars moving off.

'She's gone,' said Dorothea, 'I do believe she has,' and at that moment Nancy and Peggy came racing across the lawn towards the boathouse.

'They're somewhere quite near. Bound to be. *SCARAB AHOY! AHOY!* Come out, you Picts!'

It was the first time for ten days that they had heard Nancy let herself go with a proper yell.

'Ahoy!' shouted Dick and Dorothea, and jumping over rocks and clumps of heather raced down the steep side of the ridge just as Timothy came slowly round the corner of the house, reading a letter as he came.

'Well done, the Picts!' cried Nancy. 'Well done! Well done! If you hadn't had the sense to bolt we'd have failed after all.'

'Has she gone?' asked Dorothea.

'Of course she has. Didn't you hear them giving her a send off?'

'Did she find out about us?'

'She didn't find out about anything. We thought she was bound to. The doctor and the postman and everybody were on the very edge of blurting it out but she didn't give anyone a chance. We thought it was all up again and again. But luckily there was Colonel Jolys and Timothy and the police, and she was pretty busy squashing them. The worst moment of all was when she wanted to thank you for bringing her home. And when she looked round for you you were gone and it turned into the best moment instead.'

Nancy turned to Timothy who had come up to them but was still looking at the letter. 'I say, it was jolly good of you to sit tight and say nothing when she said such unfair things about the burglary.'

'I couldn't do anything else,' said Timothy. 'Worse for all of us if she'd known they were in it. And anyhow it was my burglary in a way and my fault they ran into her. Good thing they did as it happened. I told them to go to the houseboat. What I can't make out is how on earth she got there.'

'I know that,' said Nancy. 'She told us. She says she met Mary Swainson, and Mary took her across. I can't think why. The G.A. was keeping something dark herself. It was something to do with her thinking the Swallows were here when we'd told her they hadn't yet come.'

'Is everything all right now?' asked Dorothea.

'All right? Much more than all right. You look at the letter she's written to Mother. She left it open and told us we were to read it. Hi! Timothy! Let's have it.' She took the letter from him and pushed it into Dorothea's hands. 'Read it! Read it! And then you'll see.'

'But ought we?'

'Of course you ought. Timothy's read it. It's a sort of public testimonial.'

'She's given you a pretty good character,' said Timothy. 'She's a bit hard on me, but I must say I did like the way she polished off the police and Colonel Jolys. If you ask me, I think your Great Aunt is remarkably like her Great Niece. And the way she dealt with Jolys's notion of taking his whole gang to see her off at the station! ... Did you hear her tell her man not to drive at more than ten miles an hour?' Timothy chuckled, threw himself on the slope of the lawn, and put his hands behind his tired head.

Dick and Dorothea were reading the letter together.

My dear Mary,

On hearing, by the merest accident, that you and James had thought fit to make a voyage for purposes of pleasure leaving your daughters, my great nieces, alone at Beckfoot, I felt it my duty to take charge of them in your absence. I have no doubt that you would yourself have suggested this arrangement if you had not been unwilling to inconvenience me. I should like to say that I have been pleasantly surprised by the notable improvement in both Ruth and Margaret. They were, I may say, most attentive and obedient, and in every way did all they could to make my visit pleasant. They have, besides keeping up their practice upon the pianoforte, made remarkable progress in their holiday tasks, so that they will be the better able to enjoy your companionship on your return. Ruth, in particular, at a moment when a slight misunderstanding on my part had brought about circumstances that might have been embarrassing to me, showed that she possesses much of the tact that was characteristic of your grandfather. I wish I could give as good a report of the person to whom, it seems, James had unwisely lent his houseboat. I hope James took the precaution of having an inventory made of his possessions before he left them in the hands of a man who is not above breaking into the house at night to obtain something that I suppose he thought I might otherwise have denied him.

I leave today to rejoin my dear old friend, Miss Huskisson, who, in accordance with her usual summer routine, is to take the waters at Harrogate. I should otherwise have been glad to prolong what I undertook as a duty but found to be a most delightful visit.

I hope that you and James had a pleasant voyage.

I am, my dear Mary,

Your affectionate Aunt,

Maria Turner.

'What about that?' said Nancy. 'I knew we'd bring it off. Mother'll be most awfully pleased. And when you think that the G.A. came here all bristling and meaning to be piggish to Mother. And in spite of her being here, we've done everything we'd planned to do. And now it's over, and you can stop being Picts and we haven't got to be angels any more.'

'But you don't know what she's done,' said Dick. 'She's thrown overboard all the samples from the mine.'

'That's all right,' said Timothy. 'Very kind of her. Saved me the trouble. Those samples don't matter now. We've done with them. What matters is the results we got, and they're all in my pocket. The only samples we need now are the two we got yesterday and they're safe in my knapsack. And if you like to come along tomorrow morning we'll get those done and then we'll have finished. Jim and Mrs Blackett can't be here till the afternoon.'

The load was lifted that had been on Dick's mind ever since he had known that the Great Aunt had been busy in the houseboat. He knew what tidying meant when people wrapped things round their heads and really went at it. He had thought that the burglary had been in vain and that Timothy and he had done their work for nothing.

'I'll sail down first thing,' he said.

Cook was coming across the lawn.

'You'll be stopping for lunch, Mr Stedding,' she said. 'I'm laying for five. And you should NOT be lying on that damp grass even if the sun is shining. Eh, but I'm glad that's over. And to think of Miss Turner spending the night in yon old boat, as comfortable as you please, with us thinking of inquests and all.'

'She's written to Mother to say we've been awfully good,' said Nancy. 'And so we jolly well have. But I say, Cooky, you aren't really going to leave?'

'Oh that,' said Cook. 'She asked me to take my notice back, and I was that pleased to see her alive I told her I didn't mind if I did. And now, lunch'll be ready as soon as I ring the gong, and you come in sharp. You've everything to bring down from that old ruin. We must have them in their bedrooms like Christians again, ready for Mrs Blackett coming home. We must have everything just right. And so it would have been all along if Miss Turner'd left well alone.'

Cook went off back to the house.

*

It was oddly peaceful on the Beckfoot lawn. Only a coach call now and again, far away by the head of the lake, told of the firefighters going home after the hunt.

'Thank goodness that's over,' said Timothy, still lying on the grass in spite of what Cook had said.

'Yes,' said Nancy with a new look in her eyes. 'And only ten days gone after all. An awful ten days, but worth it to save Mother. And now at last we're free to start stirring things up. We'll hoist the skull and crossbones again the moment we've had our grub. We'll get things moving without wasting a minute . . .'

Timothy sat up suddenly. 'Oh look here,' he said, 'I'm all for a quiet life after this.'

'Well, you won't exactly have one,' said Nancy. 'Not yet. You can't expect it. Not with the Swallows coming, and Uncle Jim, and five whole weeks of the holidays still to go.'

Other Books by Arthur Ransome

SWALLOWS AND AMAZONS

'Watch the effect of the first hundred pages on your own children. If they want no more, send for a doctor' – *Daily Telegraph*

SWALLOWDALE

'If there is a nicer book this side of *Treasure Island* I have missed it' – *Observer*
'A perfect book for children of all ages, and better reading for the rest of us than are most novels' – *Spectator*

PETER DUCK

'One of those rare books which come from time to time to enthral grown-up people and children at once with the spell of true romance. A book to buy, to read, to give away – and to keep' – *The Times*

COOT CLUB

'There is a satisfactory realism about all that happens to the Coot Club, and the atmosphere and detail of the odd part of England where they navigate are conveyed with a charm and accuracy that only this author perhaps could bring to bear' – *Guardian*

WINTER HOLIDAY

'One could hardly have a better book about children' – *The Times*

PIGEON POST

'In its own class, and wearing several gold stars for distinction, *Pigeon Post*, by Arthur Ransome, stands head and shoulders above the average adventure book for and of children' – *The Times*

WE DIDN'T MEAN TO GO TO SEA

'This book is Ransome at the top of his form; and so needs no further recommendation from me' – *Observer*
'This is the seventh of the Arthur Ransome books about the Swallows, and I really think it is the best' – *Sunday Times*

SECRET WATER

'Once more the Swallows and Amazons have a magnificent exploring adventure, once more Mr Arthur Ransome has kept a complete record of their experiences, terrors, triumphs, and set it down with the cunning that casts a spell over new children and old' – *The Times Literary Supplement*

THE BIG SIX

'The setting is once more the Norfolk Broads, about which Mr Ransome obviously knows everything that can be known. As usual every single detail of the boatman's art and craft is meticulously explored. . . . Mr Ransome once again equals or perhaps excels himself, and every boy who enjoys him – and every boy does – will vote this detective story super' – Rosamund Lehmann in the *New Statesman*

MISSEE LEE

'*Missee Lee*, by Arthur Ransome, seems to be his best yet. Not only are there pirates in it, but a super female pirate, Missee Lee herself, whose very surprising behaviour creates a situation far too good to be given away. This new Ransome like all the other Ransomes, is a book to buy, to read, and to read again, not once but many times' – *Observer*

GREAT NORTHERN?

'What is that something possessed by Arthur Ransome that most of the others haven't got? I suppose really it is the old spell-binding stuff, the ability to weave and tell a story simply, directly, vividly and swiftly, and with that extra magic quality that raises the first-class story-teller so far above the rest. . . . Here's the perfect boat and bird story for this Christmas, for any age and for those who like their books well produced and well illustrated too' – *Time and Tide*

All illustrated, and published by Jonathan Cape and Puffins

Also by Arthur Ransome

OLD PETER'S RUSSIAN TALES

Outside in the forest there was deep snow, and the sound of more falling down from the branches, but the little hut where Old Peter lived with his grandchildren Vanya and Maroosia was snug and warm, and there was nothing cosier in the world than sitting by the stove and listening to his stories.

These tales of fire-birds and flying ships, cruel stepmothers and patient step-daughters, about Sadko the poor merchant and his river-bride, little Martha who never complained of cold even to Frost himself, and one of the most eerie of all, about Prince Ivan and his terrifying iron-toothed baby sister the witch, touch the imagination and haunt the memory in a way that only the cream of one's childhood reading does.

THE LOSS OF THE NIGHT WIND
Sylvia Sherry

'The day trippers' cars had all left by eight and nobody up on the caravan site gave him a lift,' said the policeman. 'No, George Telford went out on the *Night Wind*.' And that same night the fishing coble the *Night-Wind* had capsized, presumably taking all her crew with her.

But *how* could a boat capsize on a calm night, and had John's friend Fordie really been aboard, or had he run away as he had always talked of doing? However unpopular it made him, John was determined to go round asking questions until he proved to his own satisfaction what had happened.

THE CHILDREN OF THE HOUSE
Brian Fairfax-Lucy and Philippa Pearce

Tom, Laura, Hugh and Margaret were happiest when they were together and their parents were away. It's true that they were Hattos of Stanford Hall, living in one of the grandest houses in England, but no one outside would ever have guessed what it meant to be one of the children, the economies that were made in their schooling, their clothes, and even their food, the lack of love or interest from their parents, and how they had learned to play in silence and never to pass in front of their father's study in case he saw them. So they turned for affection to the butler, the groom, the gardener and the maids, until the First World War came along and ended their story.

For readers of twelve and over, particularly girls.

TO THE WILD SKY
Ivan Southall

Everyone waited for the engine to stop. It was bound to run out of fuel some time, and the six children seemed to have been sitting in this plane, imprisoned, for days, waiting to die. And Gerald, who had taken over the controls when disaster struck their pilot, just flew on and on almost as though he didn't know how to go down. Tomorrow was his fourteenth birthday, but he hadn't much hope of seeing it.

And if they did land, where would it be? On the mountains? On the sea? Somewhere near habitation, or in the desert wastes, or even in New Guinea, where the savages were? It would take a miracle now to save the party who had set off that Friday afternoon to visit a sheep station in New South Wales.

This book, which won the Australian Children's Book of the Year Award for 1968, is suitable for readers of eleven and over.

THE DIDDAKOI
Rumer Godden

'Diddakoi,' said the other children after the Schools Inspector came and ordered poor Kizzy reluctantly to school. 'Gypsy, gypsy joker, get a red hot poker, Diddakoi.' Maybe Kizzy *was* a diddakoi, only half a gypsy, but she had her own opinion of those children and their gorgio ways, 'living in brick' and taunting her for living in a wagon and having funny old clothes which smelt of wood smoke. 'What about gorgios for dirt?' she thought, letting dogs into their houses and getting hair on everything, and using the same washing bowl for clothes and dishes? Never mind, though, as long as she had her Gran and Joe the old horse and the wagon to go home to, she was all right.

Then Gran died, and somehow her cousins seemed unable to care for one extra little girl themselves, so it was decided that Kizzy must go to the gorgios and faithful old Joe to the knackers. But luckily for Kizzy, in the midst of all this misery and interference there were some people who were prepared to love her for herself.

WHAT THE NEIGHBOURS DID
Philippa Pearce

What is it like to be a fly on the wall in our neighbours' houses, to see their real selves at home, instead of the polite people who say good morning and disappear through the front door to who knows what? Philippa Pearce sees the neighbours with human, sympathetic understanding and without fuss or drama she lifts the lid from our neighbours' houses, shows us the feeling lives within, and helps us understand them.

There's the story of a blackberrying expedition that might have been such fun but is no such thing when Dad is bossing the troops, one about a never-to-be-forgotten midnight feast, and a boy's thrilling afternoon exploration ruined by a little girl tagging on. Simple things, told with sincere, simple artistry.

GOLDENGROVE
Jill Paton Walsh

The one fixed point in Madge's young life has always been Goldengrove, her Grandmother's seaside home in Cornwall. There she and Paul meet and spend their summers, swimming, fishing, climbing the cliffs, walking on the beach, listening to the roaring surf, loving the sound and smell of the sea.

But this year is different. First there is the disturbing stranger who sits in the garden overlooking the beach. Why does he stare at them? What does he want? And this year Madge is not quite a child any more. She discovers the stranger's need, and Paul's resentment, and learns all too soon that some things cannot be mended, some things are too late to put right.

WILKINS' TOOTH
Diana Wynne Jones

OWN BACK LIMITED — it seemed a marvellous scheme! Frank and Jess had set up the business because they needed money. Their father had put a quick stop to ERRANDS RUN, so they tried something else and put up a notice on the potting shed — REVENGE ARRANGED, PRICE ACCORDING TO TASK, ALL DIFFICULT TASKS UNDERTAKEN, TREASURE HUNTED, ETC.

The first customer to take the idea seriously was Buster Knell, who wanted revenge on Vernon Wilkins, who'd knocked his tooth out — what Buster wanted was one of Wilkins' teeth in return. That was a bit of a problem, but luckily Vernon's small brother was just losing a tooth . . . Quickly news of the business spread and more children became entangled in the web of plots and mystery.

Heard about the Puffin Club?

... it's a way of finding out more about Puffin books and authors, of winning prizes (in competitions), sharing jokes a secret code, and perhaps seeing your name in print! When you join you get a copy of our magazine, *Puffin Post*, sent to you four times a year, a badge and a membership book.

For details of subscription and an application form, send a stamped addressed envelope to:

The Puffin Club Dept A
Penguin Books Limited
Bath Road,
Harmondsworth
Middlesex UB7 ODA

and if you live in Australia, please write to:

The Australian Puffin Club
Penguin Books Australia Limited
P.O. Box 527
Ringwood
Victoria 3134